"Cole, why me?" Maddy sighed. "I've got baggage. A lot of it. I'm prickly."

Cole chuckled and she felt the vibration of the sound through his chest and into her back. "You're not the only one with baggage," he admitted. Before she could ask what he meant, he continued on. "Listen, what happened to you just made you cautious. You're not prickly. You're scared. I would be, too."

They let the thought sit for a few minutes, and then Cole spoke again. "I don't know, Maddy. I got thinking about how you're young and pretty and so damned strong and then...and then I couldn't stop thinking about you."

She looked up into his face. "The last thing I was looking for was a date. Maybe it just snuck up on both of us."

She licked her lips, which suddenly felt dry, and saw his gaze drop to where her tongue had wet the surface. Desire surged through her, terrifying by its very presence and exhilarating at the same time.

"It snuck up on me for sure," he admitted quietly, smiling. "You snuck up on me."

His Christmas
Baby Bonus

DONNA ALWARD
&
JENNIFER FAYE

Previously published as *The Cowboy's Christmas Family* and *Her Festive Baby Bombshell*

ISBN-13: 978-1-335-47147-5

Recycling programs for this product may not exist in your area.

His Christmas Baby Bonus
Copyright © 2020 by Harlequin Books S.A.

The Cowboy's Christmas Family
First published in 2015. This edition published in 2020.
Copyright © 2015 by Donna Alward

Her Festive Baby Bombshell
First published in 2016. This edition published in 2020.
Copyright © 2016 by Jennifer F. Stroka

This edition published by arrangement with Harlequin Books S.A.

For questions and comments about the quality of this book, please contact us at CustomerService@Harlequin.com.

Harlequin Enterprises ULC
22 Adelaide St. West, 40th Floor
Toronto, Ontario M5H 4E3, Canada
www.Harlequin.com

Printed in U.S.A.

CONTENTS

Donna Alward lives on Canada's east coast with her family, which includes her husband, a couple of kids, a senior dog and two crazy cats. Her heartwarming stories of love, hope and homecoming have been translated into several languages, hit bestseller lists and won awards, but her favorite thing is hearing from readers! When she's not writing, she enjoys reading (of course), knitting, gardening, cooking...and she is a *Masterpiece Theatre* addict. You can visit her on the web at donnaalward.com and join her mailing list at donnaalward.com/newsletter.

Books by Donna Alward

Harlequin Romance

South Shore Billionaires

Christmas Baby for the Billionaire
Beauty and the Brooding Billionaire

Destination Brides

Summer Escape with the Tycoon

Marrying a Millionaire

Best Man for the Wedding Planner
Secret Millionaire for the Surrogate

Heart to Heart

Hired: The Italian's Bride
How a Cowboy Stole Her Heart

Visit the Author Profile page at Harlequin.com for more titles.

The Cowboy's Christmas Family

DONNA ALWARD

To my family—the reason for everything.

Chapter 1

There were days when Madison Wallace felt like a single-mom Cinderella.

She blew at a few strands of hair that had escaped her messy ponytail, then tucked them behind her ears for at least the tenth time in the past half hour and checked her watch yet again.

Six twenty. The library closed at eight. The meeting was due to start in ten minutes and she didn't even have the coffeepot going yet. The boys were in a playpen in one of the smaller meeting rooms, and her brain was on the verge of shutdown, with her body not far behind.

Whoever came up with the idea of Snowflake Days needed their head examined.

Oh, right. That would be her.

Of course, she'd put forth that proposal last winter, and the mayor and council had loved the idea. She'd thought she'd have tons of time to help with the planning committee. The babies would be a little older, she'd be back at work, Gavin would be home at night to lend a hand, and life would be back to normal.

And then everything had changed.

She couldn't think about that now. She didn't have time. And playing the what-if game was a waste of energy, anyway.

The meeting room where the twins were was quiet except for the odd babble, so she rushed around as committee members started arriving and gathered in the foyer, chatting. There were twelve altogether, a blend of male and female, young and old, business owners and retirees and anything in between. She put tablets of paper at each spot at the conference table as well as pens that said Gibson Public Library on them. A separate table held coffee, now dripping merrily into the pot, ice water, and an array of muffins and breads, which she'd baked just this morning while the boys were napping rather than taking from the library's petty cash, which was always pretty tight.

"Maddy, this is just lovely, dear." Pauline Rowe stopped and patted her arm. "Thank you for setting it up. Now that Thanksgiving is over, we're really going to get into the nitty-gritty of the planning. Lots of coffee required."

Maddy smiled at Pauline, who owned the town's only dry cleaning and alterations shop. "Thanks, Pauline. Let me know if you need anything else, okay?"

An ear-splitting scream punctuated the relative quiet and Maddy winced. "Sorry. I'll be right back."

She rushed to the meeting room and found Liam and Lucas in the playpen. Liam was hanging on to the edge for dear life and crying, while Lucas whimpered softly in the corner, big crocodile tears on his cheeks.

Her boys. Best friends one moment, fighting like cats the next, and at a year old, with no verbal skills to tell her what was wrong. She hadn't been prepared for motherhood, let alone times two. And going it alone? Since Gavin died, she'd really had to fight against despair at times. Like tonight, when she was bone weary.

"Hey, sweetie. Mama's here." She picked up Liam and settled him on her arm. He burrowed into her neck and stuck his thumb in his mouth, his wet face sticking to her skin. Her heart melted just a little bit. He was such a snuggle bug.

"You had to bring the twins?" Pauline asked gently. Without missing a beat, she went to the playpen and lifted out Lucas, who stared at her with owlish blue eyes and sucked in his lower lip as he fought against crying.

"Mom's down with the stomach flu as of this morning. It was...short notice to find a replacement."

Short notice was her excuse. The truth was, she didn't have the money to pay someone for child care today. It had come down to food and lights as far as priorities went. Filled tummies and running water were pretty important, and the holidays were coming.

She gave Liam a bounce and smiled, and he placed a chubby, if damp, hand on her cheek. Despite the troubles and challenges, she wouldn't trade her babies for anything. Things would work out the way they were supposed to. When times got rough, she found it difficult to remember that, but it was what she truly believed. Something good was around the corner for her. It was going to be okay. How could it not be?

"Hello, is the meeting in here?"

Maddy looked up and went dumb for a few seconds.

Cole Hudson, all six feet of him, stood in the doorway. He'd taken off his hat and held it in his hand...of course he had, because he had impeccable manners. His dark hair was cut short, just long enough for his fingers to leave trails as he ran his hand through it, in what Maddy assumed was a gesture of tidying it but really gave it a mussed look. And blue eyes. Blue with little crinkles at the corners. Like the Texas bluebells she'd seen once on a trip she'd taken with her parents.

A girl had to be blind not to get a little tongue-tied around Cole Hudson.

"Sorry," she said as she found her wits again. "The meeting's across the hall."

In her rush to get to the boys, the door to the meeting room had closed and locked, so she dug in her jeans pocket for the keys on one of those stretchy wrist things all the librarians used. She fumbled and Cole reached around, took the key from her hand and put it in the lock. He was standing awfully close to her, and she suddenly found it difficult to take a full breath.

"Allow me. You have your hands full," he said kindly, swinging open the door.

She adjusted Liam on her shoulder. "Let me get a door stopper so you don't get locked out again," she said, looking around, feeling unusually flustered. Pauline still held Lucas in her arms and he was starting to squirm, wanting to get down. Both boys were walking now, but unsteadily, which meant they were an accident waiting to happen when let loose.

She put the stopper in the door, committee members started filing in—still chatting—and she took Lucas from Pauline, so she held a child in each arm.

"Is there anything more you need?" she asked the group at large, holding tight as Lucas twisted and fussed.

"We're fine, Maddy. Truly." Lacey Duggan came forward, a smile on her face. "This is wonderful. And you have your hands very full. We'll come find you if we need something, but really, don't worry about a thing."

"Thanks, Lacey." Lacey was new to Gibson, Montana, and new wife to Quinn Solomon up at Crooked Valley Ranch. Maddy let out a small sigh. "I was kind of hoping to be involved, but…" She let the sentence trail off and gave a small shrug with her aching shoulders.

"Your boys are adorable," Lacey added, ruffling Liam's hair.

"Thanks. I'm not usually this discombobulated." She boosted Lucas on her hip, getting him in a better position. "Work and babies don't go together very well."

"Everyone understands," Lacey offered sympathetically.

Yes, they did. And it burned Maddy's biscuits that she was reminded of it so very often. As if she could forget what had gotten her in this position in the first place.

Gavin had been a cheater. And a liar.

"Well, I'd better get back to the desk. Holler, okay?"

She pasted on a smile and went back to the room where she'd set up the boys. She dug in her bag and pulled out a sleeve of arrowroot cookies and two sippy cups of milk that had been sitting against an ice pack. "Okay, boys, please be good for Mommy. Please. I have to check the front desk and then I'll be back."

For the moment, the promise of a cookie and milk pacified the children and Maddy zipped out to the front desk. The library was quiet; other than the meeting there were no other special activities tonight, thank goodness.

Two or three people browsed the stacks, and Maddy quietly went to them and told them to ring the bell at the circulation desk when they were ready to check their books out.

A quick breath and back to check on the boys.

And so went the next hour and a half. A quick check, back to the front. Change a diaper, back to the cart to put books back on the shelves. Slipping the twins into their pajamas, and then back to the drop box to scan the returned books into the system. She could hear the committee laughing behind the door and her shoulders slumped. She should be in there. She wanted to help. Last Christmas the boys had only been a month old. This year they were old enough to be excited at the bright lights and the sound of ripping paper, eating a real Christmas dinner even if half of it had to be mashed.

Maybe she could make next week's meeting. As long as her mom could babysit…

At five minutes to eight, the conference room door opened and the noise got louder, just as Liam had nodded off and Lucas was finally starting to settle, curled up with a blanket and rubbing his eyes. The sudden change in volume startled them both, and Maddy closed her eyes for a second, let out a breath. It was nearly done. She could close up the library and take the boys home and maybe, finally, get some sleep.

And for right now she was going to let the boys fuss and whimper for two minutes while she saw everyone out and locked the damn doors.

The place was nearly empty when she turned from the circulation desk and saw Cole come around the corner, a very grouchy Lucas on his arm. She felt a definite pang in her chest, seeing her fussy boy being held by a strong man, like a father would. Only Lucas didn't have a father. He was going to miss out on all of that.

Then there was the impact of seeing Cole Hudson holding a baby. Men and babies… Maddy didn't know if there was an evolutionary, biological reason for finding it so attractive or not, but there was no denying her heart softened just a little bit and her pulse started beating just a little faster.

"Cole, I'm sorry. I was going to get back to the boys as soon as I locked up." She gave a small smile. "It doesn't hurt them to fuss for a few minutes, you know."

"The other one's back to sleep. I thought I'd get this little guy out before he woke him up again." Cole smiled, and her heart went all mushy again.

Stop it, she reminded herself. *Pretty is as pretty does.* And Gavin had been darned pretty. He'd given her pretty babies. And in all likelihood he'd fathered another one that was due any day—Laura Jessup's baby.

She had a long way to go before she trusted anyone ever again. Even Cole, who had such a stellar reputation in the community that it seemed he could do no wrong.

"Thanks. I'll take him. You probably want to get going."

But Cole didn't move. "You're not leaving right away, are you?"

Her cheeks heated. "Well, I have to spend a few minutes tidying up. It won't take long."

Cole shifted Lucas's weight, and to Maddy's consternation, Lucas's eyes were drifting shut, cocooned in the warm curve of Cole's arm. "It'll take you longer if you have him in your arms," Cole reasoned. "I can stay for a few minutes. Give you a hand."

"That's generous of you, Cole, but…"

"But nothing." He chuckled. "I heard you were stubborn. Accept the help, Maddy. It's no big deal."

It felt like a big deal to her. "I'm perfectly capable of handling it. Thank you." She moved forward and took Lucas out of Cole's arms, close enough to Cole that she could smell his aftershave and feel the soft cotton of his shirt as her fingers brushed against it. The last thing she wanted was more pity. More sympathetic looks. All it did was remind her of how stupid she'd been. How duped. She'd been an inconsolable wreck when she'd gotten the news about the car accident. Three days later she'd gone to Gavin's funeral as the grieving widow, devastated that they'd never have the chance to fix their marriage, that her boys would grow up without their father.

And two days later she'd heard the rumors. And remembered that Laura had been at the funeral and offered her condolences...

Maddy brushed past Cole and left him to exit the library on his own, and she went to the conference room and began putting muffins back in the tin with one hand.

No one would make a fool of her that way again.

Cole sat at the kitchen table, sipping a glass of water and reading one of his latest cattle magazines. He knew he should go to bed. Tomorrow was an early start, and there were things he wanted to get done before snow hit, as it was forecast to do tomorrow night. He turned another page and realized he hadn't really been reading. He'd been thinking about Maddy Wallace, how tired she'd looked, how she tried to cover it with her work face and how defensive she'd gotten when he'd tried to help.

And then he'd called her stubborn and that had been the end of any assistance he might have offered. That really stuck in her craw. He'd make a point of not saying that again. He was certain to see her, as the meetings for the committee were always at the library. Besides, Gibson was pretty small. Their paths crossed now and again.

And as such, Maddy's story was pretty common knowledge. Her husband had been killed in a car accident several months before, leaving her widowed with the twins. Which would have been bad enough, but rumors had spread that Gavin Wallace had been having an affair. He didn't blame Maddy for being defensive. It wasn't nice having your dirty laundry hung up for everyone to see.

The exhausted, hopeless look on her face tonight had reminded him of someone else, too. Someone he tried not to think of much anymore...

He hardly noticed when his mother came into the kitchen. It wasn't until the fridge door opened that he jumped and spun in his chair, looking over his shoulder at her.

Ellen Hudson was still a beautiful woman at fifty-seven. Her gray hair was cut in a wispy sort of bob and while she had crow's-feet at the corners of her eyes, they still twinkled as blue as ever. She gave a light laugh at Cole's surprise and took a carton of milk from the fridge.

"You're up late. I didn't mean to scare you."

"Just reading. Winding down." Thinking too much.

She went to the cupboard and got a mug. "Me, too. I couldn't sleep so I thought I'd try some warm milk." She poured the milk into the mug and put it in the microwave. Cole watched as she took it out again, added a splash of vanilla and a spoon of brown sugar, and took a sip.

"I don't know how you drink that disgusting stuff," he commented, closing his magazine.

She grinned and sat down opposite him. "I drank it when I was pregnant with Tanner and was off the caffeine." She cradled the mug and looked up at him. "Something on your mind, son?"

"Not really. Probably just too much coffee at the meeting tonight."

"How'd that go?"

"Good," he answered, leaning back in his chair. "Things are coming together."

"I'm sorry we're going to miss it," his mother said. "We'll be in St. Thomas by then."

Cole grinned. "You're not that sorry. You and Dad have been waiting for this trip for years." They were flying to Florida to spend a week, and then taking a two-week cruise through the Caribbean. "Besides, you'll be back for Christmas."

"Of course we will. With a suntan." She laughed a little. "I'm not sure if my sleeping problems are from excitement or anxiety."

It was Cole's turn to laugh. "Mom, I promise Tanner and I aren't going to throw any ragers while you guys are out of town."

"Smart-ass." But she laughed, too. "You both are grown men. And good men. Still, I hate leaving you to manage both the ranch and the house."

"We're big boys. We know how to clean and cook. You go and don't worry a bit about us. We'll eat steak every night. It's Tanner's specialty."

If Tanner was ever home, that was. He always seemed to find somewhere to go, something to do. And when he wasn't being a social butterfly, he was putting in hours as a volunteer EMT. Maybe it was because Tanner was younger, but he had an energy that far surpassed Cole's. Or maybe Cole was just more of a homebody.

"You know, if you'd hurry up and get married…"

"I know, I know. You and Dad would downsize and you wouldn't worry about me so much. And while I'm at it, get to work on some grandkids for you to spoil."

It was a well-worn refrain. And one he understood, but he didn't need to have it mentioned quite so often. It wasn't that he had anything against settling down. He just hadn't met the right one yet. Every girl he dated seemed great for a while, but then the novelty fizzled out.

Lately he'd started to wonder if the problem was that he was afraid of getting too close to someone. When Roni left him, he'd felt like such a failure. He'd tried over and over to help her, but nothing had worked. He had no idea where she was now, or if she was even okay. Truth be told, he hadn't been in love with a woman since she'd trampled on his heart. And that had been eight long years ago.

His mind went back a few hours to Maddy and the way she'd shut him out so quickly. She was living proof of what happened when a marriage went wrong. The last thing he'd want to do is rush into a marriage and end up making a mess. "I'm not in a big hurry," he replied, frowning into his water glass. "I take marriage seriously, Mom. Isn't that what you want?"

"Of course." She reached over and touched his hand. "You know we just want to see you happy. You'd be such a good dad, Cole. A good husband. You're a good man."

Ugh, she made it sound as though he was such a paragon, when he knew he wasn't. He supposed she was looking at him through mom goggles.

"Hmm," he answered, thinking again of Maddy and

how stressed she'd seemed. It had to be hard at the best of times, handling twins. Doing it on her own must be an extra challenge. He remembered what she was like before. A hard worker, always with a smile, with an extra glow once she met Gavin and they got engaged. In Gibson everyone pretty well knew everyone else, even though she'd been a few years behind him in school. It sucked that her vibrancy, that glow, had disappeared.

"Thinking about anything in particular?" his mom asked.

"Just Maddy Wallace. She was working at the library tonight and her babysitting fell through and she had the twins. She was run ragged."

"Maddy's had a rough time, that's for sure." She nodded. "Losing her husband, finding out he was cheating. She's one strong girl, picking herself up the way she has. But the whole situation has to be hard."

"I got the impression that she doesn't appreciate a lot of pity," he said, raising an eyebrow.

"Would you?" his mom asked simply. "If your dad had stepped out on me, and the whole town knew about it? I'd be humiliated. And really angry. Honey, Maddy hasn't got anyone to be angry with anymore, except herself, really. I'm sure she'd rather forget all about the whole thing."

He hadn't thought of it in quite that way before. The one person she'd probably like to ask most about the affair couldn't answer. And as far as he could gather, Laura wasn't talking. Which was to her credit, really. But it didn't help stop the gossip.

"Son," she said, taking the last drink of her milk, "this is one time I'm not going to do any urging or matchmaking. Maddy has a truckload of baggage to sort through.

But if you ended up in a position to give her a helping hand, that wouldn't be amiss, either. The holidays are coming up and she has those two babies to think about. Maybe your committee can think about that, too, amid all the festival stuff."

It wasn't a half-bad idea, though the idea of Maddy accepting any form of charity was ludicrous. She wouldn't even accept his help in cleaning up the room tonight, which was just dumping some garbage cans and emptying the coffeemaker.

It would have to be something secret, something she wouldn't expect, something that seemed random.

What in heck would that be?

"I'm a guy. I don't do well with this sort of thing."

His mom laughed, got up and put her mug in the sink. Then she came over to him and dropped a kiss on top of his head. "You're probably better at it than you think. And now I have to get to bed. I have a lot of packing to do tomorrow. I'm not letting your father anywhere near those suitcases."

After she left the room, Cole fussed with the corner of the magazine pages, thinking, It wasn't a bad idea, actually, helping one of their own. Besides, up until the last few months, Maddy had always been active in Gibson, helping out with fund-raisers and activities with a smile.

Life had handed her some huge lemons. Maybe it was up to them to give her the lemonade. It was the season of giving, after all.

What could go wrong?

Chapter 2

Maddy was trying to space out her shopping and minimize her babysitting bills, so she hit the town's rather small department store on a Tuesday after work to pick up a few things before she was due to get the boys.

She had forty dollars today. That was it. And there was another payday before Christmas where she might be able to squeeze a bit more out of her check. It wasn't as though the boys were old enough to know they were getting less than most other kids. It was that *she* knew. She knew she couldn't provide the type of Christmas she wanted to and it bugged her to no end.

As she pushed the metal cart toward the baby section, she took a deep breath. Thinking about finances just made her angry at Gavin again, and that didn't serve any purpose. In the new year, she was going to make a new plan, that was all. Maybe downsize to a smaller house, for one. The three of them didn't need two thousand square feet, really. A smaller bungalow would suit them fine and the upkeep would certainly be easier.

She stopped by the baby clothes, searching for discounts. Pajamas were on sale, cute little blue and green ones with the feet in them and a brown-and-white puppy on the front. She put one of each color in the cart. She picked up fuzzy socks, new slippers with the traction dots on the bottom and two soft white onesies.

Calculating in her head, she had about fifteen dollars left. Barely.

At the toy section she was utterly daunted. How could she buy two toys with what she had left?

She'd decided on the rock-a-stack rings she knew the boys loved from the church nursery, and was deliberating the wisdom of wooden alphabet blocks when a voice startled her.

"I just need help getting it down from the top shelf."

Maddy looked across the aisle and felt her face go redhot. Laura Jessup was smiling at an employee, pointing at a crib set on a high shelf. She was everything Maddy wasn't, it seemed— petite, red haired, creamy complexioned, young.

And carrying Maddy's husband's baby. There was no mistaking the roundness at her middle. At Maddy's best guess, Laura had to be close to seven, eight months along. Not that she was about to ask the exact due date. Gavin had died five months ago, which meant that he'd been seeing Laura pretty much since she'd showed up in town last spring.

With the plastic case containing the comforter in hand, Laura turned around and caught Maddy staring at her. For a brief second she looked embarrassed and awkward, but then she put on an uncertain smile. "Madison," she began, and started walking toward Maddy.

Hell, no, Maddy thought, her throat tightening and heart pounding. *This is not going to happen.*

She wasn't going to have a panic attack, but it was damned close, and she hustled the cart across to housewares, down the center and straight to the cash registers.

A quick glance behind her as she put her items on the belt reassured her that Laura hadn't followed her. Thank God. Maddy wasn't interested in anything Laura had to say.

"Is that all today, Mrs. Wallace?"

She nodded at the girl behind the counter. Young and fresh faced and wearing a Santa hat, she looked innocent and happy. "Yes, that's it, Stephanie. Thanks."

"It's forty-one dollars and ten cents," Stephanie said, and Maddy dug out the extra dollar and change. She'd stayed pretty close to budget after all.

"Is the library still having the tree lighting?" the cashier asked, chatting as if unaware that Maddy wanted to be just about anywhere else right now.

"Yes, on the thirteenth," she answered. "To kick off Snowflake Days."

"It's so much fun every year. Last year when I went, I—"

Maddy grabbed the shopping bags and flashed a hurried smile. "Sorry, Stephanie. I was supposed to pick up the boys ten minutes ago. I've gotta run."

"Oh, sure, Mrs. Wallace. Have a nice day."

The air outside the store was bitter, a distinct change from the crisp bite of earlier. It felt as if snow was in the air. She'd like to get home before it started, since she didn't have her winter tires on yet. She should probably do that soon...

"Afternoon, Maddy."

She had her head stuck in the trunk, stowing the bags, and the sound of her name being spoken prompted her to stand up too quickly and smack her head on the hood.

She now understood why people called it seeing stars. Little dots swam in front of her eyes as she held on to the lip of the trunk for support.

"Whoa, there!" A strong hand gripped her arm, steadying her. "I didn't mean to scare you. Sorry about that."

She blinked a few times and her vision cleared, though the pain was still sharp in her head. Cole Hudson stood before her, a frown of concern on his handsome face.

"I'm fine. You just scared me, is all." She pushed away from the car, and then reached for the hood, giving it a good slam.

"Maddy, hold still." He reached into his pocket and took out a handkerchief. "I think you cut your head."

Now that he mentioned it, there was a funny feeling on the right side of her head, as if a raindrop had fallen on her hair and was trickling toward her ear.

He reached forward and pressed the cotton to her head with a firm but gentle touch. "Wow, you really smacked it."

He took the handkerchief away and she saw a decent-sized blot of blood. "I've been preoccupied all day," she admitted, letting out a breath. "And I'm late to pick up the boys." It was a white lie, but he didn't know that. It sounded better than *I'm running away from my husband's mistress*.

"I want to make sure you're all right first," Cole insisted. "Or I could drive you over there myself. They at your folks' place?"

"No, at the day care. I can't expect Mom to keep them all the time, and it was a workday for me. Besides, the day care is closer." Maddy's mom and dad lived on a pretty lot on the other side of the river. They'd been absolutely wonderful over the past few months, but Maddy was determined to stand on her own two feet.

He dabbed at her head with the kerchief again. "It seems to be stopping. Not too deep, then. Still, it looks like you had your bell rung pretty good."

He'd raised one eyebrow and looked slightly roguish, a small smile flirting with his lips. She couldn't help it—she laughed a little. "So, my secret is out. Now you know I'm the world's biggest klutz."

"Oh, I wouldn't say that big." He was genuinely smiling at her now. "Listen, I've been meaning to call you. I wanted to talk to you about the festival. Why don't we grab a coffee or something?"

It surprised her to realize that she wanted to accept. Generally she took her own tea bags or hot chocolate to the library rather than spend money on the extravagance, and she really did need to pick up the boys…though it had been a complete fabrication to say she was running late, since she was paid up until five, which was another hour and a bit away.

"I probably shouldn't," she said, pushing her purse straps more securely on her shoulder.

"Hey," Cole said quietly. "When was the last time you let someone buy you a cup of coffee, huh? It's got to be hard being a single mom. Heck, my ma raised two boys and she had my dad and she said we were exhausting. You've got twins…phew."

"Great, now I'm a pity date?"

"Good Lord, woman, you're exasperating." Cole stepped back and tucked his hands into his jacket pockets. "I actually do want to talk to you about the festival. Over coffee sounded kind of nice, that's all. Look, I admire all your independence and stuff, but not everything comes from pity around here. Sometimes people genuinely want to help people they care about, that's all."

Was he saying he cared about her? They didn't even know each other that well. Of course, he must be speaking in far more general terms, right?

His words made her feel sheepish, too. It was no secret she had a chip on her shoulder. She'd always liked Cole. He was well-known in town, and had been only a couple of years ahead of her in school. He and Gavin had been in the same class from kindergarten right through graduation. Not that she truly trusted Gav's judgment anymore, either.

She sighed, met Cole's gaze. "I get defensive. I'm sorry, Cole. I was kind of stressed out when you came up behind me and then I whacked my head and you're right about the pity thing." She shrugged. "I tell myself every day that I should get over being bitter. It's just hard."

"Of course it is. And you're bringing up two rambunctious boys on your own. You'll find people in this town have a lot of respect for you, Maddy. Now what do you say? Do you want to stop at the diner, or maybe the Daily Grind?"

Why shouldn't she go have a cup of something? Didn't she deserve something for herself? Maddy nodded and felt a weight lift. "The Grind would be really nice, actually. I haven't been in there for ages."

She locked the car and walked beside him as they made their way down Main Street to the coffee shop. It had opened fairly recently, a somewhat trendy spot in a town steeped in old-time traditions. He held the door for her and she stepped in, loving the scents that hit her nose the moment she entered—coffee, chocolate, cinnamon—lovely, cozy, warm scents that wrapped around her and eased some of the stresses of her day.

"What will you have?" Cole asked. "My treat."

"I can get my own," she insisted, but Cole cut her off.

"What did I just say outside?"

"Sorry." She hoped she wasn't blushing again. "Um, what kinds of tea do you have?" She looked at the girl behind the counter.

"The list is here." The girl gestured, pointing to a sign on a glass display front. "But this month we have a special flavor called Country Christmas, if you would like to try it. It's kind of like mulled cider, only with black tea."

"That sounds lovely. I'll have that," Maddy said. She looked longingly at the apple cinnamon pastries, but it would only be a few more hours and she'd have dinner. Besides, she was letting Cole buy her tea. She wouldn't presume to order anything to eat.

He ordered coffee and Maddy added honey to her tea while he waited for his order. To her surprise, he came over to her and put down a plate with two pastries on it before reaching for the cream to add to his coffee.

"Don't say it," he said before she could even open her mouth. "My mom and dad left a few days ago for their trip and there's no baking in the house."

"Let me guess. Chronic sweet tooth?"

He stirred his coffee, dropped the stir stick in the trash and picked up both mug and plate. "Yeah. I think I'm spoiled probably, because my mom always keeps the kitchen well stocked for us."

"Hungry boys working the ranch need good home cooking."

"Yep." He grinned. "And my mom's is the best."

They found seats not too far from the window. Maddy looked around. The Christmas decorations were up, with boughs and pretty white lights draped around the dark wood rails and beams. Someone had sprayed fake snow on the corners of the windows, and a huge poinsettia was on a small table in the corner. Some sort of new-agey Christmas music played on the speakers, with a bluesy-sounding saxophone and a reassuring bass line. Maddy took a sip of her tea— delicious—and let her stress levels drop another notch.

"See?" he said, pushing the plate toward her and handing her one of the forks. "Time out for Maddy."

She laughed a bit. "I've been so cranky lately that you're probably doing a public service," she joked. Sort of joked, anyway. All work and no play and all that…

"Aw, darn, you saw right through me," he quipped, cutting a huge corner of the pastry with the edge of his fork. "Of course not. I just realized last week at the library that you really had your hands full. It got me thinking, that's all."

Again she got the weird swirly sensation at the idea of Cole thinking about *her*.

"Well, whatever the reason, thank you. This is delicious."

"That's better. And you're welcome."

She took a bite of turnover and closed her eyes. The pastry was light and flaky and beautifully buttery. "This is going to ruin my supper, and I don't even care," she said, licking the caramelly residue on the fork.

"I'd say mine, too, but it's Tanner's night to cook. If he's home. I'll probably end up making myself a sandwich or something later tonight."

"Your mom really does spoil you." She met his gaze again and grinned.

"And I let her, so I'm as bad as she is." He smiled, too. "Honestly, there are some pros to still living at home. And it doesn't make sense to pay for two households when there's more than enough room. But yeah, I'm a thirty-three-year-old man living with his parents. Whoo-ee, look at me."

Maddy wondered why he'd never married, but she sure as shootin' wasn't going to ask. It was none of her business, and she didn't like it when people pried into her personal life. Besides, Cole was hardly the stereotypical live-at-home type. The Hudson ranch was solid, respected in the town and state, with a reputation for quality stock and fair dealing. Definitely a family operation.

Before she could reply, he continued, "Of course, there are some disadvantages, too. Like no privacy. And it can be a little tough on the ego."

"You've got big shoulders," she said, cutting off another bite of pastry. "You can handle it. If I remember right from our school days, you always seemed to handle just about anything."

He'd had a reputation then of being solid, stable, smart. Reliable. The girls all swooned over him, he was well liked in general and he'd never gotten into any trouble, to her recollection. His brother, on the other hand…

"Wow. Maybe I should check my back to see if I've sprouted wings."

"Naw, you could just take out another hanky and polish your halo."

He laughed again. "How is your head, anyway?"

She touched the spot gingerly. "Tender, but not bad. Just a teensy goose egg."

"Good."

They each drank again and then Maddy put down her cup and pushed the plate aside. "So, you said you wanted to ask me something about the festival. What can I do to help? I know I haven't been much help on the committee."

Cole nodded. "Well, we're looking for volunteers. I don't know what your plans are with regard to the boys, but I thought I'd mention a few things. If it's too hard on your schedule, maybe you could suggest someone."

"Okay."

"First up is the night of the tree lighting. We're planning a food drive and need someone to just keep things organized at the collection site. When it's over, I've offered my truck to load up the food, and I'll deliver it the following day."

Maddy thought for a minute. "I'm going to take the twins, but I know my parents always go to it, too. I'll double-check with them to make sure they can watch the boys."

"That's great. The volunteers are all parking in the side lot at the fire station to free up room for attendees."

Maddy really wished she'd been able to sit in on the

meetings. "That's a good idea. It's so close but will help with congestion."

"It was Mike Palmer's idea." Mike was part of the fire department and sat on just about every committee in Gibson. Maddy wasn't surprised.

"Your name came up when we were discussing another event, too." He finished his coffee and put the empty mug down on the table. "The Duggans have offered a wagon and horse team to do a sleigh ride on the walking pathway."

"A sleigh ride with wheels?" She smiled a little, and despite her earlier Scrooginess, she was intrigued.

"If we get a big dump of snow, Duke says they can drive the team down Main Street instead. So far there's only about an inch on the path. The idea is to leave from the library, go past the bridge down to the park, turn around and come back, and then have hot cocoa and cookies and story time inside. You're good with kids. Are you up for a sleigh ride and storytelling?"

It sounded magical. Maybe too magical. Still, the idea of bundling up the boys and taking them on a wagon ride with jingling bells and carols…maybe she couldn't have piles of presents under the tree, but they could still enjoy the season.

"Someone would have to stay at the library to make the cocoa and set out the cookies."

"Pauline's offered to do that. She has it all planned out. Sleigh ride at two, cocoa at two forty-five, story at three."

Maddy smiled again. "She is always so organized. She's a good chair for this event."

"I hear you're the one who did up the proposal last

year," Cole said, his voice a bit softer. "You planned to be on the committee, didn't you?"

"Yeah." She looked up at him. "Hey, if I've learned anything this year, it's that sometimes things don't work out exactly as you planned."

"I'm really sorry about that, Maddy."

"Me, too. It is what it is."

Cole hesitated, but she could tell he wanted to say something. "What is it?" she asked. "You might as well say it. You won't hurt my feelings. I'm past that."

His gorgeous blue eyes held hers. "I was just wondering how you're managing, that's all. It's none of my business, I know that." He raised his hand as if to say, *tell me to back off if I'm overstepping.* "It's just... I don't know what I'm trying to say. Well, I do, but I know how you feel about pity and charity."

Embarrassment slithered through her stomach, crept up her chest and neck in the form of a blush. "We're getting by, so don't worry about that. In the new year I'm going to sit down and make some decisions, I think. But we're not cold and we're not starving, Cole. There are others out there a lot worse off than we are." Who was she to complain? Her children had clothes and food and love and a roof over their heads. More than anything, Maddy had learned that the rest was just gravy. Window dressing. She knew she needed to spend a lot more time being thankful and less time being bitter.

"Maybe you could use some extra cash for Christmas?"

"What do you mean?" She frowned. "I considered looking for some extra retail shifts in town for a few weeks, just during the busy time. But by the time I factored in child care...it didn't seem worth it."

"What if you could take the boys with you and didn't have to pay for day care?"

She laughed. "What employer would go along with that?"

He leveled his gaze at her. "I would."

"You?"

The idea of working for Cole Hudson was so strange and, frankly, made her stomach flip over nervously. "Cole, if this is some make-work project to, I don't know, make you feel good or something…"

Something flitted through his eyes, but then she wondered if she'd imagined it, it was gone so fast. "It's not," he assured her. "Tanner and I are on our own until the twenty-third. I'm a terrible cook and Tanner's unreliable, frankly. I can't eat fried steak every night for three weeks. I was thinking that I'd like to hire someone just until then, to come in and do some cooking and light cleaning every other day or so. Without Dad, Tanner and I are putting in some extra hours. Not having to do the wash or make dinner at night would be awesome."

"You want a housekeeper."

"I just thought, since you're part-time at the library, and with Christmas coming up, it might work out well for you. I'll pay ten bucks an hour, for four hours every other day."

The annoying thing was that he was right and the temptation of the money was great. Still, it was a pity job, wasn't it? And that grated.

She wasn't sure she had room for pride right now. Forty dollars a day times, what, eight days? That was three hundred and twenty dollars. She could buy the boys' presents for sure, and have leftover to catch up on bills. How could she say no to that?

He tapped her hand, bringing her attention back. "Hey," he said. "I can probably hire a student who's home for Christmas to do it. But I thought of you. And you can bring the boys with you. I don't mind."

"You'd want me to tidy up, do laundry, do some cooking?"

"That's it. It would be helping us out a lot, and maybe giving you some fun money at the same time. Win-win."

"I never saw myself as a housekeeper," she muttered. "Not that there's anything wrong with that. I'm not too proud for it. I just…well, damn, Cole. My life has just done a one eighty in the last few months. It's like I hardly recognize it anymore."

Cole put his hand over hers. "It's okay. When something so unexpected happens, so life altering, it takes a good while to adjust to a new normal."

The knot of tension eased inside her. His hand felt warm and strong over hers, and his words were exactly what she needed to hear. Rather than looking at her life as a chaotic mess, it was a search for a new normal. She'd get there. She just had to be patient.

"When would you want me to start?"

He laughed. "Tomorrow? Three days and I'm already sick of Tanner's cooking and the laundry's piling up."

She checked her watch, realizing that time had flown and she truly did have to pick up the boys soon. "Would mornings be okay? I usually work afternoons at the library, and on my days off I'd still be able to get the boys home for a good afternoon nap. You have no idea how much that helps their temperament."

"Mornings are fine. I'll leave the front door open, but I'll try to be in around…nine? I'll show you around, get you set up. Then you're done by one."

"Sounds good." She pushed out her chair and reached for her coat. "I really should get going, though. The day care gets miffed if parents are late. But thank you for the tea. You were right. It was nice to just get out and sit for an hour or so."

"It was my pleasure. And thanks for helping me out." He stood and took his jacket off the back of his chair. In moments they were bundled up against the cold and headed for the door.

To her surprise, he walked her back to her car, too. The snow had started, just light flakes drifting lazily, and Maddy hoped they didn't get much. She had to drive out to Cole's in the morning, and without winter tires. Maybe the first thing she should do with Cole's money was have them installed.

He shut her door for her and waited until she'd started the car before stepping back. Maybe she should feel crowded or patronized by his behavior this afternoon. But she didn't.

She felt cared for and protected. Which was silly. It was a few hours of work, and a request for volunteering, and a cup of tea. And she was fully capable of looking after herself.

But it was the fact that he'd looked at her—really at her—that had made the difference. And she didn't think he'd simply seen Maddy Wallace, charity case.

If nothing else, she was extremely grateful for that.

Chapter 3

Cole knew he shouldn't be nervous.

So why was his gut a tangle of knots? He'd come to the house at eight thirty, after the first of the morning chores were done, and he'd washed up, combed his hair—twice—and considered changing his shirt.

It was just Maddy. He'd known her his whole life. And this was just his way of helping her out over the holidays. It was funny, he realized, that the whole committee for Snowflake Days talked about helping the less fortunate at Christmas but Maddy's name hadn't come up once. It didn't take a genius to do the math. Unless Gavin had left her a hefty life-insurance policy—which Cole doubted he had—part-time hours at a small municipal library wouldn't house and feed a family of three. Plus day care. Maddy had to be struggling, and far more than she let on.

She wouldn't accept help, so offering her work was really the only solution. He didn't even really need it. He knew how to run a washing machine and a vacuum perfectly well. And he wasn't the greatest cook, but he could bake a potato, make a chicken breast, heat some vegetables in the microwave. Hell, last night he'd gone into the market and picked up one of those rotisserie chicken meals for fifteen dollars and it had done him and Tanner for supper and there were still leftovers in the fridge.

He wasn't as inept as he'd led her to believe, but she didn't need to know that.

Movement out the front window caught his attention and he looked closer, saw her car crawling carefully up the drive. Fool woman still had her summer tires on, and it was December. With the three inches of snow that had fallen last night, the road probably had tricky spots.

Cole ran his hand over his hair once more before reaching for the doorknob. He swung it open just as she climbed the steps, carrying a diaper bag and play-pen in her arms.

"Thanks!" she huffed out, putting them down just inside the kitchen. "Just a sec. I'll get the boys."

Her head disappeared inside the car again, and when she withdrew she had a boy on each arm. At least it looked like the boys—the snowsuits in blue and red were so puffy that Cole could hardly see the babies inside.

It occurred to him that she must have really great biceps, and he grinned at the thought.

"Here, let me take one of them," he offered as she climbed the steps. She leaned to one side, handing him one of the boys—he couldn't tell which one. Once inside she sat her cargo on the floor and began the process of pulling off boots and unzipping snowsuits. Cole hadn't done such a thing ever in his life, but he followed her lead, and before too long two identical boys stood before them dressed in little jogging suits with crooked socks and staticky hair, a pile of winter gear at their feet.

"How do you tell them apart?" Cole asked. "I mean, as their mom, you must just know or something. But… well, how do I tell the difference?"

She laughed. "Luke is a little bigger than Liam, and his eyes are just a little different. He's more independent, too. Liam's the one who likes to cuddle and be held all the time." She looked over at him and her eyes twinkled. "Which means one is in my arms, making it hard for me to get anything done, and the other one is off getting into trouble—"

"Making it hard for you to get anything done." Cole chuckled, "I get it." He looked directly at the boys and nodded. "Hi, Luke. Hi, Liam."

They both stared at him with owl eyes, but one raised a hand and opened and shut his fingers in a sort of wave. The other popped his thumb in his mouth.

"So this one is Luke," he said, pointing at the waver, "and the other is Liam."

"Bingo. Let me set up the playpen and get them into a confined space, and then you can show me where things are."

It seemed to take no time at all and she had the playpen set up. A few solid jerks and snaps and it popped into a square. Without any fuss she deposited the boys inside, added a handful of soft toys from the bag she'd brought, gathered up their outerwear and stowed it neatly on a bench by the door, and was ready to go.

"Are you sure they'll be okay there?" Cole was skeptical. It seemed like such a small space, after all.

But Maddy nodded. "I'm sure. Until they're not, and I'll deal with that when we get there." She smiled at him. "Okay. Give me the nickel tour."

He led her through the house, showing her the upstairs first, where the bedrooms and bathrooms were. "The washer and dryer are in the mudroom off the garage," he said. "Tanner and I put our dirty laundry there this morning, but normally we keep it in a clothes hamper in our rooms."

On the way downstairs he added, "Mom keeps her cleaning supplies in the laundry room, too, in a carry basket. You should be able to find everything you need there."

"Sounds fine," she said, following behind him.

They went to the mudroom next and he opened a closet to reveal a vacuum cleaner and broom and dustpan. "For the floors. The big freezer is out here, too, if you start supper or anything and are looking for stuff."

They ventured back into the kitchen. To Cole's surprise, the boys were stacking up soft blocks on the floor of the playpen and then knocking them over, giggling. It took no time at all to give her the rundown of the cupboards. "I'd better go and get out of your way, then," he added, feeling suddenly awkward. He couldn't help but notice she'd worn a soft hoodie in dark green, a color that set off her fair skin and blue eyes. And Maddy Wallace looked damned fine in a pair of dark-wash jeans, too. He had the sudden thought that she'd be very nice to cuddle up to...

"Hey, are you okay?" Her voice interrupted him. "You just kind of drifted off there for a sec."

Could he feel more foolish? He remembered his mom's words a few days before they left, when he'd mentioned Maddy's name. She'd actually discouraged him from any romantic notions where Maddy was concerned. And after speaking to Maddy yesterday, he knew for sure that she was still hurting from the events of the last year. He had no business thinking about being near her in any way other than being a good neighbor.

"I'm fine. Sorry."

"It's no problem. Will you and Tanner be in for lunch?"

She was all business, and he should be glad, but he was a little annoyed. Clearly she wasn't as distracted by him as he was by her.

"Yes, around noon or a little after. But we can get ourselves something to eat."

"Let's just see how it goes." She smiled at him. "I'll be fine, Cole. I'm going to start some laundry before the boys start demanding attention, and I think I'll run the vacuum over the floors and get some cooking started."

"Right." It was what he'd hired her to do, but he had to admit it felt strange, having her and her babies in the middle of the normally quiet house. And not strange in a bad way, necessarily. Just very, very different.

While she traded toys for the boys in the playpen, Cole went to the mudroom and put on his jacket and boots. He had his hand on the doorknob when she appeared, heading straight for the two laundry hampers standing in front of the dryer.

She laughed. "Seriously, Cole. I can run a washing machine."

He shook his head. "Sorry. I don't know what's wrong with me today. Of course you can. I'll see you in a few hours. I'll be at the barn if you need anything."

"If you keep talking, you'll be here until lunch. And I won't get any work done."

He swallowed against the lump in his throat, annoyed with the route his thoughts had taken. That wasn't what this was about. It was helping someone who needed a hand. Nothing more.

He stomped outside and shut the door behind him, then hurried through the snow to the barn. Maybe the fresh air would get his head right. In any case, he'd better get himself together for when he went back to the house at noon.

Maddy breathed a sigh of relief as Cole left the house. She could see him walking to the barn, his hands shoved in his jacket pockets and his shoulders hunched against the cold. He'd lingered this morning, and she wasn't sure what for, but there'd been a moment in the kitchen when his eyes had gone all soft and dazed and little alarm bells had gone off in her head.

Cole was a nice guy. He was giving her a helping hand and she appreciated it. But oh, my, she was so not in a place for romance. She hoped that wasn't what he had on his mind. She had her hands full enough just trying to keep her life together.

It didn't help that he was so flipping handsome, either. Stupid dark hair that set off his stupid blue eyes so that a girl couldn't think straight. Well, she was smarter than that now, and her only reason for being here was to make a little extra Christmas cash to give her sons a special holiday.

Speaking of, she needed to get that load of laundry in the washer if she was going to get two loads done in the time she had left.

By the time she'd sorted the clothes and gotten the washer started, the boys were getting bored. She took them out of the playpen, and then moved the bulky structure to the stairs, blocking them from doing any climbing—and falling. Then she turned on the television and found the station and programs that they liked. Even at barely over a year old, the sounds and colors were intriguing and Maddy laughed to herself as Liam bobbed on his knees a bit, out of time to the music but dancing, anyway. Luke took one look at his brother and joined in with a big toothy smile.

"Please, stay this good," she breathed as she spread out a blanket and added toys, making it a play mat in the middle of the living room.

In deference to Cole's professed sweet tooth, she wanted to bake something for them to have on hand, and she figured a cake was as fast as anything. It didn't take long to find a recipe book and the ingredients in Ellen's tidy cupboards, and while the boys played and sang away to the program on TV, she whipped up a chocolate cake and had it in the oven. A quick trip to the mudroom showed the laundry on the spin cycle, so she searched the freezer and took out a ham and put it in a slow cooker to bake for the afternoon. By the time she'd changed laundry over, the boys needed diaper changes and then a snack. The cake came out of the oven and she put it to cool, then sat with the boys for a few minutes and read them three stories, including their favorite, *Mole in a Hole*, twice.

After settling them again with a Thomas the Tank Engine DVD, she built a casserole of scalloped potatoes, which she put in the oven to bake, and prepared a pot of carrots that Cole and Tanner could simply turn on and cook. She put the second load of laundry in the dryer, made frosting for the cake and checked her watch. It was nearly noon. Where had the morning gone?

She fixed a plate of sandwiches and put it on the table, along with sliced pickles and a pitcher of water. Coffee was brewing and she was doing the dishes when she heard the mudroom door open and boots stomping on the mat.

The boys paused in their playing and looked at her as if to say, "What's that noise?"

Tanner came in first. Maddy hadn't seen Tanner in some time, but he looked the same as ever. A bit slighter than Cole, and a bit younger, with crinkles at the corners of his eyes that spoke of a devilish nature. He'd been a bit of a hellion in his younger years, though Maddy hadn't heard anything remarkable about him lately. Cole followed behind, tall, steady, a grown-up, serious version of his brother. Where Tanner's eyes had an impish gleam, Cole's held a certain warmth and steadfastness. Luke wobbled to his feet, tottered over to Tanner and lifted his arms. "Bup! Bup!"

Maddy laughed, and Cole spoke up. "Tanner, meet Luke."

"You got it right!" she praised. "You're a quick study."

Tanner reached down and picked up Luke, unfazed by the sight of kids in his home. "Hey, there." He settled the boy on his arm and looked at Maddy. "Nice to see you. Let me guess, this is your extrovert?"

She nodded. "Liam's my serious one." A quick glance showed Liam holding back, his eyes troubled. "He's more…reserved."

"Sounds like Cole and me," Tanner observed. "Here, partner. I'm gonna put you down now. Looks like your mama made lunch, and I need to wash up."

"Me, too," Cole said, a strange look on his face.

"Mum mum mum mum," Liam hummed after the men had gone to wash up. "Unh."

Maddy was looking forward to actual words. As it was she had to translate, and she knew what Liam wanted—his share of the attention, and something to eat. With a sigh, she put him on her hip, then dug in the diaper bag for a few small covered dishes. When Cole and Tanner returned, she was sitting at one end of the table, a boy on each knee, with a dazzling array of Cheerios, tiny cheese cubes and banana scattered on the surface.

She raised an eyebrow at Cole. "Now you see why I leave vacuuming for last."

He smiled warmly. "They'll learn table manners in time."

"I know. But I'm about to wear a fair bit of that banana. Those cute little hands will have it smeared all over my shirt in seconds."

Tanner took a chair. "This is great, Maddy. Thanks for making lunch."

"I hope it's okay. I wasn't sure how big a meal you ate at noon."

"This is fine," Cole said, reaching for a sandwich. "It's usually something like this, or some leftovers or something." He looked over at the counter. "Is that cake?"

"Yes, chocolate, with peanut butter frosting. For your sweet tooth." She smiled a little, teasing him.

"I should never have told you that."

"Well, you did. So now I know how to get around you. Just keep you flush with baked goods."

He pointed his sandwich at her. "You think it's that easy?"

They were openly teasing now, and she realized Tanner was looking from his brother to her and back again. Luke patted his hand against a beautifully soft circle of banana and Liam shoved three Cheerios awkwardly into his mouth.

Her smile faded a bit. "I'm not going to incriminate myself by answering that question. You are my boss, after all."

Tanner chuckled and reached for a few pickle slices. "Nice one."

The meal continued, but Maddy got the feeling Cole was put out about something. He didn't say much and there was a stubborn set to his mouth she hadn't seen before.

"I take it you boys can handle cooking some carrots tonight? I have a ham in the slow cooker, and scalloped potatoes in the oven. All you need to do is heat up the potatoes and boil the carrots and you're done."

"Ham and potatoes? Damn, that sounds good." Tanner leaned back in his chair and stretched. "I'm going out, but I might just have to eat before I go if that's on the menu."

Same old Tanner. She looked over at Cole. He'd finished his meal and was wiping his fingers on a paper napkin. "Thank you, Maddy. That sounds terrific."

"You're welcome. I wasn't sure what clothes belonged to whom, so everything is folded and in the laundry basket. You and Tanner can sort it out."

"Sounds good."

Luke started to squirm on her knee while Liam still methodically ate Cheerios. Maddy realized she'd left hand wipes in the bag, and when she reached for a paper napkin to clean Luke's hands, all she did was smear the stickiness around.

Without a word, Cole got up, opened a drawer, took out a cloth and wet it at the sink.

"Here," he said quietly, handing it over.

She took it gratefully, surprised that she hadn't even had to ask. In a few quick movements she'd wiped both of Luke's hands and his face and put him down on the floor. He went into the living room, his tottering gait so typical of a child new to walking, and grabbed a stuffed cow that mooed when he shook it up and down. Which he did. Several times.

"Ooo. Ooo." Liam's attention was shot now, so she wiped him off and let him go, too.

Tanner got up from the table and took his plate to the dishwasher. "Hey, Cole, I'm going to run that errand we talked about earlier."

"Sounds good. I'll see you back here later."

"Thanks for lunch, Maddy." Tanner smiled and headed for the mudroom. "'Bye, boys," he called cheerfully.

"Tanner hasn't changed a bit, has he?"

Cole shook his head, a sheepish smile on his face. "Not much. Though he tends to be a little more discreet than he used to be. Thank the Lord for that."

Maddy had heard stories of how Tanner had gotten married in Vegas when he was younger, and that the marriage had only lasted a few days. But she wouldn't ask about that and she wouldn't judge. She knew how it felt to be on the receiving end of that sort of talk.

"He's just a bit reckless, that's all. But he's still young. Hell, he's only twenty-five."

She smiled. "And your thirty-three is so old."

"Older than your thirty-one."

A squeal and cry erupted from the living room and Maddy got up to sort it out. By the time she'd returned, Cole had cleared the table and loaded the dishwasher—including wiping the mess her sons had made on the kitchen table.

"That's supposed to be my job," she said.

"Whatever. It's nearly time for you to be off the clock, anyway."

"The boys have been really good," she said, turning back to the remaining bowls in the dishwater she'd left. It had cooled, but there was still hot water in the kettle and she added it to the sink. "They're going to get tired soon. One o'clock is a good quitting time."

He picked up a towel and started to dry the last of the dishes.

"Cole, I know you want to get back to work. Really, I've got this. You're set for today and I'll be back day after tomorrow. There should be ham left that you can have for tomorrow's dinner."

"Do you have to be so, I don't know, businesslike?"

There was an edge of irritation to his voice that surprised her. "Isn't that what I'm here for?"

He huffed out a breath. "It just feels weird." His gaze caught hers and the intensity of it made her catch her breath.

"If you didn't want me to work for you, you shouldn't have offered me the job."

He opened his mouth to say something, but then shut

it again, as if he thought better of it. She narrowed her eyes. "What were you going to say just now?"

"Nothing. It's not important."

"Okay, then." The kids were tuning up again, starting to fuss as nap time neared. "I really want to run the vacuum over the floors, Cole. I'll see you Friday. Okay?"

But his eyes didn't let her go. They held her, tethered there, for long seconds while the boys played with toys, a whiny undertone to their chatter. For the briefest of moments he dropped his gaze to her lips and back up again. But it was long enough for heat to rise to her cheeks. The last thing she wanted to do was be bashful, to acknowledge such a small thing could affect her in any way. So she lifted her chin just a little and kept her shoulders straight.

Unless she was imagining things, there was a new light of respect in his eyes.

"I'll see you Friday," he said, stepping back and giving her a nod.

"Yes, and at the tree lighting, too," she added. "That's Friday night."

"Right."

And still he didn't leave...until the silence grew awkward.

"Well, 'bye." He smiled, a little uncertainly, and then went to the boys and knelt down. "'Bye, boys," he said. He held up a hand and Luke rushed forward and gave him a sloppy high five. Liam hung back and stared.

Cole looked over his shoulder at her. "He's going to be a tough one to win over."

And then finally, blessedly, he was gone to the mudroom. Maddy let out a breath and counted to ten, then busied herself around the kitchen and living room, picking up as much as she could so that they'd be ready to go once the floors were done. Once she heard the door slam behind Cole, she ventured into the mudroom and got the vacuum from the closet. She sat the boys on the sofa, and they were just tired enough they stayed put for the ten minutes it took her to finish tidying and put the vacuum away.

Then there were snowsuits and boots to put on and mittens and the trip to the car to fasten them inside and by the time Maddy was on the road back home she was exhausted. She really should do some baking for Sunday's coffee break after church, but she thought she just might have a nap instead when the boys were asleep. The idea sounded decadent and very, very lovely.

Instead the boys fussed and resisted being put down until, worn-out, they finally collapsed, sprawled on her bed so there was no room for her. She covered them with a blanket, then tiptoed down to the sofa to try to settle her frayed nerves. She was just drifting off, in a hazy half-conscious state and thinking about Cole's finely shaped lips, when the phone rang. And rang, and rang because she couldn't find the handset to the cordless. It went to her voice mail, but not before Liam woke up and started crying.

At that point Maddy felt a bit like crying herself.

She was just so completely overwhelmed. With everything. With handling it all on her own. Yes, she was still so incredibly angry and hurt by Gavin's deception. But most of all she missed him. After all he'd done, she still missed him, and his smile, and the way he'd take one of the boys and share the load with the kids and step in and cook dinner if she'd had a crazy day. Maybe his betrayal hurt all the more because in so many ways she'd thought they'd had a strong marriage. A partnership.

She missed his help, missed having someone to talk to at the end of the day, missed having someone to tuck her against his side in bed at night and make her feel secure and safe and not so damned alone. Even though things had been strained during the final months of their marriage, she'd thought they'd work through it. She'd thought it was just the adjustment to having twins and being parents and not having as much time for each other.

Tears were streaming down her face as she went to get Liam, who was snuffling and wiping his eyes with a fist. She took him downstairs so Luke could still sleep, and put him down before she sank into the couch cushions.

He was a year old, couldn't speak, didn't understand a bit of why she was upset. But at that moment, he patted her on her knee, lifted his arms for up, and when she picked him up and held him in her arms, he didn't fuss. He just snuggled in against her chest, tucked his face against the warm curve of her neck and put his pudgy little hand on her cheek.

"I love you, little man," she said softly, sinking back into the corner of the sofa and folding her legs yoga-style. She turned her head a little and kissed his soft hair, and he patted her cheek with his fingers, a move she knew he found consoling. Like a constant reassurance that she was there. Not going anywhere.

Five minutes later she stretched out her legs, slid down in the cushions and looked down at Liam's sleeping face.

Safe. Secure. Not alone.

She could provide that for her son. And she was living proof that she could make it on her own. But sometimes she wished someone was there to take away her loneliness, too.

Chapter 4

The Gibson Christmas tree lighting was a big event. In past years, it had been a simple one-hour community occasion that was decently attended. But this year, with the advent of Snowflake Days, it was bigger and better. As Maddy parked her car in the fire department lot, she was amazed at the crowd already gathered. The lighting wasn't for another forty minutes.

Her mom was in the passenger seat and her dad was squished in with the boys and their car seats in the back. "Are you guys okay with the stroller and stuff? I didn't think I'd be needed this early."

Her mom, Shirley, laughed. "Honey, the boys will be fine. We'll just sneak a little rum and nutmeg into their milk and…"

"Mom!"

Her dad's chuckle came from the back. "Maddy, you

go. Leave us the keys, though, will you? So we can make sure we have everything and can lock it?"

She nodded and handed over the keys. "No candy canes for the boys, okay? I don't want them to choke."

She hopped out of the car and left the diaper bag behind for her parents. No candy canes? Ha. She'd learned one thing about grandparents very quickly. They nodded and agreed and then spoiled kids as soon as Mom's back was turned. Maddy reminded herself that her mom had raised three kids and they'd all survived. Besides, she was too grateful for the help to say much at all. Since her brothers both lived out of state, she figured that one day she'd be able to repay the favor when her parents got older and needed help.

Cole was at the food donation station already, and he looked up and smiled as she approached. "Hey, there," he greeted, and she couldn't help but smile. He was bundled up in a heavy jacket and boots and mittens, but wore a ridiculously plush Santa hat on his head. "Sorry I missed you at the house today. I had errands for the festival and didn't get back in time."

"It was no problem. I hope the chili was okay."

"It was perfect." He took a bag of food items from one family and thanked them. "Okay. So here's what I've done. Canned goods in one box, paper and cleaning items in another, pasta and rice and all the other stuff in this box. There are extra boxes under the table here if you need them." He grinned, showing his perfectly white teeth. "And by the looks of this crowd, you're gonna need them."

She'd been half happy, half disappointed Cole hadn't been at the house when she'd dropped by, and when Tanner had come in for lunch she'd kept busy making the chili while he ate rather than sitting and talking. And now she had this overjoyed feeling at seeing Cole again. She was a little embarrassed, bashful when their eyes met, a delicious twirly sensation tumbling in her stomach when she heard his deep voice. She surely wasn't ready to move on, so why did she constantly feel like a schoolgirl around Cole Hudson? She reminded herself that he tended to have this effect on girls. He always had, even when they were in school. And yet he'd never had the reputation of being a ladies' man. Not like his brother.

She stepped forward and accepted a grocery bag of donations from a family, finding an assortment of toothpaste, soap and shampoo inside. She put it in the proper box and jumped in surprise when she turned around and Cole put his Santa hat on her head.

"What are you doing?"

"Whoever works the station has to wear the hat," he decreed.

"I've got a knitted one," she protested, but then realized she'd left it in the diaper bag. With her parents.

"Is it invisible?" he asked.

She smiled at a teenage couple who came over, holding hands, and offered a jar of peanut butter and another of jelly. Cute.

"Don't you have somewhere to be?" she asked, annoyed. And amused, damn him. She let the hat sit atop her head where he'd awkwardly placed it.

"Sure do. I get to plug in the lights. Let's hope I don't have one of those Clark Griswold moments where I plug them in and nothing happens."

She did laugh at that. *Christmas Vacation* was one of her favorite holiday movies.

"I don't want to keep you. Maybe you'd better check

each one individually. And definitely make sure they're twinkling."

He leaned forward, a devilish look in his eye that made her realize that he and Tanner really did resemble each other. He touched the tip of her nose with his finger. "You are cheeky tonight," he said, and he winked at her. Winked! "I like it."

Her lips fell open and she scrambled for a crushing response, but before her brain kicked back into gear, he was gone.

The hat was warm from his head and she tucked it closer around her ears as the crowd grew and the food donation boxes filled. She greeted neighbors and friends, people she knew by sight but not by name by virtue of working in the library, and nearly everyone wished her a merry Christmas. The high school band teacher conducted a few instrument ensembles for background music, the trills of flutes and jazzy notes of saxophones brightening the air. Several feet away the business association, small though it was, had a table set up with cookies from the market and huge urns filled with hot chocolate and mulled cider. The rich, spicy scent was delicious.

At 7:00 p.m. sharp, Cole stood on a podium and got everyone's attention with a sharp whistle. "Merry Christmas, everyone!" he called out.

Holiday wishes were returned enthusiastically by the crowd, along with clapping.

"I don't have a microphone, so I'll keep this short and sweet. Welcome to Gibson's first ever Snowflake Days! Tonight we're going to light our tree and sing a few carols and have an all-around good time. Tomorrow there's a craft sale at the church, and you won't want to miss it. I heard Gilda Turner's made her famous fudge."

There were laughs through the crowd. Gilda was getting close to ninety and every boy and girl who'd grown up in Gibson had, at some point, tasted Gilda's fudge. There was none like it anywhere.

"And at the library tomorrow afternoon, we've got wagon rides for the kids, plus treats and story time. Finally, tomorrow night at the Silver Dollar, we have a dance for the grown-ups. Admission is ten dollars at the door and all the proceeds are going to the playground fund for a new structure to be built in the spring."

A round of clapping filled the air.

"Now," he said, his voice echoing over the crowd, "I'm going to turn things over to Ron here—" he nodded to his right "—and we can start the caroling. But first…can we have a drumroll, please?"

Maddy snorted, the scene from *Christmas Vacation* still in her head. Someone from the band did a roll on the snare and at the moment Cole went to plug the tree into the extension cord, he looked over in her direction, a goofy expression on his face. She half expected him to break out in "Joy to the World."

Then the tree was lit, all thirty feet of it, top to bottom in beautiful colored lights that reflected off the snowy evergreen tips. A collective *ooh* sounded, and then clapping, and then the choir director, Ron, took the podium and started the crowd singing "Santa Claus Is Coming to Town."

Cole jumped off the podium and disappeared into the crowd. Maddy let out a sigh and hummed along with the song. Donations had slowed to a now-and-again occasion, so she tidied the area and packed the boxes more efficiently for delivery. She half expected Cole to show up again, and when he didn't she pushed down the disappointment. She had no business looking for him. Sure, they'd seen a lot more of each other in the past few weeks, but she shouldn't make that into anything.

She had to worry about Liam and Luke, and that was all.

At eight o'clock she finally caught sight of him again, coming around the perimeter of the crowd. Things were wrapping up now; the crowd was down to about half, and the hot chocolate and cider were being packed up and the garbage put into bags. She hadn't even seen her parents or the boys, but she hadn't heard them fussing, either, so everything must have gone just fine.

"Wow, you've got everything ready to go," Cole remarked as he stepped up to the table. "Once the crowd disperses, I'll bring the truck down and we can put everything in the back."

"It was a good turnout, I think."

"I think so, too." He grinned at her. "I saw your mom and dad with the boys. They were sound asleep. The boys, I mean," he added, making her laugh.

"Fresh air and moving in the stroller will do that," she replied. "Unfortunately for me, that means they'll probably fight going to bed tonight."

"I never thought of that."

She raised an eyebrow. "Cole, there are many times that that's *all* I think about." She chuckled. "Sleep suddenly takes on a life of its own when you're not getting enough. Though to be honest, it's better now. They do sleep through the night. It's more getting them down at a decent time." Maddy put her hands into her jacket pockets, her fingers chilly despite the gloves she wore.

"I find I like to have an hour or so to myself to unwind. To read a book or watch a movie uninterrupted."

"Maybe the boys can have a sleepover at your parents' place sometime."

She frowned. "Oh, Cole, I couldn't ask them to do that. They do so much already."

The caroling ended with a rousing version of "We Wish You a Merry Christmas" and then everyone headed for their cars, chatting and laughing. Maddy held the sound close to her heart. She loved living here. Loved the goodwill of the town, even despite the whispers she knew still happened behind hands. Eventually they'd forget, wouldn't they? Maybe, just maybe, if she found a way to let it go and move on, everyone else would, too.

She looked over at Cole. He didn't seem to care about the rumors at all. "Cole, can I ask you something?"

"Sure." White clouds formed from his breath as he looked over the crowd, lifting his hand in a wave at someone he knew.

"When Gavin...well, when it came out that Gavin had been seeing Laura, were you surprised?"

The question certainly surprised him. His gaze snapped to hers and his face flattened into a serious expression. "Wow. Okay. To be honest, yes, I was surprised. I thought you guys were solid. And Gavin never struck me as a cheater."

Tears stung her eyes. "Me, too. I think that's what keeps me from moving on. How could I have been so wrong about him?"

"I don't know," he answered honestly.

"They dated in high school. You knew that, right? Maybe he never got over her."

"Have you asked her?"

Maddy's blood ran cold. "Of course not. I can't do that."

"I understand. She might be able to give you some answers, though. It might help."

"I... I just can't, Cole. It's too humiliating. Besides..." She looked up at him. He was watching her earnestly, as though he was really trying to help. It had been a long time since Maddy had truly felt as if someone was on her side. Most people were angry on her behalf, thinking they were being supportive. And they were...to a point. But this was different. This wasn't righteous indignation. It was genuinely trying to help her sort through her feelings, and she appreciated it the most out of all he'd done for her lately.

"Besides," she continued, "I'm not sure I want to know the details. I just want to find a way to let it go, so it doesn't matter anymore."

He lifted his gloved hand and put it on the side of her face. "You will," he said with a quiet confidence. "When the time is right, you will. You're a strong woman."

She suddenly felt like the Grinch, whose heart grew a few sizes. Hers felt warm and full as she looked into his face, illuminated by the light of hundreds of Christmas bulbs on the tree.

"Maddy, are you ready to go?" Her mother's voice came across the clear air and Maddy quickly stepped back and away from Cole's innocent touch. He dropped his hand and schooled his features quickly.

"I'll go get the truck," he said, and set off to the parking lot.

The stroller wheels squeaked on the snow as her parents approached. The twins were tucked in with blankets, sleeping peacefully. A tender feeling stole over

Maddy as she looked down at them. Tired as she could be, and stressed with supporting the three of them, she loved them so much. There was nothing better than hearing their big baby belly laughs or getting sloppy kisses and warm cuddles.

"Cole's gone to get the truck. I wanted to help him put the boxes in the back before I took off."

"Cole, huh?" her dad asked, his blue eyes twinkling at her. "He's a nice guy."

"Yes, he is. And that's all he is, Dad."

"Well, shoot."

Her lips fell open. "I thought you always liked Gavin!" How could they be rooting for a new…whatever? Boyfriend? That sounded ludicrous.

"Honey, we did. We were so shocked when…well, you know. But you're too young to be alone."

"And it's too soon for me to be thinking of anything else," she reminded them. Gavin had been gone less than six months.

Cole's truck crept toward them and Maddy turned away from her parents, hoping they couldn't see her hot blush. Maybe she was reminding herself as much as them?

Cole hopped out and Tanner got out of the passenger side. "Hey, Maddy," he said easily. He gave a nod to her parents, shot a smile down at the sleeping boys and then, with the boundless energy he always seemed to have, let down the tailgate and reached for the first box.

"You probably want to get those boys home and out of the cold," Cole said, picking up a box. "I found Tanner, so there's no need for any help loading this up. We'll have it done in no time."

"You're sure?"

"I'm sure. Go home and have a glass of wine and I'll probably see you around tomorrow at some point. I'll be out and about at the different events."

"All right." She was tired, and tomorrow she wouldn't have any help with the boys. Hopefully they'd sit quietly while she was reading stories at the library. They did tend to love story time, thankfully.

They made their way back to the lot and Maddy's brow puckered in confusion. "I thought I parked over there?" she said, pointing at an empty area of the fire station lot.

"Your car's right there," her dad said, pointing to the right. "Long day, sweetheart?" His voice was teasing, but Maddy was certain she hadn't parked there.

"Do you have the keys, Dad?"

"Right here." He pulled them out of his pocket and handed them over.

As they approached her car she noticed something stuck under the windshield wiper. Closer examination showed it to be a promotional Christmas card from McNulty's Auto, just a few doors up the street. She took it from under the wiper, thinking it a simple holiday advertisement, but there was a piece of paper stapled to the top.

Merry Christmas, and drive safely—from Santa Claus. Then there was a receipt, rung up for zero dollars but showing four brand-new winter tires.

New tires?

She stepped back from the vehicle and looked down. Sure enough, there were brand-new tires on her car. It was exciting, on one hand, but on the other, she didn't like charity. "Dad? Did you and Mom do this?"

There was a gleam in her father's eye. "No, we didn't. Must've been Santa."

"Don't be ridiculous." She frowned. "And is this why my car was moved? You have to know something. You had the keys."

Her dad merely shrugged. "Maybe we should get the boys out of the cold?"

"Mom?"

Her mom, too, was trying hard not to smile but looking as pleased as the cat that got the cream. "It is chilly for them to be out so long."

She wasn't going to get anything out of her parents. She recognized the expression on their faces, and they could keep a secret like nobody's business.

The whole way back to her parents' place, Maddy wondered who would have gifted her with the tires. The only person she could think of was Cole, and that was a stretch at best. It was a long way from talking more often to spending hundreds of dollars for such a present. He was already helping her out by giving her the extra work. It couldn't be him.

Besides, he'd been at the tree lighting all evening, and it must have been a very fast job to get it done in the little over an hour she'd worked the food-bank booth. It had to have been her parents. It was a very nice, very practical Christmas gift.

"Thank you both," she said, once she'd pulled into their driveway. "I've been meaning to put tires on and should have done it weeks ago."

"Santa," her father reiterated with a grin. "Drive safely."

Drive safely. The same words as on the note. She had

to admit, she was relieved. It was easier to accept such a thing from her parents than someone else.

Once she got home, she wrestled the boys inside, changed them into pajamas, gave them each a drink of warm milk and tucked them into bed, taking a few minutes to sing softly beside their cribs, hoping to soothe them back to sleep. It took about a half hour, but when they were finally asleep she sneaked out the door and let out a deep breath.

Cole's parting words echoed in her head. Feeling indulgent, she did just as he suggested. She poured herself a glass of wine, ran a hot bath and dug out the book she'd been reading about twenty pages at a time.

Maybe it was high time she started pampering herself a bit.

And if she thought about Cole Hudson while doing it, she wasn't going to beat herself up about it. She'd been a wife, a widow and the object of pity for too long. Maybe it was past time she felt like a woman again.

Chapter 5

Cole felt Tanner's eyes on him the whole way home.

"If you have something to say, just say it," Cole growled. Tanner was grinning at him like a fool and Cole wasn't in the mood.

He'd been thinking too much about Maddy's smile... and knowing he shouldn't be. That didn't fit in the cat egory of "being neighborly."

"You are one sneaky bastard," Tanner finally said, leaning back in the seat and chuckling. "I wondered when you hired her to help out at the house. Hell, bro, we've managed on our own before for a few weeks."

"That's not it at all," Cole protested. "Gavin left her in a hell of a mess, and she's trying to make a Christmas for those boys."

"And the winter tires? You went to a lot of bother to have them put on without her knowing. Not to mention the expense."

"She's driving out to the ranch with just those all-seasons on. It's not safe."

"Sure."

Cole's annoyance grew, and he knew it was because his brother was right. This did go beyond being good neighbors. But what did it mean? Or what did he want it to mean? "Look, let's just say I'm playing secret Santa for a family who could use a hand this Christmas, okay?"

"Sure," Tanner repeated, in that same smug, infuriating voice.

Cole glanced over at Tanner. "The committee for the festival has a list of families who applied for some help to get through the holidays. Know who's not on the list? That's because she's too damn proud. And I can't blame her. Her private life has been the topic of conversation around this town for the last half of the year, probably longer. I can't imagine she'd like her financial situation made public, too. She's a good person who got a raw deal and if you don't want to help, that's fine, but you can get off my case about it."

Tanner's teasing smile disappeared. "Damn, Cole, calm down. I was just riding you a bit. You don't usually give me ammunition. I was just having a little fun."

Cole sighed. "Look, I'm a bit touchy. Maddy's a nice woman. But people can be judgy."

"No judgment here." Tanner lifted a hand in peacemaking gesture. "I'm the last person to pass judgment on anyone. If you want help, say the word. I like Maddy, too, and her boys are something."

They sure were. Busy and rambunctious when awake, but little angels when they slept.

Tanner lowered his hand and spoke again. "Just so we're clear, if you did happen to have feelings for Maddy,

I wouldn't say a word. Hell, it's the first time I've seen you fired up over a woman since—"

"Don't." Cole bit out the word. He didn't want to talk about Roni. He'd given her everything he had, and she'd cut and run, leaving nothing more than a note behind.

"Hey," Tanner said, quieter, "I like Maddy. She's always been real nice. My only caution would be to say you've got your work cut out for you. Can't imagine she's too fond of romance right now."

"You got that right." Cole tapped his hand on the steering wheel. "Which makes this a nonissue. Anyway, the only job I've got for you tomorrow is to give me a hand delivering all this to the food bank."

"You got it."

The cab of the truck was quiet for a while, and then Cole posed a question that had been on his mind for some time. "Hey, Tanner? You ever think of getting married again?"

Tanner laughed. "Again? I'm not sure three days in Vegas really constitutes being married in the first place. Legally? Yeah, I guess it was. But it wasn't like we, uh, had a marriage. It was a stupid idea and I'm not in any hurry to repeat it. If that answers your question."

"Sorta," Cole replied. But he wasn't going to pry further. Tanner had a right to his privacy, too.

The topic was completely dropped as they arrived home, locked the truck in the garage and headed inside where it was warm. But even as they sat down to watch TV, Cole couldn't get Maddy off his mind. The way she'd smiled up at him tonight had made his chest feel weird, as if it was expanding or something. He wished he could have seen her face when she realized she had four brand-new tires on her car.

He'd made her parents promise not to tell. He didn't want her knowing they came from him. But he wished he could have seen her smile anyway.

He could call himself Santa Claus or a good neighbor or however he wanted to put it. But Tanner had been closer to the truth.

Cole was getting sweet on Maddy Wallace, and he wasn't at all sure what he wanted to do about it—if anything.

Sometimes Maddy wished the boys were older so they could walk on their own and didn't always need to be in a stroller or in her arms. Of course, she reminded herself, that also meant that she'd end up having to chase them around. Still, as she carried a backpack with supplies and a kid on each arm, she felt like little more than a pack mule.

Snowflakes fluttered through the crisp air as she crossed the library parking lot to where a wagon and team of horses waited. Despite her weariness, she smiled at the sight of the wagon. Duke Duggan sat up front on a makeshift seat, holding the reins in his hands. The wagon's sides were decorated with swoops of red and green garland, and one of the horses stamped its feet, the sound of bells jingling through the air. Quinn Solomon was already seated with his daughter, Amber, and Rylan Duggan was waiting by a ramp that had been fashioned to help passengers aboard.

"Afternoon, Maddy." Rylan gave a roguish grin. "You and the boys goin' for a ride?"

"Apparently." She smiled back. "Where's Kailey today?"

"Working the craft show and lunch. She's handling

the cash box for the raffle, and Lacey's at one of the bake tables." He gave a nod. "I don't remember anything like this from when I was a kid."

"Are you coming on the sleigh ride, too?"

He laughed. "Naw, I'll leave that up to Duke. I get to do crowd control."

She did laugh then. She'd just bet Rylan would be a great bouncer, but there wasn't a lot of need for muscle at a Christmas sleigh ride.

"Ma'am?" he said, holding out his hand.

"I got this," said a voice behind her, and a delicious shiver went down her spine. *Dammit.*

She schooled her features and turned around, pasting on a platonic smile that she hoped gave no hint of the sudden rapid beating of her heart. "Oh, hi, Cole."

"Hi." His smile warmed her clear through. "You've got your hands full, as usual." He reached out and took Liam into his arms, the movement looking strangely natural for a bachelor. Liam stared up at him with big blue eyes, most of his face shadowed by his thick hat and scarf.

"I thought I'd take the boys on the ride before story time," she said.

"That's a great idea. Let's get on and get good seats."

Let's? As in the both of them?

He gestured with his free hand and she had no choice but to go up the ramp ahead of him. Once on the wagon, she moved toward the front and perched on a bale of hay covered with a dark blue blanket. Quinn was across from her, listening to his daughter chatter on a mile a minute. Cole sat beside her and settled Liam on his knee. "So," he said conversationally, "did you enjoy the tree lighting last night?"

"I did. The committee did a great job."

"Are you going to the dance tonight?"

She laughed. "Right. I'll probably be in bed by nine o'clock. These guys went to sleep okay last night, but they got up at five."

"Don't you ever get to go out, Maddy?"

The question hurt a little. She and Gavin had gone out quite often before the boys had come along. Their social life had been part of a perfect marriage. The nights out had become more infrequent after the twins had been born. Now she was too tired to go out, and even if she did want to, it was hard to justify the extra expense.

Never mind the whole third-wheel thing.

"Oh, I go now and then." She offered another smile, though it was harder to keep it on her lips. Luke fussed in her arms, and she looked away from Cole and focused on making her son comfortable.

The wagon was filling up and happy kid chatter eliminated the need for more conversation. Within minutes Rylan secured the gate at the back and Duke clucked to the horses, setting the wagon in motion. The bells on the harnesses jingled merrily and the boys perked up, looking around as they sensed the movement and heard the noise. They moved through the end of the parking lot and over a little curb, then the twenty yards or so to the walkway that followed the river.

There was a skim of ice on the water, making it dark and still, though it wasn't quite frozen enough for skating yet. The recent snow clung to the branches on the trees, and the passengers were full of holiday spirit as they jingled their way west.

Someone started up a chorus of "Jingle Bells" and soon everyone was singing along—some definitely louder than others, a few slightly off-key but making up for it with enthusiasm. Beside Maddy, Cole's tentative baritone joined in. He kept Liam on his lap, and she relaxed quite a bit, seeing as the boys were content to babble along with the singing and were busy looking around them.

"This is really nice," she commented as the song ended and the wheels squeaked against the thin layer of snow on the path. "I'm glad we came."

"Me, too." Cole smiled down at her and she got that weird weightless feeling again. He was a friend. He was technically her employer. It wouldn't do to have a crush, would it?

She blinked, looking away from his gaze. That was silly. A woman her age—a widow—had no business getting a crush. Crushes were for teenagers.

A little voice intruded, though. She was only thirty-one. Not quite in her dotage yet—even if she did feel it most of the time.

"Hey, guess what happened last night?" she asked, changing the subject. "I got new tires. The note said from Santa, but I know it was my mom and dad."

His face lit up. "You did? That's great!"

"I've been meaning to put my old ones on. But one more winter would have been pushing it. It's really a godsend."

"That was really thoughtful of them." He shifted Liam on his knee, settling him more into the crook of his arm as the group started a rendition of "Frosty the Snowman."

She nodded. "I don't know what I would have done without them the last few months. They've stepped in so much. I feel guilty about it sometimes, but it's not forever."

"Your parents are great. I remember your dad keeping hard candies behind the counter at the hardware store. Whenever I went in with Dad, he'd sneak me one."

She laughed and bounced Luke up and down on her knee, as he was getting restless. "He still keeps them there. Make sure you ask him for one the next time you go in."

He laughed. "Pretty soon these guys will be asking him for candies. I'm sure your parents don't mind helping you, Maddy. According to my mom, grandkids are really important."

He said it with just a touch of acid in his voice, and Maddy laughed. "Getting pressure to settle down, are you?"

"Don't even." He lifted an eyebrow.

"Well, you are good with kids. I mean, the boys like you."

"They like Tanner, too." His eyebrow arched higher. "Though you can't fault a one-year-old for bad taste."

She giggled. "Funny. Tanner's…charming."

"And he knows it." Cole was grinning, too. "I shouldn't give him such a hard time. He's a good brother. A little…unreliable now and again, that's all."

Maddy sighed. "Aw, he's just not as weighed down with responsibility as some of us."

Cole shrugged. "Sometimes I wish I could be more like him."

Maddy thought for a minute. Yes, Tanner was charming, but she liked Cole's serious side. "You're fine the way you are, Cole."

His gaze touched hers, and she thought she saw a

flicker of surprise in the depths. "What?" she asked. "Has no one told you that before?"

He shrugged. "Not really. Not that it's a big deal. I just... Oh, never mind. Let's start another carol."

He started everyone singing "Santa Claus Is Coming to Town," and Maddy marveled that he'd rather lead a carol in his tentative voice than talk about himself. Then again, guys weren't much into talking about feelings, were they?

She gave a derisive huff under her breath. Maybe if Gavin had talked about his real feelings earlier, he might not have felt the need to reconnect with his high school girlfriend.

They turned around at the other side of the bridge and started back toward the library, singing more carols and their breath forming clouds in the air. Liam was getting sleepy, and he cuddled into the lee of Cole's arm. Even Luke had mellowed out, resting his head against the chest of her puffy winter jacket. Cole looked over at her as they neared the parking lot. "God, they're sweet kids, Maddy. You're doing such a good job with them."

There was nothing he could have said that would have been a bigger compliment.

"You've held things together in a nasty situation," Cole said, his voice low so the rest of the people on the wagon wouldn't hear. "I know it can't be easy. I just... Don't let what happened make you feel bad about yourself."

She sighed. "I've tried over and over to figure out if I did something wrong, you know? I was so blindsided. I just can't figure it out. Maybe if I could, I'd stop being angry. Instead I feel..."

She stopped. This was more than she'd said to anyone

before, even her parents. Certainly not her friends. She hadn't even asked if they'd known about the affair. She didn't want confirmation that she was the last to know.

"You feel what?" Cole leaned over a bit, his shoulder buffering hers a bit, creating a sense of intimacy.

She swallowed against a sudden lump in her throat. "Truthfully?" she murmured, her voice barely audible. "Stupid. I feel stupid."

He reached over with his free hand and squeezed her wrist. "You're not stupid."

"Whether I am or not is kind of irrelevant. I still feel like I am. It's like everything I thought I knew got turned upside down."

"Can I make a suggestion?"

"You're going to anyway, so go ahead." She aimed a lopsided smile at him.

He squeezed her arm again. "Don't be so hard on yourself."

She laughed. "That's it?"

"That's it." He gave a small nod. "Truth is, Maddy, if Gavin didn't want you to know, he would have hid things from you, so how were you supposed to figure it out?"

"Shouldn't I have seen the signs?"

Cole's gaze softened. "Honey, you trusted him and you believed in him. That says a lot about the kind of person you are."

"Gullible." She rolled her eyes.

"Kind," he contradicted. "Someone who looks for the best in people. More people should be like you."

He shifted Liam just a little, adjusting his weight as the boy's eyes grew heavy. "Like I said, your boys are lucky to have you."

His words sent a warmth through her, a confidence

that she hadn't felt in many months. She tried to be a good mom, and she tried to stay positive. Maybe Cole was right. Maybe she should stop feeling foolish and stupid and just…move on.

It wouldn't be that easy, of course, but she had to stop looking for what she'd done wrong. It really didn't matter anymore, did it?

The horse team plodded into the library parking lot, bells still jingling. Maddy checked her watch and saw that it was 2:40, perfect timing for returning and getting everything set up for story time. Rylan was waiting in the parking lot and released the gate on the wagon, helping rosy-cheeked children disembark. Cole and Maddy were nearly last, since they were sitting up front, and Cole kept Liam in his arms.

"Thanks for your help, Cole. I'd better get inside."

"I'll help. After that I could use some hot chocolate."

"Cole, I can manage. If this is a veiled way of trying to give me a hand, I've been managing the twins on my own for a while now."

"Maybe I want to spend more time with you."

The words were such a surprise that she had no response. Her cheeks felt hot despite the bite in the air and she kept her feet moving toward the library doors. Up until now Cole hadn't actually come out and said that he was putting himself in her path. But what he'd just admitted was pretty clear, wasn't it?

And now she didn't really have time to decide how she felt about it. The crowd at the library was growing, she had a sneaking suspicion that the boys needed a diaper change, and she needed to take a breath before sitting down to entertain a bunch of kids.

Once inside she wordlessly took Liam from Cole's

arms. He fussed a bit but she bounced him on her elbow and got him into better position before heading straight for the bathroom. Once both boys were taken care of, she made her way through to the reading corner at the back. It was decorated for the occasion, with a little artificial tree and twinkly lights. There was a rocking chair at the center, where she'd sit while reading, and several little cushions scattered around the carpet, waiting for children to get comfortable. A table was stationed nearer the entrance, where the floor wasn't carpeted, and Maddy saw hot chocolate being ladled out and cookies being consumed in huge quantities. Her stomach rumbled, but right now she hoped to sneak a few minutes to feed the boys so they'd be content during story time.

Maddy retrieved their sippy cups from her pack and sat one child on each knee, rocking in the chair as they gripped the cups in their chubby hands and drank away. She would have killed for a shortbread cookie or two—she'd missed lunch—but she was accustomed to waiting. Luke squirmed a bit to get settled, and more than a little milk dribbled down his chin, but Liam cuddled in like an angel.

Cole was over by the table, a cup of cocoa in hand, smiling and chatting with Pauline, who was jotting something down on a pad of paper as they spoke. Her heart gave a little stutter just seeing him there. Clearly he'd seen her reaction when he'd said he wanted to spend time with her and was giving her some space. Maybe she should have been cool about it, but this wasn't the same as before. Before, they'd run into each other by accident. Or she'd been at his house because he'd hired her...

She heard his laugh, singling it out from the other noise in the room. Who was she kidding? The job offer had been thinly veiled at best. It had just been easier to excuse away. Now, though, it seemed he was seeking her out.

She should probably just back away. He had no idea what he was getting himself into. She was an emotional wreck at best, exhausted all the time, and a good day was one where she didn't have evidence of motherhood smushed into her shirt. She came as a total package... and one that wasn't gift wrapped with a big bow, either.

She was messy. And altogether unsure if she was really, truly interested.

Luke had stopped squirming and when she looked down, she saw his eyelashes lying against his cheeks. A wave of tenderness washed over her. Her precocious one played hard and slept hard, and right now he looked like an angel.

Eloise Parker, Maddy's boss, picked her way through the crowd collecting on the carpet. "Looks like you're going to have a full house," she remarked, smiling down at Maddy.

"This should be easier with the boys settled down," Maddy agreed. "Believe me, I'm getting used to reading with a kid on each knee."

"You know I have spare arms. And it's been a while since I've had a chance to cuddle my favorite boys." Eloise looked down at the twins, her expression soft. "With mine in college now, it seems forever since I had small ones. And it'll be a few more years before we have grandkids."

Maddy smiled back. El was such a wonderful boss. Since Gavin's death, she'd been more than accommodating with the scheduling and Maddy's child-care quandaries. It was another reason why Maddy couldn't imagine leaving Gibson behind.

"Maybe just Luke?" Maddy shifted in her seat a little. "He's down for the count, I think. Liam's not quite there yet."

"He won't wake up?"

Maddy shook her head. "Reach into the bag. There's a little blanket there. If you put it over him, he should stay asleep for a good half hour or more. But only if you have time, El. I know it's a busy day."

"Aw, I just came in to supervise. I'm doing more enjoying than working. It's fine." She grabbed the blanket from the pack, then carefully extricated Luke from Maddy's arms. With barely a snuffle, he nuzzled into her shoulder. She covered him with the soft fleece and he didn't stir.

That left Liam, and he was still taking the odd drink from his sippy cup. Eloise moved away with Luke, and with only one child on her lap Maddy was free to pick up the storybooks she'd requested.

"Good afternoon, everyone," she said in a clear voice.

"Good afternoon, Miz Wallace," the kids chorused, and Maddy grinned. Oh, goodness, this felt just like years in the past when she'd sat on the story mat in her elementary school library. Only then she'd been the child and she'd looked up at the librarian as if she were some sort of superhero.

Even then she'd loved the library. It wasn't much wonder she'd chosen this as her profession.

"Did everyone enjoy the sleigh ride?"

There was a chorus of chatter and Maddy grinned at the excitement. She looked for Cole but couldn't see him anywhere. Disappointment weighed surprisingly heavy, but she pushed it aside. The next half hour was all about the kids, anyway.

She picked up a book and opened it to the first page. "We're going to start with a few special stories today. This first one is a real favorite of mine." She looked down at the beautiful illustrations. "*The Polar Express*, by Chris Van Allsburg."

The room quieted and she began to read. By the time she turned the first page, the audience was rapt.

She read about the adventures to the North Pole, the train, the special gift from Santa. And when that one was done, she picked up the second book: *How the Grinch Stole Christmas*.

As she made her way through it and the tongue-twisting words, Liam was also sound asleep, his tiny head drooped on her shoulder. She smiled down at the children. "Should I read one more?" she asked, knowing full well what the answer would be.

Once more there was a chorus of tiny voices urging her to continue. She looked up and saw Eloise sitting in a comfy chair, Luke still conked out. She picked up the book she'd been saving for last, trying not to notice Cole's absence but noting it anyway.

""Twas the night before Christmas,'" she began softly, "'and all through the house, not a creature was stirring. Not even a mouse.'"

A little girl in the front, who'd been a little antsy through the other stories, bounced up and down on her bum, her hand in the air. "I know, I know!" she said loudly. "The sthockingth were hung by the chimbley!"

Maddy tried not to laugh. "That's right. But we need to try really hard not to interrupt, right?"

"Thorry, Mith Wallath."

The lisp was too adorable for words. The girl couldn't be more than four, with strawberry blond pigtails and big blue eyes.

"Thank you, Darcy. Now, where were we? 'The stockings were hung by the chimney with care, in hopes that St. Nicholas soon would be there.'"

Another hand shot up and Maddy figured the attention span that had carried them through the first two stories was starting to waver. "Yes, Nathan?"

"Why is it St. Nicholas and not Santa Claus?"

Rather than get into the whole folklore, Maddy opened her mouth to explain when Bobby Rathbone called out, "Haven't you seen *The Santa Clause*? He has a whole lot of names besides Santa."

Maddy leaned forward a bit. "Boys and girls, how about we save our questions for the very end, okay?"

All faces turned to her again and she continued, grateful that the story wasn't too long, and putting lots of expression into the words.

When it was over, she closed the book and put it down by her side. "Thank you, everyone, for being such a wonderful audience. I hope you all have a merry Christmas, and make sure you write your letters to Santa so he knows what to bring you under your tree."

"Why write a letter when I'm right here?" came a booming voice, and Maddy looked up, startled, to see Cole's twinkling eyes staring at her from within a white bearded face and a hugely padded belly.

Oh, my sweet Lord. How on earth was she supposed to keep her distance from Santa Claus?

Chapter 6

"Santa!" The library echoed with excited screams, mingled with Cole's robust "Ho, ho, ho!" Liam's eyelids fluttered open at the chaos, but he didn't wake all the way. Maddy got up from her chair, more flustered than she cared to admit. "Santa, would you like my chair?" she asked.

"Why, thank you, Ms Maddy. I'm mighty tired from my trip and could use a sit-down." He winked at her and she willed herself not to blush—and failed. Even in the ridiculous suit with all the padding, he was remarkably handsome.

He plopped himself down in the rocking chair and put his big red sack on the floor beside him. "Well, what have we here? I heard there was a special group of children here today. Did everyone like Ms. Maddy's stories?" Cole made his voice deep and jolly.

"Yeah!"

Maddy couldn't stop the smile that curved her lips. He was such a natural. So willing to step in and help out with whatever needed doing. Now she knew where he'd disappeared to. He'd gone to get into the Santa suit. Wasn't he just full of surprises?

"Now," he cautioned, leaning forward in the rocking chair and adopting a serious expression, "since today isn't actually Christmas Day, whatever is in my sack is just a little something fun. The elves are still working to have all the presents ready to deliver on Christmas Eve. Santa's pretty good with names, so when I call yours, come on up and tell me what you want for Christmas and get your gift."

Every eye in the place was glued to Santa's face as he reached into his sack. He held up a little package. "Ho, ho, ho! Says here this one is for Dillon Graves," he called out, and a little boy of about five or six came forward.

"That's me."

"Come on up here and tell Santa what you'd like for Christmas."

Dillon was a bit shy, but he came forward anyway, sat on Cole's knee and confessed he wanted a new Lego kit and a belt buckle like his uncle Gary's. Cole gave him his present and picked out the next package. "Let me see. This one is for Darcy McTavish."

The strawberry blonde with the lisp. Maddy hid her smile behind her hand as the girl rushed forward, her pigtails bouncing. "That'th me, Thanta!"

Even Cole struggled to keep a straight face. "Of course it is!" He patted his knee. "What would you like for Christmas, Darcy?"

And so it went, through twenty or more kids, each one taking a turn and accepting their token gift. The sound of ripping paper filled the air, and Maddy could see that each child got something fun and holiday themed—a make-an-ornament kit, or a Christmas activity book and markers—as well as a treat like a candy-cane reindeer or a gingerbread cookie. It had taken plenty of planning to add this to the afternoon's agenda, and a rush job, she suspected, to add names to each package so that there was one for each child.

Maddy had had no idea this was even part of the plan, but it was the perfect ending to the afternoon activity. When every child had received something, Santa bade the group farewell and disappeared out the library's main doors. Maddy wondered where his clothing was stashed, but she didn't have time to think about it much since Liam woke up and, being refreshed, squirmed to be put down.

It gave Maddy a few quick moments to pack up her stuff and help tidy the story corner, as well as grab a couple of cookies from the table. During all the commotion she'd forgotten about the hollow feeling in her belly, but now it was nearly four o'clock and she was starving.

By the time she had the boys straightened away and ready to go, the crowd had thinned out considerably. Dog tired now, Maddy herded them toward the car, wondering if she dared splurge on some takeout just this once. If she got fried chicken from the diner, she could share the fries with the boys and have a piece of chicken or two left for her dinner tomorrow.

"Maddy! Hey, Maddy, wait up!"

She turned around and saw Cole jogging toward them. *Maybe I want to spend more time with you*, he'd said. Her pulse did a little leap.

She looked up into his face as he drew near. His chin

was red, presumably from where he'd removed the white beard, but his eyes were as twinkly as when he'd sat in the chair and pretended he'd just arrived from the North Pole.

How did a person manage to be so…happy?

"Looks like we both had a busy afternoon," she commented lightly. "You're a man of many talents."

"I've never been so scared in all my life," he admitted, stopping in front of her. He must have washed his face and gotten some water on his hair, because his hairline was turning frosty white in the cold air. "I kept thinking one of those kids would recognize my voice or something or say that I was too young to be Santa. Or that my beard was fake and know that I had a pillow stuck in the suit."

Maddy laughed again. She seemed to do that with alarming regularity when Cole was around. "Most people believe what they want to believe. Kids included."

Once the words were out, she considered them. She'd said them off-the-cuff, but now they rang with truth. She was as guilty of it as anyone, wasn't she? Believing what she wanted to?

"So what are you doing now?" Cole asked, interrupting her thoughts.

"Oh, just getting the boys home, I guess. I thought about stopping at the diner for some supper. I'm not sure I feel like cooking tonight."

"Me, either," he said, putting his hands in his jacket pockets. "It's Saturday night, so Tanner's probably taken off to the city for the evening." Cole's eyebrow took on an arch that Maddy figured was the equivalent of rolling his eyes. "Guess I'll just be sitting home flipping through channels, with a sandwich for company."

This was leading somewhere, Maddy could feel it.

And she welcomed it, though she wasn't about to take the reins.

Luke twisted around in her arms, restless with being held so long. "Sorry," she said, turning to open the car door. Cole reached around her for the door handle and opened it, and she put Luke into one seat and with one hand snapped the buckle into place. Then she went around to the other side and put Liam in his seat.

"Everything takes twice as long, huh?" Cole asked as she straightened and shut the door.

"You get used to it." She shrugged. "One of the girls at day care has three under five. That's two car seats and a booster seat. Besides, it won't be long and they'll be older and able to hop in themselves and all I'll have to do is buckle them in." And boy, was she looking forward to that.

"So, getting back to boring Saturday nights…why don't I pick up dinner and you take the boys home and I'll meet you there? It's got to be better than both of us eating alone, right?"

She hesitated, wondering if she should just ask the question on her mind. Was there any point in dancing around it? She'd always been a straightforward kind of person. "Cole, are you asking me on a date?"

His blue gaze held hers. "Well, technically, going out on a date would mean we actually, you know, went out somewhere."

He was skirting the topic. "Untechnically, then?"

"Is *untechnically* a word?"

"Cole." She said it meaningfully and his lips quirked.

"Okay. So if I said yes, that this was a date, would it change your answer?"

The idea of sharing a meal with him, with a grown-up…sounded lovely. And she needed to keep this in perspective. It was just a date. It wasn't as if he was proposing marriage or anything. Now that *would* be foolish.

"No."

"No is your answer? Or no, it wouldn't change it?"

She couldn't help it—she chuckled. "Are you being this way deliberately?"

He took a step closer to her. Her pulse leaped again. "It depends. Do you find it annoying or endearing?"

He looked so cute and hopeful she lost all her willpower. "Fried chicken. And I like extra coleslaw."

His answering grin lit his face, making him look boyish. How could a woman stay immune to that? Besides, he didn't know what he was getting into. The boys were terribly messy eaters. Cole was bound to get food on him somewhere.

"Great. I'll see you in half an hour or so?"

Half an hour. It might give her enough time to get home, do a quick five-minute tidy and freshen up. Because this was a date. No matter how they twisted the circumstances, no matter how casual…this was Maddy's first date since she'd become single again.

Holy crap.

"I'd better get going, then," she said, feeling a little breathless. "The boys hate sitting in their seats if we're not going anywhere." As if on cue, Luke started fussing, loud enough they could hear him through the closed windows. "Wait. Do you know how to get to my place?"

"It's on Oakleaf, right?"

She nodded, wondering how he knew that.

"See you soon," Cole called before she could ask, and with a parting smile, he turned around and headed across the lot for his truck.

Maddy got behind the wheel and took a deep, fortifying breath. Once she started the car, got the heater going and put it in drive, Luke quieted. And it was a good thing, because in her head she kept hearing the words *I have a date. I have a date. I have a date...*

The drive took ten minutes, and by the time she got home she wasn't sure if she was excited or nervous or both. So her frayed nerves really weren't prepared for what she found on her front doorstep.

A Christmas tree. A beautiful, full spruce that stood about seven feet tall, just tall enough to fit in her living room and put the angel on top without hitting the ceiling. A white tag fluttered in the wind.

She took both boys inside and deposited them in the living room on their play blanket surrounded by toys. Happy to be free to do as they pleased, both started pulling toys from the big yellow tub in the corner. Maddy stepped back outside and looked at the tag. *To the Wallace family. From your secret Santa.*

First the tires, and now a tree. Had her dad delivered it this afternoon? God bless him. Her parents had to know that Christmas was particularly difficult this year, and she loved how they were trying to make it better. She'd have to call them later and thank them. But right now Maddy worried more about the state of the kitchen and bathroom. Tomorrow would be time enough to dig out the decorations and the stand and have a go at the tree.

The surprise tree put her in an extrafestive mood, though, and she hummed as she put the dishes from the sink into the dishwasher and hurriedly wiped off the countertops. The pile of clean sippy cups in the drying rack got put away in the cupboard, and she hung the dish towel over the handle of the oven door instead of leaving it in a crumple. Then it was off to the bathroom to pick up dirty pajamas, give the sink a wipe and tidy the vanity.

A quick check on the boys and then she was zooming off to the bedroom. She hesitated, then pushed away the idea that Cole would ever see the inside of this room. She peeled off her sweater and put on a new one, a light blue one with a soft cowl neck. Her hair was a staticky mess from being under her hat. She dragged a brush through it and frowned. It needed…something. She tried a ponytail—too casual. Leaving it down—too limp. Up in a bun—too uptight. In the end she grabbed a thin white headband and slid it behind her ears. Hair down was good, and off her face made her feel less straggly.

Makeup. Maddy was well and truly flustered now, wanting to look nice but not wanting to look as though she'd put in a lot of effort and give Cole the wrong idea… or the right one, as the case might be. A quick reapplication of mascara and some tinted gloss brightened her eyes and lips without being overdone, and she left on the same jeans she'd worn to the library.

She shut the door to her bedroom as she left, then stepped into the boys' room and made a mad dash through the clutter, throwing dirty clothes in their hamper, straightening the bedding and dumping the diaper pail into the garbage in the garage.

It had taken her exactly fifteen minutes.

"Mama! Mama!"

Back in the living room, Liam was bobbing up and down, holding a fabric book in his chubby hand. "Mama," he said, one of the few words he could manage at only a year old. He waved the book in the air.

Luke had a plastic truck and was on his hands and knees, making *vroom* noises as he ran it over the carpet.

Cole's truck was pulling into the driveway.

Oh, Lord, oh, Lord, oh, Lord, she thought.

"Boys, how about some supper? Are you hungry?"

That got their attention. Luke's truck zoomed off course and careened into a chair; Liam dropped the book and Maddy tried to hold her composure as Cole got out of his vehicle carrying two paper bags.

He had no idea what he was walking into. And the trouble was, neither did she. And what freaked her out the most was realizing she desperately wanted to find out.

Cole clutched the paper bags as if his life depended on it. The cashier at the diner had folded them over neatly and stapled the tops, but his death grip had crumpled them completely. A date. With Maddy Wallace.

With Maddy Wallace and her children, he reminded himself. But instead of making him feel better, his stomach tied up in even more knots. He was smart enough to know that when you dated a woman with kids, you dated the whole package. In the past few weeks he'd somehow gone from wanting to lend a helping hand to a neighbor to wanting to do a lot of things that weren't neighborly at all. And over it all was the sinking feeling that he'd been here before—that he was a fool to even think she'd want him.

The tree he'd had Tanner deliver was propped up outside the door, he'd noticed. Tanner had done a great job, too. The tree looked green and full and the perfect height. And Maddy would never suspect him as being her secret Santa, because he'd been at the library with her all afternoon.

He'd thought to take a moment to gather his wits before ringing the bell, but Maddy opened the door and smiled at him. Holy doodle, she looked good. If his memory served, she'd changed into different clothes from this afternoon, and her hair fell in silky waves to her shoulders. Her eyes were incredibly blue, her cheeks bright in a porcelain face, and her lips were pink and puffy and begging to be kissed.

And all around him was the scent of fried chicken, pulling him back to reality. God, he had to get a grip.

"Take-out delivery," he announced and held up the bags.

"Come on in." She stepped aside, making room for him to enter.

The first thing he noticed was how lived-in her house looked. Not in a bad way, but in a cozy kids-live-here way that made him instantly comfortable. He thought of his great-aunt Gertrude's from when he'd been a boy. No one was allowed to touch her knickknacks, and they'd gotten in trouble for sliding in sock feet on her perfectly polished hardwood floor. Maddy's house was comfortable, with a chocolate-brown corduroy sofa and chair, beige carpeting, and a wooden entertainment unit with rounded corners. The boys ran around, but their toys were centered on a large colorful blanket on one side of the room.

"Excuse the mess," she apologized. "It's impossible to keep the place neat with two tornadoes blowing through at any given moment."

"It's great," he commented. "And perfect for a family." He handed her the bags and unzipped his jacket. "Know what I like about your kids, Maddy?"

"What?"

He took off his jacket and hung it on a hook beside

the door. "They're happy. It wouldn't be right to bring them up in a museum where they couldn't touch anything, you know?"

"Well, what you see is what you get around here." She smiled. "Take off your boots and come into the kitchen. I've got to get a few things ready for the boys."

He put his boots on the mat and followed her into the kitchen. "I see you got a Christmas tree," he commented lightly, stepping into the brightly lit kitchen. Her comment about the tires earlier told him she didn't suspect, and it was kind of fun playing along.

"It must be from my dad. He's been doing this secret Santa thing this year. First the new tires on my car, then the tree." She got plates out of the cupboard, turned around and smiled. "I think they knew that Christmas spirit was in short supply this year and they're trying to do something fun."

Well, the motive was bang on, but the identity was all wrong. It was what Cole wanted—anonymity—but he felt a little bit jealous knowing she thought her father was responsible. Still, telling her up front would have just made her refuse. He could live without taking credit. He wasn't doing it for gratitude, after all. He just wanted to help, and he was in a position to do it.

"It was here when I got home this afternoon," Maddy continued, putting a dish in the microwave. "I'll have to search the basement for the tree decorations and stuff. Maybe I'll put it up tomorrow."

Cole went to the table and started taking takeout containers from the bags. "I suppose the twins don't remember last Christmas."

She shook her head. "Not hardly. They were so little." She took the dish from the microwave and tested the food inside with her finger. "Yummy, right?" She sent him a goofy smile. "They only have a few teeth, so I still have to keep things pretty mashed up for them. I'll feed them some carrots and peas and chicken, and then they can pick at cut-up fries while we eat. Hope that's okay."

Cole watched the process, intrigued.

Maddy had two small bowls, each with a rubber-tipped spoon. The boys were seated in high chairs, bibs over their clothes, excited that they were about to eat. Cole chuckled as Maddy filled the spoon for Liam, touched it to her lip to test the temperature and then moved the spoon in his direction. Just like a baby bird, he opened his mouth wide, very ready to eat.

She managed two spoonfuls before Luke demanded his turn by banging his hands on his high-chair tray. Calmly, Maddy put down Liam's bowl and picked up Luke's, repeated the process, and started to go back and forth.

Twins, Cole thought, and not for the first time, were a lot of work.

"Um, maybe I could try? That way you won't have to go between them."

Maddy looked up at him, her face blank with surprise. "You? Want to try feeding one of the boys? Have you ever fed a baby before, Cole?"

"How hard can it be?" He'd watched her. Food on spoon, spoon in mouth, repeat.

She laughed. "All right. Here, you take Luke's bowl. Not too fast."

"I got this." He pulled up a chair and took the bowl from her. Put some mushy green peas on the spoon and held it to Luke's mouth. As predicted, Luke opened wide and took the peas in one gulp. Cole looked over at Maddy and smiled widely. "See?"

"You're a pro," she replied, a silly smile on her lips. He liked seeing her smile, he realized. She looked so young and pretty when she did that.

He scooped up more food and sent it Luke's way. He soon realized that Luke wasn't as fond of the ground-up chicken as he was of the vegetables. Luke grabbed the spoon with a chubby hand and started pulling on it with surprising strength. "Come on, open up for chicken," Cole urged him, but Luke just moved his fist up and down until he suddenly let go—and the chicken on the spoon went flying. Straight onto Cole's shirt.

He heard Maddy snicker, but he refused to look at her. It was just a little chicken. He'd had far worse on his clothes.

"Put the chicken on first," she suggested quietly, "and then put the vegetables on over top. You have to be tricky sometimes."

Cole did what she suggested and Luke opened up immediately. Scamp.

They continued feeding the boys, who seemed to be big eaters considering the amount of pureed food they ate. "Do you make all your own food?" Cole asked, scraping along the side of the bowl.

"They're eating more table food now, being a year old," she commented. "But yeah. I make my own. Usually on a Saturday I'll cook stuff up, puree it in my little blender and freeze it in ice cube trays. Then I just pop them in a dish or baggie and they're good to go."

"Smart."

"Cheap. Cheaper than buying the bottled stuff. And now I can get by with just mashing it if it's smooth enough."

Cole looked over. "And better for them, too, right?"

He kept the spoon moving, the last few mouthfuls accepted eagerly by Luke. "You're a good mom, Maddy."

"Thanks." She smiled sweetly, and he felt something warm and pleasant infuse him. "Um, you might want to slow down, though."

"What?" He looked at Luke. The poor kid's cheeks were puffed out with food. Cole had been so focused on Maddy that he'd just kept mindlessly shoveling it in.

"Oops," he said, sitting back. "Sorry, buddy."

Luke began to cough. And cough some more. And then his little blue eyes watered and he gave a big cough and…

Cole added carrots and peas to the chicken on his shirt.

There was stunned silence for a minute, and then Maddy started to giggle. And giggle. And before he could help himself, Cole was laughing back until the kitchen rang with their laughter and the sound of babies thumping their fists on their high chairs.

It was definitely the strangest first date he'd ever been on.

Maddy wiped her eyes on her sleeve. "Oh, gosh. I'm sorry. You just… Oh, you were so sure of yourself. And now you've truly been initiated."

"You warned me they were messy. I forgot." He grinned, grabbed a paper napkin from the takeout bag and dabbed at the mess on his chest and sleeves.

"You wait." She picked up the bowls and went to the sink. "Now I let them feed themselves. Sometimes I think I need to get a dog so it can do floor cleanup."

He chuckled. "It really is an adventure, isn't it?"

She shrugged. "It just is what it is. Come on, let's eat. I'm hungry."

Together they unpacked the chicken and fries and the large container of coleslaw, just as she'd requested. He'd added a couple of sodas to the order, too. "Wow, I think I must really be impressing you with the fine dining on this date," he joked, watching as she cut up a few handfuls of fries and put them on the trays for the boys.

"Were you trying to impress me?" she asked, and that little nervous bubble started rolling around in his stomach again. He hadn't dated in a long time. Hadn't felt like it. But Maddy had definitely captured his interest.

"Honestly?" He met her gaze. "Not really. I get the feeling if I tried to impress you, you'd see right through me."

Her smile faded. "I know. I'm cynical. It was much nicer when I was naive and oblivious."

She looked so down that he reached over and put his hand over hers. Hers was much smaller than his, and softer. "Maddy," he said quietly, "you are way too hard on yourself. And far from being oblivious."

"This is my first date since Gavin," she admitted, looking away.

"I know," he answered, a lump forming in his throat. "And it must seem strange. It's kind of why I wanted to keep it low-key. I get it. I get that you're scared and I get that the boys come first." He squeezed her fingers. "Maddy, look at me."

She looked up. Her eyes were wide and glistened a little. The lump in his throat grew bigger. For a moment Cole considered Gavin Wallace and felt the urge to put his fist through the other man's face simply because he'd hurt her this badly. Of course, that could never happen.

"We can go as slow as you need," he assured her. Beside them the twins made babbling noises as they played with their fries, but Cole kept his eyes locked with hers. "I like you. I like hanging out with you. It can be as simple as that, okay?" He wasn't sure he was ready for more than that, either. Being with her brought back all kinds of memories—good and bad. The wonder of being in love, tempered by the frustration at wanting to help and not getting through. Shit, he'd figured it was ancient history. Maybe he hadn't moved on as much as he'd thought.

She nodded. "I'm sorry for being such a downer."

He smiled a little, knowing if she could read his mind she'd see he was being the killjoy. "Seriously, if you apologize one more time..."

"Sorry," she said, and then put her fingers to her lips and smiled a bit.

"The chicken's getting cold. Let's just eat and take it from there, okay?"

"Okay," she agreed.

He slid his fingers off hers, and they relaxed a bit, biting into the crispy chicken and dipping fries in ketchup. She hadn't been kidding when she'd said she liked the slaw, because Cole watched as she used a fork to dump half the container on her plate.

When the meal ended, Cole took the dishes to the dishwasher while Maddy wiped sticky hands, let the boys out of their chairs and went to work wiping the trays and sweeping the mess off the floor.

As Cole collected the garbage from their meal and took it to the trash can, he realized how incredibly domestic it all felt.

And how he really didn't mind it at all.

Chapter 7

Bath time was the perfect excuse for Maddy to get some breathing space. The boys were splashing happily while she knelt before the tub, making sure no one slipped. She grinned as Liam's hand smacked the surface of the water, making a loud slap noise and sending water everywhere. He looked so proud of himself.

And Cole was out in the living room. She'd been so surprised when he'd asked to feed Luke, and their shared laughter had felt wonderful for her soul. Oh, she'd missed that sort of scene so terribly. It might have made things simpler if Cole weren't good with the boys, or if he tried to exclude them from stuff. But he didn't. He dived right in and appeared to enjoy it.

Being good to her kids carried a lot of weight.

But the part that stuck in her mind the most was how he'd put his hand over hers and told her they could go as slow as she wanted. That courtesy and understanding had had the opposite effect, actually. Instead of being relieved and taking things back a notch, Maddy found herself wanting to turn her hand over and link her fingers with his. Found herself focusing far too much on the shape of his lips and wondering what it would be like to kiss him.

Oh, she was interested, all right. But she didn't really want to be. She wasn't sure she was ready yet, and Cole was too nice a guy to mess around with.

Still, she reasoned, he was a big boy. And she'd been very up-front with her feelings. If he asked her on another date…perhaps on a real date…she'd be tempted to say yes. The one thing holding her back would be what people would say. She was so tired of having her personal life be the topic of conversation, and dating Cole would be sure to spark up the chatter again. One of the drawbacks of small-town life…

Once the boys were dried and changed into their fuzzy pajamas, Maddy let them loose while she quickly tidied the bathroom. When she finally ventured into the living room, she found Cole sitting cross-legged on the floor, his lap piled with toys from the box. She stood in the doorway and just watched, smiling. Both her boys were running to the toy box and grabbing something and then showing it to Cole. He made the appropriate noises of approval, which just urged them on. Some of the toys they didn't even use anymore, like the rattles and plastic key ring. She laughed when Luke, always the excited one, reached in and nearly fell on his head trying to retrieve something. And when he ran to Cole, he tripped in his haste and landed on the carpet with a thump.

"Whoops," Cole said. "Easy, partner."

Luke's lower lip quivered and Cole got a look of panic on his face. Maddy was just about to step in when Cole said, "Whatcha got there, Luke?" and it was just distraction enough to keep the tears at bay.

Plus he could tell Luke from Liam without much trouble. Not everyone could, but Cole paid attention.

"Having fun?" she asked softly, still standing with her shoulder resting on the doorway woodwork.

"Apparently I get to see the entire contents of that toy box."

She pushed herself away from the wall and went over to the play corner. "Congrats. They've hit bottom." She turned to Liam and Luke. "Boys, let's put everything back in the box!"

To demonstrate, she picked up a stuffed dog and carried it to the tub and dropped it in. Liam got the idea and took a plastic school bus, toddled over and flung it into the box. Not to be outdone by his brother, Luke grabbed something else and the game was on.

"They're pretty little to be doing so much, aren't they?" Cole asked. "Not that I have a lot of experience with kids."

Maddy laughed. "I think because there are two of them, and they have this competition going on. Luke can't stand for Liam to be one up on him. They were both walking at nine months. I was grateful and terrified all at once."

"I can see why."

She looked at him and noticed the food had dried on his shirt. "Would you like to change that, Cole? I think I still have one of Gavin's old sweatshirts around here somewhere."

He looked down. "I'm fine. It's just a little food."

"It's no trouble, really." She'd given most of Gavin's things away, but she'd kept his law school hoodie. He'd loved it and she couldn't bear to part with it. No matter what he'd done.

She went to the bedroom and got it out of the closet. Considered for a moment. It was just a hoodie. She wasn't transferring any feelings for Gavin to Cole. She knew that with certainty as she held it in her hands, felt the thick, soft fabric in her fingers. Gavin was gone. Maybe she should just let go and move on. And lending a sweatshirt didn't have to have any deeper meaning than that.

Back in the living room, Cole's lap was nearly empty and Liam was standing rubbing his eyes. She handed Cole the shirt. "Here, you can borrow this. It's the least I can do considering you're wearing my son's supper."

Cole grinned. "Thanks."

"I'm going to get them each a bottle. They still like one at night before bed. I'll be back in a few minutes, okay?"

"Sure. We're just going to hang out here, right, guys?"

Luke went over to Cole, plopped down on his leg and started to babble.

He liked her sons. And her sons clearly liked him.

She filled the bottles and was heading back to collect the boys when she stopped dead in her tracks. Cole was changing out of his shirt, probably thinking she was in the kitchen and he had privacy. Maybe she should turn around and go back…but she didn't.

He stood in front of the sofa and unbuttoned the denim shirt, starting with the cuffs and then down the front. When he shrugged it off her mouth went dry. She'd known he was lean, but he had muscles *everywhere*. It was winter and his skin had lost its summer tan, and his pecs had a sprinkling of dark chest hair. He reached for the hoodie and she watched, fascinated, as his shoulder muscles shifted and bunched with the simple movement. Arms went inside sleeves, his head poked through the top, and the shirt slid down over his flat belly.

Whew. There was no denying that she was attracted to him in the most elemental way possible. Sure, she'd found him nice and kind and good with her kids…but just now, as she'd watched him change, she'd responded like a woman.

It felt good. Really good.

Maddy cleared her throat and put on a bright smile as she stepped into the room as if nothing had happened. "Okay, who's ready for a bottle?" she asked.

Both boys ran to her and she laughed as she sat on the sofa, making room for each of them beside her. "Go get a book, Liam," she said, and Liam turned around and picked up one of their favorites from the pile, called *Bear Feels Scared.*

"Come on up, pumpkin," she said softly, hefting them up beside her and giving them each their bottle. "Okay. Ready?"

She was a little self-conscious as she read the story, knowing that Cole was listening, too, but this was part of their nighttime ritual, and she loved reading to her kids. As all of Bear's friends found him again, Liam crawled down off the sofa and got another book, a longer one called *Are You My Mother?* By the time she finished that one, eyelids were getting droopy and most of the milk was gone.

"I'm going to try to get them settled in bed," she murmured, looking over at Cole. He was sitting a few feet away, in the corner of the couch, his ankle crossed over his knee. The hoodie made him look cozy and comfortable and sexy in a weird, casual sort of way.

"Need help?" His voice was deep in the quiet of the room.

"I'm okay. I'll be back out in a few minutes. I hope." And he'd be waiting, wouldn't he? And they wouldn't have the twins between them, or be in a coffee shop, or have his brother sitting at the kitchen table.

They'd be alone.

She swallowed against the sudden nervousness that rushed through her.

She picked up Liam, who was fading faster than Luke, and then reached out for Luke, who helped by putting his hands up and around her neck.

They slept in separate cribs, and Maddy had a rocking chair situated in between them. Tonight, though, with the busy afternoon, short nap and fun evening, they both seemed tired and ready to be tucked in. She covered them with their blankets, tucked their favorite stuffed animals around them and made sure the nightlight was turned on. And then, when everything was quiet, she began to sing in a soft voice.

Luke stared up at her with wide eyes, as if absorbing every single syllable of the lullaby. Liam's lashes began to flutter straight away, and he rubbed his eye for a second before shoving his thumb in his mouth. Maddy knew from experience that once he was asleep, his lips would slacken and his thumb would pop out, forgotten.

When the song was done, she made sure she said, "Good night, sweeties," as she always did. Keeping to the routine seemed to help them settle.

And then, with her heart pounding madly, she left

the bedroom, closed the door quietly behind her and returned to the living room.

The single corner lamp was burning, enveloping the room with a cozy glow. Cole was sitting in the same spot, his head leaned back against the cushion of the sofa, his ankle still crossed over his knee. "Get them to bed okay?" he asked quietly.

She nodded. "They were tired. It's been a busy day today, and tonight they had an audience for their antics." She smiled, stepped closer. "It's a big compliment, you know. Them wanting you to see all their toys. You're in the club."

He chuckled. "I can see why you're so crazy busy, though. My mom always said the two of us were four times the work of each of us individually."

"Sometimes," Maddy admitted. "And sometimes they have each other to keep themselves occupied and it gives me a break. I'm quite a bit younger than my brothers, John and Sam. They both left home when I was barely a teenager. We weren't that close, but I think Liam and Luke will be."

"And what about other kids? Do you want any?"

She sat down beside him, her pulse thundering in her ears. "That's . . . well, putting the cart before the horse. I haven't really thought about it much. That would mean I'd be remarried."

"Too soon, huh," Cole said.

"I like to ease into these things," she replied, and then laughed a little. "Cole, we have the strangest conversations. And I'm sorry I talk about the kids so much. It must get terribly boring."

"It's not." He moved his arm so it rested along the back of the sofa. "Believe me. The last girl I dated used to be a pageant queen. It probably sounds awful for me to say, because she was a nice girl for the most part. But when she launched into a good old pageant-days story, my eyes kind of glazed over."

Hmm. The last girl. She seemed to remember him being fairly serious about someone several years ago, though she couldn't quite remember the details. Now that she thought about it, she couldn't remember him being paired up with anyone since. Not for any amount of time. She wondered why.

He shifted lower in the corner of the sofa. "Come on over here and relax a little."

She was shy and nervous both as she wiggled closer to him on the sofa and tentatively leaned back against his shoulder. It was strong and warm and he left his arm along the sofa rather than dropping it down, keeping the embrace open. He was letting her take it slow, she realized, and she released a long breath.

"There," he said, a bit of humor touching his voice. "Nothing bad happened."

She laughed a little. "Sorry. I'm a bit nervous."

"Me, too. But it's just talking on the couch. Baby steps, remember?"

She nodded. He really did feel lovely and warm and cozy. She snuggled in a bit closer and this time his arm did come down from the top of the sofa and curled lightly around her. She closed her eyes. It had been so long since she'd been held. And with Cole it was only a little bit scary.

"Good?"

"Mmm-hmm." She closed her eyes. "Cole, why me? I mean, I've got baggage. A lot of it. And I'm prickly. I know it."

He chuckled and she felt the vibration of the sound through his chest and into her back. "Maybe I like a challenge. Besides, you're not the only one with baggage," he admitted. Before she could ask what he meant, he continued on. "Listen, what happened to you just made you cautious, that's all. You're not prickly. You're scared. I would be, too."

They let the thought sit for a few minutes, and then Cole spoke again. "I don't know, Maddy. I saw you that night at the library and I got thinking about how you're young and pretty and so damned strong and then…and then I couldn't stop thinking about you."

She turned a bit in his arms so that she could peer up into his face. "So the job offer? Was it because you were interested in dating me and that was your way in the door?"

He blushed. She saw the color infuse his cheeks, but his gaze held steady on hers. "That sounds so shallow. I just wanted to give you a helping hand because I like you. Christmas is such a rough time. Lots of people take on extra work over the holidays to help with expenses, you know."

And she'd considered just that, except she'd worried about babysitting. She nodded her acknowledgment and sat back in his arms again. "I know. And I appreciate it. To be honest, the last thing I was looking for was a date. But here we are. Maybe it just snuck up on both of us."

He shifted on the sofa, then turned her so she was facing him better. In the soft light she could make out the tiny scar just above his right eye, the way his irises seemed outlined with a black ring, the bow shape to his lips. She licked her own lips, which suddenly felt dry, and saw his gaze drop to where her tongue had wet the surface. Desire surged through her, terrifying by its very presence and exhilarating at the same time.

"It snuck up on me for sure," he admitted quietly. "You snuck up on me." And before she could think of anything to say, he dipped his head and touched his mouth to hers.

He was gentle, and took his time, and simply let himself linger for a while, teasing her lips with his until she felt herself start to relax a bit. She hadn't kissed anyone other than Gavin in...a lot of years. This felt different, strange and new, but exciting, too. As though she was transported back to a different time, when she was nineteen again or maybe twenty. There was a delicious flutter in her stomach and she tentatively lifted her hand and touched her fingers to the hair just above his ear.

That simple touch was all it took for Cole to shift his weight a little, moving closer to her on the sofa, intensifying the kiss and taking it a bit deeper.

It blossomed into something beautiful.

Cole's arm slid around her ribs, his wide palm on the hollow of her back as he pulled her close. Maddy lifted her arms and twined them around his neck, opening her lips a little to let him in. There was desire between them but something more, too. She couldn't label it, but when Cole smiled against her lips, something in her heart rejoiced.

And when their mouths parted, he pulled her in close and just held her there in a hug. The backs of her eyes stung at the tenderness in his embrace.

"Was that okay?" he murmured softly.

She nearly said it was perfect, but truthfully she was a bit shaken by it all and didn't trust herself not to sound like an idiot, so she merely nodded.

"Want to try it again?"

She did, so much. So much, in fact, she thought it was probably a good idea if they didn't. "Baby steps," she whispered, resting her cheek on the curve of his shoulder. "I have a lot to think about."

He moved his head so it angled down to look at her. "Don't think too hard, okay? You're likely to talk yourself out of…well, whatever."

"You might be surprised." She lifted her chin. "I wasn't expecting this, Cole. I need some time to process. That's all."

"Sure." He ran a finger down her cheek. "Can't blame a guy for wanting more of a good thing."

And oh, wasn't that a lovely confidence boost?

"Can I tell you a secret?" she asked, feeling a little insecure but wanting him to understand.

"Of course."

"After Gavin died, and I heard the rumors, I… I wondered if maybe I was undesirable. If that's why he went to her."

His gaze softened. "Honey," he said, his voice smooth as silk, "you are one of the most desirable women I've ever met."

She laughed then. "You don't have to lay it on thick, Cole."

The soft look in his eyes hardened, and he sat back, taking her by the arms. "Look at me," he said firmly, and she obeyed. "Don't mistake me here. I know you want to move slow, and when you say slow down, I slow down. That has nothing—absolutely nothing—to do with what I want."

Her eyes widened and her chest cramped. He was so commanding right now, and she found it incredibly sexy. Cole was easygoing as far as she knew, but right now there was an intensity about him that was awesome.

"Maddy," he said, and his fingers tightened on her arms. "You're not ready, but that doesn't mean I don't want to kiss you again. To touch you." His eyes searched hers. "To carry you to your bed and make love to you."

"Cole," she murmured, awed and frightened at the same time. Not frightened of Cole, but of the fire that sparked to life between them as he said the words. Common sense was the only thing keeping her from throwing herself at him right now, peeling off that hoodie, feeling his skin on hers.

"You're desirable, Maddy, and don't you ever doubt it. And now I think I'd better go before we do get in over our heads."

But before he got up from the sofa, he put a hand along her cheek, rubbing his thumb on her cheekbone. And he smiled a little smile, one that went right to her heart. In that moment she realized that she couldn't have asked for a better person for her first romantic involvement after Gavin. And it wasn't just because he was sweet and sexy. Cole Hudson was kind and generous. He was a good man. And when Maddy was with him she felt safe.

She walked him to the door and got his coat off the peg as he pulled on his boots. "Thank you for supper," she said quietly, holding out the jacket so he could put his arms in.

"Thank you for the whole evening," he replied, shrugging it over his shoulders.

"Even the food on your shirt?" she joked, but he nodded.

"Especially the food on my shirt. Highlight of the night."

He was teasing again and she liked it, a lot. "Oh, really. I guess I know where I fit, then."

And then he surprised her. His arms came around her so fast she barely had time to react, and he planted a searing kiss on her mouth that made her weak in the knees and stole the breath from her lungs.

"That should clear up any confusion," he replied once he'd let her go.

Dazed, she stared up at him. "Okay, wow."

A grin spread across his face. "Thanks. There's more where that came from, just say the word."

"Get going, you nut."

He had his hand on the doorknob when she stepped forward. "Cole?"

"Yeah?" He turned back.

"Did you still want to, you know, help me get the tree inside tomorrow?"

His eyes glowed at her as he nodded. "If you'd like."

"Come around one thirty or so. That'll give me time to dig out the stand and stuff."

"Sounds good." He nodded again. "Good night, Maddy."

"Good night."

She watched him go down the walkway to his truck and climb inside. Once he was gone she closed the door and rested her back against it, trying to process everything that had happened today. She touched her fingers to her lips, feeling them tremble there just a bit. She'd had a date. A date! And the boys had been good and she'd been kissed and she was going to see him again…

Forget the tree outside. This was tantamount to a Christmas miracle!

Chapter 8

It didn't take Cole long to figure out he was in big, big trouble.

He sat on the edge of his bed and put his head in his hands. Kissing Maddy had been a mistake. He'd foolishly made that comment on the wagon ride about wanting to spend time with her, testing the waters for her reaction. And he hadn't actually expected her to accept his offer of supper, low-key as it was.

He really hadn't prepared himself for how she'd looked when she came out of the bedroom after putting the boys to bed. Her sweater was soft and her hair a little bit mussed from dealing with the twins. He'd heard her singing in there, too, in the dark, and when she'd come out she'd had a contented, sleepy look about her. Cuddling on the couch had been the start, but her kisses… man, she kissed like an angel. All light and sweet and soft and with a pliancy that made a man want far more than he should expect.

She was so different from Roni. That fact had really hit home last night, leaving him temporarily defenseless. Roni's life had been dull and loveless, and he'd wanted to open her eyes to something more, to show her all the possibilities life had to offer. But Maddy's situation was different. She already knew love and kindness. She showed it every day in the tenderness and devotion to her kids, in the little things she did, the care she gave others. And that nurturing spirit was what drew him in and made him forget all his self-cautions about getting too close.

Now he was acting like a damned teenager, sitting on his bed and wondering what the hell to wear to her house to put up a Christmas tree.

Plaid shirt or sweater? Button-down dress shirt and jeans, perhaps? He got up and went to his closet, eliminating possibilities. He'd finally decided on the jeans and had tried on his third shirt when Tanner wandered into his room, his hair pushed to one side from sleep, dressed in sweats and a T-shirt.

"What's up, bruh?"

Cole gave him a sour look. "I've been up for hours. And did the chores. By myself."

Tanner ran his hand over his head. "Yeah, sorry. Late night." At Cole's wry smile, he added, "Not that. I was on call last night, and I ended up attending a couple of accidents thanks to black ice." He looked at Cole and frowned. "Where are you off to, anyway?"

"Out."

"Clearly. You've got on your good jeans and from the looks of your bed, you're trying to decide what to wear. What's the occasion?"

"Just, you know. Hanging out."

"So cryptic," Tanner replied, stepping inside the room. "So, what are you and Maddy up to today?"

"Who said I was seeing Maddy?" he asked, a little sharper than he meant to.

Tanner chuckled. "I've seen the way you look at her. And don't forget, I've been helping you pull off that secret Santa thing. So?"

Cole sat down on the bed, letting out a sigh. "I'm just helping her set up her tree."

"Right. And she issued this invitation when?"

Cole looked up at his younger brother. Cole was the older brother, but when it came to women he deferred to Tanner. His little bro never had a hard time getting the attention of the fairer sex. "Last night. We had some takeout at her place after the library thing."

"You dog."

"Careful, Tanner."

Tanner came in and picked a shirt off the bed, a deep red one with a fine plaid in navy and gold. "Wear this one. It's new and it's a good color without looking like you're trying too hard."

Cole took the shirt from his hands. "Am I an idiot? I mean, Maddy's great. But boy, is she gun-shy. Not that I can blame her. And she's got the kids… There's nothing simple about her, you know?"

Tanner put his hand on his brother's shoulder. "There's never anything simple about caring for a woman, Cole. If it's simple, it's not worth it."

"And you know this how?" Cole lifted an eyebrow. "From your three days of experience with marital bliss?"

"Ouch." Tanner took his hand away. "You want to know how I know? Because for me it's always been simple and it's never really been worth it. Not even with Brittany. Which was why it only lasted three days, and that's all I'm going to say about that."

"Sorry. That was kind of a low blow."

Tanner shrugged. "No worries. I'm used to it."

Still, Cole felt guilty. No one liked having their past mistakes thrown up in their face all the time. "So you think Maddy's worth it?"

"I have no idea. Do you think she is?"

Cole thought about how she'd looked at him last night, as if he hung the moon and the stars. How she'd confessed that she'd worried about whether or not she was desirable, when his blood had been pounding through his veins all because of a simple kiss.

"She might be. She's different from any woman I've ever dated."

Tanner laughed again. "That's because she makes you work. Cole, you're a good-looking guy. And you're a nice guy. You've never had trouble getting female attention when you actually wanted it, and from what I can see you just sort of pick and choose, and date for a while, and then go your separate ways when you get bored. None of the women I can remember you dating was any sort of real challenge."

"Are you saying I'm only interested in Maddy because she's a challenge?"

Tanner shrugged again. "I don't know, are you?"

"You're sounding like a shrink." Cole slipped his arms into the shirt Tanner had picked. Darn, his brother was right. It was a good one. He started to do up the buttons.

"I don't mean to. She's just not the kind of woman

to mess with. She's been through enough and deserves better."

Cole stopped buttoning his shirt and looked closely at his brother. "Shit. Are you sweet on her, Tanner?"

Tanner shook his head. "No. But I'm not the insensitive jerk everyone seems to think I am, either."

"Aw, Tan…"

"Oh, for Pete's sake, I'm a grown man. And I haven't done a lot to change people's minds, have I?" He grinned. "All I'm saying is, think about why you're interested. And if you really, really care for her, I'm behind you one hundred percent."

Cole undid his jeans and went to work tucking in his shirt. "Mom warned me off her before they went on their trip. Said she had too much baggage."

"It's your life, not Mom's. Besides, she'd have instant grandkids."

"Don't even. The boys are cute, but I'm not sure I'm ready to be a dad. Hell, I'm just going over to put up a damned tree."

"Sure you are," Tanner said, and then with a whistle he left the bedroom, leaving Cole with a lot to think over. Including what his motives were. Because he knew that Tanner was wrong—it wasn't about getting bored and it wasn't about the challenge. The reason he never stuck it out was because he was scared of getting his heart handed back to him again.

One thing was becoming clear in his mind. There could be no more kissing. No more romance where Maddy was concerned. Because for the first time in a very long time, someone actually had the means to hurt him. He'd do better to keep his heart locked up where it belonged, wouldn't he?

Then he thought about kissing her and the soft sound she'd made when he'd pulled her close, and realized that sometimes things were far easier said than done.

Maddy was ready this time when Cole arrived. The boys were fed and cleaned up and dressed in adorable denim overalls and flannel shirts. The kitchen was tidied of lunchtime mess and Maddy had spun around the house this morning like something possessed, dusting and vacuuming and scrubbing the bathrooms. And yes, she'd used the playpen and the boys' favorite cartoons as babysitters, but she didn't do that very often and she wasn't going to feel guilty about it.

Right now they were on the floor playing with plastic farm animals. Maddy had made them a fenced-in area from the pieces of the set that clicked together. Liam put all the animals in the pasture, Luke threw them all out, they both giggled and then they started all over again.

It was exactly one thirty when Cole pulled up in her driveway. Maddy's pulse took a leap and she pressed her hand to her tummy. All morning she'd thought about last night's kiss and whether or not she was really ready to date someone. She wanted to—it had been so amazing to actually feel like a woman again instead of a frazzled mom. Desirable, rather than an object of pity.

And yet there was still a part of her that was unsure. She was smart enough to know it was all to do with her and her own insecurities. She'd been so wrong about Gavin; how could she possibly trust herself to get it right this time? She second-guessed everything. Even now, as Cole approached her front door, she wondered if she'd made a mistake inviting him today. If it was too much, or at least too soon… If he was really as awesome as he seemed, or simply too good to be true.

The doorbell rang and the boys froze, looked at Maddy and then scrambled to their feet. The arrival of company was always a cause of excitement.

Well, there was no backing out now. Maddy went to the door and opened it while the twins thumped about behind her. "Right on time," she said brightly. "Come on in."

Cole came in and removed his boots, then hung up his jacket, sticking his gloves in the pockets. "It's a bit warmer today," he commented.

The weather. Maddy didn't know if he was as nervous as she was, or if it was one of those forced to start a conversation things. "I heard we could get some more snow tonight." She led the way inside, on the way picking up Luke, who seemed intent on getting himself in the middle of things. "You're not busy with the festival today?"

Cole shook his head. "No. Today is an open skate at the park and snow golf. There's a carol sing tonight at the church. But I'm not required to be at any of them. Tomorrow, after everything's done and collected, we'll do the raffle draw from the shopping thing yesterday."

"It's ticked along like a good watch, then."

"So far, so good."

Luke strained from her arms and held his hands out to Cole. "Hey, buddy. You wanna come up?" He took him without missing a beat and settled him on his arm.

"Luke really likes you." There was something both comforting and unsettling about seeing her baby so happy with Cole. "I never thought about it much, because they're so little. But maybe they really miss having a guy around."

Cole gave Luke a bounce, the expression on his face unreadable. "It's more likely that he recognizes me as the guy who got sprayed with food last night. It was a real bonding moment."

Liam pulled on her pant leg and she picked him up. "Do you want something to drink? I made a pot of coffee not long ago."

"Coffee sounds good," he replied, and they went to the kitchen.

She held Liam on her hip as she took out two mugs and spoons. "How do you take yours?" she asked, getting cream out of the fridge.

"One sugar, no cream," he replied.

She added his sugar, then just cream for herself, and suggested they go into the living room. Once there, she put Liam down on the floor. "Go play with your cows, sweet pea."

He scrambled down and Luke pushed out of Cole's arms to follow. Careful to not spill, Cole let him down and they ran back to their farm. Before long they were bouncing cows, horses and sheep through the pasture, making entertaining noises.

"Nice farm," Cole said, taking a seat at the end of the sofa and sipping his coffee.

"Thanks. It's one of their favorite toys. Sometimes they add dinosaurs to the mix." She grinned. "I was thinking we'd wait until nap time and then bring the tree in. Probably easier when they're not underfoot."

"You're probably right."

"I found the stand and decorations this morning, though." She sat back against the cushions. "I'm looking forward to the boys seeing it, actually. Last year they were too little."

A chicken went flying and dinged Luke in the head, and he started to wail. "Liam, gentle. Luke, come here, Mommy will kiss it." Luke toddled over, Maddy kissed his forehead and the crying ceased immediately.

"Wow, like magic," Cole said drily.

"Wouldn't it be nice if a kiss could always fix up hurts?" Maddy sighed. "It's a lot simpler when you're a kid, that's for sure."

"Isn't that the truth."

Maddy felt the need to change the subject, so she took another sip of her coffee and asked, "How's your parents' trip going?"

They chatted for the next twenty minutes about their families and the festival and basic small talk. When it was nearly two, Luke came over with a board book and crawled up on her knee. "Buh," he said, holding it out.

"You want me to read you a book?"

"Buh," he repeated.

She looked over at Cole. "Yesterday was busy and they've been up since seven thirty. It's just about nap time."

She started reading the little book and when she got to the end and gave it back to him, he handed it to her again.

So she read it a second time. This time Liam came over and climbed up on the sofa beside them. Both boys were mellowing out substantially, and when Luke asked her to read it a third time, she laughed and obliged. By that point, Liam had leaned back against Cole and his eyelids were drooping. Luke's were nearly closed, his head doing an unstable bobble now and again.

"Come on, bubba. Let's put you to bed." She cradled him in her arms and walked softly to their room, where she gently put him down and covered him up. "Have a good sleep, Luke."

He stared at her for a moment. One thing she did appreciate about the boys was they'd learned to be patient right from the start, that sometimes they'd have to wait or soothe themselves. There wasn't a peep out of him as she went back to get Liam.

His eyes were wide-awake now, though he still leaned against Cole's strong body. Maddy reached for him and he came willingly, curling his hands around her and tucking his face against her neck. She rocked back and forth for a few minutes, crooning softly. Cole smiled up at her. "He's out."

"They've been so busy lately, they've been sleeping really well. And when they're busy, I'm exhausted," she joked. She swayed back and forth a few more times. "I'll be right back, I hope."

She tucked Liam in and made sure the thermostat was set to a comfortable temperature, and then shut the door and went to join Cole.

"There. They should be good for ninety minutes or so. Should we get this set up?"

"By all means." Cole put his mug down on the table. "Where do you want to put it?"

"Right in front of the window." She smiled. "I generally just move that chair a bit to the right and move that speaker, and it sits right in the middle."

"Well, let's do that first and then bring it in."

It took no time at all to adjust the furniture, and then Maddy retrieved the tree stand and skirt while Cole went out to the doorstep and brought in the bushy tree. Needles dropped as he moved it across the floor, and more still as she got on her hands and knees to hold the stand and help him guide the trunk into the hole. As he held it steady, she tightened the wing nuts until they were tight and the tree was straight. "How's that look?" she asked.

"Good. Tanner..." He stopped talking abruptly, and she sat back on her knees and looked up at him.

"Tanner what?"

"Tanner will be jealous," he said, brushing his hands together. "It's a great tree. Nice and full all the way around."

"Hand me that tree skirt, will you?"

Cole handed her the wedge-shaped folded fabric and she spread it out. She loved this skirt. It had a creamy gold satin background, with appliquéd holly and berries and stars all over it, bordered by a rich red fringe. She smoothed it out, tied the ribbons at the back to hold it in place around the stand, and slid out from beneath the tree.

"Wow. That didn't take any time at all," she said, hopping to her feet. "Thank you so much. It would have been a real circus trying to get that in the stand by myself. And I do still love a real tree, even though the new artificial ones are so practical."

"Me, too. Dad suggested one of those pre-lit ones a few years ago and Mom had a fit. We've always had a real tree." He smiled at her. "Dad has a chipper. We just chip it up and send it back to nature."

Maddy admired the tree, imagining how good it was going to look with the decorations on. "Know what one of Mom and Dad's neighbors do? They have a tree-burning party. They set up a bonfire pit in their backyard and invite everyone to bring their trees over, and they have drinks and food and light it up. It's really fun."

Cole reached for his coffee, which had to be lukewarm at best right now. "Is that what you're doing for Christmas? Spending it with your family?"

Maddy sighed. "Probably. I've been meaning to ask my parents if they want to come over Christmas morning and watch the boys open their presents. Dinner's at their house, so we can have breakfast here." To be honest, the thought of Christmas morning was both exciting and, well, depressing. Maddy loved the holiday, but she had a hard time rustling up a lot of Christmas spirit. It was all about making it good for the boys. But the holiday was pretty lonely on her own.

Now the task of decorating the tree was before her and she blinked. Last year it had been a real production, with the four of them in the living room, carols playing, the perfect little family. As she stared at the green branches, her vision blurred. It was time she faced a truth she'd been putting off. The past and her rosy memories of it had been a lie, and she needed to accept it and, more importantly, move past it. The anger and bitterness were cutting her up inside. That wasn't good for her, or the boys, and she had to start getting on with her life.

Maybe Christmas was the perfect time to do that.

"Hey, are you okay?"

Cole's soft voice interrupted her thoughts. She quickly swiped a finger beneath her lashes. "Actually, yes. I think I am." She turned to him and smiled, feeling lighter than she had in months. "I've had such a hard time letting go. Holding on to the past, you know? And then getting angry about it. I'm tired of being angry, Cole. I think it's time I start over."

"That sounds very healthy," Cole replied, but he didn't smile. His expression was completely sober. He could have no idea how much she appreciated him taking her seriously and not giving her a patronizing smile or some platitude.

She blinked away the remaining moisture in her eyes. "You know, I think I'm just so hurt that nothing is going to be the way we planned, and I dealt with it by being mad and passing blame. But it doesn't make sense to live my life mad at someone who isn't even here, does it?"

Cole shook his head. "Not really." He sighed. "You know, I think we're more alike than either of us realized."

"We are?" She was puzzled. Cole never seemed mad or angsty or any of the things she'd felt over the last months. He was always so *together*.

"I was in love once." He gave a dry chuckle. "It seemed like everything was great, and then she was just…gone. I'd like to say I'm over it, but I'm more gun-shy than I care to admit."

"Roni, right? I seem to remember you being in a relationship for a couple of years."

He nodded. "Yeah."

He didn't say more. She supposed it was a big thing that he'd even said anything about it.

"Did you think she was the one?"

Maddy held her breath after she asked the question. They were getting really personal here. But it was good, too. She'd felt so alone in her misery and Cole had seemed too perfect. No flaws, no vices. Knowing he understood from experience made him seem a little more…normal.

"Yeah," he said softly. "I did."

"What happened?"

He didn't answer for so long that she thought perhaps he wasn't going to. But finally he let out a big sigh and met her gaze. "I gave her everything I had. But it wasn't enough. Or at least, it wasn't what she wanted. So she left. It's been pretty hard for me to open up to anyone since."

Maddy's heart ached for him. She knew exactly how that felt, and it was so, so lowering to a person's self-esteem. "I'm really sorry, Cole."

He tried to smile. "Hey, it was a long time ago. Don't sweat it."

She smiled back. He passed it off as being nothing, but she knew it wasn't. "Don't kid a kidder. It's no fun when someone hands your heart back to you with a *no, thanks*."

"True enough. Anyway, I thought maybe you should know. I really do understand when you talk about moving slow." He reached over and squeezed her fingers, and then let her hand go.

A new strength started to build within her, and it felt good. It felt as if she was starting to be in control of her own life again rather than lamenting the current state of affairs, looking forward to the future rather than being mired in the past. "Cole, neither of us can change what's happened. But there's one thing we can control, and that's what we do right now, in this moment. And you know what? Today I choose simple holiday joy and goodwill. How about you?"

Cole chuckled, the mood lightening. "Joy and goodwill, huh? That sounds easy enough. I'm in. What's first on the agenda?"

She looked up at him. Lordy, he was so handsome. Neither of them was ready for anything serious. Their conversation had just proved that. And yet there was no denying that they liked each other, so she treated him to a huge grin. "Decorations. And we only have about an hour, so roll up your sleeves, bucko. It's time Christmas got real around here."

They left the heavy topic of broken hearts behind; Cole actually did as she asked and started rolling up his sleeves. She dashed to the basement for the first box of decorations and came upstairs again, depositing it on the sofa. "Come on, there are three more. Time to use those muscles."

Together they brought up the decorations, and then Maddy started going through them, seeing what was what. "Lights," she announced, pulling out a bag. "Lights go on first. Let's test them."

She was on a roll now. Cole started stringing the multicolored lights on the tree as she plugged in each set and made sure they worked, replacing bulbs when necessary. It was the longest part of the process, but once he had all the lights at his feet, she dug through the box and got out other decorations. A pretty wreath for above the fireplace, some holiday knickknacks for the mantel. Cute candy-cane place mats for the kitchen table, handcrafted Advent calendars for the twins that Maddy and Gavin had bought last year with the intent to use them this Christmas. Plus plastic dishes—little trays and bowls and a mug and plate set for Santa's milk and cookies, as well as Frosty and Rudolph plates and cereal bowls for the boys.

She bustled around, putting everything out, thinking how she wouldn't have to worry about putting things up high as the years went on.

"The lights are done," Cole announced, getting up from his knees, where he'd been putting the last ones around the bottom. "What do you think?"

"They look great!" Maddy saw he'd taken care to

keep the spaces even so there weren't any blank spots. "Okay. Now the garland." She reached into the box and took out ropes of the red metallic stuff. "I'll do this part if you'll check in the box for the star that goes on the top? You're taller than me, anyway."

He dug around in the box while she looped the garland in festive swoops, working her way all around the tree. She ran out one row short of the bottom, but merely shrugged. This tree was a little fuller than last year's, and the stuff on the bottom would only attract little fingers, anyway. Beside her, Cole reached up and put the star on the top and plugged it into the first set of lights.

"It's getting there."

"It is." She grinned at him. "Know what? We need some Christmas music." She dashed off to the bedroom for the little portable stereo she kept in there, brought it out and plugged it in and then went to the CD cabinet in the corner to pluck out some of the old Christmas CDs.

"There's holiday music on its own channel, you know," Cole said. "You could just turn on the TV."

She would not be embarrassed; Cole already knew her financial situation was tight. "I canceled most of our cable a few months ago," she admitted. "We just get the basic channels now."

Cole was the one who blushed. "Oh."

She shrugged. "I didn't really need it, anyway. I've got my phone, too, but the stereo doesn't have Bluetooth, so that's out. But it doesn't matter." She was determined that nothing was going to dampen her enjoyment today. "The oldies are the best versions, anyway. This CD will be perfect."

She hit play and then reached for the first box of ornaments as Bing Crosby's smooth voice quietly sang

"White Christmas." The sunny day turned cloudy in anticipation of the coming snow, and the lights from the tree created a cozy glow as they hung ornaments on the tree. Bit by bit it came together until they stood back and viewed the finished product. Maddy got a lump in her throat. It was beautiful. And it was hers. And she was going to get a jump on New Year's resolutions and make one right now: from now on she was going to live in the present, and do it on her own two feet.

"Hang on," she said, and dashed to the kitchen. Moments later she joined him again and handed him a glass. "Eggnog," she said, grinning. "I splurged at the grocery store."

"It only comes once a year," he agreed. "The tree looks great, Maddy."

"It does. When we were standing here looking at it, I made a resolution that I'm going to start living in the present. So..." She held up her glass. "To new beginnings."

They clinked glasses and his gaze held hers while the delicious feeling of anticipation began to spread over her again. When she'd said "New beginnings," she hadn't exactly meant new relationships, but he was standing here before her, looking all hunky and gorgeous, and they'd decorated the tree together and Nat King Cole was crooning on the stereo...

"You forgot something," he said softly, and after taking a drink of his eggnog he put the glass down and reached into the last box.

When he straightened, he was holding a sprig of plastic mistletoe in his hand.

"Oh," she said, and her voice sounded just a bit breathless.

He took the glass from her hand, put it beside his

on the side table and returned to stand in front of her. Right in front of her. So close that if she lifted her hands they'd be pressed against the front of his shirt and his broad chest…

She looked down. Her hands *were* pressed against his chest, the warmth of it against her skin as his breathing quickened. He held the mistletoe up over their heads. "Be a shame to break a tradition," he murmured, his eyes dark and mesmerizing.

"A shame," she echoed.

He took his time, and when his lips finally touched hers she could barely breathe. It was as good as last night…no, better. There was anticipation and nerves but not the first-time nerves that had made her so jumpy. There was a sweetness and purity to it that reached in and wrapped around her heart. It was a perfect Christmas kiss, under the mistletoe, in front of a Christmas tree, with the taste of eggnog still on their lips and a soft carol on the air.

Their lips parted and she let out a blissful sigh. "Cole," she whispered. "What are we starting here?"

He didn't answer, but he dropped the mistletoe on the floor and pulled her into his arms for a deeper, more satisfying kiss. Her head was swimming with it all. The feel of his strong arms wrapped around her, the scent of his cologne on his clothes, the way his teeth nipped gently at her lower lip, causing a dart of desire straight to her core.

A cry echoed down the stairs, muffled by the distance and the bedroom door, but definitely an impatient howl.

It was the worst—and best—time for the boys to wake up from their nap.

Chapter 9

Maddy pulled away, her eyes still dazed and her body humming. Cole, too, had a look of surprise about him, as if this was more than he'd expected, somehow. As if reality had smacked him in the face like a splash of ice-cold water. Maddy wasn't sure which boy was crying, but they were really tuning up now. Had they been awake for a while already and she hadn't heard their fussing?

"I have to go," she whispered, stepping back. "Get the boys."

"And show them the tree." The words were innocuous enough, but there was a strain in Cole's voice that hadn't been there before.

Right. Big mistake and he was regretting it, wasn't he?

She rushed off to the bedroom, her emotions in turmoil as she opened the door and saw both Luke and Liam standing up in their cribs having a shouting contest. "All right, you two, I'm here," she said, stepping inside.

The noise changed from shouting to delighted squeals and bouncing on the mattresses. "Let's get you changed first," she said, picking up Liam. In no time flat she had him in a fresh diaper, deposited him in Luke's crib, picked up Luke and repeated the process. All the while she was thinking about Cole.

Their kisses today had been amazing. Phenomenal. Unburdened, she realized. It seemed that a weight had lifted, allowing a new intimacy. Could it be that a change of attitude had accomplished all that? But then…when the boys had started crying, Cole had looked almost upset. Lordy, she'd been out of the dating scene for so long that she had no idea how to read the clues.

With both babies in her arms, she took a deep breath. "You ready, boys? Mama has something to show you." She started out of their room and down the stairs. "We've got a Christmas tree. Look, isn't it pretty?"

She turned the corner and there was Cole, standing in front of the tree, his eggnog in his hand again. Her pulse picked up at the sight of him. But then she looked at her sons and her heart simply melted.

Eyes as big as saucers, they stared at the tree. Two little mouths formed perfect O's, and the lights were reflected in their huge blue eyes.

"Do you like it?" Maddy put them down. "Don't touch, now. Just look. Pretty."

Liam approached it carefully, stared up to the top, then back to the bottom and a particularly shiny ornament. "Buh," he said. It was his favorite almost word. As far as Maddy was concerned, it showed his approval.

Luke took a few steps forward, then raced back to Maddy. "Up," he said, holding out his hands. She lifted him up and took him over to the tree, where he pointed at individual ornaments and made unintelligible but what sounded like approving noises.

She looked over at Cole.

"You are so good with them," Cole said. "So patient."

She laughed and put Luke down again. "Not always. Believe me. I just try to hold it in until I'm alone."

"You put them first. And they know it, because even at their age they're happy and secure."

"They'll always come first," she vowed, lifting her chin a little to look up at him.

"Maddy, you asked what we were starting. The truth is, I don't know." His gaze searched hers. "Maybe your idea of living in the present is a good one. Just take it day by day."

Maddy considered. She wondered if seeing Cole was a mistake. There was a big possibility that neither of them was emotionally ready for romance. But then, day by day was a pretty small commitment when all was said and done.

"Day by day sounds nice," she answered. She broke eye contact briefly to make sure the boys weren't getting into trouble, then looked up at him again.

"So how about I take you to dinner sometime next week? I'll pay for a sitter. We can have an evening out, just the two of us."

Maddy bit down on her lip. "To dinner?" The idea of an actual date, a public one, gave her a lot of misgivings. Kisses in private were one thing. But going out, particularly in a place like Gibson, made a statement. When you did that, you were a *couple*.

"You know, where people order food and it's brought to them and they eat it?"

She couldn't help but smile a little. "Yes, I know. I'm just… Well, I'm not sure that's a good idea."

When Cole didn't say anything, she elaborated. "It's just that for the past six months, I've felt like people were whispering behind my back all the time. And not always bad stuff, but my life became news. I don't want this to be news, Cole. At least not yet, until we're sure. Or ready. Or…heck, I don't know. I think I'd be on edge, though, and not much fun to be around."

"We've been out together before. Yesterday, on the wagon ride. Coffee at the Grind. The only difference is how we categorize it. Heck, we don't even have to call it a date. It could be sharing a meal or hanging out." He smiled and she thought again how he could be so darned charming.

He was right in a way, too. Maybe the perception was all in her head. But then, maybe they'd already provided fodder for gossip. "People might already be talking," she said plainly. "I just want to keep things more private. At least for now. Can we do that?"

Disappointment marked his face and she felt bad about it. "Cole, you didn't do anything wrong. I love that you asked me. I'd just rather stay out of the public eye for a while."

He nodded, but she could tell there were things he wasn't saying. It was in the way his jaw was set and his lips were pursed.

She put a hand on his arm. "I'm sorry. I know this must seem exactly the opposite of what I said earlier about letting go of the past. I've been the topic of conversation and speculation enough, and I just want some privacy. That's all."

"What if I come up with a compromise?"

She hesitated. "If I say yes that means I'm committed. Sneaky." She smiled a little. "How about I say maybe? It'll depend on what it is."

"I'll let you know. Now, I should probably be going. Tanner's going to go crazy if I leave him to do the chores on his own tonight. Even though I did them by myself this morning." He grinned. "You'll be by the house tomorrow, though?"

"You still want me there?"

"Of course, why wouldn't I?" His brows pulled together in the middle.

Maddy could have bitten her tongue. She'd assumed that it had been a pity position, a made-up way to give her some help. But he looked sincerely perplexed. Maybe the offer had been genuine all along.

"Oh, never mind. I'll get there around nine. I work at one instead of two, though, so I'll have to leave by twelve fifteen to get the boys to day care and then on to work."

"Sounds perfect to me."

They looked around at the boys. Luke had found Maddy's eggnog glass and had taken sips from it, leaving a streak of creamy white down the front of his shirt and the glass as well, which was forming a ring on the table. Liam was sitting on the floor, playing with a plush ornament he'd plucked from the tree.

Maddy sighed. "See what happens when I get distracted? And this is why the soft ornaments are at the bottom of the tree. I see it's going to be an interesting few weeks."

"But fun, I hope. With lots of that Christmas spirit you've been looking for."

His eyes held a twinkle. It seemed the earlier awkwardness was forgiven, or at least forgotten for the time being. She liked that about Cole. He was easygoing, and that was something she particularly needed right now.

"It's getting there," she admitted. "Today helped."

"Then I think you should help us decorate our tree when the time comes. Mom and Dad are home in nine more days and it'd be nice to have the house decorated for when they return."

"Now that I can do." She grinned up at him, then reached down and took the ornament from Liam and hung it back on the tree. "Don't touch, Liam."

She walked Cole to the door, waited as he put on his coat and boots. "Thanks for coming over. For the help and for the company. It would have sucked decorating the tree alone."

"I'm glad I could help."

She reached out and took his hand. "You have. More than you know. Thanks for being understanding."

Cole leaned down and kissed her lightly. "I'll see you in the morning," he murmured, then reached for the door handle. At the last minute he looked up and at the boys. "'Bye, Luke and Liam."

Maddy's heart gave a stutter as both of them stopped what they were doing and looked at Cole. And then Liam, bless him, grinned a toothy smile and flapped his hand in goodbye.

"In the morning," she parroted, and held the door as he went outside into the cold afternoon.

Cole huddled against the bitter wind as he guided his horse out of the pasture and toward home again. Tanner rode behind him, neither of them saying anything in the frosty morning. After morning chores they'd gone out on horseback to move part of the herd to a different pasture with new stacks. Normally it was fun, but the wind chill had bitten at his face and his fingers were cold inside his gloves. He was glad that job was over and he could do something else for the afternoon. Something inside where it was warm.

"Hey, hold up," Tanner called, and Cole reined in a little, allowing Tanner to catch up to him.

"A cup of coffee is sure gonna be good," Tanner said, hunching his shoulders. "It's a cold one today." The white cloud of his breath seemed to hang in the air as he spoke.

The mention of coffee reminded Cole that Maddy was going to be at the house when they went in. God, he was so mixed up about that. Not even twenty-four hours ago he'd resolved that nothing could happen. He'd been certain they would be just friends—and then he ended up kissing her under the mistletoe and asking her to dinner.

Was it the challenge? Maybe Tanner was right and Cole was wrong. He looked over at his brother and took a deep breath. They didn't usually talk about this sort of thing. But he found he needed a sounding board, and Tanner, for all his faults, was not one to judge.

"Hey, Tanner? What you said yesterday, about me getting bored with women… Do you think I'm interested in Maddy just because she's, well, she's hard work?"

"So she hasn't fallen into your arms at the snap of your fingers?"

Cole wondered if it was possible to blush when he was this cold. "Be serious."

"I am serious. This is about Roni, isn't it? You never got over her leaving you."

The words stung. "That was a long time ago, Tanner. Granted, I'm not in a hurry to give someone the ammunition to hurt me, but there's nothing wrong with being cautious."

Tanner started laughing. "Cole, this is the first time I've seen you tying yourself in knots over a woman in years."

"Glad you think it's funny." He wiggled his fingers inside his gloves, relieved when the barn came into view.

"I think it's awesome. What's funny is that you don't get it."

"Don't get what?"

"Why it's so hard for you. Cole, I don't know if you've noticed, but you have a bit of a rescue complex."

Cole frowned and looked over at Tanner. His brother seemed serious now, no laughing at all. "What on earth are you talking about?"

Tanner sighed. "I know you loved Roni, but what you really loved was being her knight in shining armor. Or leather, as the case may be." He smiled briefly at his own joke. "Roni's life growing up was rough. We all know that. You swept in and tried to take care of her and make everything better. And for a while it worked and you guys were happy. But it wasn't enough to base forever on, you know?"

"What was I supposed to do, then? Not help?" Hell, Tanner knew little about it. Roni's mom had been abused by her husband before they split up. They'd had hardly any money, and Roni hated being at home. She used to say that it smelled like stale cigarettes and disappointment.

"Of course not. But it's not your job to fix things for everyone, either. You can't take all that on yourself. After a while it…"

He hesitated.

"It what?"

The air was clear, so for a few moments the only sound on the wind was the steady but muffled clopping sound of hooves on hard-packed snow and dirt. "You mean well. But it can make the person on the receiving end feel like a burden. Or…well, incapable. Like you don't trust them to fix things for themselves."

That was a little too insightful for it to be out of the blue or off-the-cuff. "Do I do that to you, Tan?"

Tanner shrugged. "Maybe a little. I know you're the responsible one and I'm the goof-off, but I can handle more than you think."

Cole didn't know what to say. Tanner was younger than he was. He'd always felt protective and responsible for him, but maybe he'd been too protective. Looking back, he realized Tanner had tried a lot of unexpected things. Like his brief marriage, and doing his EMT training. "I've held you back, haven't I?" He felt like a heel even asking.

"Hell, Cole, you're my big brother. You just… Well, you cast a long shadow sometimes. It makes it hard to live up to, so I acted out a bit from time to time." Tanner's sideways grin was back, though, and Cole felt relief slide through him. His brother didn't harbor hard feelings, at least.

"Anyway," Tanner finished, "hopefully I've grown up enough to figure out it's not a competition."

"I never realized," Cole said, shifting in his saddle. The leather creaked in the cold.

"Of course you didn't. The thing is, Roni was young and at a disadvantage, and you were a little older and had your shit together. At first I bet it was really great. But in the end it was probably too much, you know? I know the breakup hurt you. You felt like you gave her everything and she threw it back in your face."

That was it exactly.

"The problem is," Tanner informed him, "that you're doing the same thing with Maddy. Riding to her rescue. But you're also guarding your heart and it's creating this tug-of-war that's driving you crazy."

Cole tugged on the reins and halted the horse. "Shit."

Tanner stopped, too. "What?"

Cole let out a sigh, a cloud of breath puffing in the air before his face. "Do I really do that? Try to fix everything?"

Tanner rested his reining hand on the saddle horn and lifted his other hand, raising his fingers as he itemized the list.

"You offered her the job at the house, even though we could have managed just fine until Mom and Dad got home. You put new tires on her car. You bought her a Christmas tree. You bought her dinner and then went back to help her decorate the tree. I'm running out of fingers here, Cole, and it's only been a few weeks."

"Am I wrong to want to help?" He suspected his brother had hit the nail on the head, too. Every time he found himself getting close to Maddy, he backed off in a hurry. Only to discover he couldn't seem to stay away.

Tanner nudged his mount, starting along the lane again. "Are you wrong? No, of course not. You're a good, generous, upstanding guy. I like Maddy, and I told you that. But you might want to sort out *why* you're doing it. Is it because you need to be needed? Or do you really, honestly care about her?"

They were quiet for a while as they rode back to the ranch yard. They were nearly to the barn when Cole spoke up. "Hey, Tanner? How'd you get so smart about that stuff?"

Tanner looked back at him, but the expression on his face was tight and grim. "We're cut from the same cloth, or didn't you realize that? You're not the only one in the family to mistake how someone feels. For me it was Britt. For you it was Roni. It makes a man a little gun-shy."

Cole thought about Tanner's most public mistake—his brief Vegas marriage a few years back. Now he volunteered as an EMT and helped people that way. Cole had always thought it was rather noble of his brother, but now he wondered if it was something else. A form of rebellion, perhaps, or Tanner's way to help people while keeping himself detached from them on a personal level.

Either way, Tanner had given him lots to think about.

They were at the barn now and they halted, each dismounting quietly and gathering reins in their hands to lead the horses inside. "Hey, thanks for being a sounding board this morning," Cole said as he tied the gelding and reached for the cinch strap.

"That's what brothers are for," Tanner answered, and clapped a hand on Cole's shoulder in solidarity before moving away. "But that's enough of the touchy-feely crap for one day. When's the farrier due out again?"

The subject was changed and the focus returned to ranch operations—at least for the time being. When lunchtime arrived, the strange, weightless feeling returned to Cole's stomach, simply from knowing that Maddy was waiting inside.

And he still had no idea what he was going to do about it.

Chapter 10

The morning at Cole's was the most difficult Maddy had had yet.

Luke appeared to be teething, and his slight fever and whiny temperament grated on Maddy's nerves. She tried cooling teething rings and numbing gel, which only created more drool until she simply left a bib around his neck all the time to keep his clothing dry. Baby acetaminophen helped after a while, and he crashed on the floor on the blanket, but by then Liam was bored of being by himself and begged for attention. Trying to get the sheets washed and the beds made up was nearly impossible, and she burned the first pan of cookies she baked and needed to open a window to let out the smoky stench. By noon she was ready to pull her hair out, but at least she'd managed the bedding and baked the rest of the cookies without incident, and there was a batch of spaghetti sauce on the stove so Cole and Tanner just had to make pasta for dinner.

And then she realized she hadn't made lunch. For anyone. And she had to get the boys to day care and be at work by one.

When Cole came in, she was frantically flipping grilled cheese sandwiches on a griddle and stirring tomato soup on the stove. "I'm so sorry," she said, pushing the hair off her face that had come out of her ponytail. "Luke is teething and Liam's clingy and I lost track of time..."

"Relax," he said, walking into the kitchen and taking the spatula from her hands. "Tanner's making a quick run into the hardware store, so it's just me. And you've got four sandwiches on the go." He checked his watch. "Besides, weren't you supposed to be out of here soon?"

She checked her watch. Twelve twenty. "Dammit," she muttered, reaching for a plate. "I'm sorry, Cole. I should have had this done and cleaned up for you."

"Maddy. It's fine. Have you and the boys eaten?"

She shook her head as she rushed around, slamming things back into cupboards.

"Here." He shoved a sandwich into her hand. "Take two minutes and eat a sandwich. I can't eat four. What do the boys need?"

"I can leave their lunch at the day care. I don't like to, but I can."

She looked at the sandwich. She shouldn't, but it was a heck of a long time until dinner. She sighed, took a bite. Grilled cheese was perhaps the best comfort food on the planet. Something about crispy bread and butter and melted cheese just soothed.

"See?" Cole took a bite and chewed about a quarter of one sandwich. "Food. Breathing. Necessities of life."

She swallowed. "Everything just seemed to work against me today."

He smiled. "Well, some days are like that. I can wash up from this. And there are cookies. And something in that pot over there. It's all good."

She was chewing again. "Spaghetti sauce," she said around her mouthful of sandwich. "And I stripped the beds and washed the sheets."

"Perfect. Finish that and I'll dress the boys."

She wanted to protest, but he had already grabbed the blue and red suits and proceeded to put Liam's on Luke. It didn't matter. She shoved the rest of the sandwich into her mouth, wiped her hands and went to help.

There was no time for anything remotely romantic or intimate or…anything. Maddy wasn't sure if she was disappointed or relieved. She still had so many mixed feelings where Cole was concerned. Mostly that she liked him, probably too much, and felt as though she shouldn't. And today he was acting as if nothing had ever happened between them. He was just being friendly and helpful and that was it.

"There. All ready. Do you want some help getting them to the car?"

"That'd be great, Cole. I really am sorry."

"Will you stop apologizing?" He shrugged into his coat and pulled on a pair of winter boots but left them untied. "Oh. And I forgot to pay you for last week." He reached into his pocket and pulled out some bills. "Here. Three days, right?"

She hesitated, and he held out his hand. "Maddy, come on. You're not cooking and cleaning in my house and not getting paid for it." He shook the bills.

When he put it like that, she couldn't argue. It just felt

strange and wrong, considering how they'd been kissing lately. Reluctantly she took the money and tucked it in her pocket. She swallowed against a tightness in her throat. It was almost as though those intimate moments between them had never happened at all.

"Okay, slugger. Here we go." Cole picked up Luke, shouldered the diaper bag and left Liam for Maddy. At the car he helped fasten them in and opened her door.

It all happened so fast that she barely had time to breathe. At this rate she was going to get to work spooled up like a top.

"Hey," he said, standing in front of her door so she couldn't get in. "Drive safely. Don't speed, okay? Tanner's been to too many accidents lately."

"I will."

"Nothing is so important that a few extra minutes will matter, you know?"

Some of the tension left her body. "I know. This morning just got me all discombobulated."

"Okay. Oh, and you forgot something else, too."

"I did?" She ran her list through her mind. Yes, she'd hoped to do a bit more cleaning today, but what had she forgotten?

He leaned forward and cupped his hand around her neck. "One of these," he said, and touched his lips to hers.

It only took a few seconds of delicious contact for her to melt against him. The tension in her muscles eased as he took his time, giving her a thorough goodbye kiss that would leave her body humming for a good long time.

Their lips parted and she took a nice, slow breath. "That was nice."

"I know. You better now?"

She looked up into his eyes, feeling slightly dazed but much calmer. "Yes, thank you."

He smiled. "Then get going. I'll call you later."

"Okay."

"Okay."

She got in the car and he shut the door behind her, then headed back to the house, his untied boots scuffing in the snow. She refused to worry about the time as she drove away. Five or ten minutes wasn't going to get her fired, and she went in early or stayed late often enough that it bought her some leeway. She dropped off the boys at Sunshine Smiles, leaving instructions to give Luke another dose of medicine if he needed it and their containers of lunch that they'd missed. Then on to the library, where she quickly stowed her coat and bag and joined Eloise in the day's work.

"You look frazzled," Eloise noted. "Everything okay?"

"Yeah." Maddy smiled. "Crazy morning. And Luke's teething." She didn't mention anything about Cole. No one knew she was working for him and she'd like to keep it that way.

"That'll try anyone's patience," Eloise replied with a sympathetic smile. "Why don't you take a few minutes, grab a tea from the lunchroom?" Her gaze darted to Maddy's hair. "Redo your ponytail."

"Oh, am I a mess? Darn it…"

"Like I said, just a little frazzled. I'll man the desk for a few minutes. Go get some mint tea."

"Thanks, El."

The beverage and few moments in the staff bathroom were just what she needed. She came back to the front feeling slightly refreshed and much more relaxed. The mint tea was soothing and she went to work at the circulation desk with a renewed energy.

At three-thirty there was an influx of people; school let out for the day and several students came in with textbooks in hand to find tables for study groups. A few parents came with kids to pick out new books, and several returns were dropped in the drop box. Maddy was in the process of issuing a new library card to a very excited first grader when a deliveryman came through the doors holding a big basket.

She looked up. "Hi, can I help you?"

"Are you Maddy Wallace?"

"That's me." She looked at the basket in his arms. It was wrapped in clear cellophane with tiny snowflakes on it and tied with a sparkly silver ribbon.

"Delivery for you. Can you sign for it, please?"

"Excuse me just a moment," she said to the mom and daughter. She took a pen and signed the delivery slip. "You're sure this is for me?"

"Positive. Says Maddy Wallace at the Gibson library. If that's you, this is yours." He gave a wide smile. "Merry Christmas."

"Thanks."

The basket sat on the corner of the desk and the little girl who was waiting for her library card looked at it eagerly. "Are you going to open it?"

"Do you think I should?" Maddy asked.

The girl nodded vigorously.

There was no one waiting in line, so Maddy untied the ribbon and folded it carefully, then peeled back the plastic wrapping. Inside the basket was an assortment of her favorite things from the Daily Grind. There was a little pot with a built-in strainer for tea leaves, three small tins of different teas, a package of biscotti tied with a ribbon, a box of shortbread cookies, a bag of scone mix and four fresh pieces of strudel, the crisp pastry flaked with coarse sugar and with caramel and crimson fruit showing through the slits in the dough. Apple and cherry—her favorites.

And a little card. But she already knew what it was going to say.

"'To Maddy, from your secret Santa,'" she read aloud, shaking her head with amazement.

"That's lovely," said the girl's mother. "What a gorgeous basket."

Maddy beamed. "I've got a secret Santa this year. This is the third present I've received."

"What's a secret Santa?" the girl asked.

"Well, someone is giving me early Christmas presents, and they aren't telling me who they are. It's a mystery."

"I like mysteries."

Maddy looked at the assortment of books the girl had chosen to check out and smiled. "I see that. So, I've been looking at clues and I've been trying to figure out who my secret Santa is. I'm pretty sure it's my mom and dad. But it's nice getting surprises."

"Presents are always fun," she agreed.

In the basket were some assorted individual chocolates, and Maddy took one out and looked at the mom for approval. "Is a chocolate okay?" She nodded and Maddy held it out. "I think sharing is fun, too. Would you like one?"

Her smile lit up the room. "Thanks."

"You're welcome." Maddy ran the plastic card through the scanner once more and activated it. "And now you have your very own library card. Keep this safe, okay?"

She scanned the books' bar codes and handed them over. "When you finish them, come back and tell me what you think."

The girl nodded vigorously. Her mom leaned over and quietly said, "Thank you, Ms. Wallace. She's had a rough time with reading, and I'm trying to make it fun and find stuff she likes."

"Keep an eye on events, then," Maddy suggested. "In the new year we'll be starting up a new children's reading club, and there are always special activities over spring break and the summer."

"We will. And merry Christmas."

When they were gone, Maddy sneaked away to the break room and treated herself to one of the cherry strudels. The pastry melted in her mouth and she closed her eyes in appreciation. The tires had been practical and expensive; the tree was for the family. But this…this present was just for her, and a wonderful treat that she would never have splurged on for herself. After her crazy morning, it turned the day completely around.

With a quick glance at her phone, she realized she had about two minutes to make a call. She dialed the number quickly and her mom answered right away.

"I got the delivery," Maddy said. "It's wonderful."

"What delivery?"

"Come on, Mom, I know you and Dad are my secret Santa. The basket from the Grind is exactly what I would have wanted. Right down to my favorite kinds of tea. Only you could have known that."

"Honey, I'm glad you like it, but we're not your secret Santa."

She grinned. "You keep saying that. Anyway, fine,

I won't bug you about it again. Just know that I love it and I love you both."

There was a light laugh at the other end. "We love you, too."

"I've gotta get back to work. Talk soon."

"Of course. 'Bye, sweetie."

When Maddy hung up, she knew there was nothing that could ruin her good mood.

She was wrong.

Maddy finished work at six and rushed straight to the day care, where the boys were the last children to be picked up. Luke was crying and his nose was running, a sure sign of full-on teething, and Liam didn't look that happy, either—probably because his brother was miserable. Maddy got them home as quickly as possible and sat them in their high chairs while she heated some supper for them.

They'd just been fed and Maddy had taken a bite of the last leftover piece of cold fried chicken when Luke began to fuss and threw up. She hurried to clean up the mess—thank God it was in the kitchen and not on any carpet—and tried to soothe him, all the while herding Liam along to the tub. They both loved bath time and needed to be cleaned up, and once she got them in the warm water with some rubber ducks and frogs, she let out a big breath. Poor Luke's cheeks were bright red, and he grabbed the washcloth and shoved it in his mouth, sucking on it to ease the pain of his gums.

She couldn't keep them in the tub forever, though, and she got them into pajamas, put a fresh bib around Luke's neck to absorb the drool, and put a little more numbing gel on his gums. She could feel the hard bump of the tooth trying to poke through and felt terribly sorry for him, but it seemed his fussiness put everything off-kilter. Liam fell and hit his head, and his crying set off Luke again, and by the time she got them both settled in bed she was ready to sit down and have a right good cry herself.

When the phone rang, she grabbed it after the first ring so it wouldn't disturb the hard-won peace.

It was Cole.

"You sound tired. Busy night?"

"You might say that."

"I wondered how Luke was feeling. Still fussy?"

She sighed, leaning her head back against the sofa. "Yeah. He's got a tooth that's almost through."

"That doesn't sound like fun."

"For either of us. He threw up his supper, was clingy, Liam fell and bumped his head..."

"Sounds like you could use a break."

"Yeah. I think I'm going to go run myself a bath and go to bed. I have an eight-hour day tomorrow."

"The day care is okay with Luke being so out of sorts?"

"For the most part. I'll send stuff with him." While Cole's money was helpful, she didn't want to say that a day off work meant the loss of a whole day's pay. Even if most of it went to child care, it was a necessity.

"Well, sorry you had a rough day. If you need to miss your next morning here, don't worry about it."

She let out a relieved breath. She wouldn't take him up on it, but it was very understanding of him to offer. "Thank you, Cole."

"No problem. I hope you and the boys all feel better. Maybe you should make a cup of tea and just relax for a few hours."

She thought of the new tea in the basket in the kitchen and smiled. "I just got some new tea. Maybe I'll do that."

"I'll let you go, then. Oh, before I do, I had an idea today."

"What sort of idea?"

"Well, it'll depend on how the boys are feeling, of course. But I heard what you said about going on a date here in town and I think I found a compromise."

"You did?"

"The theater in Great Falls is showing *It's a Wonderful Life* on the weekend. I'll arrange for a sitter if you'll go with me Friday night."

She loved that movie. And a movie was fun but not overly intimate, and chances were they'd never see anyone they knew. But a sitter? Maddy was used to leaving the boys with the day care or her parents. She wasn't sure she trusted Cole to work out that detail. "Who did you have in mind to babysit?"

"A kid at a nearby ranch. Oldest of five and with tons of experience. If they're free, of course. I haven't asked. I wanted to see if you'd say yes first."

She hesitated.

"Maddy, come to a movie with me. I'll buy you popcorn. Don't you deserve a night out?"

She was so tempted. She hadn't had a night out like that in so long. When she did have a chance to go out alone, she took it to run errands without having to drag car seats and diapers along. But a movie…and popcorn…and fun…

"If your babysitter is available. And you'll have to come early so I can make sure I'm comfortable leaving the boys."

"Of course." She could hear the smile in his voice. "So you're in? It's a date?"

Her heart gave a little flutter. "Yes, it's a date."

"Perfect. And now I'll let you get to your peace and quiet. Good night, Maddy."

"Good night, Cole."

She hung up the phone and sat in the silence for a few minutes, and then a smile spread across her face. Maybe she shouldn't be so excited, but she was. Between today's surprise gift and her Friday plans, she was starting to feel like a human being again.

As the week wore on, so did the glow. Luke's tooth came through, to everyone's relief, Maddy made it to Cole's as previously arranged, and she even managed to sneak a few hours of shopping and bought some adorable things for the boys for Christmas, as well as a lovely sweater and scarf for her mom and a DVD box set for her dad. On Thursday, during her afternoon shift, another delivery arrived at the library for her, and this time it was a present for the boys. She tore off the wrapping to discover a plush snowman and penguin, each about twelve inches high. Delighted, she pressed a button on the penguin's wing and he sang a song to the tune of "I'm a Little Teapot." She quickly turned it off again—it was abnormally loud in the quiet library— but she was enchanted just the same.

The card simply said, "To Luke and Liam, from Santa."

This really had to stop. But surely, with Christmas only a week away, the gifts would quit arriving.

She tucked the parcel under the desk, but there was no denying it. The Christmas spirit was definitely starting to catch hold.

Chapter 11

Cole tried not to be nervous as he arrived at Maddy's with sixteen-year-old Will Fletcher in the passenger seat. Fletch, as his friends called him, was tonight's babysitter. Cole had promised Maddy he'd look after the arrangements, and he had. And then they were going to Great Falls to a movie. Not just any movie, but a showing of *It's a Wonderful Life*. Cole figured if anything could give a boost of Christmas spirit, that was it.

"So, Maddy will give you the lowdown on the boys. They're great kids. Busy, but good."

Fletch looked over at Cole. "Dude, relax. I've been looking after my brothers and sisters for a long time. I got this."

"Right. I know that."

"You got some nerves, bro?"

Cole gave a short chuckle. Was he going to get dating

advice from a kid now? This was what his life had come to—picking up babysitters and getting love life advice. Maybe Tanner was right. If he'd been seeing anyone else, he would have bailed by now. But he hadn't. He was still trying. And that was both encouraging and scary as hell.

"Maybe a few," he admitted.

"Just keep it chill. She's a mom, right? Just having a night out without kids is a big deal. Believe me, I've heard my mom say it enough." Fletch rolled his eyes. "Which is why I started babysitting as soon as I was old enough. Happy Mom equals more good stuff for me."

Cole chuckled. "Sounds like you have it all figured out."

"Not hardly. Right now moms are easier to figure out than sixteen-year-old girls, know what I mean?"

"Amen, brother." Cole turned off the car and took the keys out of the ignition. "All right, let's go."

The walkway was lit up with the twinkly lights he'd installed, and he could see the tree through the front window. When he got to the front door, he knocked and stepped back.

When she opened the door, he caught his breath.

It wasn't that she'd dressed up in her finest. She was wearing black trousers and a red top that seemed to gather beneath her breasts before flowing down over her waist and hips. He'd seen lots of women wear the same sort of outfit to work around town, but on Maddy it looked different. Special. A delicate necklace lay at her throat, and she'd pulled her hair back from the sides and curled the rest in big, tumbling curls.

She'd made an effort. As if tonight was an occasion. And it was. Their first real, official date where they went somewhere and he paid and…yeah. This was the real thing.

"Hi," she said simply, and smiled, and his world turned upside down.

"Hi," Fletch said, holding out his hand. "I'm Fletch, your babysitter for tonight."

"You are?"

"Yes, ma'am."

Cole finally found his tongue. "Sorry. Right. This is Will Fletcher. He's got lots of babysitting experience, don't worry. Plus the boys might like playing with another guy, right?"

"My brother always liked to get all his cars together and play smash-up derby," Fletch joked.

"Well, come in. I'll introduce you to the twins, show you where everything is."

She stood aside to let them in, showed Fletch where to hang his coat and watched as he went straight to the living room, where the boys were playing. "Are you sure about this?" she asked, her eyes worried.

"You mean because he's a guy? Positive. His family lives close to the ranch, and he's the oldest of five. He's looked after his siblings lots and gave me references for other babysitting jobs. The boys are going to be fine, Maddy."

"And I'll have my cell."

"That's right. And we're not that far away, either. He seems to be making himself at home."

They looked over. Sure enough, they were playing farm with the animals and the boys had taken right to him. He sat on the floor, legs crossed, and Luke ran over and shoved a horse into his hands.

"I should give him the rundown so we won't be late."

"That'd be good." Cole smiled down at her. "But before you do that..."

He reached for her hand and made sure she was looking at him. "You look really pretty tonight, Maddy."

A blush colored her cheeks. "Thanks. I'll be right back."

He took a seat in a chair as she went over contact
numbers and routines with Fletch, showed him the boys'
room and where everything was. "If there's any trouble,
just text me. We're going to a movie, but I'll keep my
phone on vibrate."

"We'll be fine. We're going to have fun, right, guys?"
He looked at her and grinned. "Though I'll admit, I
might have trouble telling them apart."

She laughed. "A lot of people do at first. Liam's a little
shyer than Luke, and Luke's a tad bigger."

"Got it."

"And you've got all my numbers?"

"Yes, ma'am."

"In bed by eight, okay?"

Fletch nodded and Cole admired his patience. "Eight
sharp. Go have fun."

Cole held her coat as she shrugged it on and then put
on heeled knee-high boots that made his mouth water,
they were so sexy. "Ready?"

She let out a deep breath. "Ready."

They escaped outside into the cold air and Cole held
her elbow as they went down the walk, just in case there
was any ice. At the truck he opened her door and shut it
again after she hopped up. When he was inside he started
the engine and cranked on the heater. "I think winter is
definitely here to stay," he remarked.

"Me, too."

As she fastened her seat belt, he casually observed,
"New lights on the hedges. Nice."

"Mom and Dad strike again," she said lightly, smiling. "They really went crazy this week. I got a basket at work and then the cutest plush animals for the boys, and I came home from work yesterday to this. I could get used to having a secret Santa."

"I bet." He smiled back. She was enjoying being spoiled a little bit, and she deserved it. And if she never knew it was him, it didn't matter. He loved Christmas, and knowing he'd made hers a little more fun was all the thanks he needed.

"I do feel a little guilty, though," she said with a sigh. "It seems pretty one-sided."

"But that's probably why it's a secret. Knowing would take the fun out of it, wouldn't it?"

"Maybe." She shrugged as they backed out of the driveway and started down the street. "But at this point it's just a technicality. They keep saying they aren't doing it, but I know it's them."

Once they hit the highway it was just the two of them and the songs on the radio. It felt strange, going somewhere alone. They hadn't, not since the day he'd run into her and they'd gone for coffee. He'd gotten used to the boys being around, and now he felt a gap of silence with their absence.

"It feels funny without the kids," he commented.

She smiled. "I know. Sometimes I think I'm going to have to have them surgically removed." A light laugh followed. "This is really nice, Cole. Thanks for asking me."

"It seemed a fair compromise." He grinned. "Besides, you, me, in a dark movie theater? Hard to complain about that."

"Cole!" She looked over at him. "I haven't made out in a movie theater in over ten years, and I'm not about to revisit that activity."

He laughed and put a hand over his heart. "Don't worry. I'll be the soul of gentlemanly behavior."

As much as it killed him, he would.

They spent the rest of the drive into Great Falls talking about the holidays, what was going on around town and his parents' vacation, which was rapidly coming to a close. "Are you still coming over on Sunday to decorate the tree?"

"Of course, if you still want me to."

"You know I do."

He pulled into the parking lot, which was already filling up. "Well, here we are. Let's go get our tickets and a big tub of popcorn."

He held her hand as they crossed the lot to the doors. The theater was a popular spot on a Friday night, and after they bought their tickets and concessions, they discovered the seats were filling up fast. The top rows were completely packed, and the best seats left were about a third of the way up. Closer to the screen than Cole liked, but it would have to do. They made their way down the row and took turns holding food while they hung their coats over the seats.

"I don't remember the last time I went to a movie," Maddy said, settling into her seat and reaching for her soda. "Over a year for sure. Probably over two."

"Me, either," Cole admitted. When he did go, black-and-white holiday films were last on his list of must-watches.

But this year he was Santa Claus. And he'd known it was something she'd like.

The lights dimmed and he saw Maddy smiling at him as the screen came to life with current previews.

"Do you know I've never actually seen *It's a Wonderful Life*?" he whispered, leaning over.

"What? Really?" She took a drink of her soda and looked so very young. "But it's a classic."

He shrugged. "That every-time-a-bell-rings stuff never made me want to."

"So why now?"

He didn't answer. Just looked into her eyes and held her gaze. Watched her expression soften as she understood. For her. He was doing it for her.

"You're going to love it," she whispered and turned to face the front fully before reaching into the tub for a handful of hot, buttery popcorn.

She was right, he did enjoy it. It wasn't anything like he expected, and Jimmy Stewart's lovable comedy was perfect. Near the end, when everyone was parading through the house giving back to the man who'd always sacrificed for Bedford Falls, he looked over and saw Maddy sniffling and wiping her eyes. He smiled, feeling an unexpected tenderness in the moment, and handed her a napkin. She gave him a rueful smile, then dabbed at her tears. The popcorn bucket had been put on the floor long ago, and Cole reached over and took her hand in his, rubbing his thumb over hers.

It was a far cry from making out, but there was something about it just the same, something that reached in and confirmed something he'd suspected all along: Maddy Wallace was different.

She was worth it.

As the credits started rolling, he looked over at her. She looked back, and they gazed at each other for several long moments as the crowd began to filter out. It wasn't until another couple said, "Excuse me," edging past them to the end of the row, that they broke eye contact and hurried to stand up and let the people pass. The moment gone, they put on their coats and gloves and prepared to make their way out into the cold again.

"Did you want to do something else?" he asked as they made their way outside.

"I should probably get home. I don't leave the boys with someone new very often."

"Did Fletch call or text?"

She shook her head. "No."

"Then let's go get a coffee. Or hot chocolate or something. It's early. It's only nine thirty."

"Okay."

Once more he opened her door, closed it, got in and started the truck. But there was a different feeling than he'd had before. Bigger, scarier, amazing. After all this time, he figured he'd better face the truth. He'd done a lot of soul-searching after talking to his brother, and the conclusion he'd reached was that it was possible he was falling in love. With the most complicated woman in Gibson. Wasn't that just a kick in the pants?

Falling in love. That was so not what he'd intended when he'd started all this. It scared the hell out of him and felt amazing and exciting all at the same time.

Before leaving the parking lot, he slid across the seat and cupped her face in his hands. "I've been waiting over two hours to do this," he murmured, and then he kissed her.

Despite her misgivings about being in public, Maddy didn't hold back much. He kept the kiss decent, of course, and kept his hands where they should be in public. But that didn't mean there wasn't a wealth of passion and longing in that one kiss. "You sure you want to go for coffee?" he asked breathlessly. "We could go parking like a couple of teenagers."

She laughed against his mouth. "Coffee," she said, kissing the corner of his mouth. "All we'd need is to get caught by some cop making out in your truck."

"Damn," he muttered. But he grinned, anyway.

He drove them to a little coffee shop near the highway and they ordered peppermint hot chocolates instead of something loaded with caffeine. Maddy took a sip and licked whipped cream off her upper lip. "Cole, do you suppose we're getting old, worrying about drinking caffeine at night?" Her smile was impish and anything but old.

"Naw. We're wise. Besides, we both have to get up early in the morning."

She nodded. "Yeah. Responsibilities."

He reached across the table and took her hand. "Do you ever wish you were eighteen again, with everything before you?"

Maddy lifted her cup, took another drink and paused before answering. "Sometimes I miss having the freedom to just pick up and go somewhere, you know? But honestly? Despite everything, I wouldn't trade those two boys for any do-overs."

He smiled. "I know. They're pretty special."

"It doesn't scare you, that I have kids?"

Cole met her gaze. "Scare me? No. Make me be careful? Oh, yes. Dating a single mom is serious business."

He took a drink of his cocoa, rich chocolate and bright peppermint. Maddy laughed and wiped his lip with a napkin. "So in your estimation, we're dating?" she asked.

Why did that particular question make his stomach knot up with nerves, as if he was seventeen again? "Aren't we? Let's see. We've had coffee—twice now—and we've taken a wagon ride in the snow. Then there's dinner, and Christmas tree decorating, and a movie. In the space of about three weeks. What would you call it?"

Her cheeks pinkened. "Dating."

"Maddy," he said quietly, understanding all too well where she was coming from. "I know you want to keep things low-key in Gibson. But eventually people are going to figure it out."

"I know. I know," she repeated meaningfully. "Just not yet, okay?"

"Okay."

"That's it?"

He shrugged. "Sure." Then he smiled. "For now, anyway."

They finished their cocoa and it was ten thirty by the time they hit the road for Gibson. When they got home, the porch light was on and so were the Christmas lights, but the house seemed quiet. They found Fletch in the living room, watching something on TV. Every toy was picked up and put away and she didn't see any dirty dishes, either. Definite bonus points for the sitter.

"Hi," she said quietly. "Any troubles?"

Fletch turned off the TV and stretched. "Well, eight was more like eight thirty by the time I got them to settle down, but nothing since then. They really like playing with that farm, don't they?"

Maddy nodded. "Thanks, Will."

"I'll give you a ride home," Cole said, nodding. "Here's the keys. I'll be right out."

Fletch gave him a knowing smile but hastened to put on his coat and shoes. "'Bye, Ms. Wallace. Anytime you need a sitter, let me know."

"Thanks, Will, I'll do that."

Fletch slid outside and the lights of the truck lit up the driveway as he turned on the engine.

"So," Cole said, wishing he had all night, but knowing that it was probably better that he had to drive Fletch home. "I guess this is where we say good-night."

"I had a really good time," she said quietly, turning her soft eyes up at him.

"Me, too."

The kiss this time seemed as natural as snowflakes falling to the ground. Their lips met easily, with a growing familiarity.

"I'll see you on Sunday, then?" he asked, wishing he could find an excuse to see her tomorrow but realizing she had to work.

"Sunday. Why don't I bring lunch over for you and Tanner?"

"That'd be great. Can I have a couple of these for dessert?" He kissed her again, thinking she tasted sweeter than any candy cane or cookie.

"Fletch is going to know exactly what we're doing."

"Well, I would hope so, or I'll have to give that boy an education."

She laughed. "Go. I'll see you Sunday."

"'Bye, sweetheart." He leaned forward and kissed her forehead, and then ducked out the door.

Yep, he was in big trouble. And the greatest part was that he didn't even really seem to mind. Maybe it was truly time for him to move forward and take the next step. The fact that he was taking that step with pretty, gentle Maddy just made it that much sweeter.

Chapter 12

"Beef stew coming through," Maddy called out as she entered the warm house.

"We're in here," Tanner replied from the living room. She looked over and saw that he and Cole had already put the tree in its stand. So much for Tanner being jealous. Their tree was at least a foot taller than hers, and fuller, too, to accommodate the larger room and higher ceiling.

She put the slow cooker on the table. "Be right back. I've got to get the boys."

She went to the door, but Cole stepped inside with a boy on each arm and the diaper bag over his shoulder. "Looking for these?"

"I was just going to get them. Thanks, Cole."

"No problem. I saw you drive in from the barn. Here you go, slugger." He handed Liam to Maddy and then put Luke on the floor and started undoing his snowsuit. Together they got the boys undressed and soon the pair was standing in the middle of the kitchen with twisted socks and hair sticking up at odd angles.

"They've already eaten, so let me get them settled with some toys and we can eat, too." She busied herself plugging in the slow cooker to make sure everything was hot, then reached for the bag, taking out a variety of toys.

"I found something when I was looking for the decorations," Cole said. "The old VHS movies Mom had for us when we were little. Including Christmas ones. I can put one on for them."

She laughed. "You mean you still have a VCR?"

"Yeah, I found that in the attic, too, and it still works." He grinned as if he was immensely proud of himself. "We have an assortment of classics. Rudolph, Frosty, Charlie Brown and the Grinch."

His face looked so boyishly excited about it all that she said, "Pick your favorite. We'll start there."

The boys wandered around the living room, familiar now with the lower level of the house, while Cole set up the video and Maddy got out dishes and put the buns she'd brought on a plate. The television was larger than hers, and as soon as the Charlie Brown music came on, the twins' attention was grabbed. Between that and the toys, Maddy figured she had about twenty minutes to eat before she'd have to referee something.

They all sat down to beef stew and crusty buns and the mood was definitely festive. The warm feelings from Friday night's date had stayed with her all weekend long. She liked being with Cole—liked it a lot. As she split a bun and buttered it, she listened to him tease Tanner about some girl he'd been seeing. Cole was sweet to her and so good and patient with the boys. Dating hadn't really been on her radar, but she wasn't sorry. As long as he was content to take it slow.

She still didn't quite trust herself yet. Her mood took a little dip as she remembered how happy she'd been before. She'd been so sure things were great only to find out she'd been wrong all along. It was going to take a while for her to get past that.

But if Cole could be as patient with her as he was with the boys...

"You got quiet all of a sudden," Cole observed.

"Oh. Sorry. Just thinking."

"I've heard it's bad to do too much of that," Tanner said, grinning.

"You could stand to do a little more," Cole shot back at his brother, a crooked smile on his face.

"Yeah, yeah. Someday I might surprise you all," Tanner said, scooping up some stew. "This is really good, Maddy."

"Thanks. It's my mom's recipe."

Maddy had barely scraped the bottom of her bowl when the kids started winding up. As she tended to them, Tanner and Cole took over tidying the lunch mess. Then Maddy put in another video—as much for Cole as for the boys—and cuddled with them on the sofa as Cole and Tanner debated over the lights for the tree.

Her heart hurt a bit, listening to them bicker good-naturedly. It felt like a real family moment, only this wasn't her family. It was lovely to be included, and of course she cared for Cole. How could she not? But it wasn't the same.

Why was she so melancholy today, anyway? Hadn't she promised herself to live in the present? She let out a deep breath, trying to send her negativity with it. Her beautiful sons were snuggled up on her lap, a Christmas movie was playing, she was with friends decorating their tree. She had way too much to be thankful for.

Rudolph was nearly done by the time the lights were perfect, and both boys had fallen asleep. Maddy eased them down on to the sofa and covered them with one of Ellen's crocheted afghans, pausing a moment to study their little faces. How she loved them…even when they made her tired and crazy. Looking at them as they slept chased away all the bad things.

Cole came over and looped his arms around her from behind, surprising her. "They're pretty cute, huh."

"Cole, your brother's here."

"Tanner's not stupid. He knows we've been seeing each other."

Somehow the embrace felt like more, though. Simply because it was in the presence of someone else. "It's just new, that's all," she whispered.

"You'll get used to it. I'm a hugger."

She couldn't stop the smile that touched her lips. "I'll keep that in mind."

"Okay, lovebirds, I've got some stuff over here I have no idea what to do with."

Maddy knew she was blushing a little when she turned back. Tanner was holding rolls of gold mesh in his hands, looking a little helpless. She laughed. "You want some help?"

"Please," he said. "Our mom usually does this part."

She took the mesh from his hands and played with it for a few moments, getting the feel of it in her fingers. "Okay. I'm going to start here." She went to the top and back of the tree. "Is there a step stool or something?"

Cole brought her the stool and she climbed up, then twisted the wire mesh and anchored it to a branch. "Tanner, unroll this as I go so I have some slack to work with." She handed him the roll and they made their way around the tree, with Maddy making puffs with the mesh before gathering it around a branch. It was finicky work, and it took a good amount of time and some joking around to get it done, but in the end the gigantic tree was adorned with what looked like lovely gold ribbon. Their tree had white lights instead of multicolored, and the effect was stunning.

"Wow," Cole said, admiring. "That looks good. I think we should say that we did it ourselves, Tanner." He nudged Maddy's elbow.

"Mom will never believe it," Tanner said.

"You're right."

They were in the middle of putting on the ornaments when Tanner's cell rang. He answered and Maddy heard Tanner say he'd be right there. When he hung up, Cole asked, "What's going on?"

"Jimmy's on call this weekend, but his car won't start. We've got a run to the hospital."

"Accident?"

Tanner went to the closet and took out his EMT jacket. "Baby's coming. Hopefully we'll have lots of time to get to the hospital. The roads are good."

Maddy's blood ran cold for a moment, but then she told herself it was silly. The only reason she was thinking of Laura was because Laura was the only pregnant woman she knew. But then, she was due around Christmastime and the holiday was only a few days away... coincidence?

"Who is it?" Cole asked, and Maddy held her breath.

Tanner had the grace to look uncomfortable. "It's Laura Jessup."

Maddy could feel Cole's gaze on her. She refused to look at him right now, instead taking the ornament in her hand and hanging it on the tree with calm precision.

"You'd better get going, then," Cole said, and no one spoke as Tanner dressed and headed out the door.

"Are you okay?" Cole asked quietly.

"I don't know," Maddy answered honestly. She reached for another ornament and hung it, not knowing what else to do but needing to keep her hands busy.

"I'm sorry I asked. I never thought about Laura…"

"The problem is, I think about her too often." She picked up another ornament and looked for an empty space to hang it. "She's having my husband's baby."

"Maddy, do you know that for sure?"

She turned on him then, annoyed with his placating tone. "The rumors have been around for months and not once has she denied it. Come on, Cole. If you were accused of having an affair with a married man and carrying his child, and it wasn't true, don't you think you'd clear the air?"

Cole didn't say anything.

She tossed the ornament she was holding back into the box. "I'm sorry. I didn't mean to ruin a nice afternoon. I know I promised to live in the present. But it's hard when reminders of the past sneak up to slap me in the face, you know?"

"Sure."

His brief agreement only made her more annoyed. "You think I'm being unreasonable."

His jaw hardened. "What I think is that I want you to move past this so we might have a chance at something great. Because I really care for you, Maddy. More than I expected to."

Oh, Lord. Her emotions were already a disaster zone, and adding his feelings to it only made it worse. She didn't know what to think or say. On one hand, knowing he cared for her felt so good, but on the other hand, it only added to the pressure.

She took a step back. "Cole, I told you I needed to go slowly."

"I know. But there's slow and then there's slow, and I've really been trying here. I tell myself to just be a friend. A good neighbor. That neither of us is ready, but honest to God, Maddy, every time we're together I feel like I'm falling in—"

"Don't say it." She cut him off. "Just don't. We've been out together a handful of times over the course of a month. Not even."

He went to her and grabbed her forearm. "It's more than that. You know it. There's something real between us. Something awesome, and I'm willing to name it. But I can't keep fighting against a ghost. Surely you can see that, right?"

She was starting to feel overwhelmed. Over on the sofa, the boys slept soundly. They'd lost their father. Right now Tanner was on his way to help bring their half brother or sister into the world. Did Cole not understand how hard that was for her to bear? Did he want her to pretend that it had never happened? That it wasn't happening right now? Impossible.

"Look," she said, trying to remain calm. "There *is* something between us. But I can't just turn my feelings on and off. And I can't just snap my fingers and say I'm over it. Don't you think I would if I could?" Her heart hurt just saying the words. "Don't you get that Gavin and I said vows and then they turned out to be meaningless for him? How could I have been so wrong about him? How can I ever be sure of anyone again?"

"What are you saying?" He pressed on, staying in front of her, not letting her escape the conversation. "Are you saying that there's never a chance for us because you don't trust me?"

"I don't trust anyone, don't you see?" she blurted out.

She looked into Cole's eyes, saw the hurt register there and felt terrible about it. She lowered her voice. "Cole, I've enjoyed being with you. It's been wonderful in so many ways. But when I said baby steps, I really meant it."

He swallowed, his Adam's apple bobbing. "I know that, so I tried to show you in any way I could. I didn't want to use words, and so I tried to show you with my actions. Why else would I have done all the secret Santa stuff? And I really started caring for the boys and—"

"Wait. *You're* my secret Santa?" Something inside her froze at the knowledge. "It wasn't my parents?"

As if he sensed he'd put his foot in it, he spoke carefully. "I…swore them to secrecy. They were in on it and so was Tanner."

Maddy turned away. The tires. The Christmas tree. The lights on the hedge and the gift basket at work. The presents for the boys. That had all been Cole, in addition to paying her for the scant amount of housework she'd done here. And the dates themselves…dinner, movies, coffee…

"Wow," she said quietly, taking a step back. "I must have seemed really pathetic to you."

"Of course not! Maddy, come on…"

She held up a hand. "That first night at the library, when you wanted to stay and help, I should have known. Poor Maddy Wallace, with two babies and no husband. You know, for a while I wondered if you asked me out because you like a challenge. But that's not it, is it? You've got a rescue complex. You want to swoop in and fix everything. Well, here's a news flash, Cole. I don't need to be rescued. And I sure as hell don't need to be fixed. The boys and I were managing fine on our own."

She must have touched a nerve, because instead of the imploring expression he'd had before, he was starting to look angry. His lips thinned and his eyebrows knit together as he frowned at her. "Have you been talking to Tanner?"

She frowned, confused. "Of course not. Except when you were both here. Why would you ask that?"

"Because he asked me the same damned thing in almost those exact words. You want to know why I did the Santa thing? Because I knew damn well that you wouldn't accept help any other way."

"Maybe I didn't *want* the help."

"Maddy," he said, and his tone said clearly, *Don't be ridiculous.* Which only added fuel to both her temper and her humiliation.

"So this job...it really was made-up, then. You didn't need me..."

"Could we have managed around here? Sure. But having you here has helped out a lot. I told you it was mutually beneficial."

"I want to know and I want you to answer me honestly," she demanded. "Did you come up with this job as a way of helping me without it being 'charity'?"

He didn't answer right away, which was answer enough.

"You wanted to give the boys a good Christmas," he defended.

She closed her eyes. "Not at the expense of my pride."

"Pride can be overrated."

"Not when you've had yours taken away." Tears pricked her eyelids. "I had so little pride left, Cole. And good intentions or not, you took more of it away from me. I felt guilty enough thinking it was my parents helping out, but I figured there'd come a time when I could repay the favor. They're my folks. But this…"

She sighed heavily. "You went behind my back. You lied because you knew I wouldn't accept the truth. How can you possibly think that would be okay after what I've been through?"

He stared at her as though she were crazy. "You're mad at me because I helped. Ouch."

"I'm mad at you because you went behind my back! How am I supposed to trust you after this?"

Cole swore and ran his hand over his hair. "For God's sake, Maddy, that's crazy. I played Santa Claus and you're making it out to be a capital crime. I helped out a friend who was having a hard time making ends meet, and I did it in secret because I knew she'd hate feeling like it was charity. So sue me for caring and trying to help! You know what? I don't think the problem is that you don't trust me. I think you do. I think you have feelings for me just as much as I do for you. And I think that scares you to death, because the person you really don't trust is yourself. You don't trust your own judgment and so this is the perfect excuse to drive me away."

Her mouth dropped open. "That's ridiculous." But

even as she said the words she knew she was wrong. Hadn't she just been thinking the same thing only minutes ago?

"Is it? Every time we get close, either you pull back or I do so I don't push you further than you want to go. You're very careful to only give little pieces of yourself. Maybe I did like the feeling of helping you and seeing the smile light up your face. But you know what? I can't wait around forever for a person who's only going to ration out their affection according to how afraid they are at the moment. I've done that before, and in the end I was the one sitting there alone."

"I knew it would come to this. The whole take-it-slowly thing never works. Someone always wants more…"

"I'm not asking for much."

"You're asking for everything."

Once more silence fell over the room.

Cole met her gaze. There was sadness in his eyes, she thought with a bit of wonder. And inevitability. She almost wished she could take back the words, but she couldn't, and besides, they'd been the truth.

The truth.

"You're not ready for everything," he murmured. "Even if I wanted to give it to you. And now I realize you might never be. You loved Gavin and he betrayed that trust. For the rest of your life you're going to look at a man and ask yourself one question—do I believe the words coming out of his mouth?"

"Cole."

He shook his head. "Maddy, you are sweet, and kind, and hardworking. You're a wonderful mother and your boys…they're a little crazy and a whole lot cute. You're beautiful and I know you stopped me from saying it before, but I'm pretty sure I've fallen in love with you. I didn't expect it. You just had a way of making me want to make your life better. To see you smile more. Maybe I went about it the wrong way, I don't know. All I know is the thought of the three of you sharing Christmas with me has been on my mind for a while now. I want to see the boys' faces Christmas morning when they open their presents. I want to kiss you under the mistletoe again and drink Christmas morning coffee with you. I've never, ever said that to another woman, Maddy. Never."

She felt as though her heart was weeping, and what he said must have been true, because tears streaked down her face. "But we never made Christmas plans…" It was a dumb thing to say, but at such a moment she didn't know what to say. She was so full of conflicting emotions nothing seemed clear.

"I wanted to. I wanted you three to spend Christmas Eve here and maybe I could share Christmas morning with you."

"My parents are coming over Christmas morning." It would have meant making their relationship official to her folks.

"I know," he answered, and she knew that had been his intention all along.

He was asking too much. As heartrending as his plea was, she simply wasn't ready. "I can't," she murmured. "I'm sorry, Cole. I've enjoyed these last few weeks, but you want more than I can give. You always have. And I can't escape the feeling that somehow you bought your way in." She held up a hand when he started to protest. "Oh, I know you didn't intend it that way. I do respect you enough to believe that. But you weren't honest, and that's the one thing I need."

"Let me be honest now, then. I love you, Maddy."

She hated that she couldn't say the words back. And it wasn't that she didn't care. She did. So much. Things wouldn't have progressed this far if she didn't. But it was a long way to love and the kind of relationship he was looking for.

"I'm sorry, Cole," she answered, and to her chagrin she saw his jaw muscle tighten for just a second before he took a breath and let it out.

"Me, too," he replied, turning away.

There was a charged silence and then Maddy knew she had to go. "I'd better get the boys together and head home."

"Let them sleep out their nap. I can leave…"

He'd leave his own house rather than stay a moment longer. She couldn't blame him. She wished she could give him what he wanted. Wished it with all her heart. Instead she went to the kitchen and gathered up her things, then gently dressed the boys in their snowsuits for the drive home. On the tires he'd bought. To the house with the lights he'd put up and the tree he'd had delivered.

No matter what he said, she still felt like one big charity case.

"I'll help you take everything to the car," he said quietly.

"Thanks."

It was a quiet and sad procession they made to her car. She put the slow cooker and bag in the front, buckled the boys in the back and was about to get in the driver's side when Cole reached for her arm and pulled her back.

"Maddy," he said, his voice rough with emotion. "Tell me what to do and I'll do it. I'm not giving up on us."

She wrenched her arm away, choking on a sob. "Don't, Cole. Please. Just let me go."

She got in and shut the door, started the car. And as she drove away she saw him in the rearview mirror, looking about as lonely as she'd ever seen a man.

She'd done that. She had. She'd hurt him terribly. And that was the last thing she wanted to do.

Maddy had heaped a fair bit of criticism on herself over the past months, but today she was as bad a person as she'd ever felt. And she was the only one to blame this time. She was the one running scared.

Cole sat on the sofa and put his head in his hands. Well. He'd definitely botched that up. What had he been thinking, saying that he loved her? Telling her about his ridiculous fantasy of spending Christmas together?

It was all true, though. That was the real kicker. Every single thing he'd said had been true.

The cushions were still warm from where Luke and Liam had been sleeping, and Cole sighed. If he were honest, those little guys had wormed their way into his heart, too. Today when he'd opened the car door, their little faces had lit up, and Liam, always a bit more reserved than Luke, had put his arms up first. They were pretty special kids. So was their mama, but he'd said the *L* word and she'd panicked.

He didn't realize how long he'd been sitting there until Tanner came in the door, stomping his feet. "Hey," he greeted. "Tree's all up. Where's Maddy and the boys? I figured they'd still be here."

Cole looked up at him and Tanner's face fell. "Shit. What happened?"

"I fell in love with her, that's what happened," Cole said. "I know, you don't have to say it. It's only been a few weeks. She mentioned that several times. And she went ballistic when she found out I was her secret Santa."

"She's got a lot of pride," Tanner said. He went to the fridge and grabbed two beers, popped the tops and went to sit by Cole, handing him one of the bottles. "And I'm guessing she found out in the middle of an argument rather than a *guess what?* moment."

Cole chuckled a little. He loved his little brother. Who else could make him laugh at a time like this? "Yeah. You're right."

"So are you just giving up?"

"She's not over her ex. Or at least, what he did to her. I wish she could see that I'm not him. That I wouldn't do that."

"Yeah, but she probably thought the same thing about Gavin. And that's the problem."

"I know. Dammit, I know."

"I'm sorry, Cole. I know you felt differently about her."

He nodded. "I've never told another woman that I loved her."

"What?" Tanner stared at him. "First of all, never? Not even Roni?"

Cole shook his head. "Roni asked me not to. Long story." One that had more to do with what she'd heard and seen at home than wanting to go slow. In her house, *I love you* had been an excuse, not an endearment.

"Wow. And you actually told Maddy that today?"

He slapped himself in the forehead. "No wonder she took off."

"It's so bad to say *I love you* to a woman?"

Tanner shook his head. "Most women, when you're dating, are dying for you to be the one to say it first. But as you said, Maddy's different. And you haven't been seeing each other that long. She probably freaked."

"She did."

Tanner took a swig of beer; Cole did the same.

"Maybe you can just give her some time. She'll come around."

Cole wanted to take encouragement from the words, but he wasn't feeling very optimistic. "She was mad at me on so many levels that I think the ship has sailed. It's really over."

"I'm sorry," Tanner said quietly, and for a few minutes they simply sat, nursing their beers and thinking.

"By the way," Cole finally said, "what happened with Laura?"

"She'd waited awhile to call us, and by the time we got out there and to the hospital, the baby was crowning. She was delivered right in the emergency room. A healthy little girl."

A girl. Gavin's daughter, in all likelihood. Cole thought for a minute about how that would make Maddy feel in years to come. The little girl would be a year behind her brothers in school. They'd meet on the street. There would always, always be a reminder of his infidelity.

He'd pushed too hard and expected too much. Maybe he'd been particularly blessed, and while he was a whiz at helping out, maybe he wasn't so good at empathizing. All this time he'd blamed Roni for taking so much from him and leaving him with nothing in return, but maybe he hadn't been blameless, either. As Tanner had said when they'd been out riding, maybe helping so much sent a message that he didn't think she could manage on her own, and as a result he'd pushed Roni away. He'd pushed both of them away.

Maddy had surely humbled him today.

Tanner looked at Cole, his expression guarded. "I hope you don't mind me saying, but Laura reminded me a lot of Maddy."

"Don't tell Maddy that. She'll flip her lid."

Tanner let out a soft laugh. "Anyway, what I'm saying is that it's got to take some guts to bring a child into the world all on your own. And she knows what they say around town."

"Makes you wonder why she stays."

Tanner shrugged. "It's home. She probably has her reasons, which are none of our business. Sometimes people are stronger than we give them credit for, Cole."

"I know. My intentions came from a good place, you know what I mean?"

"Then give it some time and tell her that. You're not just going to give up, are you?"

Cole didn't know. Maddy had seemed pretty sure of herself when she left.

After a while they turned on the TV and looked for a hockey or football game. Tanner got up and put on a few steaks for supper, his specialty; Cole threw some frozen fries in the oven. Tomorrow their parents would be back, then it would be Christmas Eve, and Christmas Day.

He'd been looking forward to it this year, but not so much now. Not when the people he really wanted to be with were across town in their own house.

Chapter 13

The library was open until 2:00 p.m. on Christmas Eve, and Maddy was scheduled to work. The boys were at her parents'; they'd bring them over later once Maddy was done with her errands. She'd forgotten croutons for the salad for dinner, and she'd made a pie for dessert and forgotten the ice cream. In fact she'd been forgetting things for the last two days. All because Cole Hudson had told her he loved her.

Well, he was a fool.

There wasn't much traffic at the library, either, which made her shift drag on endlessly. A few people came in to check out books for the holidays; a few more brought books back so they wouldn't be overdue during the break when the library was closed. Maddy was more than ready to leave when two o'clock came and she could lock the doors and log off the computers. They wouldn't open again until the twenty-seventh, so she went through and made sure everything was secure and turned off before leaving.

Cole's final pay to her was in an envelope in her purse. She wasn't sure whether she could spend it or not. She felt guilty taking it now. She was still deliberating when she parked between the grocery store and the drugstore. And she was so preoccupied that she didn't hear the female voice calling her name until it was too late.

"Maddy. Madison. Madison Wallace."

When she finally clued in, she saw Laura Jessup bearing down on her, on her way out of the drugstore. Good Lord, was she out of the hospital already? There was nowhere to run. Maddy simply froze, feeling like the proverbial deer caught in the headlights.

Laura was carrying the baby in a carrier against her chest, underneath her jacket. *Gavin's baby*, Maddy realized, and her knees felt a little bit wobbly.

"Maddy," Laura said again, finally arriving, a little out of breath. Maddy noticed she wasn't wearing a speck of makeup and her hair was pulled into a hasty ponytail.

"You're out of the hospital already?" Maddy asked, not knowing what else to say.

"They sent me home this morning, so I could be home for Christmas."

"Oh."

God, could this be any more awkward...

"Look, Maddy, I've wanted to talk to you for a long time, but I got the feeling you weren't ready."

Maddy gave her a sharp look. "I don't think I'll ever be ready." She was all too aware of the baby, who seemed so very tiny. How was it possible she'd forgotten how small newborns were? All she could really see was a pink hat peeking out from beneath Laura's jacket. A girl. Something twisted inside her, thinking of Gavin having a daughter.

"I know. Which is why I figured, when I saw you, that now is as good a time as any. Maddy, you need to know the truth."

"No, I don't want to hear the details. Please, spare me that." Maddy wanted to run away, but the lot was packed with last-minute shoppers. A few were giving them funny looks. But the cart corral was on one side of her, her car on the other, and Laura in front. To escape she'd literally have to turn tail and run.

"That's just it. There are no details."

Maddy scoffed. "After all this time, you haven't denied a thing. Now you honestly expect me to believe that you and Gavin never had an affair? Is that what you're saying?" She stared pointedly at the lump of pink beneath Laura's jacket, and had a perverse urge to want to see the baby's face, to find out if she bore any resemblance to Gavin's family.

Laura's face reddened. "Maddy, just give me two minutes and hear me out."

Her expression was so earnest, so desperate, that Maddy paused. Maybe they needed to have this conversation. Maybe it was one of the things keeping her from moving forward. Either way, she found herself reluctantly agreeing. "Two minutes, Laura."

Relief showed on the other woman's face, and her right hand was pressed against the bundle inside her jacket. "I'm going to trust you with something. Something I trusted Gavin with, and I know he loved you something fierce."

"Don't presume to tell me about my husband," Maddy replied acidly.

"He did love you," she insisted, "and he said so all the time. He was helping me because I was an old friend. Nothing more. The only secrets we shared were because of lawyer-client privilege."

"Then the baby? How do you explain her?" Maddy looked down at the bundle sleeping beneath the jacket and instantly felt guilty. It wasn't the baby's fault that she was caught in the middle of all this ugliness.

"If I tell you, I need your word you won't tell anyone," she said. "Maddy, I know you hate me. But I need you to promise me this. You do and I know you'll understand."

Maddy paused, looked at Laura's face. She was pleading with her. There was no craftiness in her expression. Never had been. And Maddy remembered how Laura had tried to talk to her a few times, even as recently as a few weeks ago when they'd been in the department store together...

What she saw in Laura's expression now was fear, and Maddy had a difficult time dismissing it.

"Okay. You have my word."

Laura looked around, as if ensuring they wouldn't be overheard. "Gavin was just being a friend and giving me some advice. You see, I ran away from the baby's father before I even knew I was pregnant. I was so afraid he'd come after me, and I didn't want him to know where I was."

"You were pregnant when you came to Gibson?" Now that was a shock. She counted back months. It had been one of the things that had bothered her most. By doing basic calculations, it had looked as though her husband had fallen into bed with his high school sweetheart the moment she came back to town.

"Just. I hadn't even taken a test. As soon as I found

out, I called Gavin at his office. He met me at my place because I wanted privacy."

"And you kept meeting that way?"

"Yes. The baby's father…you see…he's in jail. I made a lot of mistakes, Maddy, but coming home to Gibson wasn't one of them. I never intended for rumors to start about Gavin and me. He was a good friend." Tears welled in her eyes. "I was so shocked when I heard of the accident. And I wanted to set the record straight, but I was afraid. I don't want this guy to ever find me or risk anyone saying something they shouldn't, and so I let people believe what they wanted to believe. But I'm sorry about what that did to you. I can never make that up to you."

"You tried to tell me sooner," Maddy admitted. "Right after the funeral…"

"Yes. Horrible timing."

"And a few times since."

"Yes."

"God." Maddy let out a huge breath, the implications of what this meant swimming around in her head. "This changes everything. It's so… I don't know… Wow."

"I can't imagine what it's been like for you, thinking that he had an affair. And so many times I wished I could set the record straight. But it's just safer for me this way." She looked down at her daughter, her face wreathed in worry. "Safer for her."

And as a mom, Maddy understood that a child's welfare always came first.

"What was Gavin helping you with? Legally?"

"I don't want Spence to find me. Or know about Rowan."

Rowan. The baby's name was Rowan. Maddy looked down again and instantly thought, *not Gavin's. Not his daughter.* It shouldn't have made a difference. But it did. There was relief, and a lot more that Maddy would really have to sit and think about later.

"And Gavin was doing that?"

Laura nodded. "Family law wasn't his thing, he said, but he referred me to someone in the office he trusted. And he made sure I had what I needed, particularly when I felt so rough the first few months here and I was trying to find someone to hire me. No one wants to hire someone who's only available for six months."

Laura sighed and looked at Maddy. "You know we dated in high school. I trusted him...but I didn't trust anyone else. And I still don't. But I'm trusting you because you need to know. Your husband didn't cheat on you. What you two had was real. He didn't tell you he was helping me because I asked him not to, and Gavin Wallace was a man of his word."

Maddy's eyes stung. "I'm sorry," she said quietly. "I had no idea. You've borne your share of gossip, too, and it can't have been easy."

"I thought about leaving and starting over somewhere new. But Gibson is all I have right now. I still have a few friends who are behind me." She blushed a little. "And my grandparents are here.

"Anyway," Laura continued, "I don't expect us to be friends or anything. I just wanted to clear the air. To let you know you weren't wrong to believe in him." She gave a small sniff. "Gavin was so good to me, and all I've done is tarnish his reputation. That's my biggest regret, you know. I've been just sick about it. The only reason I haven't spoken up has been because of Rowan."

"Maybe someday you'll be able to," Maddy said. "If things are safer for you."

"I hope so," Laura said, meeting her gaze. "I truly do."

"I'm glad," Maddy replied, swallowing against a lump in her throat. "I'm sorry I made it so difficult for you. If I'd known…"

"Who can blame you? I'm lucky you didn't come banging on my door, ready to tear a strip off me."

Maddy couldn't help it, she laughed. And thought in different circumstances she probably would have liked Laura quite a bit.

"Do you have everything you need? For you and the baby?" she found herself asking.

Laura's face registered surprise. "Well, yes. Most of the necessities, anyway." She smiled. "Funny how I wasn't planning on being a mom, but now I'm so excited. And scared. It's a huge responsibility, isn't it?"

Maddy nodded. "Thank you, Laura. For telling me."

There was a general sense of the conversation winding up; they weren't going to magically become good friends all of a sudden. "You're welcome. Merry Christmas, Maddy. To you and your boys."

"To you both, too," Maddy replied.

Laura walked off, and Maddy watched as she went to her car and carefully extricated the baby from the carrier and tucked her into the car seat in the back.

Not Gavin's baby. Not Laura's lover. After months of trying to get used to the idea of her husband being a stranger, to find out that he was innocent put her entirely off balance. She frowned, then checked her watch. Three o'clock on Christmas Eve and she still needed to get those last-minute items. And she had a lot to think about. Because in the space of a ten-minute conversation, everything she thought she knew had been turned upside down. For the second time this year.

* * *

To Cole, it didn't feel much like Christmas Eve. Not even with his mom and dad home and the traditions in full swing. He couldn't stop thinking about Maddy and what she must be doing and how he'd blown it and shouldn't have said the things he did...

Except he'd just told the truth. It might have been rotten timing and the wrong words, but he hadn't lied. He'd fallen for Maddy, and it was too soon for her. What hurt was the knowledge that it might always be too soon. He could try to prove himself over and over, but until she was willing to trust herself and her own judgment, she'd never trust *him* to keep his word.

For the second time in the last month, he had the thought that he'd gleefully punch Gavin Wallace in the mouth—if he were still alive to take a beating.

"Is this some weird experiment where you try to light the tree on fire with the sheer power of your brain?" Ellen asked, sitting beside him on the sofa.

"What?"

She sighed. "You've been sitting here scowling for the better part of an hour. I asked Tanner what was going on with you and he shut up tighter than a clam."

Cole smiled for all of a millisecond at that. They might have their differences from time to time, but he and his brother always had each other's backs.

"What is it? You've been quiet ever since we got back yesterday. The house and ranch are fine, so something's going on with you." She peered closely at his face. "If I didn't know better I'd say it was a woman, but we were only gone three weeks."

He looked at her, feeling miserable, then back at the tree as he let out a sigh.

"A girl? Really?" His mom perked up at that. "Who?"

He might as well talk. His mom would keep at him with as much tenacity as a dog with a bone until he told her everything. "You warned me, and you were right. I took a liking to Maddy Wallace, but it's not going anywhere. The whole thing with her husband has shaken her too much to take a chance on me."

"Oh, honey." She put her hand on his knee. "On you? Or on love in general?"

"What does it matter? The end result's the same, isn't it?"

"What happened?"

He gave her the abridged version, with enough detail for him to realize how deeply he'd gotten himself into it and how, despite the short amount of time, he and Maddy had really shared a lot. "Those boys, too," he said glumly. "God, they're cute. And a lot of work. But then when you hear their belly laughs, it's like the whole world smiles along."

He looked over at his mom, who was studying him with tears in her eyes. "Oh, man, don't start with tears. I don't think I can handle it." Not because he couldn't handle a woman crying, but because it made him feel like crying himself. Which was ridiculous, but the stinging behind his nose was a good indication.

"I warned you, you stupid idiot," she half laughed, half lamented. "I should have known better. Maddy's a good person, and you've always been one to help someone who could use a hand."

"It's not that I don't understand where she's coming from. I do. But I can't compete with Gavin. I can't make up for his wrongs. I pushed too soon and I hurt her with what I said."

"Then say you're sorry."

"It's not that easy."

"I know. It never is."

He was quiet for a minute. Then he rubbed his hand over his face and stared at the tree some more. "She told me I took her pride. It wasn't what I intended, but I didn't really consider how she'd feel. I hired her to work here and told myself I was doing her a favor because she wouldn't have accepted the money outright. I did the secret Santa thing for the same reasons. But no matter how I did it, Maddy's one point of pride in everything was that she was making it on her own two feet. And by jumping in and taking over, even in those small ways, I took that away from her. And yeah, I did it to help a friend, but it also made me feel like I was something special, you know? So how does that make my motives that pure?"

Ellen chuckled a little bit. "Oh, honey, altruism is seldom completely pure. It's satisfying to know that you've helped someone who needs a hand. It's a positive thing in a world dominated by selfishness and *I, I, I.* Don't be too hard on yourself."

"I miss her. Two days and I miss her. And the boys. I was going to ask her to bring the boys over for Christmas Eve and now it just feels like there's no point to Christmas. None at all."

"Give it time, Cole. For all anyone knew, Maddy and Gavin were happy with two precious babies as recently as seven or eight months ago. She's dealt with a lot since then."

"I know." He looked at his mom and felt a rush of love. She was so steady. So strong. He realized that all this time the reason why no other girls had held his interest was because they'd been mere shadows compared to his mom's grace and strength. Maddy was the first to come close. "It's just that I finally fell in love and I don't want to wait."

She leaned over and gave him a hug. "You," she said quietly, "are one in a million. Just you remember that."

"Thanks. And thanks for the talk. It didn't really fix anything, but at least the tree is probably safe from spontaneously combusting. For the time being."

She smiled and patted his knee again. "Your dad and I are going to the church service at seven. Are you coming?"

He shook his head. "Naw. I'll do a last check on the stock. Tanner's on call—again. But he'll be home around nine. I think we should all meet back here, have a Christmas toast, and just be thankful for our family. How does that sound?"

"Perfect," she replied. "Now, I'm going to go wake up your father. He says he needs a vacation to recover from vacation. And if I don't get him up now, he won't sleep tonight."

Cole laughed and watched his mother disappear. But when she was gone the heaviness settled in his heart again. He wanted what his parents had. He'd thought he'd found someone to have it with. But as his parents always said, it took two. And he was sitting here alone.

Chapter 14

Christmas Eve church service was tradition in Maddy's family, and her parents had stayed for dinner and were going to church with her and the boys before heading home again. They'd be over in the morning around eight to see the boys, and Maddy was dreading the few hours when she'd be home alone, staring at the tree, looking at the few presents beneath it. Two from her parents, one from Gavin's folks that they'd sent up from Florida and two envelopes from her brothers, both of which she was pretty sure contained gift cards.

It wasn't that she was ungrateful. She just suspected that the magical part of her Christmas was over, done with the end of her secret Santa surprises. The anticipation was gone, and in its place she simply felt lonely.

The service was lovely as usual, with lots of carols and candlelight and smiles. Maddy sat and listened to the Christmas message and let her thoughts drift to Gavin, and Laura, and Cole, and all the stuff that had created such havoc in her life the past half year. She was so torn. She felt guilty for believing that her husband had been cheating and had fathered another child, but on the other hand, she understood that with the absence of denial came doubt. She thought about Cole and the wonderful things he'd done for her in the past month and then remembered that she'd wanted to stand on her own two feet. Was he right? Did she just have too much pride and was it getting in the way of her happiness? Or was it insecurity? She looked over at her boys, one on each of her parents' laps, and felt as if she'd let them down, too.

Laura had said that Gavin had been devoted to their marriage. Tears welled up in Maddy's eyes. She'd loved him, too. And perhaps that was why she'd been so stuck since his death. Everyone had been so convinced of his guilt that she hadn't felt free to love him, or grieve for him, or really let him go. She'd been outraged, and she'd let that take over to get her through. Because it was expected.

But she could examine those feelings, because now he was the husband she remembered. Kind, caring, willing to help a friend, even if it meant keeping a secret. Somehow, it had felt as though there'd been a final piece that just didn't fit into the puzzle, but now it slid into the empty space easily, completing the picture. And it was a good picture. Maddy understood now what Laura had meant this afternoon. She, too, had promised to keep Laura's secret, and she would. It meant that Gavin's reputation couldn't be restored. And that seemed cruel and unfair.

But she knew the truth, and that was all that mattered right now.

"Are you okay?" her mom whispered.

"I really am," she murmured back. "And I'll explain everything tomorrow." She smiled at her mom, feeling more at peace than she had for a very long time.

When the service was over, she put on her coat and reached for the boys' outerwear. Before she could get them dressed, however, Ellen Hudson approached, her silvery hair perfectly styled, the golden tan of her face evidence of her vacation in the sun. "Maddy, I wanted to come over and thank you for the help you gave out at the house while we were away."

Maddy felt awkward and miserable as she looked at Cole's mom. "You're welcome. Your home is lovely, Mrs. Hudson."

Ellen put her hand on Maddy's arm. "You've always called me Ellen. No need to stop now. Do you have a few minutes to talk?"

She looked around for her parents. "I came with my mom and dad," she said weakly. She wasn't sure if she actually wanted to talk to Ellen or if she just wanted to escape.

"We can give you and the boys a lift home. Please, Maddy. It's important."

She swallowed, anxious. If only one of the kids would fuss or something. But they were good as gold, sitting on the pew, playing with a few little toys.

"I guess it would be okay. Let me tell my parents."

"I can sit with the boys for a moment if you like. They're adorable."

They really were, Maddy admitted to herself. She'd bought them little trouser, shirt and vest outfits for church and they were scrumptious in them.

"I'll just be a moment."

And of course her mom and dad had no objection, so she had no real excuse not to talk to Ellen. Chalk it up to the second awkward conversation of the day...

She returned and sat in the pew on the other side of the boys. "Did you have a good vacation?" she asked politely.

"It was wonderful. We were so overdue for a trip away, and neither of us had been south before. We're thinking we might try to get away every year or so now."

Maddy nodded. But there was no sense avoiding the topic. "I'm guessing you want to talk to me about Cole."

Ellen met her gaze. "We had a long talk this afternoon." She shook her head a bit and gave a soft chuckle. "I warned him away from you, you know. Not because I don't like you, because I do. But every time I saw you I could see the hurt in your eyes and I knew losing Gavin had left some deep, deep scars. Particularly after certain things came to light."

Maddy wished she could defend him now. It hurt that she couldn't.

"But Cole has a thing for wounded birds." She folded her hands in her lap. "One time when he was little I found him with a crow in his lap, thinking he could help nurse it back to health. It was deader than Moses and I was pretty disgusted and washed him from top to toe, but that's the kind of kid he was. If there was a stray kitten, he wanted it for a barn cat."

Maddy's heart gave a pang. "One of the things I like about Cole is his kindness. And his gentleness."

"I'm glad you see that side of him. So you must know that he's hurting right now."

"It's only been a few weeks," Maddy began, but Ellen shook her head.

"Cole's funny that way. When he sets his mind on something, it's a done deal. And when he sets his heart on something...or someone...well, there's no halfway for him. He didn't say it exactly, but I'm sure he's fallen in love with you."

"I know."

The two words settled in the air between them.

"Maddy, I know finding out what you did about Gavin had to turn your world upside down. But loving someone means taking that risk that they'll let you down. And I get you not wanting to take that chance again, but is it worth being alone? That is, if you care for Cole. Maybe his feelings aren't returned in the same way."

Maddy picked up a stuffed toy Liam had dropped and gave it back to him. "Ellen..."

She wanted to say more but she couldn't. It was all too much right now. There were still people in the church, including Cole's father, who was sitting patiently, reading some pamphlet or something in the very back pew. The lights were soft and the Christmas tree glowed and her boys were playing and she should have been happy. But she thought about Cole and all the moments they'd shared in the past weeks and her heart just hurt. She pictured his eyes when he teased her, heard the sound of his laugh. The way he looked when he wanted to kiss her.

She thought about all the things she'd said to him and what she'd accused him of and the pain intensified. She tried taking a breath and found herself letting out a sob. He had been kind, funny, sexy, loving, generous and understanding. So many good things. And Ellen was right. She didn't want to be alone. She wanted more afternoons in the snow with the boys between them. Oh, he was so good with the boys. Another sob broke forth as she remembered Liam putting his arms up for Cole. Liam, her shy boy, who accepted him so easily. Who trusted and felt safe.

The way she did when she was in his arms.

And the way he kissed her as if she was the last woman on earth and making her toes curl.

And how he'd suggested that she might want more children someday. She did. She still wanted what she'd always wanted—a big family, a home of brothers and sisters and laughter and arguments...

And she had turned it all away not because he'd done anything wrong but for the simple reason that she was scared...and she'd blamed it all on a reason that didn't even exist. Because he'd been too kind and too helpful.

Ellen held out a tissue. "I'm sorry. I didn't mean to upset you."

Liam came over and crawled into her lap, offering quiet comfort the way she often offered it to him. Oh, her boys. And she knew without a shadow of a doubt that if she dropped her damned pride and fear for two seconds and asked Cole to comfort her, he'd be there as soon as humanly possible with a kiss and a strong shoulder for her to cry on.

Because Cole Hudson was the kind of man a woman could rely on.

"I'm sorry." She sniffed and wiped at her eyes. "I don't know why that just happened."

"Could it be because you miss my son almost as much as he seems to miss you?"

She met Ellen's eyes. She recognized them. They were Cole's—full of compassion and understanding. And steel, when required.

"You almost sound like you want me to say yes."

"That's because I do. You're a good woman and a fine mother, Madison. You were always a nice girl. You seem down-to-earth and friendly and warm. My hesitation was because of exactly what happened. That you might not be ready for love. Yet, anyway." She smiled, a sentimental little flicker across her lips. "Cole is like his father, you know. I knew when he fell, it'd be hard. That's why we've been together for thirty-five years. And will be for many more, God willing."

"I said some harsh things," Maddy admitted. "I'm so scared, Ellen. And there are things you don't know…"

"Of course there are. As there should be."

Maddy took heart from that. "I don't want to hurt him," she continued on, holding Liam close. Luke had climbed down from the pew and was rummaging around in the diaper bag, his little white shirt untucked from his black pants. "Things happened so fast. It just scared me so much. I never imagined this happening."

"Love can be like that. Maddy, I'm just asking for you to talk to him. Come home with me and talk to him and hear him out. If he cares about you like I think he does, and you care about him the way I think you do, you need to talk. And maybe try again."

Ellen looked at the boys and her gaze softened even further. "And the twins…my word, they're sweet. I wouldn't mind having them around now and again. Will you do it, Maddy? It's Christmas Eve. There's no need for you both to be miserable."

Could she do it? Go to Cole's and ask for forgiveness for all she'd said?

Was she ready for that?

In the end she knew only one thing. If she didn't try,

she'd regret it. Because the idea of not trying to make things right with Cole felt so wrong.

She'd promised to stop living in the past. Start living in the present. And she'd failed. Maybe this was the first step she needed to take to finally, finally move on. Didn't everyone deserve a second chance?

"I'll come with you," she agreed. "I can't promise to make things right. But I promise to talk to him."

"That's all I ask. I think seeing you is the only Christmas present he wants, to be honest."

They collected Cole's dad, packed up the diaper bag and put coats and hats on the boys. Maddy's mom had left their car seats in the vestibule, and the five of them left just as the last members of the women's group shut off the lights for the night.

Maddy sat in the back, in between the car seats, and politely asked about the vacation so that any potential awkward silence was filled with tales of the Caribbean. Nerves jumbled around in her stomach, wondering what she'd say to Cole, wondering what he'd say to her, wondering if she'd see him and all her words would just scatter at the sight of him. And Lord help her, there was anticipation, too. She wanted to see him again.

When she walked in the door—carrying Luke, with Liam in Ellen's arms—it seemed as though the world stopped moving. Everything went silent. Tanner was in the kitchen getting something out of the fridge and he stopped, the fridge door open and the soda can forgotten in his hand. Cole was coming through the door from the mudroom, but he halted and simply looked at her, first with numb surprise and then with the slightest flicker of hope in his eyes.

Ellen was the first to speak. "Look who I found at church tonight?"

The three of them made their way inside. "Tanner, I wanted to take a quick look down at the barn and make sure everything's secure for the night," their dad said.

"I'll come with you."

There was no real pretense; everyone was on the same page with giving Cole and Maddy privacy to talk. Ellen undid Liam's jacket and took off his mitts and Maddy figured she should do the same for Luke. And as she did Liam ran, stumbled his way over to Cole and lifted his arms joyously. "Bup! Bup!"

"Hey, little man," he said softly, picking him up, and Maddy's hands fell still on Luke's jacket. "Aren't you handsome tonight?"

Luke squirmed and she took off his jacket as Ellen disappeared to…somewhere. It was just the two of them—well, four of them. As soon as Luke was free, he, too, made his way to Cole, who sat down on the sofa and lifted them onto his knees.

"They missed you," she said softly.

"The first time I met them they just stared at me," he marveled. He bounced his knees up and down and the boys laughed. Cole smiled and Maddy silently thanked Ellen for urging her to come tonight.

"Cole…"

"My mom put you up to this, didn't she?" He didn't wait for an answer. "She pried a lot out of me this afternoon. Maddy, I'm sorry. You said time and time again that you weren't ready and I didn't listen. I pushed and drove you away. It's my fault."

She smiled. She couldn't help it. This really wasn't his fault, not at all. What he'd expected wasn't all that unreasonable. She went to the sofa and sat beside him, taking one of the boys onto her own lap. "You're a good person, Cole. Strong and kind."

"It's not that I'm afraid of working at a relationship. I know how to work hard. It's like Tanner told me a while ago—when you find the one who's worth it, then it takes work. It's not going to be easy because it's not supposed to be. And I got caught up in wanting everything right now."

"You and the rest of society," she commented. "But I wasn't fair, either." She debated on what she was allowed to tell him. She didn't want to betray Laura's confidence, especially if this wasn't going to work out. But it was so tied up in her reasons that she couldn't avoid it completely.

"Cole, I learned something recently that flipped everything I knew upside down. I'm not at liberty to explain a whole lot, but I learned that Gavin isn't the father of Laura's baby, and they weren't having an affair. I believe the source."

His mouth fell open. "Holy…wow. That's big news. How do you feel?"

"Mixed up," she admitted. "I realized that I was angry all these months, and I didn't want to believe he'd done it, but there was this weird pressure on me to accept it. I was already poor Maddy. I would have been poor Maddy who still believes in her cheating husband." It hurt to say it. She ran her hand over Luke's soft hair. "I feel relieved that the faith I had in him wasn't misplaced. And guilty because I let doubt get the better of me." She laughed softly. "I feel a lot of things. But most of all, right now, I realize that I hid behind all of that to avoid admitting how I was feeling about you. Especially with Gavin being gone such a short time."

"And me rushing you didn't help."

"Maybe, but you were so right about a lot of things."

Maddy looked down. Both kids were getting drowsy. It was past their bedtime and they were getting good snuggles and it seemed they were ready to take advantage of it.

"You were right about some things, too, Maddy. Like how I shouldn't have taken it upon myself to do all those things like I was some stupid white knight or something."

"Those things have been the best part of my Christmas," Maddy protested. "All the sweet surprises…no one has ever done anything like that for me before." It was absolutely true. "And I was completely ungrateful."

"They've been the best part of my Christmas, too," he whispered. "Because I got to see your face light up or hear your voice and I knew that for a few minutes, I'd made you happy."

Tears filled her eyes. "Oh, Cole."

She leaned over and kissed him, just a light grazing of lips, but it was the beginning of healing and starting over.

She sat back, wishing she could curl up in his arms, but she couldn't because they had the boys.

"Know what I discovered?" Now that they'd started, she felt the need to say everything. "I learned that saying you want to leave the past in the past is a lot easier than actually doing it. But it's the actions that really count, not the words. I know now that you tried to show me you cared, Cole, instead of just telling me or paying me compliments. I wasn't fair to you, but you stuck with it, anyway. And I'm so glad. Knowing the truth does change things, because you were right. It was me I didn't trust.

"But I was right all along. My faith wasn't misplaced. And I know, deep down, that Gavin would want me to be happy, to find love again and find someone who cares about the boys. And here you are. If you're willing to give me another chance."

She bit down on her lip. She'd been doing all the talking; she figured she had the most apologizing to do. But now the ball was in Cole's court.

He reached over and put his hand on top of hers. "That is the easiest thing in the world to do," he replied, squeezing her fingers. "And I promise I won't rush you. I just want us to be together. We can take our time. I just want to be with you, whatever that looks like."

Her heart soared. Never could she have imagined this happening, not even a few months ago. But it was Christmas Eve and maybe a time for miracles. A time for truly looking ahead instead of behind. All Maddy knew was that she felt more hopeful than she had in a long, long time, and it was all because Cole Hudson had turned up at the library one day and offered to help take out the trash.

The twins were nearly asleep, and Maddy knew she should get them home, but she couldn't bear the thought of the evening being over just when they were getting somewhere. She looked into Cole's eyes and found him waiting…patiently. And she found she suddenly didn't want to be all that patient. She wanted to start on the next chapter of her life.

"Maybe you could drive us home?" she asked, swallowing against a lump in her throat. "And maybe you could stay awhile? Talk some more?" Truthfully, she thought she might like to do more than talk. Like kiss him some more without worrying about the kids between them or someone walking in.

The very idea sent whorls of anticipation coursing through her.

"Of course I can."

"Your family won't mind? It's Christmas Eve."

"They'll probably send up a cheer. I haven't been very good company the last few days." He smiled, and it had a sweet edge to it that she loved.

She put the boys' jackets back on while he went to tell Ellen he was leaving. In no time they'd fastened the boys into the truck and made the trip into town and her house. She'd left the outside lights on, and when Cole cut the engine, Liam woke. Luke stayed asleep until she took him out of his seat, but then his eyes opened, too. Maddy unlocked the door and led the way inside, keeping the rooms dark.

"They really do need to get to bed," she murmured. "I'll get their jammies on."

Cole followed her down the hall with Liam on his arm. "I'll help."

And he did. Maddy felt a strange new contentment as they got the boys ready together. She did the diaper change while Cole fastened up their onesies and dressed them in soft sleepers. When she got bottles ready for one last drink, he cradled one child in his arms and gave the bottle while she fed the other, the two of them on opposite sides of the sofa. Maddy looked over, saw his eyes shining at her in the dark, and melted. All she'd ever truly wanted was a partner and a friend. How blessed to have found one—twice. Because Cole was that guy.

Even though their relationship was in the fledgling stage, she knew, deep down, that this was it.

Together they walked up the stairs and put the boys in their cribs, covering them with their blankets. When Maddy turned around, Cole held out his hand, and she took it, lacing her fingers with his.

Once in the hallway, she quietly shut the door, and then there was a moment where she had to decide. She could lead him back down the stairs to the living room, or ten feet down the hall to her bedroom. Indecision kept her feet rooted to the spot, but now that they were alone, Cole gently pulled her closer and cupped his hand along the curve of her jaw.

"I love you, Maddy. You don't have to say it back—you don't have to do anything. I just want you to know. I love you. I'm rapidly falling in love with your kids." He smiled, then touched his lips to hers. "But right now, I'm more focused on you. You inspire me. You make me want to be a better man. I can't promise it'll be easy, but I promise I'll do the best I can to make you happy."

She could use words at this moment, give assurances. But she remembered that words were just that and sometimes it was actions that were required. And right now she wanted to show him how she felt. Needed him to know that she was willing to meet him halfway, that he wasn't alone in this.

She wanted him to know that their relationship was a shared responsibility, not one where he gave and she did all the taking.

So she reached for the buttons on his shirt and started to undo them, one by one, pulling the tails of his shirt out of his jeans. Desire and excitement curled through her, urging her fingers on as she pushed the open shirt wide across his chest and pressed a kiss to his warm skin. He shuddered beneath her touch and she closed her eyes for a minute, being wholly in the moment.

"Maddy," he whispered, and she took his hand and led him down the hall to her room.

Quietly, reverently, they undressed in the dark, and Maddy pulled down the covers of the bed. Cole stood on the opposite side of the bed, a hungry look in his eyes. She held out her hand and they met in the middle on the soft sheets: mouth to mouth, skin to skin, heart to heart.

And when Maddy fell back against the pillows, it truly felt like a new and awesome beginning.

Chapter 15

She sneaked out of bed while Cole was still sleeping. Months of being a mom meant she could hear the boys stirring; she silently slipped on a robe and tiptoed out of the bedroom, quietly padding down the hall and opening their door.

There was nothing like waking in the morning and being greeted by their smiles. Well, maybe one thing was nicer, she amended in her head. It was pretty darn fantastic waking up next to Cole.

As quietly as she could, she got the boys up and changed their diapers before taking them downstairs to get ready for Christmas morning. She turned on the tree lights and got them each a sippy cup of juice to hold them over until breakfast when her parents got here…

Her parents. Oh, Lord, she'd forgotten. And Cole was upstairs in bed…and she'd forgotten to stuff the stockings for the boys. Thank goodness they were too young to realize! She darted off to the closet for the little bags of stuffers she'd bought and hurriedly tucked them inside the little stockings.

She made a pot of coffee and figured she should get Cole up soon so he could at least be dressed before her parents arrived. But there was no need. His footsteps sounded on the stairs and he arrived, fully dressed in his jeans and shirt from last night. There was a shadow of stubble on his jaw and to Maddy he looked perfect.

"Merry Christmas," she said softly as he got to the final step.

"It is, isn't it?" He grinned at her. "And look what's under the tree."

She turned around and saw that the twins had crawled underneath the lowest branches and had each grabbed a stocking, pulling the contents out left and right.

"And this is why nothing got put under the tree until just before we left last night!" Maddy laughed and jumped into the fray, trying to make some order out of the chaos. The boys thought it was a game and items went in and out of the stockings for several minutes until everyone was laughing.

"My parents are coming over. I understand if you want to get home." Maddy handed him a cup of coffee with one sugar. "But if you want to stay…"

"If?"

"Well, I am making Christmas breakfast. And dinner is at Mom and Dad's tonight, and I know you'd be welcome. I can't believe they were in on the secret Santa thing all along."

"They want you to be happy, too."

She curled up against his side. "Well, lucky for them,"

she observed. So far the boys were ignoring the presents and playing with the contents of their stockings, so she let well enough alone. "I just feel badly that I don't have anything for you." She'd thought about it, right up until the day they'd parted ways. Now she wished she'd bought some little trinket he could unwrap.

"Are you kidding? Having you and the twins under the tree today is just what I wanted. But that does remind me..."

He extricated himself from her embrace and went to where his coat was hanging on the hook. "I seem to have a little something in here for you."

Cole took a small rectangular box from the pocket. It was white and tied with silver ribbon, and Maddy accepted it with trembling hands. "Cole, you shouldn't have. Oh, gosh. When did you..."

"I bought it a week or so ago and grabbed it before we left last night. Open it."

She did, and it was a heart shaped silver pendant on a fine chain. Nothing overly extravagant, but sweet and thoughtful and a bit sentimental. Just like him, apparently, and she was incredibly touched.

"It's beautiful," she said, laying the pendant against her palm, "Thank you so much."

He took it from her hands and unhooked the clasp, putting it around her neck. "There," he said, dropping a kiss on the back of her neck. "Perfect."

She turned around and pressed a kiss to his lips. "This Christmas keeps getting better and better," she teased, and they forgot about the stocking stuffer carnage as they kissed long and deep.

And when the kiss ended, he hugged her, which was almost as good.

"There's one thing I meant to ask you last night," he said when they finally went to the sofa to sit down. "How did you find out what you did about Gavin?"

Maddy tucked one leg beneath her and thought about what she could say and what she couldn't. The fear in Laura's eyes had been real. That much she was sure of.

"I can't tell you. And it's not that I want to have secrets. I don't, Cole. But I promised I wouldn't say a word, and I have to keep that promise until I'm told otherwise. No one is even supposed to know, and you can't say anything. I do hope I can tell you someday, though." She paused, took his hand in hers. "All I can say is that it doesn't matter now. I mean, I wish I could exonerate him. But I understand why I can't. And I know that doesn't help you at all." She gave a short laugh. "I guess what I'm saying is, the important thing is that it's all good. And it really is." She lifted his hand and placed a kiss on his knuckles.

"If it's good enough for you, it's good enough for me. Whatever happened, I'm glad."

"Mummm mummm mummm."

Maddy looked down to find Luke holding a square box, bouncing on his chubby knees. "Hold on, sweetie," she said, taking the box from him. At the same time she saw her parents' car pull in behind Cole's truck. "Mom and Dad are here."

"Well, then let's wish them merry Christmas." He got up and pulled her close for one last kiss. "To tide me over until we're alone again," he said, nipping at her lip.

She stood on tiptoe and gave him a tight hug. "Cole?"

"Hmm?"

"I thought of something I can give you for Christmas."

He waggled his eyebrows. "I thought you did that last night."

Her parents were coming up the walk. "Not that." She put her hand on the side of his face. "I love you, Cole."

His smile was wide and joyous. "And that," he replied, "is the best gift ever."

* * * * *

Award-winning author **Jennifer Faye** pens fun, heartwarming contemporary romances with rugged cowboys, sexy billionaires and enchanting royalty. Internationally published, with books translated into nine languages, she is a two-time winner of the *RT Book Reviews* Reviewers' Choice Award. She has also won the CataRomance Reviewers' Choice Award, been named a Top Pick author and been nominated for numerous other awards.

Books by Jennifer Faye

Harlequin Romance

The Bartolini Legacy

The Prince and the Wedding Planner
The CEO, the Puppy and Me

Greek Island Brides

Carrying the Greek Tycoon's Baby
Claiming the Drakos Heir
Wearing the Greek Millionaire's Ring

The Cattaneos' Christmas Miracles

Heiress's Royal Baby Bombshell

Once Upon a Fairytale

Beauty and Her Boss
Miss White and the Seventh Heir

Snowbound with an Heiress
Her Christmas Pregnancy Surprise

Visit the Author Profile page at
Harlequin.com for more titles.

Her Festive Baby Bombshell

JENNIFER FAYE

For Nancy F.

To a wonderful lady I'm honored to know.

Thanks so much for the encouragement.

Prologue

"What are you doing here?" a rich, deep voice called out from the shadows of the executive suite.

Holly Abrams froze. The breath caught in her throat. The pounding of her heart echoed in her ears. She searched the darkness for the mysterious man.

And then he stepped into the light. She immediately recognized him. It was the CEO of Lockwood International, Finn Lockwood. The air whooshed from her lungs.

This wasn't the first time their paths had crossed, but they weren't by any stretch of the imagination what you would consider friends. And he didn't sound the least bit happy to see her, but then again, why should he?

When her gaze met his, her palms grew damp. "Hi." Why did her voice have to be so soft—so seductive? She swallowed hard.

"Isn't it a bit late for you to be working?"

Overtime was nothing new to Holly. After a failed engagement, she'd sworn off men and instead focused all of her energy on her career. When she was working, she felt confident and driven.

"I…uh, have these papers for you." She held out the large manila envelope to him. "I was told you wanted this contract right away." When he went to retrieve the envelope, their fingers brushed. A jolt of awareness arched between them. The sensation zinged up her arm and settled in her chest.

"Thank you." As the seconds ticked by, he asked, "Is there something else you need?"

Need? Her gaze dipped to his lips—his very kissable lips. She remembered their last meeting in the elevator. They'd been alone when she'd dropped a slip of paper. They'd simultaneously bent over to retrieve it, bringing their faces so close. When they'd straightened, he'd stared at her as though seeing her as a woman instead of as a paralegal in Lockwood's legal department. She knew when a man was interested in her, but when the elevator dinged and the doors slid open, the moment had passed. It had left her wondering if it'd been a product of wishful thinking on her part.

And now, before she made a further fool of herself, she needed to make a speedy exit. "I'll just let you deal with that." She turned to retrace her footsteps back to the elevator when she remembered her manners. She glanced over her shoulder. "Good night."

"Wait."

With her back to him, she inwardly groaned. Her gaze moved to the elevator at the end of the hallway. Her escape was so close and yet so far away. Suppressing a resigned sigh, she turned.

"Come with me." Without waiting for her response, he strode into his office.

What in the world did he want with her? Her black peep-toe platform pumps echoed as she crossed the marble floor. She couldn't tell which was louder, the *click-click* of her heels or the *thump-thump* of her heart. Most people didn't make her nervous, but Mr. Lockwood was the exception.

When Holly entered the spacious office, she had to admit she was awed. While he read over the document, she took in her surroundings. Behind Mr. Lockwood's desk stood a wall of windows. Being so high up, it provided the most amazing view of Manhattan. She longed to rush over and stare out at the bustling city, but she didn't dare.

The sound of a desk drawer opening distracted her. Mr. Lockwood appeared to be searching for something. While he was preoccupied, she continued her visual tour of his office. It reminded her of a museum with its impressive sculptures as well as a baseball collection ensconced in glass cases. But the bookcases spanning an entire wall were what drew her in.

She struggled not to gape at the large collection of books. He liked to read. They had that in common. She wanted to slip across the room and examine the titles, but when she glanced over at Mr. Lockwood, he pointed to one of the two chairs in front of his desk. Without a word, she complied.

"What do you think of the office?"

"It's very nice." She indicated the floor-to-ceiling bookcases. "Have you read them all?"

"I have. And what about you? Do you like to read?"

"Oh, yes." She laced her fingers together to keep from fidgeting with the hem of her skirt. "I read every chance I get."

"Is that why you're not downstairs at the company's fiftieth anniversary celebration? Would you prefer to be at home reading?"

Was this some sort of test? She hesitated. Was there a right and a wrong answer? Her clasped hands tightened as his gaze probed her. Could he tell how nervous his presence made her?

"I missed the party because I needed to finish the contract." She indicated the document on his desk. "I was just going to leave it for you before I headed home." She wasn't the only one not attending the party. What was his excuse for skipping his own celebration? "I figured you'd be at the party."

"I already made a brief appearance. No one will let their guard down around the boss so I made a quick exit, letting everyone get back to having a good time."

She could totally understand people being nervous around him. He was an intense man, who insisted on only the best from his employees. "That can't be much fun for you."

He shrugged. "I'm fine with it."

She looked at him in a new light, realizing for the first time that the privilege of working up here in this ivory tower was also a sentence of isolation. "It doesn't seem right that you're working instead of celebrating your family's accomplishments."

He shook his head. "This is the way it must be."

Well, now, that was an odd comment. It was on the tip of her tongue to question him about it, but she thought better of it. She had a feeling his pleasantness had its limitations.

Quietness settled over the room as Mr. Lockwood scanned the twenty-one-page document. Holly struggled to sit still—waiting and wondering why he wanted her to remain there. Her index finger repeatedly smoothed over the chipped nail polish on her thumb.

There was something about this man that turned her into a mass of jittery nerves. But what? It wasn't his billions or his power. It was something more intrinsic, but she couldn't quite put her finger on it.

"This exhibit isn't right." He gestured to a page in the contract. "Do you have your source material?"

"Not on me. But I double-checked everything." In actuality, she'd quadruple-checked the figures, but she didn't want to sound like she'd been trying too hard to impress him.

His brows drew together into a formidable line. "You had to have made a mistake. This doesn't make sense."

"Prove it." The words slipped past her lips before she could stop them.

Mr. Lockwood's eyes widened as though unaccustomed to being challenged. She continued to hold his gaze. She wasn't going to back down—not when the one thing she greatly valued was in question—her reputation.

"These exhibits are skewed. I'm positive of it." His eyes darkened. "I'll log in to the system and then you can show me where you pulled your numbers."

For the next hour they worked side by side, going over the figures in the exhibits. In the end the contract was wrong, but to Holly's relief, it hadn't been her fault. The numbers on one of the source files had been transposed. After printing a revised copy, Finn signed it. Holly used his personal assistant's scanner to email the contract to the designated party.

"Thanks for the assistance." Finn slipped the hard copy back into the envelope. "Sorry to take up so much of your evening and for causing you to miss dinner." He glanced at his Rolex. "We'll have to remedy that."

"That's okay. It's not a big deal."

"I insist on dinner." He stood and then moved around the desk. "You did me a big favor tonight by helping with the contract." His gaze dipped to her lips before quickly returning to her face. The corners of his mouth lifted into a sexy smile. "And I'd like to show you how thankful I am for the help with meeting that deadline."

Oh, he definitely had more than dinner on his mind. The thought sent a new wave of nervous tremors through her stomach. She glanced away. Her initial inclination was to turn him down. Her experience with men was less than impressive. But did that mean she had to live in solitude?

What was wrong with a little company? A little laughter and perhaps flirting? And maybe a little more. Her gaze met his once more. It'd all be fine as long as neither of them had any expectations. After all, it wasn't like it would ever happen again.

"Dinner sounds good."

"Great." He made a brief phone call and then turned to her. "It's all arranged. I'll just drop this envelope on Clara's desk and then we'll be off."

A little voice inside Holly said to be cautious. Finn Lockwood wasn't just any man and she knew nothing of his world. But another part of her was drawn to him like a moth to a flame—and boy, was he hot.

The sizzling tension smoldered between them as they quietly rode down in the elevator. When they stepped into the parking garage beneath the building there was a sleek black town car waiting for them. A driver immediately alighted and opened the door for them.

Holly climbed in first, followed by Finn. When he joined her, his muscular leg brushed against hers. Her stomach shivered with excitement. When their hands came to rest side by side on the leather seat, neither pulled away. It felt as though the interior of the car was statically charged. Every nerve ending tingled with anticipation.

As the car eased into the Friday evening traffic, she glanced over at Finn. She was surprised to find him staring back at her. Her heart *thump-thumped*, loud and fast.

"Where to, sir?" the driver asked.

"The penthouse." Finn's darkened gaze returned to Holly. "I thought we would dine in. Unless, of course, you have something else in mind."

She had something on her mind, but it wasn't food. Perhaps she had been spending too much time working these days because there had to be a reasonable explanation for her lack of common sense. Because all she could think about was how much she longed to press her lips to his.

Chapter 1

Seven weeks later...

Bah, humbug...

Finn Lockwood didn't care if the saying was cliché. It was how he felt. Even though this was the first week after Thanksgiving, the holiday festivities were in full swing. He wanted no part of having a holly jolly Christmas. Even though he'd turned off the speakers in his office, the music still crept down the hallway, taunting him with its joyous melody.

He did his utmost to block out the mocking words. Instead, he focused on the stack of papers awaiting his signature. He was so close to being out of here—out of the office—out of New York City.

"I just love this." His longtime assistant, Clara, strode into his office with a hefty stack of papers.

"Love what? The endless phone calls and this mess of paperwork?"

"Um, no." Color filled her cheeks as she placed the papers on his desk. "I meant this song, 'Home for the Holidays.' It puts me in a warm fuzzy mood."

His pen hovered over the document as he paused to listen. The sentimental words about home and family stabbed at his scarred heart. "To each his own."

She swept her dark bobbed hair behind her ear. "Although it never feels like the holiday season until that first snowflake falls. Don't you think so?"

He frowned at her. "How long have you known me?"

"Almost eight years."

"And by now I'd have thought you'd realize I don't do holidays."

"I… I just keep hoping—"

"Don't. It's not going to happen." An awkward silence ensued as he glanced over a disbursement and then signed it.

"Oh. I almost forgot. These came for you." She handed over two tickets for the Mistletoe Ball.

He accepted the tickets. Without bothering to look at them, he slipped them in a side desk drawer with other tickets from years gone by. When he glanced back at his assistant, unspoken questions reflected in her eyes. "What?"

Clara hesitated, fidgeting with the pen in her hand. "Why do you order tickets every year but then never use them?"

"Don't you think it's a worthy cause?" When Clara nodded, he continued. "I want to do my part." His voice grew husky with emotion. "If everyone does their part, maybe they'll find a cure for leukemia. The damn disease steals lives far too soon." His hand tightened around the pen. "It leaves nothing but devastation in its wake."

Clara's eyes widened. "I… I agree. I, um, just can't afford the tickets."

Finn realized he'd said too much. No one knew he was the sole sponsor of the ball and that was the way he intended for it to remain. But he just couldn't attend—couldn't face the guilt. If it wasn't for him and his actions, his mother and father would still be alive. They'd be attending the ball each year just like they'd always done in years past.

Finn pulled open the desk drawer and removed the tickets. "Here. Take them. It'd be better if they were used rather than sitting around gathering dust."

Her gaze moved from the tickets to him. "But I couldn't. You should give them to someone else."

When she rattled off the names of people who headed up his various divisions and departments, he said, "I want you to have them."

"Thank you." She accepted the tickets with a hesitant smile.

"Now back to business. I hope this is the last of what I need to sign because we have a trip to prepare for."

"A trip? When?"

"Tomorrow morning." This wasn't the first time he'd sprung a spur-of-the-moment trip on her. "And I'll need you there—"

"But…" Clara worried her bottom lip.

"But what? Surely you can reschedule anything on my calendar for some time after the first of the year."

"It's not that."

Color stained her cheeks as she glanced down at the tickets. She remained quiet, which was so unlike her.

Something was definitely amiss and he didn't like it, not one little bit. They were set to leave in the morning for his private island in the Caribbean for a secret business meeting. When it concluded, Clara would return to New York while he remained in the sun and sand until after the New Year—when life returned to normal and people were no longer gushing with the holiday spirit.

Clara's continued silence worried him. He leaned back in his chair, taking in the worry lines bracketing her eyes. "What's the problem?"

"I got engaged last night." She held up her hand. A sparkly diamond now resided on her ring finger.

"Congratulations."

"Thank you."

"I'm sure you'll have lots of planning to do after our trip—"

"Well, um…that's the thing." Her gaze dipped again. "We're eloping this weekend."

"What?" She couldn't be serious. He had everything worked out. His business associates were meeting them on his private island in two days. "You can't back out on me now."

"I'm really sorry. But Steve, my fiancé, he, um…surprised me with tickets to fly to Vegas."

Finn resisted rolling his eyes. *Could things get any worse?* His plans had already hit a major snag, prompting this emergency meeting, and now his trusted employee was running off to Vegas to get hitched by some Elvis impersonator. *This is just great!*

"You can't bail on me." He raked his fingers through his hair. "I need your assistance for this meeting. It's important."

"Oh. Um…" She wrung her hands together.

He caught the shimmer of unshed tears in Clara's eyes. This was not good—not good at all. He was so used to having Clara at his beck and call that he hadn't anticipated this scenario. He hated being put in this position—choosing between his work and his associate's happiness. There had to be a compromise.

After a bit of thought, he conceded. "If you can find a suitable replacement, you can have the time off. But it'll have to be done pronto. My meeting can't be delayed."

Clara's eyes widened. "I'll get right on it. I'll have someone by this afternoon."

She turned and rushed out the door, leaving him alone to scowl about his plans being upended. Normally he'd have insisted on being involved in the selection of a temporary PA, but these weren't normal circumstances. His private jet was already being fueled up for tomorrow's flight.

He tapped his pen repeatedly on the desk. Why did Clara have to pick now to elope? Not that he wasn't happy for her. He was. He just wasn't happy about the surprise. Okay, so he didn't like surprises and certainly not when they caused his plans to go awry.

Just like his evening with Holly. Talk about everything going sideways—in a mind-blowing way. It'd been weeks since they'd been together and he still couldn't get her out of his system. Though they'd agreed there would be no repeat of the amazing evening, he regretted letting her go more than he thought possible.

What had she been thinking?

Holly Abrams stood alone in the elevator at Lockwood International. She pressed the button for the top floor—Finn's floor. The last time she'd visited the executive suite things had spiraled totally out of control. One moment they were talking work and the next she'd been in Finn's luxury penthouse. The memory made her stomach dip.

There'd been candles, delicious food, sparkling wine and honeyed compliments. It'd been quite a heady combination. And when at last he'd pressed his lips to hers, she'd have sworn she'd fallen head over heels in love with him. It was though this thing had been building between them since they first met. Love at first sight?

She didn't believe in it. This thing, it had to be infatuation—a great big case of it. And even though they'd mutually agreed to go their separate ways, her oasis at the office had turned stressful with reminders of Finn at every turn.

The elevator dinged and the door slid open. She stepped out. Taking a deep, steadying breath, she started down the hallway toward Clara's desk—toward Finn's office. However, Clara wasn't at her desk. Holly's gaze moved to Finn's closed door. She had a moment of déjà vu and her heart raced.

The door swung open. Who was it? Finn?

And then Clara stepped into the hallway. Holly sighed. She dismissed the disappointment that assailed her as Clara headed toward her.

The young woman's eyes reflected an inner turmoil. "There you are. Thank goodness you came."

"What's the matter?"

"Everything."

"Whoa. It can't be that bad."

"You're right." The frown on Clara's face said otherwise. "I… I need to ask you for a huge favor. And I'll totally understand if you can't do it. I just don't know anyone else who can help. And this just has to work out—"

"Slow down. Tell me what it is." Holly thought of Clara as a friend ever since they met on the charity committee. The woman was always generous in word and deed.

"My boyfriend proposed last night." A smile lifted her lips as she held up her left hand.

"Wow! Congratulations! I'm so happy for you." She gave Clara a brief hug.

Clara pulled back. "Thank you. It really was a surprise. We've been together for over five years now. I'd pretty much given up on him ever proposing. Anyway the plan is we catch a plane tomorrow and elope in Vegas followed by a honeymoon in Napa Valley. I can't postpone it. I don't want him changing his mind."

"Don't worry. Everything will work out." She was happy that Clara was finally getting her happily-ever-after. Holly didn't see such a rosy future for herself, but it didn't mean she didn't believe it could happen for others. "What can I do to help?"

"I know this is a lot to ask, but I need you to fill in for me while I'm off on my honeymoon."

"What?" Clara wanted her to be Finn's assistant? No. Impossible. Finn would never agree. She must have misunderstood. "You want me to be Mr. Lockwood's assistant?"

Clara nodded. "It won't be for long."

Her friend had absolutely no idea what she was asking of her. None whatsoever. She'd given Finn her word that she'd stay clear of him just as he'd agreed to do the same for her.

Now it appeared she had to make a very difficult

choice—keep her word to Finn or keep her friendship with Clara. Holly's stomach plummeted into her Louis Vuittons. She desperately wanted to do both.

But that wasn't possible.

Chapter 2

There had to be a way out.

But how? Holly couldn't bear to hurt Clara's feelings. But Holly acting as Finn's assistant for even the briefest time would be at the very least awkward. It'd raise too many memories—memories best left alone.

How did she explain that this arrangement would never work? No one knew about that special evening she'd spent with Finn. And it had to remain that way.

Holly smoothed a nonexistent wrinkle from her skirt. "I can't just move up here. What about my work in the legal department?"

Clara sent her a pleading look with her eyes. "If that's all you're worried about, I worked it out with your boss. You are temporarily transferred here. But don't worry. Working for Mr. Lockwood comes with benefits."

She'd already sampled Mr. Lockwood's benefits and

they were unforgettable, but she was certain that was not what Clara meant. "Did you talk this over with F... ah, Mr. Lockwood?"

Clara's eyes momentarily widened at Holly's slip of the tongue. "I did and he's on board."

He was? Really? She was running out of excuses about why this wouldn't work. But maybe this was the break she was looking for. If Finn was open to taking her on as his assistant, would it be such a stretch to think he'd consider giving her a personal referral?

It was time she left Lockwood International. And like a sign, there was an opening at another *Fortune 500* company for an assistant to the lead counsel. She'd heard about the position through a friend of a friend. But the attorney was older and wanted someone closer to his age with top qualifications.

The cards were stacked against Holly as she was in her twenties and her experience was so-so, depending on what the position required. But it would be a big boost for her and it would make it possible for her mother to make her time off permanent.

Holly had come up with one thing that just might make gaining the new position a real possibility, a letter of recommendation from Finn—a well-respected businessman. Although she hadn't quite figured out how to approach him. But then again, it appeared he'd taken that problem out of her hands.

After all, she'd only have to be his PA for one week and then he'd be on his annual holiday. She'd have the office to herself. In the meantime, it wasn't like they were going to be working in the same office. He'd be down the hall behind a closed door and she'd be out here. If he could make it work, then so could she.

"I'll do it."

Clara's face lit up like a Christmas tree. "I was hoping you'd say that. I can spend the rest of today going over current projects with you, but first let's go get you introduced to Mr. Lockwood."

On wooden legs, Holly followed Clara down the hallway. Her morning coffee sloshed in her stomach, making her nauseated. *Keep it together. Just act professional.*

Clara knocked on the door and then entered. Holly followed her inside. Her heart picked up its pace as her gaze eagerly sought him out. His hair appeared freshly trimmed. And the blue button-up accentuated his broad, muscular shoulders. Holly swallowed hard.

He glanced up from his computer monitor. Was that surprise reflected in his blue-gray eyes? It couldn't be. He'd approved this scenario. In a blink, the look was gone.

"Mr. Lockwood, I'd like to introduce Holly Abrams." Clara's voice drew Holly from her thoughts. "She's from the legal department."

"We've met." His gaze moved between the two women. "The question is what's she doing in my office?"

Clara sent him a nervous smile. "She's agreed to step up and fill in for me while I'm away on my honeymoon. Her boss in legal gave nothing but rave reviews about her."

"I see." Finn's gaze moved to Holly.

What was she missing here? Hadn't Clara said Finn had approved of this temporary assignment? She forced a smile to her lips as his intense gaze held her captive. Her heart continued to race and her palms grew damp. She should say something, but the jumbled words in her mind refused to form a cohesive sentence.

Clara spoke, breaking the mounting silence. "She'll do a really good job for you."

"I don't know about this." Finn leaned back in the black leather chair. "Why don't you give us a moment to talk?" Clara made a discreet exit. It wasn't until the door snicked shut that Finn spoke again with a serious, no-nonsense tone. "Okay, we're alone now. Please explain to me what happened to our agreement to keep clear of each other."

"Clara said that she okayed this with you. I figured if you were big enough to deal with this awkward situation for Clara's sake then so was I. After all, Clara would do most anything for anyone. And it is her wedding—"

"Enough. I get the point. But this—" he gestured back and forth between them "—it won't work."

"That's fine with me. Do you have someone else who can fill in?"

Finn cleared his throat. "No, I don't."

Holly clasped her hands together to keep from fidgeting and straightened her shoulders. "I know that we've never worked together, but I think I can do the job."

Finn leaned back in his chair and crossed his arms. "Tell me why I should give you a chance."

Holly swallowed hard, not expecting to have to interview for the position, but when she recalled the desperation in her friend's voice, she knew she couldn't let Clara down. "I'm a hard worker. I'm the first through the door in the morning and I'm the last out in the evening."

"Are you sure that's a good thing? Perhaps you just don't get your work done in a timely manner."

Her gaze narrowed. Why exactly was he giving her such a hard time? A smart retort teetered on the tip of her tongue, but she choked it back, refusing to let him provoke her. "No. I like to be punctual. I like to have the coffee brewing and a chance to take off my coat before the phone starts ringing. And I don't rush out the door at the end of the day simply because I can't. I usually have a task or two dropped on my desk by my boss as he's leaving."

Finn nodded as though her answer pleased him. "And you think you're up to the challenges of being my PA?"

"I do."

"You do realize that what happened between us is in the past. It will have no bearing on our working relationship."

"I wouldn't have it any other way."

"Good."

"Does that mean I have the position?" The breath caught in her throat as she waited for his answer.

Seconds ticked by and still he said nothing. What in the world? She thought of all the things she could say to him to sell herself, but she didn't want to look desperate because she wasn't. Oh, maybe she was just a bit. She had a plan and he played a pivotal role.

"Okay. You've convinced me. We'll do this."

The breath rushed from Holly's straining lungs. "Thank you. I'll go catch up on everything I need to know from Clara."

"Holly, remember this is strictly work."

Like she could or would forget. "I understand, Mr. Lockwood."

He frowned. "I don't think we have to be that formal. Finn will do."

"Yes, sir…erm… Finn."

This was it, she was in. She should be inwardly cheering or smiling or something. And yet she stood there transfixed by the man who danced through her dreams each night and left her longing for a glance of him each day. The truth was that she didn't know how to react. It was one of those good news–bad news scenarios.

The best thing she could do was leave. The sooner, the better. She turned for the door.

"Holly, there's one more thing." He waited until she turned around before continuing. "Make sure you aren't late tomorrow morning. Takeoff is at six a.m. sharp."

"Takeoff?"

Finn's brows scrunched together. "Clara didn't tell you?"

"Tell me what?"

"We're leaving first thing in the morning for the Caribbean. I have an extremely important meeting there."

This was not what she'd been expecting at all. How was she supposed to fly to a sunny destination spot with the sexiest guy alive—a man who could heat her blood with just a look? She inwardly groaned. She was in so much trouble here.

Not only was she nervous about being around him—about remembering their first night together in vivid detail—but she was also a nervous flier, as in white-knuckling it through turbulence. Exactly how long was a flight from New York City to the Caribbean?

No matter what, she wasn't about to back out of this arrangement. There was too much riding on it—too many people counting on her. Her mother's pale face flashed in her mind. After her mother's recent stroke, the doctor had warned that with her other medical conditions, if she didn't slow down, her health would be put at greater risk. Holly needed to do whatever she could to further her career in order to support her and her mother.

"Holly? Will that be a problem?"

His voice drew her from her frantic thoughts. "I didn't know. Where will we be staying?"

"On my private island."

Oh, boy! One private island. One sexy guy. And a whole lot of chemistry. What could possibly go wrong with this scenario?

Chapter 3

Twenty-two minutes late, Holly rushed through the air-
port early the next morning. Her suitcase *clunk-clunked*
as it rolled over the tiled floor.

She hadn't meant to stay up late the night before, talking on the phone, but it'd been a long time since she'd
heard her mother so exuberant. Apparently the Sunshine
State agreed with her, especially the strolls along the
beach while Holly's aunt was off at her waitressing job.

When her mother mentioned returning to New York,
Holly readily assured her there was no rush. At the same
time, she'd made a mental note to send her aunt some
more money to cover her mother's living expenses. Holly
proceeded to fill her mother in on the business trip, cit-
ing her absence as another reason for her mother to remain in Florida. Her mother actually sounded relieved,
confirming Holly's belief that she needed to do every-

thing to ensure her mother didn't have to worry about money. And that hinged on impressing Finn.

But this morning, if anything could have gone wrong, it had. As late as she was, Finn would think she was incompetent or worse that she'd changed her mind and backed out without a word. And because she'd been so rattled yesterday, she'd forgotten to get his cell number.

When she finally reached the prearranged meeting spot, Finn stood there, frowning. She was breathless and feeling totally out of sorts.

His piercing gaze met hers. "I didn't think you were going to show up."

She attempted to catch her breath. "There was an accident."

Immediately his anger morphed into concern. "Are you okay?"

"It wasn't me. It was the vehicle two cars up from my cab." In that moment the horrific events played in her mind. "One second we're moving along the highway and the next a little sports car attempts to cut off a souped-up pickup truck with large knobby tires. The car swerved wildly across the lanes as tires screeched and the driver tried to regain control, but the car lifted and flipped a couple of times." Tears welled up in her eyes. "I never witnessed something so horrific. I... I don't think the driver made it."

Finn reached out to her and pulled her close. Her cheek rested against his shoulder. "Thank God you're safe."

Her emotions bubbled to the surface. The worry. The fear. The shock. She wasn't sure how much time had passed as Finn continued to hold her. Horrific scenes of the accident played in her mind, one after the other.

She knew she shouldn't seek comfort in his arms. Although it was innocent enough, it wasn't part of their agreement. And yet, she didn't move.

It was only when she started to gather herself that she noticed the spicy scent of his cologne. It would be so easy to forget about their agreement and turn in his arms, claiming his very kissable lips. Every cell in her body longed to do just that. Just once more.

But she couldn't. Once would not be enough. Frustration balled up inside her. Besides, he was just being nice—a gentleman. She refused to throw herself at him and ruin everything. After all, she was out to prove to him that she was an invaluable asset in the office.

With great regret, she extricated herself from his arms, already missing the warmth of his touch. "I must be such a mess." She swiped her hands over her cheeks. "Sorry about that. I... I'm usually—"

"No apologies necessary." He waved away her words. "I'm just relieved you're safe."

The sincerity in his words had her glancing up at him. In that moment he'd reverted back to Finn Lockwood, the friendly man who'd taken her to his penthouse to thank her for her help with the contract. The man who'd spent the evening wining and dining her with some pasta he'd whipped up himself. The same man who'd entertained her with tales of hilarious fiascos at the office. The man who'd swept her off her feet.

"What are you thinking?"

His voice drew her from her thoughts. Not about to tell him the truth, she said, "That we should get moving. I've already put you behind schedule."

"You're right." He gestured for her to walk ahead of him.

Her insides shivered with nervous tension. She couldn't tell if it was from being held in Finn's arms or the thought of soaring through the air in his jet. Maybe she should mention her fear of flying to Finn. Then again, they'd already shared more than enough for now. She would just lose herself in her work. If all went well, he'd never even know of her phobia of heights.

What had he been thinking?

Finn sat across the aisle from Holly on his private jet. They were in midflight and Holly had been surprisingly quiet. It suited him just fine. He was preparing for his upcoming meeting, or he had been until thoughts of Holly infiltrated his mind. Truth be told, he hadn't been able to let go of the memories of their night together. She was amazing and so easy to be with. Most people wouldn't find that to be a problem, but he did.

He refused to let someone get close to him—he would do nothing but lead them to unhappiness. Because that was what happened to the people he cared about—he let them down. And Holly was too nice to get caught up with the likes of him.

The onboard phone buzzed. Finn took the call from the pilot. After a brief conversation, he turned to Holly, who had her window shade drawn. He presumed it was to cut down on the glare on her digital tablet. He, on the other hand, enjoyed being able to look out at the world around them. However, the overcast day hampered much of his view. "That was the captain. He said we should buckle our seat belts as we're about to hit some rough weather."

Without argument or for that matter a word, Holly did as he asked. She then returned her attention to the tablet as though she hadn't heard him. What in the world had her so absorbed?

He gave a shake of his head and turned back to his laptop. He'd been working on an agenda for his upcoming meeting, but he'd totally lost track of his line of thought. He started reading the last couple of bullet points when his attention meandered back to Holly.

Giving up on his attempt to work, Finn closed his laptop. He glanced over at her, which was a mistake. He was immediately drawn in by her natural beauty. He loved that she didn't wear heavy makeup, only a little bit to accent her own unique qualities.

There was just something so different about Holly, but he couldn't quite put his finger on exactly what made her so much more appealing than the other women who had passed through his life. Maybe it was that she was content with her life— not looking to him for a leg up in her career. Or maybe it was that she treated him like everybody else instead of trying to cater to him. Whatever it was, he was intrigued by her.

Realizing he was staring, he cleared his throat. "What are you reading?"

She glanced up as though completely lost in thought. "What did you say?"

He smiled, liking the sheepish look on her face and the touch of pink in her cheeks. "I was wondering what had you so deep in thought."

She glanced down at her tablet and then back at him. "Um, nothing."

"Must be something to have you so preoccupied."

"Just some work."

"Work? I don't recall giving you anything to do on the way to the island."

She worried her bottom lip. "I was doing a little re-search."

"Do tell. I'm thoroughly intrigued."

She set aside her tablet. "I downloaded some back-ground on the businessmen that you'll be meeting with."

"Really? I thought you'd prefer to read a book."

"I like to be prepared. Clara gave me their names. I hope you don't mind."

"What else did she tell you about the meeting?"

"Nothing except that it is extremely important and top secret."

He smiled, liking that Clara had emphasized discretion. Of course, Holly would learn all about his plans soon enough. "Let me know if you uncover anything noteworthy."

"I will." She once more picked up her tablet.

Why was she working so hard on this? Surely she wasn't this thorough normally. There had to be something driving her. Was she afraid of disappointing him?

Or more likely, she was doing whatever she could to ignore him.

Just then the plane started to vibrate. Finn glanced over at Holly and noticed that she had the armrests in a death grip. "Don't worry. It's just some turbulence."

She looked at him, her eyes as big as saucers. "Maybe we should land until it passes over."

"You don't fly much, do you?"

She shook her head. "Never had much reason. Any-place I've ever wanted to go I can get to by train or car."

"Well, relax. Turbulence is common. It's nothing to worry about."

"Easy for you to say," she said in a huff.

He suppressed a chuckle. She did have spirit. Maybe

that was what he liked so much about her. Otherwise, why would he have agreed to this completely unorthodox arrangement?

Perhaps if he could get her talking, she'd temporarily forget about the turbulence. "Where are these places you visit by car or train?"

She glanced at him with an *Are you serious*? look. He continued staring at her, prompting her to talk.

"I... I don't go away often."

"But when you do travel, where do you go?"

"The ocean."

It wasn't much, but it was a start. "Which beach is your favorite?"

"Ocean City and..." The plane shook again. Her fingers tightened on the armrests. Her knuckles were white.

"I must admit I've never been to Ocean City. Is there much to do there?" When she didn't respond, he said, "Holly?"

"Um, yes. Ah, there's plenty to do along the boardwalk. But I like to take a book and sit on the beach."

"What do you read?"

"Mysteries. Some thrillers."

He continued talking books and authors with her. He found that she was truly passionate about books. As she talked about a series of suspense novels she was in the process of reading, his attention was drawn to her lips— her tempting lips. It'd be so easy to forget the reason for this trip and the fact she was helping him out.

What would she say if he were to take her in his arms and press his lips to hers?

His phone buzzed again. After a brief conversation with the pilot, he turned to Holly. "The pilot believes we're past the bad weather. You can relax. It should be smooth flying from here on out."

The tension visibly drained from her as her shoulders relaxed and her hands released the armrests. "That's good news. I guess I'm not a very good flyer."

"Oh, trust me, you're doing fine. I've experienced worse. Much worse." He inwardly shuddered, recalling a couple of experiences while flying commercial airlines.

His attention returned to his laptop. He was surprised the break had him feeling refreshed. His fingers flew over the keyboard. Some time had passed when he grew thirsty.

He got up from his seat. "Can I get you something to drink?"

"That sounds good. But I can get it."

She stood up and followed him to the front of the plane where there was a small kitchenette. "I'm surprised you don't have any staff on board."

"Staff? For just me?" He shook his head. "I don't need anyone standing around, waiting for something to do. Besides, I appreciate the time alone."

"Oh."

"Sorry. I didn't mean that the way it sounded. I'm happy having you along."

"You are?" Her eyes widened. And was that a smile playing at the corners of her lips?

"I am. You're doing me a big favor. This meeting can't be rescheduled. It's time sensitive. And I didn't want to ruin Clara's wedding."

"Seems it all worked out."

He arched a brow. "Did it? Are you really okay with being here?"

"I—"

The plane violently shuddered. Then the plane dipped. A gasp tore from Holly's lips. Her body swayed forward. He sprang into action, catching her.

"It'll be okay."

The fear in her eyes said she didn't believe him.

As the pilot guided the plane through a particularly rough patch of airspace, Finn held on to Holly, who in turn held on to him. This was the exact thing he'd told himself that wouldn't occur on this trip, but fate seemed to have other plans.

He looked down at her as she lifted her chin. Their gazes met and held. Even when the plane leveled out, he continued to hold her. The emotions reflected in her eyes were intense. Or was he reading what he wanted to see in them?

He did know one thing—having her this close was doing all sorts of crazy things to his body. He caught a whiff of her soft floral scent and inhaled deeper. The pleasing scent swept him back to that not-so-long-ago night. Maybe playing it safe was overrated.

The plane started to vibrate again. Her wide-eyed gaze reflected fear. He knew how to distract her. His head dipped. His lips swooped in, claiming hers. She didn't move at first as though surprised by his actions. But in seconds her lips moved beneath his.

Holly was amazing. He'd never met a woman who intrigued him both mentally and physically. Her lips parted and his tongue slipped inside. She tasted of mint with a hint of chocolate. A moan swelled in his throat.

His thoughts turned toward the big bed in the back of the plane. Should he even entertain such an idea? But with the heat of their kiss, it wasn't out of bounds. All he had to do was scoop her up in his arms. It wasn't like it'd be their first time. Or even their second.

There was a sound. But he brushed it off, not wanting anything to ruin this moment. And yet there it was again. He concentrated for a second and realized it was the private line from the cockpit.

With great regret, he pulled back. "I better get that. It's the pilot."

Her lips were rosy and slightly swollen. And her eyes were slightly dilated. He'd never seen a more tempting sight. And yet his mind told him the interruption was exactly what they needed. It would give them time to come to their senses.

Chapter 4

"This is your place?"

Holly exited the helicopter that had transported them from the airstrip on the big island to Finn's private island. The landing zone sat atop a hill. It was the only place on the small island cleared of greenery except for the white sandy beach.

Finn moved to her side. "Do you like it?"

"I do. I've only ever seen places like this on television or on the internet. I never imagined I would one day step foot in paradise."

"Paradise?"

"Yes. You don't think so?"

"I never really thought about it." He rolled her suitcase to the edge of the helipad. "I'm afraid we have to walk to the house. It isn't far."

"No worries. This jaunt is nothing compared to the

hour I spend each day at the gym sweating my butt off."
She pressed her lips together, realizing she'd probably
shared more than he ever wanted to know about her.

When she reached for her suitcase, their fingers
brushed. He looked at her. "I can take it."

She wasn't about to be treated like a helpless woman.
She'd been standing on her own two feet since she was
ten and her father had walked out on her and her mother.
Someone had to pick up the slack. At that point in time,
her mother hadn't been in any condition.

Holly's grip tightened around the handle. "I can manage."

"You do know it'll have to be carried over the rough
terrain."

"Understood. I'll count it as exercise on my calorie
counter."

He shook his head as he stepped back. "By the way,
there's a gym at the house. Please feel free to use it. I
certainly don't make it there nearly enough."

"Thanks. I just might take you up on the offer." When
he gestured for her to go ahead of him, she said, "I'd
rather follow while I get my bearings."

With a shrug, he set off down the stone path surrounded by lush green foliage.

Her gaze followed him and he set a steady pace.

But it wasn't the beautiful setting that held her attention—it was Finn. His shoulders were broad and muscled, while his waist was trim without an ounce of flub.
And his backside, well, it was toned. A perfect package.

"See anything in particular you like?"

Heat rushed to her cheeks. Had he just busted her
checking him out? Her gaze lifted and she was relieved

to see that he was still facing straight ahead. "Lots. You're so lucky to live here."

"Only part-time. When you're done working, please feel free to use all of the facilities including the pool."

He didn't have to give her any more encouragement. She had every intention of checking it all out since she would never be back here again. "I do have to admit that this does feel strange."

"How so?"

"Leaving the snow and Christmas decorations in New York and landing here where there's nothing but a warm breeze and sunshine. Do you decorate a palm tree instead of a pine tree for Christmas?"

He stopped walking and turned to her. "I don't do either. I thought Clara might have mentioned it."

"She didn't say a word."

"Long story short, I don't like Christmas." He turned and continued along the path to the house.

He didn't like Christmas? She really wanted to hear the long version of that story. Was he a real-life Grinch? Impossible. He was friendly—when he wanted to be. Social—again, when he wanted to be. So why did he hate Christmas?

Wait. Who hated Christmas? It was full of heartwarming, sentimental moments. Twinkle lights. Snowflakes. Presents. Shopping. Definitely lots of shopping. And the most delicious food.

Whatever. His reasons for not enjoying the holiday were his problem. They were certainly none of her business. But that wasn't enough to suppress her curiosity.

"Why don't you like Christmas?" she blurted out.

He stopped. His shoulders straightened. When he turned, his forehead was creased with lines and his brows were drawn together. "Does everyone have to enjoy the holidays?"

She shrugged. "I suppose not. But I'm sure they all have a reason. I was just curious about yours."

"And if I don't want to share?"

"It's your right. I just thought after we talked on the plane that we were at the stage where we shared things with each other."

"You mean you equate our talk of books to digging into my life and finding out how my mind ticks? No." He shook his head. "My personal life is off limits." His tone lacked its earlier warmness. In fact, it was distinctly cold and rumbled with agitation. "You might research prospective business associates, but I'd appreciate it if you wouldn't put my life under your microscope."

What is he afraid I'll find?

She gave herself a mental shake. He was right. She was treading on a subject that was none of her business. His dislike of Christmas had nothing to do with her presence on—what was the name of this island? She scanned her mind, but she didn't recall him ever mentioning it.

"What did you say the name of this island is?"

"I didn't."

Surely this wasn't another one of those subjects that was off limits. Even she couldn't be that unlucky.

As though reading her mind, he said, "It's called Lockwood Isle."

Not exactly original, but fitting. "Your own island nation."

He shrugged. "Something like that. It's a place to get away from everything."

Her phone buzzed with a new email. "Not exactly everything. I see there's internet access."

"As much as I'd like to totally escape, I do have an international company to run. I can't cut myself off completely."

Holly was relieved to know that she could keep in contact with her mother. Even though she'd made financial arrangements with her aunt for her mother to make her very first visit to Florida, she still wanted to talk with her daily. Holly needed the reassurance that there weren't any setbacks with her health.

Her gaze strayed back to her host. She might not have to worry too much about her mother right now, but she did have to worry about Finn. That kiss on the plane, it couldn't happen again. He wasn't looking for anything serious and neither was she. Her focus had to be on getting his recommendation for the new job.

Finn stopped walking. "Here we are."

She glanced up at the white house with aqua shutters. The home was raised up on what looked like stilts. Each post was thick like an enormous tree trunk. It certainly looked sturdy enough.

Still staring at the impressive structure, she asked, "Why is the house on pylons? Are there a lot of storms?"

"No. But some of them bring in a high storm surge. I like to be prepared."

She had a feeling it wasn't just storms he liked to be prepared for. He struck her as the type of man who carefully plotted out not only his business but also his whole life, avoiding as many storms as possible.

"Will this do?"

Later that afternoon Finn glanced up from his desk in his study to find Holly standing there in a white sundress, holding a file folder. The bodice hugged her generous curves and tied around her neck, leaving just enough of her cleavage to tempt and tease. He swallowed hard. He should tell her to change clothes because there was no way he could conduct business with her looking so desirable.

Instead, he said, "Thank you." He accepted the file. "By the way, don't forget to pack lots of sunscreen."

"Pack? I never unpacked." Her eyes filled with confusion. "We're leaving?"

"Yes. Tomorrow morning we're setting sail on my yacht."

"Yacht?"

"Did I forget to mention it?" When she nodded, he added, "We'll be cruising around the islands for a couple of days until my business is concluded."

"Sounds great." Her voice lacked conviction.

"Have you been sailing before?"

She hesitated. "No."

Why exactly had he brought her along on this trip? Oh, yes, because her credentials were excellent. But that was when she was in a skyscraper in New York City. She didn't seem to fare so well outside her element. But it was too late to change course now. He just had to hope for the best—definitely not his idea of a good strategy, but the only one he had at this particular moment.

"Don't worry." He hoped to ease the worry lines now marring her face. "The yacht is spacious. You'll have your own stateroom." He took a moment to clarify the importance of the meeting. "I have worked for a number of months to bring these very influential men together. Discretion is of the utmost importance."

She nodded. "I understand. I've worked in your legal department for the past five years. Everything that passed over my desk was confidential. You can count on me."

He knew that. It was one of the reasons he'd agreed to this arrangement. Now, if he could just keep his mind from straying back to her luscious lips. His gaze zeroed in on them. They were painted up in a deep wine color. It was different from her usual earthy tones. But it was a good look on her.

He forced his mind back to business. "Did you reply to all of the outstanding emails?"

"I just finished them. The personal ones I've forwarded to your account as directed. I thought you might have some last-minute items you need completed before the meeting."

She was good. Really good. Normally that would be awesome, but when he was trying to keep her busy to avoid temptation, he wished she wasn't quite so competent.

"Have you returned all of the phone calls?"

She nodded. "I even called my mother."

"Your mother?"

"I just wanted to let her know that we arrived safely. She's actually off on her own holiday."

Was Holly attempting to make small talk? Boy, was he out of practice. He wasn't even sure how to respond. "That's good." He was better off sticking to business. "It sounds like you have everything under control. You can take the rest of the day off. We'll head out this evening as soon as all of our guests have arrived. Why don't you take a book and relax by the pool until then."

"I didn't bring a book. I didn't see a need since I planned to be working."

"But not from the time you woke up until you went to bed."

"You mean like you're doing?"

He glanced down at the papers littering his desk. "Guilty as charged. But you don't want to end up like me. You're young and have so much to look forward to."

"You make it sound like you're old and your life is almost over."

"My life is Lockwood International. It's the reason I get out of bed in the morning."

"I'm sorry."

"Sorry? Sorry for what?"

"That you think that's all you have to live for."

"It's the way it has to be."

The pity reflected in her eyes had him recoiling. He didn't deserve pity or sympathy. She had no idea about his life—none whatsoever. Not even the press knew the entire truth.

Living and breathing everything about Lockwood International was his punishment. He'd lived while the rest of his family had perished. It was what his aunt had told him quite frequently when he rebelled about doing his schoolwork or having to stay in boarding schools. She told him he had no room to complain. He had lived while the others had died a painful death, and then she'd glare at him like it was all his fault. And for the most part, she was right.

Holly moved to the window. "Have you looked around this place? It's amazing. When's the last time you enjoyed it?"

"I don't have time for fun."

"Everyone needs to loosen up now and then. You

don't want your guests showing up and finding that scowl on your face, do you?"

What scowl? He resisted the urge to run his hands over his face.

"I don't scowl." Her eyes widened at the grouchy tone of his voice. What was it about this woman that got under his skin? "I just need to stay on track and focus."

"Then I won't distract you any longer." She turned to the door.

She'd only tried to get him to relax, and yet he'd made her feel awkward. "Holly, wait." When she hesitated, he added, "I've been working so hard to pretend nothing happened between us that I've made matters worse. That was never my intention."

She turned. "Is it that hard to forget?"

"You know it is." His mind spiraled back to the kiss they'd shared on the plane. "But we can't go back there. It was a mistake the first time. And now that the fate of this project rests on how well you and I work together, we can't get distracted."

"I understand. I'll let you get back to work."

After Holly was gone, his concentration was severely lacking. He kept going over their conversation. Was his mood really that transparent? Usually business provided him solace from all that he'd done wrong in life and all that his life was lacking, but he couldn't find that escape anymore. He wondered if he'd done things differently, how his life would have turned out.

His chair scraped over the floor as he got to his feet. There was no point in staring blindly at the monitor. He wasn't going to get any more work done—at least not now. Maybe Holly was right. He should take a break. A run along the beach would be nice.

After changing his clothes, Finn stepped onto the patio. The splash of water drew his attention. He came to a complete halt as he watched Holly swim the length of the pool. He'd had no idea that she had taken him up on his suggestion that she go for a swim. He quietly watched, impressed with the ease of her strokes as she crossed the pool.

If he was smart, he'd head back inside before she noticed him. But his feet wouldn't cooperate. Sometimes being smart was overrated.

When she reached the edge of the pool, she stopped and straightened. That was when he noticed her barely there turquoise bikini. The breath caught in his throat.

"Oh, hi." Droplets of water shimmered on her body as she smiled up at him. "Did you change your mind about unwinding?"

He struggled to keep his gaze on her face instead of admiring the way her swimsuit accented her curves. He made a point now of meeting her gaze. "I was going to take a run on the beach."

"In this heat?" When he shrugged, she added, "You'd be better off waiting until later when it cools down."

She was right, but he couldn't bring himself to admit it. "I'll be fine."

"Why don't you come swimming instead? The water is perfect."

He moved to the edge of the pool and crouched down. He dipped his hand in the water. She was right. The water was not too cold and not too warm. "I don't want to bother you."

"You won't be. The pool is plenty big for the both of us."

He had his doubts about the pool being big enough

for him to keep his hands to himself. And with Holly in that swimsuit, he'd be so tempted to forget that they'd come to the island to work.

Finn raked his fingers through his hair. "I don't know. I really should be working."

"Your problem is that you think about work too much."

And then without warning, she swiped her arm along the top of the water, sending a small wave in his direction. By the time he figured out what she was up to, he was doused in water.

"Hey!" He stood upright and swiped the water from his face. "What was that all about?"

Her eyes twinkled with mischievousness. "Now you don't have an excuse not to join me."

Why was he letting his worries get the best of him and missing out on this rare opportunity to have some fun? After all, it was just a swim.

"Okay. You win." He stripped off his T-shirt and tossed it on one of the lounge chairs.

He dove into the pool, enjoying the feel of the cool water against his heated body. He swam the length of the pool before returning to Holly. She was still smiling as she floated in the water.

"Not too bad for an old man—"

"Old man. I'll show you who's old. Let's race."

She eyed him up but didn't say a word.

"What's the matter?" he asked. "Afraid of the challenge."

"No. I'm just wondering if an old man like you can keep up with me."

"Seriously? You have to race me now."

She flashed him a teasing grin. "First one back gets their wish."

Without waiting for him, she took off. He smiled and shook his head. And then he set off in her wake. His muscles knew the motions by heart. He'd swam this pool countless times over the years, but this time was different. This time he wasn't alone.

He pushed himself harder. He reached the end of the pool and turned. He wanted to win. Not because he wanted to be the best. And not because he couldn't be a good loser. No. He wanted to win because the winner could name their wish.

And his wish—

His hand struck the end of the pool. His head bobbed above the water. A second later Holly joined him.

"About time you got here," he teased.

She sent him a cheesy grin before sending another splash of water in his direction. He backed away, avoiding most of the spray.

Holly was about to swim away when he said, "Not so fast. I won."

"And?"

"And I get my wish." He moved closer to her.

She didn't back away. It was as though she knew what he wanted. Was he that obvious?

Her voice grew softer. "And what did you have in mind?"

His gaze dipped to her lips. It seemed like forever since he last felt her kiss. There was something about her that got into his veins and made him crave her with every fiber of his being.

His gaze rose and met hers. His heart hammered

against his ribs. Was she as turned on as he was? There was only one way to find out.

He reached out to her. Her skin was covered with goose bumps. He knew how to warm her up. His fingers slid over her narrow waist.

He'd never wanted anyone as much as Holly. And she was the last person he should desire. She was a serious kind of girl—the kind who didn't get around.

She was the type of woman you married.

The thought struck him like a lightning rod. As though she'd also had a moment of clarity, they both pulled back. Talk about an awkward moment.

"I...ah, should get back to work." Holly headed for the pool steps.

It was best that he didn't follow her, not right now. "I'll be in shortly. I think I'll swim a few more laps."

Finn groaned before setting off beneath the cool water, hoping to work Holly out of his system. He was beginning to wonder if that was even possible. He kicked harder and faster.

The one thing he knew was that he wasn't falling for Holly. No way. He didn't have room in his life for that major complication.

Chapter 5

One pounding heart pressed to the other. Heated gazes locked. Lips a breath apart.

Holly gave herself a mental jerk. Not even a night's sleep had lessened the intensity of that moment in the pool with Finn. Oh, how she'd wanted to feel his touch again.

But then she'd spotted the passion in his eyes. One kiss wouldn't have been enough—for either of them. The acknowledgment of just how deep this attraction ran had startled her. She'd pulled back at the same time as Finn.

Now aboard Finn's luxury yacht, the *Rose Marie*, Holly took a seat off to the side of the room as the meeting commenced. With a handful of notable and influential businessmen in attendance, she couldn't let herself dwell on the almost-kiss. As each man took a seat at the long teakwood table, she quietly observed. Her job was to step in only when needed. Other than that, she was to remain virtually invisible on the sidelines.

So this is the hush-hush, wink-wink meeting.

A small smile pulled at Holly's lips as she glanced around the room. Finn sat at the head of the table in a white polo shirt and khaki shorts. A very different appearance from what she was accustomed to seeing on those rare times when she caught a glimpse of him at the office.

On either side of the table sat four men. Mr. Wallace, Mr. Santos, Mr. McMurray and Mr. Caruso. All influential men in their own rights—from toys to office supplies, electronics and snack foods. No wonder there were bodyguards littering the upper deck.

"Welcome." Finn began the meeting. "I've invited you all here in hopes that we will be able to rescue Project Santa."

He'd given her the information about this holiday project just before the meeting. He made it perfectly clear that it was not to be leaked to anyone for any reason. What took place on this boat was to remain top secret for now.

Talk about surprised.

Holly stared at Finn as though seeing him for the first time. He was a man known for his shrewd business dealings, not his philanthropy. And here she thought this meeting was about conquering the world—about a major corporate takeover. She couldn't have been more wrong.

Finn and his cohorts were planning a way to bring Christmas to many underprivileged children. If it worked, it would be the beginning of an ongoing project aimed at putting food and educational materials in the hands of children.

Holly was truly in awe of Finn. He was such a contradiction at times. He worked long, hard hours, but he didn't expect his employees to do the same. He didn't celebrate Christmas, yet he planned Project Santa. At the office, he was all about profits and yet here he was planning to donate a portion of those profits to people in need.

For a man who hated Christmas, he certainly was doing a fine job of filling the boots of Santa this year. And she was more than willing to help him pull off this Christmas miracle. Although it was odd to have all of this talk about Christmas and presents surrounded by sunshine and the blue waters of the Caribbean.

Holly redirected her attention to the meeting, taking notes on her laptop and pulling up information as needed. She was tasked with running interference when tempers soared. Each of these men were billionaires and used to getting their own way, so compromise was not something they entertained often.

Some wanted to switch the Project Santa packaging to gift bags to cut costs. Others wanted to make the content more meaningful—something that wouldn't just entertain but help the recipient.

"Gentlemen." Finn's face was creased with stress lines. "This was all decided long ago. It's too late to change our plans. The gift boxes are strategically packed according to the location of each child."

Mr. McMurray leaned forward. "And how do we know these packages will get to the children?"

"Yeah, I've heard that a lot of these outreach programs are fronts for scams." Mr. Caruso, a gray-haired man, crossed his arms. "What if they steal them?"

"I hear your concerns. That's why some of my best

Lockwood employees will escort each shipment to their destination. They are each tasked with making sure the packages get to their intended targets."

There was a murmur of voices. Holly noticed that Finn wasn't happy with the distractions, but he patiently let the men voice their concerns before they moved on to the reason for this meeting.

"Gentlemen, we need to address the problem we have with the lack of transportation now that Fred has suddenly pulled out."

Thanks to her research, Holly knew Fred Silver owned a delivery company that spanned the globe. As she listened to the men, she learned a federal raid on a number of Fred's distribution centers put his whole company in peril. It seemed Fred didn't have enough controls in place and the cartel got a foothold in his distribution routes. What a mess.

"Without Fred, I don't see how it's possible to complete Project Santa." Mr. Wallace shook his bald head in defeat.

"I agree." Mr. McMurray leaned back in his chair. "It's already December. It's too late to fix this."

The other men nodded in agreement.

Mr. Caruso stared at Finn. "But we still have all of the books, toys and whatnot already allocated to this project. What do we do with it all?"

The men started talking at once. Voices were raised as each tried to talk over the other. Holly found it amusing that these men, who were well-respected in their own worlds, had a tough time playing nice with their peers. Each thought they had the right answer. And none wanted to stop and consider the other's perspective.

"Gentlemen!" Finn leaned forward, resting his elbows on the table. A hush fell over the room. "I think we need some coffee."

Finn glanced at Holly, prompting her into motion. She moved to grab the coffeepot with one hand and in the other she picked up a tray of pastries. As she headed for the table, each man settled back in their chair as though gathering their thoughts.

Holly pasted on her best and brightest smile. "Mr. Wallace, can I get you some coffee?"

The deep-set frown melted from the man's face and in its place was the beginning of a smile. "Why, yes, coffee sounds good."

She turned the coffee cup upright on the saucer and started to fill it. "I think what you all have come together to do is amazing. Project Santa will give hope to so many children." And then she had an idea. "And it will be such great publicity for your companies."

"Publicity." Mr. Wallace shook his head. "There's to be no publicity. Is that what Finn told you?"

"No, he didn't. I just presumed—obviously incorrectly." She was utterly confused. She'd missed something along the way. "Why then are all of you working so hard on this project when you each have global companies to tend to?"

They leaned back in their chairs as though contemplating her question. That was exactly what she was hoping would happen—that they'd remember why they were here and not give up. In the meantime, she served coffee for everyone.

"Finn should have told you." Mr. Santos reached for the creamer in the center of the table. "We each have so much that we wanted to do something to help those who have had a rough start in life. And with this being the season of giving, Finn came up with this idea. If we can make it work, it might be the beginning of something bigger."

"That sounds fantastic." Holly smiled, hoping to project her enthusiasm. "Too bad you can't make it work— you know, now that Mr. Silver isn't able to participate. I'm sure it's too big of a problem for you men to work around at this late date. Those poor children."

She turned to Finn, whose eyes widened. Oh, no. Had she gone too far? She'd merely wanted to remind these powerful men that they'd overcome greater obstacles in order to make their respective companies household names. If they really put their heads together and pulled in their resources, she was certain they could overcome this issue.

"She's right." Finn's voice commanded everyone's attention. "We can't stop now."

Tensions quickly rose as each powerful man became vocal about their approach to overcome these last hurdles and make the project a go. But this time they were pausing to hear each other out. And at times, building on each other's ideas.

Finn mouthed, "Thank you."

It wasn't exactly the use of her mind that she'd prefer, but the more she heard about this project, the more she believed in it—the more she believed in Finn. He was nothing like his ruthless businessman persona that was portrayed by the press. Why didn't he show the world this gentle, caring side of himself?

After spending hours to resolve the transportation problem with Project Santa, they were still no closer than they had been that morning.

Finn had just showered and changed into slacks and a dress shirt before meeting up with his associates for a card game. This trip wasn't all business. He'd learned long ago that keeping his allies happy was just as important as presenting them with a profitable deal.

He'd just stepped out of his cabin and glanced up to find Holly coming toward him. Her hair was wet and combed back. She looked refreshed and very tempting. His gaze dipped, finding she was wearing a white bikini. She must have been unwinding in the hot tub. He swallowed hard. *Look away. Concentrate on her face.*

Finn met her amused gaze. "Thank you."

"For what?" She adjusted a white towel around her slender waist.

His mouth grew dry. "For your help at the meeting. You were a big help getting everyone to work together."

"I'm glad I could help."

And then realizing they were talking in the hallway where anyone might overhear, he opened his cabin door. "But the distribution is more than we can overcome at this late date."

Holly didn't move. "Actually, I have some thoughts about your problem with the distribution. I don't think it's insurmountable."

He worried that she was a bit too confident. This was a national endeavor—coast to coast. But he had to admit he was intrigued. "Why don't you step in here a moment?"

Her hesitant gaze moved from him to the interior of his stateroom and then back to him. "I really shouldn't. I'm still wet."

"I promise I won't keep you for long. In fact, I'm due at a card game in a couple of minutes."

She noticeably relaxed. Without another word, she passed by him and entered the room. His heart thumped as he contemplated reaching out and pulling her close. What was it about her that had such a hold over him?

She turned as he pushed the door closed. She averted her gaze as her hands wrung together. Was she aware of the energy arching between them? Could she feel his draw to her? Was she as uncertain as he was about what to do about it?

"I don't think I told you, but your boat is amazing." She looked everywhere but at him. "I had no idea they were so elaborate."

"I'm glad you like your accommodations. I take it you enjoy sailing more than you do flying?"

"Definitely. I don't have to worry about falling out of the sky and—"

"No, you don't," he said, not wanting her to finish that graphic image. "If there's anything you want but can't find, just let me know."

"You know if you keep this up, you'll ruin your image."

"My image?"

At last, her gaze met his. "The one of you being a heartless corporate raider."

He pressed a hand to his chest. "I'm wounded. Do you really believe those nasty rumors?"

"Not anymore. I've seen the part you hide from the outside world." Her voice took on a sultry tone as her gaze dipped to his mouth. "Why do you do that?"

He swallowed hard, losing track of the conversation. "Do what?"

"Hide behind your villainous persona when in reality you're not like that at all."

His gaze shifted to her rosy lips. "How am I?"

"You're tough and hard on the outside, but inside…" She stepped closer, pressing a hand to his chest. "In there where it matters, you have a big heart."

"No one ever said that before."

Her hand remained on his chest as though branding him as hers and hers alone. "They just don't know you like I do."

His heart pounded against his ribs. "And do you like what you've gotten to know?"

"Most definitely."

His hand covered hers. "You do know if you don't leave right now that I'm not responsible for what happens next."

"But what about your guests?"

"They're involved in a card game."

"Oh, yes, the card game. You don't want to miss it."

By now she had to be able to feel the rapid beating of his heart. "I don't think they'll miss me."

"Are you sure?"

He nodded, not caring if they did. There was nowhere else he wanted to be at this moment. "Are you sure about this? You and me?"

"I'm sure that I want you to kiss me."

"Holly, I'm serious."

"I am, too. You do still want me, don't you?"

He groaned. "You know that I do."

His hands wrapped around her shapely hips and pulled her to him. In the process her towel came undone, pooling at her feet. He continued to stare into her eyes, watching to see if she'd change her mind, but he only found raw desire reflected in them.

She lifted up on her tiptoes and he didn't waste a moment claiming her lips. He was beginning to think he'd never tire of kissing her. The thought should worry him, but right now he had other things on his mind—things that were drowning out any common sense.

As their kiss deepened, so did his desires. Once was definitely not enough with Holly. Her beauty started on the inside and worked its way out. If he were to ever entertain the idea of getting serious with someone, it would be her.

Her fingers slid up his neck and combed through his hair. Her curves leaned into him, causing a moan to form in the back of his throat. Perhaps they could be friends with benefits. There wouldn't be any harm in that, would there?

He clearly recalled when things ended between them that Holly had said she didn't want anything serious. In fact, she was the first one to say there couldn't be anything more between them. For a moment he'd been floored and then relieved.

Now as her lips moved passionately over his, he wondered what he'd been thinking by letting her walk away. They had so much to offer each other with no strings attached.

But first he had to be sure Holly was still on board with the idea. He just couldn't have her expecting some sort of commitment from him because in the end, he'd wind up letting her down.

He grudgingly pulled back. Cupping her face in his hands, he gazed deep into her eyes. "Holly, are you sure about this?"

She nodded.

"Even though it'll never lead to anything serious?"

Again she nodded. "I told you I don't do serious."

A smile tugged at his lips. How could someone be as perfect as her? The thought got shoved to the back of his mind as she reached up and pulled his head down to meet her lips. This was going to be a night neither of them would forget—

Knock-knock.

"Hey, Finn, you coming?" Mr. Caruso's jovial voice came through the door. "Everyone's anxious to get the game started."

Holly and Finn jumped apart as though they were teenagers having been caught making out beneath the bleachers. She looked at the door and then him. Her lips lifted into a smile before she started to laugh. Finn frowned at her. She pressed a hand to her lips, stifling the stream of giggles.

"I'll be right with you." Finn ran a hand over his mouth, making sure there were no lingering signs of lip gloss. And then he finger-combed his hair.

Holly gestured that she would wait in the bathroom. He expelled a sigh of relief. He really didn't want to have to explain what she was doing in his room scantily dressed in that tempting bikini.

With Holly out of sight and his clothes straightened, he opened the door. "Sorry I'm running late. I had something come up at the last minute. You know how it is."

The man clapped him on the shoulder. "You work too hard. Come on. The guys are waiting."

"I don't think so. I really need to finish this—"

"Work can wait, your guests can't." Mr. Caruso reached out, grabbed his arm and pulled him into the hallway. "After all, you're the host."

Finn glanced back in his suite longingly, knowing the

exquisite night he'd be missing. Playing cards had never looked so dull and tedious before.

"You coming?"

With a sigh, Finn pulled the door shut. "Sure. The work can wait till later."

"Try the morning. I have a feeling this game is going to last most of the night. Should we invite your assistant?"

"I passed her in the hallway earlier. Holly—um, Ms. Abrams called it a night already."

"That's too bad. I like her."

He liked her, too—perhaps far more than was wise. Or perhaps he was blowing everything out of proportion since it'd been a while since he'd been dating. In fact, he hadn't dated anyone since his evening with Holly. No other woman had even tempted him after her. He wasn't sure what to make of that.

Chapter 6

The next morning Holly awoke late. But she didn't feel too guilty. It was work that had her burning the midnight oil—not Finn.

She ran her fingers over her lips, recalling Finn's kiss before he'd left her for the card game. If there hadn't been a knock at his door, she knew where things would have led. Part of her knew it was for the best, but another part ached for the missed opportunity.

What was wrong with her? Why couldn't she be immune to his charms? It was like once his lips touched hers any logic disengaged and her impulses took over. She wondered if he had this effect over all women or just her.

She knew this thing between them couldn't go anywhere. Her experience with men should be proof enough. First, her father walked out on her and her mother. And then while she was earning her paralegal degree, she'd met Josh. He was good-looking and charming. Deciding all men couldn't be like her father, she let herself fall for him.

Holly felt ill as the memories washed over her. Everything between her and Josh had been great for a while. In fact, it was the happiest she'd ever been. And then she'd learned Josh had a gambling problem that led to him stealing from her— the person he was supposed to love. She'd arranged to get him help and he'd sworn he would complete the twelve-step program.

She'd wanted to believe him, but after what her father had done to her mother, Holly had to be sure. And that was when she'd caught Josh in a web of lies with another woman. Holly's stomach soured at the memory.

The depth of his betrayal had cut her deep. After Josh, she'd sworn off relationships. Her independence gave her a much-needed sense of security. And with her full attention focused on her work, she didn't have time to be lonely. Guys just weren't worth the heartache. And she'd stuck by her pledge until now. Finn had her questioning everything—

Knock-knock-knock.

She had a feeling there'd only be one person who'd come calling at her door this early in the morning. Still, she asked, "Who is it?"

"It's me." The voice was very distinct. "Finn."

"Hang on." She scrambled out of bed and rushed to grab her robe. It was then that she noticed her stomach didn't feel right. It was way more than being upset about the unpleasant memories. She took a calming breath, willing the queasiness away.

She moved to the door and pulled it open. Finn stood

there freshly showered and shaved, looking like he was ready to tackle the world. "Good morning."

His gaze narrowed in on her. "Everything okay?"

She ran a hand over her hair. "Sorry. I slept in." Her stomach lurched. She pressed a hand to her midsection, willing it to stop. "I'll, ah, take a quick shower and be right with you."

"You know, you don't look so good."

Right then her stomach totally revolted. She dashed to the bathroom. Thankfully her cabin wasn't that big. She was quite certain she wouldn't have made it another step. She dropped to her knees, sick as a dog. What in the world? She hadn't even eaten that morning.

Once her stomach calmed, she heard the sink turn on. Finn? He was here? He'd witnessed her at her worst. She would have groaned, but she feared doing anything that might upset her stomach again.

"Here. Take this." He handed her a cold cloth.

"You shouldn't be here."

"And leave you alone when you obviously don't feel well?"

No matter what she said, he wasn't leaving. And at that moment she didn't have the energy to argue. Once she'd cleaned up, she walked back to the bedroom. Her stomach wasn't totally right, but it did feel somewhat better.

"I'm sorry about that." Her gaze didn't fully meet his. "You…you were quite the gentleman. Thank you."

"Do you know what's bothering you? Is it something you ate?"

"I think it's seasickness."

"I'm sure it doesn't help that we hit some rough water this morning. Are you sure that's all it is?"

She nodded, certain it had to be the constant roll of the boat.

"You should lie down."

"I don't have time."

"Sure you do." He guided her back to the king-size bed. "Stay here. I'll be right back."

She did as he asked, hoping she'd soon feel like herself. He disappeared out the door like a man on a mission. As she lay there, her mind strayed to her plan for Project Santa. Perhaps she should run it by Finn first. She didn't want to do anything to embarrass either of them in front of those powerful men.

A few minutes later Finn came rushing back into the room. "How are you feeling now?"

"Better." It wasn't a lie.

"I grabbed some ginger ale and toast. Hopefully you'll be able to keep that down. And I grabbed some medicine for the motion sickness."

"Thank you." She sat up in bed and accepted the glass of soda. She tentatively took a sip, not sure what to expect when it hit her stomach. Thankfully, it remained calm.

"I also talked with the captain and he's set course for what he hopes is smoother water."

Finn was changing his trip just for her? She didn't know what to think, except that Finn was a lot more Santa-like than Grinchy.

She took another drink of the soda. So far, so good. Anxious to get on with her day, she got to her feet. She glanced over to find Finn staring at her. "What?"

"The look on your face. Something is bothering you. Is it your stomach again?"

She shook her head. "I told you I'm feeling better."

He sighed. "You're sure? You're not just telling me this to get rid of me?"

"I'm certain. I'll just get showered and be up to the meeting soon."

"I could use your help, but I don't want you pushing yourself." His gaze searched her face and then he moved to the door. "I should be going."

"Finn?"

"Yes."

"There is something I wanted to talk to you about."

His brow arched. "Is it about your health?"

"No. It's nothing like that. It's just an idea I wanted to run past you."

He glanced at his Rolex. "I'd be happy to hear you out, but not right now. I'm late." He opened the door. "I'll see you on deck." He rushed out the door.

"But—"

The door closed. Her words had been cut off. A frown pulled at her lips. She knew how to help him with Project Santa if he'd just slow down and listen to her. She refused to give up now. There had to be a way to get his attention.

Had he made a mistake?

Finn sat uncomfortably at the end of the table, knowing if they didn't come up with a reasonable resolution to their transportation problem today that they would have to cut their losses and scrap the idea of Project Santa. The thought deeply troubled him.

He glanced at his watch for the third time in ten minutes. Where was Holly? Had she been struck with another bout of sickness?

"Listen, I know we need a solution regarding transportation, but all of my rigs are booked from now until Christmas, delivering our toys to stores." Mr. Wallace tapped his pen on the blank legal pad. "Besides, this wasn't my part of the arrangement. It's not my fault Fred wasn't on top of his business dealings and got in bed with the cartel."

Mr. Caruso sighed. "I couldn't possibly reroute all of my snack food shipments. It'd be a logistic disaster. And it would only cover the east coast. What about the children west of the Mississippi?"

All eyes turned to Mr. Santos. The guy shook his head. "I'm in the same boat. My network is on the east coast. And I have no transportation "

That left one man who hadn't spoken up, Mr. McMurray. He cleared his throat, visibly uncomfortable being in the hot seat. "And what makes you all think I can pull this off when none of you can?"

Immediately everyone spoke at once, defending why they couldn't take over the shipping part of the plan. Finn sat back quietly wondering why he ever thought they'd be able to pull off such a big project. It dashed his hopes for future projects of this scale.

At that moment Holly walked into the room. A hush fell over the men and Finn knew why. She looked like a knockout. She wore an aqua, sleeveless sundress. Her golden-brown hair had been piled on top of her head while corkscrew curls framed her face. She wore a little makeup, but definitely on the conservative side. If he hadn't known that she was feeling under the weather earlier, he wouldn't have been able to guess it by looking at her.

"Good morning, gentlemen. I'm sorry to be late. But I promise I was hard at work."

The tension around the table evaporated, replaced with smiles and warm greetings. Finn shook his head in disbelief. Who'd have thought a bunch of workaholics could be so easily swayed by a pretty face and long, toned legs?

"Don't let me interrupt your discussion." Holly moved to the chair she'd sat in the day before.

Mr. Wallace grunted. "You didn't interrupt much. Everyone was just making excuses about why they couldn't take on the shipping portion of Project Santa. We could use a fresh perspective. Do you have any thoughts on the matter?"

"Actually, I do. First, I want to say I'm very impressed with the endeavor you all are undertaking." She made a point of making eye contact with each man. "And if you would indulge me, I might have a suggestion about the transportation problem."

"Holly." The room grew silent. Finn had to give her a chance to gracefully bow out. "Perhaps I didn't make clear the enormity of this project. The gifts will need to be delivered from coast to coast in every town or city where our companies have a presence."

She nodded as her steady gaze met his. "I understood." She leveled her shoulders. "From what I understand, you have a master list of names and locations for the gifts. You also have all of the items sorted and boxed. All you're lacking is a delivery system."

Finn noticed a couple of the men had started to fidget with their cell phones. They didn't have faith in Holly's ability to overcome such a large obstacle. He had to admit he didn't know what she could do that they hadn't already considered.

"That would be correct." Finn really wanted to know

where she was headed. He didn't like surprises. "We have a sorting facility in St. Louis. From there the packages need to be distributed to numerous cities."

"And if I understand correctly, you were planning to do this by way of long-haul trucks."

"Yes, until Fred's company was seized by the government. There's no way he'll be able to unravel that ugly mess in time to help us. So do you have a lead on some other trucking firm?"

She shook her head. "My idea is a little different. I started to think about all of the modes of transport. And then I started to think about who I knew in the transportation industry. And I realized my neighbor in New York is a pilot."

Finn cleared his throat. "So you're suggesting we have your friend fly all of the packages around the country."

She frowned at him. "Of course not. That wouldn't be possible considering there are thousands of packages."

"Then I'm not following what you're telling us."

"My friend is a pilot, but he's just one of many. When he's not flying commercially, he takes part in a national flying club." She glanced around the table and when no one said anything, she explained further. "This flying club has hundreds of members around the country. If we were to enlist their help, we could get the packages to their destinations."

"I don't know." Finn had to think this over. The men started chatting amongst themselves. Finn glanced up to find Holly with a determined look on her face. When she opened her mouth to elaborate, no one noticed.

Finn cleared his throat and then said loudly, "Gentlemen, shall we let Ms. Abrams finish her presentation?"

When silence fell over the room, Holly continued.

"I've already put feelers out to see if there would be an interest in helping such a worthy cause, and I have close to a hundred pilots willing to fly the packages."

Finn rubbed his chin. "You trust these people? And they're going to do it out of the goodness of their hearts?"

"Yes, I trust them. And aren't you all doing this project out of the goodness of your hearts?"

One by one the men's heads nodded except Finn's. He didn't have faith in her plan. There were just too many moving parts. But he would give her credit for thinking outside the box. He was lucky to have her on staff at Lockwood.

Not about to discuss the pros and cons of her plan in front of her, Finn said, "Thank you for your input. We greatly appreciate your efforts. We'll need a little bit to discuss it. In the meantime, you could—"

"But don't you want to hear the rest of my plan?" Holly sent a pleading stare his way.

How could he say no when she turned those big brown eyes his way? He felt his resolve melting.

"Let her finish," Wallace chimed in.

The other men agreed.

Finn nodded at her to proceed.

"Getting the presents from the distribution center to the airstrip will take more transportation."

He was almost afraid to ask. "And what did you have in mind?"

"We'll go public and ask for volunteers."

"More volunteers?" He shook his head. "I don't think so."

"Listen, I know you were hoping to operate under the radar. And I know none of you are in this for the publicity, but if you would reconsider, this project might be bigger and better than before."

He wanted to put a stop to this, but he knew what it was like to be a child with no Christmas presents. Although his lack of presents had nothing to do with his parents' financial standing, it still hurt. He didn't want that to happen to other children, not if he could make a difference.

But he refused to put out a public plea asking for help. He didn't do it for the Mistletoe Ball, which meant so much to him—a continuation of his mother's work and a way to support the foundation seeking a cure to the horrible disease that stole his brother's life. Besides, he was the very last person in the country whom people would want to help. After all of the companies that he'd bought up and spun off into separate entities, causing job consolidation and ultimately downsizing, he was certain people would go out of their way to make sure he failed. He couldn't let that happen with Project Santa.

Finn met her gaze. "I'm not going to make this a publicity campaign."

"But at least hear me out."

He didn't want to. His gut told him she was about to give them a unique but tempting solution to their problem—but it would come at a steep price.

"Go ahead." Wallace spoke up. "Tell us how you would recruit these people?"

"We could start a media page on MyFace." She paused and looked around the table. "Do you know about the social networking service?"

They all nodded.

"Good. Well, it's hugely popular. With a page set up

on it specifically for Project Santa, we can post updates and anything else. It even allows for spreadsheets and files. So there can be an official sign-up sheet. Or if you are worried about privacy, I could set up an online form that dumps into a private spreadsheet. In fact, last night when I couldn't sleep I started work on the graphics for the media page."

Caruso smiled at her. "You're a real go-getter. I can see why Finn scooped you up. You must make his life so easy at the office."

"Actually, he and I, well, we don't normally work together."

"Really?" Caruso turned to Finn. "What's wrong with you? How could you let this bright young lady get away from you?"

Finn kept a stony expression, not wanting any of them to get a hint that there was far more to this relationship than either of them was letting on. "I already had a fully capable assistant by the time Holly was hired. She normally works in the legal department, but with my assistant eloping, Holly agreed to fill in."

"And she's done an excellent job with her research." Caruso turned a smile to Holly.

"Yes, she has," Mr. McMurray agreed. "It isn't exactly the most straightforward option, but it definitely deserves further investigation."

Finn was proud that she'd taken the initiative, but he was not expecting the next words out of his mouth. "And we need to give her presentation some serious consideration."

"Agreed." The word echoed around the table.

Holly's hesitant smile broadened into a full-fledged

smile that lit up her eyes. "Thank you all for listening to me." Her cloaked gaze met Finn's. "I have work to do. I'll be in my cabin should you need me."

Chapter 7

What had she been thinking?

Holly paced in her cabin, going over the meeting in her mind—more specifically the deepening frown on Finn's face as she'd presented her idea to distribute the gifts. Why had she even bothered? It wasn't like it was part of her job duties—far from it. But there was something about Project Santa that drew her in. She'd wanted to help.

And now she'd made a mess of things. Having Finn upset with her would not help her get the personal recommendation she needed to land the new job and get her the big pay increase she needed to secure her mother's early retirement.

She should have kept the ideas to herself. When would she ever learn? When it came to Finn, she found herself acting first and thinking later. Just like that kiss in his cabin. If they hadn't been interrupted, she knew there would have been no stopping them. Her logic and sanity had gotten lost in the steamy heat of the moment.

Going forward, she would be the perfect employee and that included keeping her hands to herself. She glanced down, realizing she'd been wringing her hands together. She groaned.

She knew Finn was going to shoot down her proposal. His disapproval had been written all over his face. She didn't understand his reaction. It wasn't like he had a better suggestion. No matter what Finn said, she still believed in her grass-roots approach.

Knock-knock.

For a moment she considered ignoring it. She wasn't in any state of mind to deal with Finn. She didn't think it was possible to paste on a smile right now and act like the perfect, obedient assistant. And that would be detrimental to her ultimate goal—leaving Lockwood—leaving Finn.

Knock-knock.

"Holly, I know you're in there. We need to talk." Finn's tone was cool and restrained.

She hesitated. He was obviously not happy with her. And on this yacht, even though it was quite spacious, she wouldn't be able to avoid him for long. So she might as well get it over with.

She took a calming breath, choking down her frustration. On wooden legs, she moved toward the door. Her stomach felt as though a rock had settled in the bottom of it. *You can do this.*

She swung the door open. "Can I do something for you?"

"Yes. I need an explanation of what happened at the

meeting." He strode past her and stopped in the middle of the room.

Was it that he didn't like her idea? Or was he upset that it had been her idea and not his? She'd heard rumors that he was a bit of a control freak.

She swallowed hard. "I presented an idea I thought would save Project Santa. What else is there to explain?"

"When did you have time to come up with this idea?"

"Last night when you were playing cards."

His gaze narrowed in on her. "You should have brought it to my attention before making the presentation." His voice rumbled as he spoke. "We should have gone over it together. I'm not accustomed to having employees take the lead on one of my projects without consulting me."

Seriously? This was the thanks she got for going above and beyond her job duties—not to mention sacrificing her sleep—all in order to help him. Maybe it was her lack of sleep or her growing hunger, but she wasn't going to stand by quietly while he railed against her efforts to help.

She straightened her shoulders and lifted her chin. "I'll have you know that I tried to tell you about my idea this morning, but you didn't have time to listen. And something tells me that isn't what has you riled up. So what is it?"

His heated gaze met hers. "I knew this was going to be a mistake—"

"What? My plan?"

"No. Your idea has some merit. I meant us trying to work together."

"Well, don't blame me. It wasn't my idea."

He sighed. "True enough."

"Wait. Did you say my plan has merit?"

"I did, but I don't think it's feasible."

Her body stiffened as her back teeth ground together. Really? That was what he was going with? Feasible?

She pressed her lips together, holding back her frustration. After all, he was the boss—even if he was being a jerk at the moment.

"I know you're not happy about this decision, but it's a lot to ask of so many pilots, and what happens if they back out at the last minute? It would be a disaster." He glanced down at his deck shoes. "I hope you'll understand. This is just the way it has to be."

"I don't understand." The cork came off her patience and out spewed her frustration and outrage. "I have given you a cost-effective, not to mention a timely solution, to your problem and yet you find every reason it won't work. If you didn't want to go through with Project Santa, why did you start it in the first place?"

"That's not what I said." He pressed his lips into a firm line as his hand came to rest on his trim waist. When she refused to glance away—to back down, he straightened his shoulders as though ready to do battle in the boardroom. "Okay. Your idea could work, but how do you plan on getting the message out to the people about Project Santa and the MyFace page?"

"We'll need a spokesperson."

"Where will you get that?"

She stared pointedly at him. "I'm looking at him."

"Me?"

"Yes, you."

"No way."

"Why not? All you have to do is a few promo spots to secure the public's assistance. What's the problem?"

His heated gaze met hers. "Why are you pushing this?"

She implored him with her eyes to truly hear her. "Do you realize the number of children you could help with your generous gifts?" When he refused to engage, she continued. "It would give them hope for the future. It might influence the path they follow in life." And then for good measure she added, "And without your cooperation, they'll never have that chance."

"That's not fair. You can't heap all of that guilt on me."

"Who else should I blame?"

A muscle flexed in his jaw. "You know, I didn't come here to fight with you."

"Then why are you here?"

A tense moment passed before he spoke again. "I wanted to tell you how impressed everyone was with your presentation."

"Everyone but you." The words slipped past her lips before she could stop them.

"Holly, that's not true." He raked his fingers through his hair, scattering it. "You don't know how hard this is for me."

"Then why don't you tell me?"

Conflict reflected in his eyes as though he was warring with himself. "I don't want to talk about it."

"Maybe you should. Sometimes getting it all out there helps." She walked over to the couch and had a seat. She patted the cushion next to her. "It might not seem like it at this particular time, but I am a good listener."

His gaze moved from her to the couch. She didn't think he would do it—trust her with his deeply held secret. But if it stood in the way of his helping with the publicity for Project Santa, then they needed to sort it out.

When he returned his eyes to hers, it was as though she was looking at a haunted person. She hadn't even heard his story yet and still her heart swelled with sympathy for him. Whatever it was, it was big.

"Christmas wasn't always good at our house." His voice held a broken tone to it. "I mean it was when I was little, but not later." He expelled a deep breath.

"I'm sorry for pushing you. I shouldn't have done it—"

"Don't apologize. I understand why you want Project Santa to succeed. And I want the same thing."

"Then trust me. A little publicity is all we need to gain the public's assistance."

"But it has to be without me. Trust me. I'm not the right person to be the face of a charitable event."

"I disagree."

"That's because you don't know me." Pain reflected in his eyes. "Appearances can be deceiving. I'm not the man everyone thinks I am. I'm a fraud."

"A fraud?" She instinctively moved away. "If you aren't Finn Lockwood, who are you?"

"Relax. I'm Finn Lockwood. I'm just not supposed to be the CEO of Lockwood International. I got the job by default."

She was confused. "Who is supposed to be the CEO?"

"My brother."

"Oh." She still didn't understand. "He didn't want the job?"

"He wanted it but he died."

"I'm sorry." She slipped her hand in his. "Sometimes when I have an idea, I don't back off when I should."

For a while, they just sat there in silence. Hand in hand, Holly once again rested her head on Finn's shoulder as though it was natural for them to be snuggled together. Her heart ached for all he'd endured. She felt awful that she'd pushed him to the point where he felt he had to pull the scabs off those old scars.

"You didn't do anything wrong." Finn pulled away and got to his feet. "I should be going. I just wanted you to understand why I can't be the spokesman for Project Santa."

She rolled his words around in her mind, creating a whole new set of questions. She worried her bottom lip. After everything that had been said, she realized that it was best to keep her questions to herself. Enough had been said for one evening.

Finn placed a finger beneath her chin and lifted until they were eye to eye. "What is it?"

She glanced away. "It's nothing."

"Oh, no, you don't get off that easy. What are you thinking?"

She shook her head, refusing to say anything to upset him further. She was certain if she thought about it a bit longer, she'd be able to connect the dots. It was just that right now it was all a bit fuzzy. "It's not important."

"I'm not leaving here until you talk to me. Whatever it is, I promise not to get upset with you. Because that's what you're worried about, isn't it?"

She took a deep breath, trying to figure out how to word this without aggravating him further. "I'm sure it's my fault for not understanding. If I just think it over some more, it'll probably make perfect sense."

He moved his hand from her face and took her hands in his. "Holly, you're rambling. Just spit it out."

She glanced down at their clasped hands. "It's just that I don't understand why the way you became CEO would keep you from getting personally involved with the publicity for Project Santa."

He frowned. See, she knew she should have kept her questions to herself. Clearly she hadn't been listening to him as closely as she'd thought. She prepared herself to feel silly for missing something obvious.

"I don't deserve to take credit for the project. I don't deserve people thinking I'm some sort of great guy."

Really? That was what he thought? "Of course you do. This project was your brainchild. You're the one who brought all of those businessmen together to orchestrate such a generous act. There aren't many people in this world who could have done something like this."

"I'm not a good guy. I've done things—things I'm not proud of."

"We all have. You're being too hard on yourself."

He shook his head. "I wish that was the case. Besides, I'm not even supposed to be doing any of this. This company was supposed to be handed down to Derek, not me. I'm the spare heir. Anything I do is because of my brother's death. I don't deserve any pats on the back or praise."

What in the world had happened to him? Was this some sort of survivor's guilt? That had to be it. She had no idea what it must be like to step into not one but two pairs of shoes— his father's and his brother's.

"I disagree with you."

Finn's brows drew together. "You don't get it. If it weren't for my brother dying, I wouldn't be here."

"Where would you be?"

He shrugged. "I'm not sure. After my brother died, I gave up those dreams and embraced my inevitable role as the leader of Lockwood."

"Did you want to be a policeman or a soldier?" When

he shook his head, she asked, "What did you dream of doing with your life?"

"I thought about going into medicine."

"You wanted to be a doctor?"

"I wanted something behind the scenes. I was thinking about medical research. My mother was always going on about how much money her charity work raised to find cures for diseases, but it was never enough. I excelled in math and science—I thought I could make a difference."

"But don't you see? You are making a difference. You gave up your dreams in order to take over the family business, but you've made a point of funding and planning charitable causes. You are a hero, no matter what you tell yourself."

His mouth opened and then he wordlessly closed it. She could tell he was stuck for words. Was it so hard for him to imagine himself as a good guy?

She squeezed his hand. "This is your chance to live up to your dreams."

"How do you get that?"

"You can make a difference to all of those children. You can give them the Christmas you missed out on. Maybe you'll give them a chance to dream of their future. Or at the very least, give them a reason to smile."

His eyes gleamed as though he liked the idea, but then he shook his head. "I'm not hero material." And then his eyes lit up. "But you are. You could be the face of Project Santa."

"Me?" She shook her head. "No one knows me. I won't garner the attention that Finn Lockwood will." Feeling as though she was finally getting through to him, she said, "Please, Finn, trust me. This will all work out.

I know you aren't comfortable with the arrangement, but do it for the kids. Be their hero."

There was hesitation written all over his face. "There's no other way?"

"None that I can think of."

The silence stretched on as though Finn was truly rolling around the idea. The longer it took, the more optimistic she became.

His gaze met hers. "Okay. Let's do this."

"Really?" She couldn't quite believe her ears. "You mean it?"

He nodded his head. "As long as the promo is minimized."

"It will be. Trust me."

He didn't look so confident, but in time he'd see that her plan would work. And then a bunch of children wouldn't feel forgotten on Christmas morning. Knowing she'd had a small part in giving them some holiday cheer would make this the best Christmas ever.

"What are you smiling about?"

She was smiling? Yes, she supposed she was. Right now she felt on top of the world. Now that she'd proven her worth to Finn, she thought of asking him for that recommendation letter, but then she decided not to ruin the moment.

"I'm just happy to be part of this meaningful project."

"So where do we begin?" Finn sent her an expectant look.

In that moment all of her excitement and anticipation knotted up with nerves. She'd talked a good game but now it was time to put it all into action. Her stomach churned. She willed it to settle—not that it had any intention of listening to her.

When she didn't say a word, Finn spoke up. "Where do we start?"

The *we* in his question struck her. They were now a team. Not allowing herself to dwell on this new bond, she asked, "What about your guests? Shouldn't you be with them?"

"McMurray said he wasn't feeling so good and went to lie down. The other guys are taking in some sun and playing cards. So I'm all yours."

She eyed him up, surprised by his roll-up-his-sleeves-and-dive-in attitude. "The first place we start is on My-Face and work on recruiting additional pilots. Do you have a MyFace account?"

"No. I'll get my laptop." He got to his feet and headed for the door. He paused in the doorway and turned back to her. "On second thought, why don't you bring your laptop and work in my suite? It's a lot bigger."

Holly paused. The last time she'd been in his room, work had been the very last thing on either of their minds. The memory of him pulling her close, of his lips moving hungrily over hers, sent her heart pounding. She vividly remembered how he'd awakened her long-neglected body. Their arms had been entangled. Their breath had intermingled. And any rational thoughts had fled the room.

"I know what you're thinking."

Heat flared in her cheeks. *Are my thoughts that transparent?*

"But don't worry, it won't happen again. You have my word."

Maybe I can trust you, but it's me that I'm worried about.

Chapter 8

She amazed him.

Finn awoke the next morning thinking of Holly. They'd worked together until late the night before. She had truly impressed him—which wasn't an easy feat. To top it off, she was efficient and organized. He knew she was good at her job, but he had no idea just how talented she was until last night.

They'd taken a long break for dinner with his associates. They updated them on all they'd accomplished and what Holly hoped to achieve over the next few days. The men promised to do their part to ensure the success of Project Santa, including putting out a call for volunteers to their employees and their families.

And to Finn's shock the two men who weren't active on social media were open to having Holly assist them with setting up a personal MyFace account. Everyone wanted to do their part to promote the project so that it was a success.

Finn slipped out of bed and quietly padded to the shower. With Project Santa underway, he had to concentrate on today's business agenda. He had a business venture that he wanted to entice these men to invest in. And thanks to Holly, everyone appeared to be in fine spirits. He hoped to capitalize on it.

Today he'd switched from his dress shorts and polos to slacks and a dress shirt. He couldn't help it. When he wanted to take charge of a business meeting, he wanted to look the part, too. He supposed that was something his father had taught him. Though his father had spiraled out of control after his brother's death, before that he was a pretty good guy, just a bit driven. He supposed his father was no more a workaholic than himself.

Finn straightened the collar of his light blue shirt with vertical white stripes sans the tie. Then he turned up the cuffs. After placing his Rolex on his wrist, he was ready to get down to business. Now he just needed Holly to take some notes.

He headed down the passageway to her cabin and knocked. There was no answer.

"Holly, are you in there?"

Knock-knock.

"Holly?"

That was strange. When they'd parted for the evening, they'd agreed to get together first thing in the morning to go over today's agenda. And then he recalled her picking her way through her dinner. Maybe he should be sure she was okay.

He tried the doorknob. It wasn't locked. He opened it a crack. "Holly, I'm coming in."

No response.

He hesitantly opened the door, not sure what he expected to find. He breathed easier when he found her bed empty. Before he could react, the bathroom door swung open and she came rushing out.

Dressed in a short pink nightie, she was a bit hunched over. Her arm was clutched over her stomach.

"Holly?"

She jumped. Her head swung around to face him. The color leached from her face. He wasn't sure if the lack of coloring was the result of his startling her or if it was because she didn't feel well.

"What are you doing here?"

"Sorry. I didn't mean to startle you. I…uh, well, we were supposed to meet up this morning. And when you didn't answer the door, I got worried. I came in to make sure you're all right."

Holly glanced down at herself as though realizing her lack of clothing. She moved to the bed and slid under the sheets. "I'm fine."

"You don't look fine."

"Well, thanks. You sure know how to make a girl feel better." She frowned at him.

"That's not what I meant. I…uh, just meant you don't look like yourself. What can I get for you?"

"Nothing."

"Are you sure? Maybe some eggs?" Was it possible that her pale face just turned a ghastly shade of green? She vehemently shook her head. Okay. Definitely no eggs. "How about toast?"

Again she shook her head. "No food. Not now."

"Are you sick?"

"No." Her answer came too quickly.

"Something is wrong or you wouldn't be curled up in bed."

"It's just the sway of the yacht. I'm not used to it."

He planted his hands on his waist. He supposed that was a reasonable explanation. "You aren't the only one with a bout of motion sickness. McMurray still isn't well. I guess my sailing expedition wasn't such a good idea."

"It was a great idea. And I'll be up on deck shortly."

"Take the morning off and rest—"

"No. I'm already feeling better. Just give me a bit to get ready."

"Why must you always be so stubborn?"

She sent him a scowl. "I'm not stubborn. It isn't like you know me that well."

"Since we started working together, I've learned a lot about you."

"Like what?"

He sighed but then decided to be truthful with her. "I know that you're honest. You're a hard worker. And you go above and beyond what is asked of you in order to do a good job."

A smile bloomed on her still-pale face. "Anything else?"

"I know you can be passionate—about causes you believe in. And sometimes you push too hard if you think it will help someone else."

She eyed him up. "You really believe all of that nice stuff about me? You're not saying it because you feel sorry for me, are you?"

Was she hunting for more compliments? He searched her eyes and found a gleam of uncertainty. He had to wonder, if only to himself, how someone so talented and sure of herself when it came to business could be so insecure behind closed doors.

"Yes, I meant everything I said. You're very talented."

Holly worried her bottom lip. When his gaze met
hers, she glanced away. What did she have on her mind?
Something told him whatever it was he wasn't going to
like it. But they might as well get it over with.

"What else do you have on your mind?"

She blinked as though considering her options.
Then she sat up straight, letting the sheet pool around
her waist. He inwardly groaned as her nightie was not
exactly conservative, and that was not something he
needed to be contemplating at this moment.

*Stay focused on the conversation! Don't let your eyes
dip. Focus on her face.*

Holly lifted her chin. "I would like to know if you'd
write me a personal recommendation."

"Recommendation? For what?"

She visibly swallowed. The muscles in her slender
neck worked in unison. "I have an inside source who
says a prime opportunity is about to open up and I'd
like to apply for the position."

"No problem. Just tell me what department it is and
I'll make it happen. But I thought you liked working in
the legal department."

"I did—I mean I do. But you don't understand. This
job isn't within Lockwood."

He had to admit that he hadn't seen that one coming.
And for a man that prided himself on being able to plan
ahead, this was a bit much to swallow. "But I don't understand. You like your job, so this has to be about us."

Her slender shoulders rose and fell. "It's too complicated for me to stay on at Lockwood."

"You mean the kiss the other evening, don't you?"

Her gaze didn't quite meet his. "It would just be easier if I were to work elsewhere."

"When would you be taking this new position?"

"At the beginning of the year. So you don't have to worry about Project Santa. It will be completed before I leave and I'll be out of Lockwood before you return to New York."

"Sounds awfully convenient." His voice took on a disgruntled tone.

He didn't like the thought of Holly going to such lengths to keep her path from crossing his. Up until this trip, they'd done so well avoiding each other at the office. He had to admit a few times he'd hoped to bump into her in a hallway or the elevator, but that had never happened.

Holly was smart for wanting to get away from him. When his ex-fiancée hadn't been able to deal with his moods and distance, she'd left. He'd never blamed her. It was what he'd deserved. He should be relieved that Holly wanted to move on, but he couldn't work up the emotion.

He told himself that he didn't want to see her go because she was a good worker. She was smart and a go-getter. She wasn't afraid to think outside the box. His company needed more innovative people like her.

Holly smoothed the cream-colored sheet as though sorting her thoughts. "Listen, I know this comes as a surprise, but I really do think it would be for the best. It isn't like either one of us wants a serious relationship. You have your company to focus on."

"And what do you have?" He knew there was more to this request than she was saying, perhaps something even beyond what was going on between the two of them. Because if her reasons extended beyond the attraction between them, then he could fix it and she would stay, he hoped.

"I have my work, and this new position will help me to grow and to take on greater responsibility."

"And you can't do that at Lockwood?"

She shrugged, letting him know that she'd already dismissed that option.

Without Holly to liven things up, he would return to a downright boring existence. Before he handed over the golden ticket to another position, he needed more time to think this over. Surely there had to be a way to persuade her into staying.

"You've caught me off guard. Can I have some time to think over your request?"

"Of course. But don't take too long. Once word gets out about the opening, the candidates will flood the office with résumés."

He could see she'd given this a lot of thought and her mind was made up. "Just tell me one thing and be honest. Is this because you're trying to get away from me?"

Her gaze met his. "Maybe. Partly. But it's an amazing opportunity and I don't want to miss out on it."

"Would you be willing to tell me what the position is?"

"That would be telling you two things and you said you'd only ask one thing."

"And so I did." He sighed. "This isn't over."

"I didn't think that it was."

"I'll go get you some ginger ale and crackers."

"You don't have to do that. You have a business meeting to attend."

"Not before I see that you're cared for."

And with that he made a hasty exit from the cabin, still digesting the news. It left an uneasy feeling in his gut. And this was why he never got involved with employees of Lockwood. It made things sticky and awkward, not to mention he couldn't afford to lose such talent.

Chapter 9

It was so good to be back on solid ground.

The next morning Holly stood on the balcony of Finn's beach house that was more like a mansion. He'd just escorted his last guest to the helipad. Their sailing trip had been cut short due to the rough waters. She thought for sure Finn would be upset, but he took it all in stride.

She shouldn't be standing here. There was work to be done on Project Santa—work that could be done from anywhere in the world, including New York.

The sound of footsteps caused her to turn around. Finn stopped at the edge of the deck. He didn't smile and the look in his eyes was unreadable.

"Did everyone get off okay?"

"They did."

The silence between them dragged on. Finn obviously

had something on his mind. Maybe this was her chance to broach the subject of her leaving.

She turned to him.

"I was thinking I should get to work. You know, there's no reason I can't complete Project Santa in New York. I can make my travel arrangements and be out of your way shortly."

"You're not in my way." His voice dropped to a serious tone. "Have I somehow made you feel unwelcome?"

"Well, no, but I just thought that, ah, well, there's no point in me staying on the island. That is, unless you still need my assistance."

"You're right." His voice was calm and even. "Any work from here on out can be done via phone or the internet."

His sudden agreement stung. She knew she should be relieved, but she was conflicted. His eagerness to see her gone almost felt as though she was being dismissed—as though she hadn't quite measured up as his PA. Was that what he was thinking? Or had he merely grown tired of her like the other men in her life had done?

"I'll pack my bags and leave tomorrow."

She moved swiftly from the large deck and into the cool interior of the house. The sooner she got off this island, the better. She'd forget about Finn and how every time she was around him she wanted to follow up their kiss with another and another.

A new job was just what she needed. It'd give her the time and space to get over this silly crush she had on Finn. Because that was all it was, a crush. Nothing more.

So much for Holly's departure and having his life return to normal.

She was sick again.

Finn paced back and forth in his study.

He didn't care what Holly said, it obviously wasn't seasickness any longer. Her illness could be anything, including something serious. He hadn't gotten a bit of work done all morning. At least nothing worthwhile. And now that lunch was over and Holly hadn't shown up, he wasn't sure what to do. He'd never been in a position of worrying about someone else.

When his brother had been sick, it had been his parents who'd done most of the worrying and the caretaking. And then there had been his great-aunt who'd taken him in after his parents' deaths, but she was made of hearty stock or so she'd liked to tell him. She'd barely been sick a day while he'd known her. Even on the few times she'd gotten the sniffles, she carried on, doing what needed to be done until her final breath.

But he couldn't ignore how poorly Holly looked. And her appetite at best was iffy. Then a thought came to him. He'd take a tray of food to her room. There had to be something she could eat.

When he entered the kitchen, Maria, his cook/housekeeper, glanced up from where she was pulling spices to prepare the evening dinner. "Can I get you something?"

Finn shook his head. "Don't let me bother you. I'm just going to put together a tray to take to Miss Abrams."

"I can do it for you."

"I've got it." There was a firm tone to his voice, more so than he'd intended. He just needed to do this on his own. "Sorry. I'm just a little worried."

Maria nodded as in understanding before turning back to her work.

Finn raided the fridge, settling on sandwich makings. It was what he ate late at night. And then he thought of something that Holly might enjoy. It was something his aunt swore by. Tea. "Maria, do we have some tea around here?"

The older woman smiled and nodded as though at last happy to be able to do something to help.

Between the two of them, they put together an extensive tray of food plus spearmint tea. And just to be on the safe side, he added a glass of ginger ale and crackers. As an afterthought, he snagged one of the pink rosebuds from the bouquet on the dining room table, slipped it into a bud vase and added it to the full tray. Hopefully this would cheer Holly up.

He strode down the hallway, up the steps and down another hallway until he stopped in front of her door. He tapped his knuckles on the door.

"Holly, it's me."

Within seconds, she pulled open the door. Her hair was mussed up and there was a sleepy look on her face. Her gaze lowered to the tray. "What's all of this?"

"It's for you. I noticed you missed lunch. I thought this might tide you over until dinner."

"Till dinner? I think that amount of food could last me for the next couple of days."

He glanced down at the sandwich. "I wasn't sure what meat and cheese you prefer so I added a little of everything. I figured you could just take off what you don't like."

"And the chips, fruit, vegetables and dip. Is there anything you forgot?"

He glanced over the tray and then a thought came to him. "I forgot to add some soup. Would you like some?"

"I think I'll get by with what you brought me."

A smile lifted her lips, easing the tired, stressed lines

on her face. His gaze moved past her and trailed around the room, surprised to find that her laptop was closed. And then he spied the bed with the wrinkled comforter and the indent on the pillow. She'd been lying down.

"I'll put it over here." He moved toward the desk in the corner of her room. When she didn't follow him, he turned back to her. There were shadows under her eyes and her face was void of color. "Holly—"

She ran out of the room. She sent the bathroom door slamming shut.

That was it. He was done waiting for this bug or whatever was ailing her to pass. He pulled his cell phone from his pocket and requested that the chopper transport them to the big island where there would be medical help.

He didn't care how much she protested, this simply couldn't go on. There was something seriously wrong here. And he was worried—really worried.

"Finn, don't forget your promise."

"I won't." He stared straight ahead as he searched for a parking spot on the big island.

Before they flew here, Holly had extracted a promise from him. If she agreed to this totally unnecessary doctor's appointment, he would help her catch the next flight home. She was certain whatever was plaguing her was no more than a flu bug. No big deal. She had no idea why Finn was so concerned.

Being an hour early for her appointment, Holly took advantage of the opportunity to meander through the colorful shops and the intriguing stands along the street. And in the end, it was a productive visit as she bought a few gifts.

When it was time to head to the clinic, Holly pleaded

that it wasn't necessary. She was feeling better, but Finn insisted, reminding her that they had an agreement. And so they did. It also meant that she was almost homeward bound...just as soon as this appointment was concluded. She'd even packed her bag and brought it with her.

In the doctor's office Holly completed the paperwork and then they took her vital statistics. An older doctor examined her. He did a lot of hemming and hawing, but he gave her no insight into what those sounds meant. When she pointedly asked him what was wrong with her, he told her that he'd need to order a couple of tests.

Tests? That doesn't sound good.

She was feeling better. That had to be a good sign. But why was the doctor being so closemouthed? Although she recalled when her mother had suffered a stroke, trying to get information out of doctors was nearly impossible until they were ready to speak to you.

So she waited, but not alone. With her exam over, she invited Finn back to the room so he could hear with his own ears that she was fine. She was certain the doctor was only being cautious.

In the bright light, she noticed that Finn didn't look quite like himself. "Are you feeling all right?"

His gaze met hers. "I'm fine. It's you we should worry about."

She studied him a bit more. His face was pale and his eyes were dull. There was definitely something wrong with him.

"Oh, no, have I made you sick, too?"

He waved away her worry. "I'm like my great-aunt. I don't get sick."

"I don't believe you."

Finn's jaw tensed and a muscle in his cheek twitched,

but he didn't argue with her. Okay, so maybe she was pushing it a bit. Doctor's offices made her uptight.

"I'm sorry," she said. "I didn't mean anything by that. I guess I don't do well with doctors."

The lines on Finn's handsome face smoothed out. "Why? What happened?"

She shrugged. "You don't want to hear about it."

"Sure, I do. That is, if you'll tell me."

Oh, well, what else did they have to do while waiting for the test results? There weren't even any glossy magazines in the small room. So while she sat on the exam table, Finn took a seat on the only chair in the room.

"It was a couple of days after you and I, you know, after—"

"The night we spent together?"

She nodded. "Yes, that. Well, I got a call from my mother's work. They were taking my mother to the hospital." She paused, recalling that frantic phone call when life as she knew it had come to a sudden standstill. "I'd never been so scared. I didn't know what was going on. I just knew an ambulance had been called for my mother. That's never a good sign."

"I'm sorry. I didn't know. I... I would have done something."

She glanced at him. "There was nothing for you to do. Remember, we agreed to stay clear of each other."

"Even so, I would have been there for you, if you'd have called me."

Holly shook her head. "I was fine. But thanks."

"I'm sure you had the rest of your family and friends to keep you company."

Holly shrugged. "I was fine."

He arched a brow. "When you said that the first time,

I didn't believe you. And I don't believe it this time, either."

"Okay. I wasn't fine. I was scared to death. Is that what you want to hear?"

"No, it isn't what I want to hear. But I'm glad you're finally being honest with me."

Her gaze met his. "Why? It isn't like there's anything between us. At least, not anymore."

"Is that the truth? Or are you trying to convince yourself that you don't feel anything for me?"

She inwardly groaned. Why did everything have to be so complicated where Finn was concerned? Why couldn't things be simple, like her life had been before she'd walked into his office all those weeks ago?

Chapter 10

Now, why had he gone and asked her if she had feelings for him?

Finn leaned his head back and sighed. It wasn't like he wanted to pick up where they'd left off. It didn't matter that they had chemistry and lots of it. In time, he'd forget about her sweet kisses and gentle caresses. He had to—she was better off without him.

He'd tried having a real relationship once. Talk about a mess. He wasn't going to repeat that mistake. Not that Holly was anything like Meryl. Not at all.

"Holly—"

The exam room door swung open. The doctor strode in and closed the door behind him. He lowered his reading glasses to the bridge of his nose. His dark head bent over a piece of paper. When he glanced up, his gaze immediately landed on Finn.

"Oh, hello." The doctor's puzzled gaze moved to Holly.

"It's okay. You can talk in front of him."

The doctor hesitated.

Holly sent the doctor a reassuring smile. "Finn's the one who insisted on bringing me here, and I just want to show him that he was overreacting."

"If you're sure."

She smiled and nodded.

"Okay then. I have the results back. It's what I initially suspected. You have morning sickness."

"Morning sickness? You mean I'm pregnant?" Holly vocalized Finn's stunned thoughts.

The doctor's bushy brows drew together. "I thought you knew."

Holly turned to Finn, the color in her face leaching away, but no words crossed her lips. That was okay because for once, Finn couldn't think of anything to say, at least nothing that would make much sense.

A baby. We're having a baby.

Disbelief. Surprise. Excitement. Anger. It all balled together and washed over Finn.

Holly stared at him as though expecting him to say something, anything. But he didn't dare. Not yet. Not until he had his emotions under control. One wrong word and he wouldn't be able to rebound from it. And to be honest, he was stuck on six little—life-changing—words.

I'm going to be a father. I'm going to be a father.

Holly turned her attention back to the doctor. "You're sure? About the baby, that is."

The doctor's gaze moved to Finn and then back to her. The question was in his eyes, but he didn't vocalize it.

"Yes, he's the father."

Finn realized this was another of those moments where he should speak, but his mind drew a blank. It was though there was this pink-and-blue neon sign flashing in his mind that said *baby*.

"I'm one hundred percent certain you're pregnant." The doctor's forehead scrunched up. "I take it you have your doubts."

"Well, I, um—" she glanced at Finn before turning back to the doctor "—had my period since we were together. Granted it was light."

"Recently?"

"The week before last."

"Was there any cramping associated with it?"

She shook her head. "None that I recall."

"A little spotting is not uncommon. Have you had any spotting since then?"

"No. I'm just really tired. Are...are you sure everything is okay with the baby?"

"I'll be honest, you're still in your first trimester, which means the risk of miscarriage is higher. But I didn't tell you that to worry you. I just want you to realize that taking care of yourself is of the utmost importance."

"The baby." Her heart was racing so fast. "It's okay, right?"

"At this point, yes. I've arranged for a sonogram." He moved to the counter to retrieve a stack of literature. "You might like to read over these. They're about prenatal care and what to expect over the next several months. I'll be back."

Finn paced. Neither spoke as they each tried to grasp the news. Seconds turned to minutes. At last, Finn sank into the chair, feeling emotionally wiped out. His gaze moved to Holly but she appeared engrossed in a baby magazine the doctor had given her.

Where was the doctor? Had he forgotten them?

As though Finn's thoughts had summoned the man, the door swung open. A nurse walked in. Her eyes widened at the sight of Finn.

The nurse handed Holly a pink gown. "The straps go in the front." Then the nurse turned to him. "You might want to wait outside."

"I think you're right." That was it. Finn was out of there. He had no idea what was involved with a sonogram, but he'd give Holly her privacy.

When he reached the waiting room, he was tempted to keep going. In here he felt as though he couldn't quite catch his breath. Outside, in the fresh air, he would be able to breathe again. But he didn't want to move that far from Holly. What if she needed him?

And so he remained in the waiting room. He picked up a baby magazine, glanced at the cover and put it back down. He picked up another magazine, but it was for women. He put it down, too.

The door he'd just exited opened. A different nurse poked her head out. "Mr. Lockwood."

He approached her, not having a clue what she wanted. "I'm Mr. Lockwood."

"If you would come with me, sir." She led him back to Holly's exam room.

When he stood in the doorway, he found Holly lying on the exam table with a large sheet draped over her legs. He did not want to be here. He shouldn't be here.

Holly held her hand out to him. "Come see our baby."

He did want to see the baby. It would make it real for

him. He moved to Holly's side, all the while keeping his gaze straight ahead, focused on the monitor. He slipped his hand in hers, finding her fingers cold. He assumed it was nerves. He sandwiched her hand between both of his, hoping to warm her up a little.

In no time at all, there was a fuzzy image on the monitor. Finn watched intently, trying to make out his child. And then it was there. It didn't look much like a baby at this point, but the doctor pointed out the head and spine.

"Wait a second, I need to check one more thing."

The doctor made an adjustment. Holly's fingers tightened their hold on Finn. Her worried gaze met his. Was there something wrong with their child?

Finn fervently hoped not. He just didn't think he could go through all his parents had endured with his brother. It was an experience he'd never forget.

"Okay." The doctor's voice rose. "Here we go. Just as I suspected."

Finn couldn't be left in the dark. He had to know what they were facing. "What's the matter?"

The doctor smiled up at him. "Nothing at all. You are having twins."

"Twins!" Holly said it at the same time as Finn.

"Yes, see here." The doctor showed them both babies.

It was the most amazing thing Finn had ever witnessed in his life. Twins. Who'd have thought? His vision started to blur, causing him to blink repeatedly. He was going to be a father—twice over.

He glanced down at Holly. A tear streamed down her cheek. His gut clenched. Was that a sign of joy or unhappiness? It was hard for him to tell. And then she turned and smiled at him. He released the pent-up breath in his lungs.

Holly squeezed his hand. "Did you see that? Those are our babies."

"I saw."

The doctor cleared his throat. "Well, you'll want to see your OB/GYN as soon as possible. But in the meantime, you need some rest and lots of fluids."

"Rest?"

"Yes and fluids. You have to be careful not to become dehydrated with the morning sickness."

"Okay. Whatever you say. I still can't believe I missed all of the signs."

"You aren't the first. Some women are in labor before they realize they are pregnant. These things happen."

Finn followed the doctor into the hallway while Holly got dressed. When they reentered the room, Holly looked different. Was it possible there was a bit of a glow about her? Or was he imagining things?

The doctor went over some suggestions on how to minimize her morning sickness and gave her a bottle of prenatal vitamins to get her started. "If you have any problems while you're in the islands, feel free to come back. I'm always here."

"I was planning to fly to New York today or tomorrow. Would that be all right?"

"I'd like to see you rested and hydrated before you travel. Get your morning sickness under control first."

Finn could feel everyone's attention turning his way, but he continued to study the random pattern of the floor tiles. He had nothing to contribute to this conversation, not at this point. This sudden turn of events was something he'd never envisioned.

The door opened and closed.

"Finn, are you okay?"

He glanced up, finding that he was alone with Holly. "Okay? No."

Her lips formed an O. "Can I say or do anything?"

He shook his head. He should be the one reassuring her, letting her know this was all going to be all right, but he couldn't lie to her. He had no idea how any of this was going to be all right. He was the last person in the world who should be a father. In fact, up until this point, he'd intended to leave all of his estate to designated charities.

But now, wow, everything had just changed. He raked his fingers through his hair. He had to rethink everything.

Pull it together. She's expecting me to say something.

He lifted his head and met her worried gaze that shimmered with unshed tears. That was the last thing he'd expected. Holly was always so strong and sure of what she wanted. Her tears socked him in the gut, jarring him back to reality. She was just as scared as he was, if not more so.

Oh, boy, were his children in big trouble here. Neither Holly nor himself was prepared to be a parent. They had so much to learn and so little time.

Finn stood. "Let's go back to the island."

Her worried gaze met his. "But what about New York?"

"You heard the doctor. You need to rest first." He held his hand out to her.

She hesitated but then grasped his hand.

He didn't know what the future held, but for now they were in it together. For better. Or for worse.

Chapter 11

What were they supposed to do now?

A few days after returning from their trip to the big island, Holly was starting to feel better. The suggestions the doctor had given her for morning sickness were helping. And she'd been monitoring her fluid intake.

She was still trying to come to terms with the fact that she was pregnant. There was no question in her mind about keeping the babies, but that was the only thing she knew for sure.

Maria and Emilio had been called away from the island. This meant Holly and Finn had the entire island to themselves. In another time, that might have been exciting, even romantic, but right now, they had serious matters on their minds.

She paced back and forth in the study. Where would she live? How would she manage a job, helping out her mother and being a mom all on her own? And where did this leave her and Finn?

The questions continued to whirl around in her mind. She would figure it out—she had to—because she wasn't going to fall back on Finn. She'd counted on two men in her life and they'd both failed her. She knew better this time around. She could only count on herself.

Deciding she wasn't going to get any more work done, she headed for the kitchen. She needed something to do with her hands and she had an urge for something sweet.

As she searched the cabinets, looking for something to appease her craving, her thoughts turned to Finn. He'd barely spoken to her since they left the doctor's office. The occasional nod or grunt was about as much as she got out of him. She couldn't blame him. It was a lot to adjust to. Her mind was still spinning. Her hand ran over her abdomen.

A baby. No, two babies. Inside her. Wow!

"How are you feeling?" Finn asked.

Four whole words strung together. She would take that as a positive sign. "Better."

"And the babies?"

"Are perfectly fine." She bent over to retrieve a cookie sheet from the cabinet.

"I can get that for you." Finn rushed around the counter with his hands outstretched.

"I can manage." She glared at him until he retreated to the other side of the counter.

She placed the cookie sheet on the counter before turning on the oven. "Did you need something?"

"You're planning to bake? Now?"

"Sure. Why not? I have a craving."

"Isn't it a little early for those?"

She sighed. Why did he have to pick now of all times to get chatty? She just wanted to eat some sugary goodness in peace. "Not that kind of craving."

"Then what kind?"

What was up with him? He'd never been so curious about her dietary habits before. Or maybe he was just attempting to be friendly and she was being supersensitive. She choked down her agitation, planning to give him the benefit of the doubt.

"These are cravings that I get when I'm stressed out." She pulled open the door on the stainless-steel fridge and withdrew a roll of premade cookie dough. "Do you want some cookies?"

"If you're stressed about Project Santa—?"

"It's not that!"

His eyes widened. "Oh. I see."

This was another opening for him to discuss the big pink or perhaps blue elephant in the room. And yet, he said nothing. Her gaze met his and he glanced away. Was this his way of telling her that he wasn't interested in being a father?

She placed the package of cookie dough on the counter before moving to the oven to adjust the temperature. Next, she needed a cutting board. There had to be one around here somewhere. The kitchen was equipped with absolutely everything. At last, she spotted a small pineapple-shaped board propped against the stone backsplash.

With the cutting board and a knife in hand, she moved back to the counter. "I'll have some reindeer cookies ready in no time. I thought about some hot chocolate with the little marshmallows, but it's a little warm around here for that."

"Thanks. But I'll pass on the cookies. I have some emails I need to get to. By the way, do you have a copy of the Cutter contract?"

"I do. It's in my room. Just let me finish putting these cookies on the tray." She put a dozen on the tray and slipped it in the oven. "Okay. There." She turned back to him. "Stay here and I'll be right back."

She rushed to her spacious guest room that overlooked the ocean. It was a spectacular view. She was tempted to take a dip in the sea or at the very least walk along the beach, letting her feet get wet. Maybe she'd do it later, after she was done working for the day.

Turning away from the window, her gaze strayed over the colorful packages she'd brought back from the big island. She'd splurged a bit, buying a little something for everyone, including her half-sisters, Suzie and Kristi.

Holly worried her bottom lip. She always tried so hard to find something that would impress them and each year, she'd failed. Thankfully she'd bought the gifts before her doctor's appointment because afterward she hadn't been in a holly-jolly spirit. The bikinis, sunglasses, flip-flops and a cover-up with the name of the island were placed in yellow tissue-paper-lined shopping bags. The girls would be all set for summer. About the same time she was giving birth.

With a sigh, Holly continued her hunt for the contract. On top of the dresser, she found the file folder. She pulled it out from beneath a stack of papers and an expandable folder when the back of her hand struck the lamp. Before she could stop it, the lamp toppled over.

Holly gasped as it landed on the floor and shattered, sending shards of glass all over the room. As she knelt down to clean up the mess, she muttered to herself. It was then that she heard rapid footsteps in the hallway.

"What happened?" Finn's voice carried a note of concern. "Are you okay?"

"I am. But the same can't be said for the lamp."

"I'm not worried about it." His concerned gaze met hers.

"I'll have this cleaned up in no time. Your contract is on the edge of the dresser."

When he stepped forward, she thought it was to retrieve the contract. However, the next thing she knew, he knelt down beside her.

"What are you doing?" she asked, not quite believing her eyes.

"Helping you."

"I don't need your help—"

"Well, you better get used to it because I plan to help with these babies."

It wasn't a question. It was an emphatic statement.

Her stomach churned. She was losing her control—her independence. She was about to lose her sense of security because her life would no longer be her own—Finn and the babies would now be a part of it—forever.

Holly sucked in a deep breath, hoping it'd slow the rapid pounding of her heart.

"Did you cut yourself on the broken glass?" Finn glanced down at her hands.

"I'm fine." She got to her feet, needing some distance from him. And then she smelled something. She sniffed again. "Oh, no! The cookies."

She rushed to the kitchen and swung the oven door open. The Christmas cookies were all brown and burnt. With Finn hovering about, she'd forgotten to turn on the timer. She groaned aloud, not caring if he heard her or not.

She turned to the garbage and dumped the cookies in it. Her gaze blurred. The memory of Finn's words and the knowledge that life would never be the same made her feel off-kilter and scared. What were they supposed to do now?

Chapter 12

He had to do something, but what?

The next evening, Finn did his best to concentrate on the details of a potential acquisition for Lockwood. Try as he might, his thoughts kept straying back to Holly and the babies. This was the time when his family would be invaluable. A deep sadness came over him, realizing that his children would never know his parents or his brother, Derek. In that moment he knew that it would be his responsibility to tell his children about their past—about their grandparents and uncle. Finn didn't take the notion lightly.

He glanced across the study to where Holly was sitting on the couch, working on her laptop. She'd been feeling better, which was a relief. Whatever the doctor had told her to do was helping. Now they could focus on the future.

His gaze moved to the windows behind her. The day was gray and glum just like his mood. He knew what needed to be done. They needed to get married.

He'd wrestled with the thought for days now. And it was the only solution that made sense. Although, he wasn't ready to get down on one knee and lay his heart on the line. Just the thought of loving someone else and losing them made his blood run cold. No, it was best their marriage was based on something more reliable—common goals.

The welfare of their children would be the tie that bound them. Finn's chest tightened when he realized that he knew less than nothing about babies. He would need help and lots of it. That was where Holly came in. He needed her guidance if he wanted to be the perfect parent—or as close to it as possible. Without her, he wouldn't even know where to start.

He assured himself that it would all work out. After all, Holly was the mother to the Lockwood heirs. Their fates had been sealed as soon as she became pregnant. They would have to marry. And he would do his utmost to keep his family safe.

Holly leaned back. "I'm almost finished with the last details for Project Santa. I've reviewed the list of volunteers, state by state and city by city. I've been trying to determine whether there are enough volunteers to transport the gifts from the airports to the designated outreach centers."

Finn welcomed the distraction. "And what have you determined?"

"I think we need a few more drivers. I've already posted a request on MyFace. I'll wait and see what the response is before I take further steps."

"Good. It sounds like you have everything under control."

The fact that they worked well together was another thing they could build on. It would give their marriage a firm foundation. Because he just couldn't open his heart—he couldn't take that risk again.

A gust of wind made a shutter on the house rattle, jarring Finn from his thoughts. It was really picking up out there. So much for the sunshine in paradise. It looked like they'd soon be in for some rain.

"Finn, we need to talk." The banging continued, causing Holly to glance around. "What was that pounding sound?"

"I think it's a shutter that needs tightening."

Holly closed her laptop and set it aside. She got to her feet and moved to the window as though to inspect the problem. "Do you have a screwdriver and a ladder?"

"Yes, but why?"

"I'll go fix it."

"You?"

She frowned at him. "Yes, me. If you haven't noticed, I'm not one to sit around helplessly and wait for some guy to come take care of me."

"But you're pregnant and have doctor's orders to rest. You shouldn't be climbing on ladders. I'll take care of it later."

She sighed loudly. "I've been following his orders and I'm feeling much better. But if you insist, I'll leave the house repairs to you. Besides, there's something else we need to discuss."

"Is there another problem with Project Santa?"

"No. It's not that." She averted her gaze. "Remember how I asked you for a letter of recommendation?"

Why would she bring that up now? Surely she wasn't still considering it. Everything had changed what with the babies and all. "I remember."

Her gaze lifted to meet his. "Have you made a decision?"

"I didn't think it was still an issue."

"Why not?"

"Because you won't be leaving Lockwood, unless of course you want to stay home with the babies, which I'd totally understand. They are certainly going to be a handful and then some."

"Why do you think I won't leave to take that new job?"

Finn sent her a very puzzled look. "Because you're carrying the Lockwood heirs. And soon we'll be married—"

"Married?" Holly took a step back.

What was Finn talking about? They weren't getting married. Not now. Not ever.

"Of course. It's the next logical step—"

"No." She shook her head as her heart raced and her hands grew clammy. "It isn't logical and it certainly isn't my next step. You never even asked me, not that I want you to or anything."

"I thought it was implied."

"Implied? Maybe in your mind, but certainly not in mine. I'm not marrying you. I'm not going to marry anyone."

"Of course you are." His voice rumbled with irritation.

"This isn't the Stone Age. A woman can be pregnant without a husband. There are plenty of loving, single mothers in this world. Take a look around your office building. You'll find quite a few. But you won't find me there after the first of the year."

Had she really just said that? Oh, my. She'd gotten a little ahead of herself. What if he turned his back and walked away without giving her the recommendation? And she didn't have the job. It was still iffy at best. And without her position at Lockwood to fall back on, how would she support herself much less the babies and her mother?

"You're really serious about leaving, aren't you?"

She nodded, afraid to open her mouth again and make the situation worse.

"Do you really dislike me that much?"

"No! Not at all." In fact, it was quite the opposite.

She worried the inside of her lower lip as she glanced toward the window. The wind had picked up, whipping the fronds of the palm trees to and fro. She did not want to answer this question. Not at all.

"Holly?" Finn got to his feet and came to stand in front of her. "Why are you doing this? Why are you trying to drive us apart?"

"You…you're making this sound personal and it isn't." Heat rushed up her neck and made her face feel as though she'd been lying in the sun all day with no sunscreen.

"It is personal. It couldn't be more personal."

"No, it isn't. It's not like you and I, like we're involved."

"I don't know your definition of involved, but I don't think it gets much more involved than you carrying my babies."

"Finn, we both agreed after that night together that

we wouldn't have anything to do with each other. We mutually decided that going our separate ways was for the best—for both of us."

"That was before."

"The pregnancy is a complication. I'll admit that. But we can work out an arrangement with the babies. We don't have to live out of each other's back pockets."

"I don't want to live in your back pocket. I want to provide a home for my children and their mother—"

"I don't need you to take care of me or the babies. I can manage on my own."

"But the point is you don't have to. I'm here to help. We can help each other."

She shook her head. "A marriage of convenience won't work."

"Sure it will, if we want it to."

Holly crossed her arms. "Why are you so certain you're right? It's not like we're in love. This thing between us will never last."

"And maybe you're wrong. Maybe the fact that we aren't in love is the reason that it will work. There won't be any unreasonable expectations. No emotional roller coaster."

"And that sounds good to you?"

He shrugged. "Do you have a better suggestion?"

"Yes. I think some space will be best for everyone."

"I don't agree. What would be best is if we became a family—a family that shares the same home as our children."

"And what happens—" She stopped herself just in time. She was going to utter, *What happens when you get bored*? Would he trade her in for a younger model?

But she wasn't going there. It didn't matter because what Finn was proposing wasn't possible.

His gaze probed her. "Finish that statement."

"It's nothing."

"It was definitely something. And I want to know what it is." He moved closer to her.

His nearness sent her heart racing. It was hard to keep her mind on the conversation. No man had a right to be so sexy. If only real life was like the movies and came with happily-ever-afters.

"Holly?"

"I honestly can't remember what I was going to say. But it's time I go back to New York."

Finn's eyes momentarily widened in surprise "What about the project?"

"The event is ready to go."

"You just said you had a problem with transportation."

"That...that's minor. I can deal with it from anywhere."

His gaze narrowed. "You're serious, aren't you?"

She settled her hands on her hips. "I am. You don't need me here. You can email me or phone, but you no longer need my presence here."

"Is there anything I can say to change your mind?"

There were so many things she wanted him to say. But she feared they were both too damaged—too cynical about life to be able to create a happily-ever-after.

And instead of trying and failing—of taking what they have and making it contentious, she'd rather part as friends. It'd be best for everyone, including the babies.

But finding herself a bit emotional, she didn't trust her voice. Instead, she averted her gaze and shook her head.

Finn sighed. "Fine. I'll call for the chopper."

"Really?" He was just going to let her walk out the door? It seemed too easy.

"It's what you want, isn't it?" He retrieved the phone.

"Yes, it is." She turned away and walked to the French doors. They were usually standing open, letting in the fresh air and sunshine, but not today. She stared off into the distant gray sky. Dark clouds scudded across it as rain began to fall.

She couldn't believe he was just going to let her walk away. A man who liked to control everything in his life surely couldn't live with just handing over his children with no strings attached.

In the background, she could hear the murmur of Finn's voice. He'd lowered it, but not before she caught the rumble in it. He wasn't happy—not at all. Well, that made two of them. But they'd have to make the best of the situation.

Her hand moved to her abdomen. It wouldn't be long now before she really started to show. She didn't even want to guess how big she'd get carrying not one but two babies. She had no doubt her figure would never be quite the same. But it would be worth it.

To be honest, she'd never thought of having children before. After her family had been ripped apart, she told herself she wasn't getting married or having children. She'd assured herself that life would be so much simpler when she only had herself to worry about.

Now she had two little ones counting on her to make all of the right decisions.

She turned, finding Finn with his back to her as he leaned against the desk. He certainly was different from Josh. Where Josh was a real charmer, Finn only gave a compliment when he truly meant it. Where Josh ran at the first sign of trouble, Finn was willing to stand by her. So why couldn't she give him a chance to prove that he truly was an exception?

He certainly was the most handsome man she'd laid her eyes on. Her gaze lingered on his golden hair that always seemed to be a bit scattered and made her long to run her fingers through it. And then there were his broad shoulders—shoulders that looked as though they could carry the weight of the world on them. She wondered how heavy a load he carried around.

Something told her he'd seen far too much in his young life. And she didn't want to add to his burden. That was never her intention. With time, she hoped he'd understand that she never meant to hurt him by turning down his suggestion of marriage.

Finn hung up the phone and turned to her. "We can't leave."

Surely she hadn't heard him correctly. "What do you mean we can't leave?"

"There's a storm moving in and with these high winds it's too dangerous to take up the chopper." His gaze met hers. "I'm sorry. I know how much you wanted off the island."

"So what are you saying? That we're stranded here?"

"Yes." He didn't look any happier about it than she did.

"What are we going to do?"

"You're going to wait here." He turned toward the door. "With Emilio and Maria away, I've got a lot of work to do before the storm. I won't get it all done tonight, but I can at least start."

"Wait for me. I want to help."

She rushed after him. There was no way she was planning to stand around and have him do all of the work. She knew her way around a toolbox and power tools. She could pull her own weight.

Hopefully this storm would pass by the island, leaving them unscathed. And then she'd be on her way home. She wasn't sure how much longer she could keep her common sense while around Finn.

Her gaze trailed down over Finn from his muscled arms to his trim waist and his firm backside. The blood heated in her veins. Enjoying each other's company didn't mean they had to make a formal commitment, right?

Wait. No. No. She couldn't let her desires override her logic. She jerked her gaze away from Finn. It had to be the pregnancy hormones that had her thinking these truly outlandish thoughts.

She was immune to Finn—about as immune as a bee to a field of wildflowers. She was in big trouble.

Chapter 13

Why was she fighting him?

The next day, Finn sighed as he stared blindly out the glass doors. No matter what he said to Holly, there was no reasoning with her. She was determined to have these babies on her own.

He knew that she wouldn't keep him from seeing them, but he also knew that visitation every other weekend was not enough. He would be a stranger to his own children—his only family. His hands clenched. That couldn't happen.

He'd never thought he'd be a part of a family again. And though he had worries about how well he'd measure up as a husband and father, he'd couldn't walk away. Why couldn't Holly understand that?

He didn't know how or when, but somehow he'd convince her that they were better parents together than apart. If only he knew how to get his point across to her—

The lights flickered, halting his thoughts. The power went completely out, shrouding the house in long shadows. After a night and day of rain, it had stopped, but the winds were starting to pick up again. And then the lights came back on.

Finn didn't like the looks of things outside—not one little bit. Normally there weren't big weather events at this time of the year, but every once in a while a late-season storm would make its way across the Atlantic. This just happened to be one of those times.

Finn rinsed a dinner plate and placed it in the dishwasher. Yes, to Holly's amazement, he did know his way around the kitchen. He was a man who preferred his privacy and he didn't have a regular household staff in New York, just a maid who came in a couple of times a week.

But here on the island, it was different. Maria and Emilio had a small house off in the distance. They lived here year-round. Maria looked after the house while Emilio took care of the grounds. They were as close to family as Finn had—until now.

He ran the dishcloth over the granite countertop before placing it next to the sink. Everything was clean and in its place. He wondered what Holly was up to. She'd been particularly quiet throughout dinner. He made his way to the study.

Though she wouldn't admit it, he could tell the storm had her on edge. He was concerned, too. The tide was much higher than normal and the wind was wicked. But this house had been built to withstand some of the harshest weather. They'd be safe here.

Now if only he could comfort Holly, but she resisted any attempt he made to get closer. He wondered what had happened for her to hide behind a defensive wall.

It had to be something pretty bad. If only he could get her to open up to him.

He was in the hallway outside the study when the lights flickered and went out. This time they didn't come back on. He needed to check on Holly before he ventured outside to fire up the emergency generator.

He stepped into the study that was now long with shadows. He squinted, looking for her. "Holly, where are you?"

She stood up from behind one of the couches. "Over here."

"What in the world are you doing?"

"Looking for candles in this cabinet."

"There are no candles in here. I have some in the kitchen."

She followed him to the supply of candles. There were also flashlights and lanterns in the pantry. It was fully stocked in case of an emergency.

"Do you think we'll really need all of this?" She fingered the packages of beef jerky and various other pre-packaged foods.

"I hope not. The last I checked the weather radio, the storm was supposed to go south of us."

"And I think it's calming down outside. That has to be a good sign, doesn't it?"

When he glanced over at the hopefulness in her eyes, he didn't want to disappoint her. He wanted to be able to reassure her that everything would be fine, but something told him she'd already been lied to enough in her life. So he decided to change the subject.

He picked up a lantern. "I think this might be easier than the candles."

"Really?"

Was that a pout on her face? She wanted the candle-light? Was it possible there was a romantic side to her hidden somewhere beneath her practicality and cynicism?

Deciding it wouldn't hurt to indulge her, he retrieved some large candle jars. "Is this what you had in mind?"

She nodded. "But we won't need them, will we?"

Finn glanced outside. It was much darker than it normally would be at this time of the day. "Come on. I have a safe place for us to wait out the storm."

She didn't question him but rather she quietly followed him to the center of the house. He opened the door to a small room with reinforced walls and no windows.

"What is this?"

"A safe room. I know it's not very big, but trust me, it'll do the job. I had it specifically put in the house for this very reason." With a flashlight in hand, he started lighting the candles. "There. That's all of them." A loud bang echoed through the house. "Now, I'll go work on the generator."

Holly reached out, grasping his arm. "Please don't go outside."

"But I need to—"

"Stay safe. We've got everything we need right here."

"Holly, don't worry. This isn't my first storm."

"But it's mine. Promise me you won't go outside."

He stared into her big brown eyes and saw the fear reflected in them. It tore at his heart. He pulled her close until her cheek rested against his shoulder.

"Everything will be fine."

She pulled back in order to gaze into his eyes. "Promise me you won't go outside."

He couldn't deny her this. "Yes, I promise."

This time she squeezed him tight as though in relief.

Seconds later, Finn pulled away. "I think we'll need some more candles and I want to do one more walk through the house to make sure it's secure. I'll be back."

"I can come with you."

"No. Stay here and get comfortable. I'll be right back. I promise." He started for the door.

"Finn?"

He paused, hearing the fear in her voice. "Do you need something else?"

"Um, no. Just be careful."

"I will." Was it possible that through all of her defensiveness and need to assert her independence that she cared for him? The thought warmed a spot in his chest. But he didn't have time to dwell on this revelation. The winds were starting to howl.

He hurried back to the kitchen where he'd purposely forgotten the weather radio. He wanted to listen to it without Holly around. He didn't know much about pregnant women, but he knew enough to know stress would not be good for her.

The radio crackled. He adjusted it so he could make out most of the words. The eye of the storm had shifted. It was headed closer to them. And the winds were intensifying to hurricane strength. Finn's hands clenched tightly.

This was all his fault. He should have paid more attention to the weather instead of getting distracted with the babies and his plans for the future. Now, instead of worrying about what he'd be like as a father, he had to hope he'd get that chance. He knew how bad the tropical storms could get. He'd ridden one out in this very house a few years back. It was an experience he'd been hoping not to repeat.

With a sigh, he turned off the radio. He made the rounds. The house was as secure as he could make it. With the radio, satellite phone and a crate of candles and more water, he headed back to Holly.

"How is everything?" Her voice held a distinct thread of worry.

He closed the door and turned around to find a cozy setting awaiting him. There were blankets heaped on the floor and pillows lining the wall. With the soft glow of the candles, it swept him back in time—back to when his big brother was still alive. They were forever building blanket forts to their mother's frustration.

The memory of his mother and brother saddened him. Finn tried his best not to dwell on their absence from his life, but every now and then there would be a moment when a memory would drive home the fact that he was now all alone in this world.

"Finn, what is it?" Holly got to her feet and moved to him.

It wasn't until she pressed a hand to his arm that he was jarred from his thoughts. "Um, nothing. Everything is secure. It's started to rain."

"The storm's not going to miss us, is it?"

"I'm afraid not. But we'll be fine."

"With the door closed, it's amazing how quiet it is in here. I could almost pretend there isn't a big storm brewing outside."

He didn't want to keep talking about the weather. He didn't want her asking more questions, because the last thing he wanted to do was scare her with the word *hur-*

ricane. After all, it wasn't even one yet, but there was a strong potential.

"I see you made the room comfortable."

She glanced around. "I hope you like it."

"I do." There was one thing about this arrangement— she couldn't get away from him. He had a feeling by the time the sun rose, things between them would be drastically different.

This was not working.

Holly wiggled around, trying to get comfortable. It wasn't the cushions so much as hearing the creaking of the house and wondering what was going on outside. Finn hadn't wanted to tell her so she hadn't pushed, but her best guess was that they were going to experience a hurricane. The thought sent a chill racing down her spine.

"Is something wrong?"

"Um, nothing."

She glanced across the short space to find Finn's handsome face illuminated in the candlelight. Why exactly had she insisted on the candles? Was she hoping there would be a bit of romance? Of course not. The soft light was comforting, was all.

His head lifted and his gaze met hers. "Do you need more cushions? Or a blanket?"

"Really, I'm fine." There was another loud creak of the house. "I… I'm just wondering what's going on outside. Should we go check?"

"No." His answer was fast and short. "I mean there could be broken glass and it's dark out there. We'll deal with it in the morning."

She swallowed hard. "You really think the windows have been blown out?"

"The shutters will protect them. Hopefully the house is holding its own."

"Maybe you should turn on the radio." Whatever the weather people said couldn't be worse than what her imagination had conjured up.

"You know what I'd really like to do?" He didn't wait for her to respond. "How about we get to know each other better?"

"And how do you propose we do that?"

"How about a game of twenty questions? You can ask me anything you want and I have to be absolutely honest. In return, I get to ask you twenty questions and you have to be honest."

She wasn't so sure honesty right now would be such a good idea, especially if he asked if she cared about him. "I… I don't know."

"Oh, come on. Surely you have questions."

She did. She had lots of them, but she wasn't so sure she wanted to answer his in return. She didn't open up with many people. She told herself it was because she was introverted, but sometimes she wondered if it was more than that.

On this particular night everything felt surreal. Perhaps she could act outside her norm. "Okay, as long as I go first."

"Go for it. But remember you only get twenty questions so make them good ones."

Chapter 14

Holly didn't have to think hard to come up with her first question. "Why did you look like you'd seen a ghost when you stepped in here?"

There was a pause as though Finn was figuring out how to answer her question. Was he thinking up a vague answer or would he really open up and give her a glimpse of the man beneath the business suits and intimidating reputation?

He glanced off into the shadows. "When I walked in here I was reminded of a time—long ago. My brother and I used to build blanket forts when we were kids. Especially in the winter when it was too cold or wet to go outside. My mother wasn't fond of them because we'd strip our beds."

Holly smiled, liking that he had a normal childhood with happy memories. She wondered why he kept them hidden. In all the time she'd been around him, she could count on one hand the number of times he spoke of his family. But she didn't say a word because she didn't want to interrupt him—she found herself wanting to learn everything she could about him.

"I remember there was this one Christmas where we'd built our biggest fort. But it was dark in there and my brother wanted to teach me to play cards. My mother would have been horrified that her proper young men were playing cards—it made it all the more fun. We tried a flashlight but it didn't have enough light. So my brother got an idea of where to get some lights."

Holly could tell by the gleam in Finn's eyes that mischief had been afoot. He and his brother must have been a handful. Would her twins be just as ornery? Her hand moved to her stomach. She had a feeling they would be and that she'd love every minute of it. She might even join them in their fort.

"While my parents were out at the Mistletoe Ball and the sitter was watching a movie in the family room, we took a string of white lights off the Christmas tree."

Holly gasped. "You didn't."

Finn nodded. "My brother assured me it was just one strand. There were plenty of other lights on the tree. After all, it was a big tree. So we strung the lights back and forth inside our fort. It gave it a nice glow, enough so that we could see the cards. There was just one problem."

"You got caught?"

He shook his head. "Not at first. The problem was my brother for all of his boasting had no clue how to play cards. So we ended up playing Go Fish."

Holly couldn't help but laugh, imagining those two little boys. "I bet you kept your parents on their toes."

"I suppose we did—for a while anyway." The smile slipped from his face and she wanted to put it back there. He was so handsome when he smiled.

"So what happened with the lights?"

"Well, when my parents got home, my mother called us down to the living room. It seems my father tried to fix the lights that were out on the lower part of the tree, but he soon found they were missing. My mother wanted to know if we knew anything about it. I looked at my brother and he looked at me. Then we both shrugged. We tried to assure her the tree looked good, but she wasn't buying any of it. My mother didn't have to look very long to find the lights. As I recall, we were grounded for a week. My father had the task of putting the lights back on the tree with all of the ornaments and ribbon still on it. He was not happy at all."

"I wouldn't think he would be."

"Okay. So now it's my turn. Let's see. Where did you grow up?"

She gave him a funny look. "Seriously, that's what you want to know?"

He shrugged. "Sure. Why not?"

"I grew up in Queens. A long way from your Upper East Side home."

"Not that far."

"Maybe not by train but it is by lifestyle." When Finn glanced away, she realized how that sounded. She just wasn't good at thinking about her family and the way things used to be so she always searched for a diversion.

"It's my turn." She thought for a moment and then asked, "Okay, what's your favorite color?"

He sent her a look of disbelief. "Are you serious?"

"Sure. Why wouldn't I be?"

"It's just that I thought these were questions to get to know each other. I don't know how my favorite color has much to do with anything."

"I'll tell you once you spit it out."

He sighed. "Green. Hunter green. Now why was that so important to you?"

"Are you sure it isn't money green?" He rolled his eyes and smiled at her before she continued. "It's important to me because I need a color to paint the babies' bedroom."

"Oh. I hadn't thought of that. Then I get to ask you what your favorite color is."

"Purple. A deep purple."

"Sounds like our children are going to have interesting bedrooms with purple and green walls."

Holly paused and thought about it for a minute. "I think we can make it work."

"Are you serious?"

"Very. Think about green foliage with purple skies. A palm tree with a monkey or two or three. And perhaps a bunch of bananas here and there for a splash of yellow."

His eyes widened. "How did you do that?"

"Do what?"

"Come up with that mural off the top of your head?"

She shrugged. "I don't know. It just sounded fun and like something our children might enjoy."

"I think you're right. I'll have the painters get started on it right away."

"Whoa! Slow down. I don't even know where we'll be living by the time these babies are born." When the smile slipped from his face, she knew it was time for a new question. "Why do you always leave New York at

Christmastime? No, scratch that. I know that answer. I guess my real question is why do you hate Christmas?"

He frowned. "So now you're going for the really hard questions, huh? No, what's your middle name? Or what's your favorite food?"

She shrugged. "I just can't imagine hating Christmas. It's the season of hope."

There was a faraway look in his eyes. "My mother, she used to love it, too. She would deck out our house the day after Thanksgiving. It was a tradition. And it wasn't just her. The whole family took part, pulling the boxes of decorations out of the attic while Christmas carols played in the background. After we hung the outside lights, my mother would whip up hot chocolate with those little marshmallows."

"So you don't like it anymore because it reminds you of her?"

Finn frowned. "You don't get to ask another question yet. Besides, I wasn't finished with my answer."

"Oh. Sorry."

"Now that my family isn't around, I don't see any point in celebrating. I'll never get any of those moments back. When I'm here, I don't have to be surrounded by those memories or be reminded of what I lost."

There was more to that story, but she had to figure out the right question to get him to open up more. But how deep would he let her dig into his life? She had no idea. But if she didn't try to break through some of the protective layers that he had surrounding him, how in the world would they ever coparent? How would she ever be able to answer her children's questions about their father?

She didn't want to just ignore her kids' inquiries like

her mother had done with her. Initially when her father had left, she'd been so confused. She thought it was something she'd done or not done. She didn't understand because to her naive thinking, things had been good. Then one day he packed his bags and walked out the door. Her mother refused to fill in the missing pieces. It was really hard for a ten-year-old to understand how her family had splintered apart overnight.

Finn cleared his throat. "Okay, next question. Do your parents still live in Queens?"

"Yes, however right now my mother's visiting my aunt in Florida. And my father moved to Brooklyn."

Finn's brow arched. "So they're divorced?"

"You already had your question, now it's my turn." Finn frowned but signaled with his hand for her to proceed, so she continued. "What happened to your brother?"

Finn's hands flexed. "He died."

She knew there had to be so much more to it. But she didn't push. If Finn was going to let down his guard, it had to be his choice, and pushing him would only keep him on the defensive.

And so she quietly waited. Either he expanded on his answer or he asked her another question. She would make peace with whatever he decided.

"My brother was the star of the family. He got top marks in school. He was on every sports team. And he shadowed my father on the weekends at the office. He was like my father in so many ways."

"And what about you?"

"I was a couple of years younger. I wasn't the Lockwood heir and so my father didn't have much time for me. I got the occasional clap on the back for my top marks, but then my father would turn his attention to my brother. For the most part, it didn't bother me. It was easier being forgotten than being expected to be perfect. My brother didn't have it easy. The pressure my father put on him to excel at everything was enormous."

Holly didn't care what Finn said, to be forgotten by a parent or easily dismissed hurt deeply. She knew all about it when her father left them to start his own family with his mistress, now wife number two.

But this wasn't her story, it was Finn's. And she knew it didn't have a happy ending, but she didn't know the details. Perhaps if she'd dug deeper on the internet, she might have learned how Finn's family splintered apart, but she'd rather hear it all from him.

"Everything was fine until my brother's grades started to fall and he began making mistakes on the football field. My father was irate. He blamed it on my brother being a teenager and being distracted by girls. My brother didn't even have a girlfriend at that point. He was too shy around them."

Holly tried to decide if that was true of Finn, as well. Somehow she had a hard time imagining this larger-than-life man being shy. Perhaps he could be purposely distant, but she couldn't imagine him being nervous around a woman.

"My brother, he started to tire easily. It progressed to the point where my mother took him to the doctor. It all snowballed from there. Tests and treatments became the sole focus of the whole house. Christmas that year was forgotten."

"How about you?" He didn't say it, but she got the feeling with so much on the line that Finn got lost in the shuffle.

He frowned at her, but it was the pain in his eyes that dug at her. "I didn't have any right to feel forgotten. My brother was fighting for his life."

She lowered her voice. "But it had to be tough for you with everyone running around looking after your brother. No one would blame you for feeling forgotten."

"I would blame me. I was selfish." His voice was gravelly with emotion. "And I had no right—no right to want presents on Christmas—no right to grow angry with my parents for not having time for me."

Her heart ached for him. "Of course you would want Christmas with all of its trimmings. Your life was spinning out of control and you wanted to cling to what you knew—what would make your life feel normal again."

"Aren't you listening? My brother was dying and I was sitting around feeling sorry for myself because I couldn't have some stupid toys under the Christmas tree. What kind of a person does that make me?"

"A real flesh-and-blood person who isn't perfect. But here's a news flash for you. None of us are —perfect that is. We just have to make the best of what we've been given."

He shook his head, blinking repeatedly. "I'm worse than most. I'm selfish and thoughtless. *Uncaring* is the word my mother threw at me." He swiped at his eyes. "And she was right. My brother deserved a better sibling than I'd turned out to be."

Holly placed her hand atop his before lacing their fingers together. A tingling sensation rushed from their clasped hands, up her arm and settled in her chest. It gave her the strength she needed to keep going—to keep trying to help this man who was in such pain.

"Did you ever think that you were just a kid in a truly

horrific situation? Your big brother—the person you looked up to—your best friend—was sick, dying and there was nothing you could do for him. That's a lot to deal with as an adult, but as a child you must have felt utterly helpless. Not knowing what to do with the onslaught of emotions, you pushed them aside. Your brother's situation was totally out of your control. Instead you focused on trying to take control of your life."

Finn's wounded gaze searched hers. "You're just saying that to make me feel better."

"I'm saying it because it's what I believe." She freed her hand from his in order to gently caress his jaw. "Finn, you're a good man with a big heart—"

"I'm not. I'm selfish."

"Is that what your mother told you?"

"No." His head lowered. There was a slight pause as though he was lost in his own memories. "It's what my father told me."

"He was wrong." She placed a fingertip beneath Finn's chin and lifted until they were eye to eye. "He was very wrong. You have the biggest, most generous heart of anyone I know."

"Obviously you don't know me very well." His voice was barely more than a whisper.

"Look at how much you do for others. The Santa Project is a prime example. And you're a generous boss with an amazing benefits package for your employees—"

"That isn't what I meant. My father...he told me that I should have been the one in the hospital bed, not my brother." Holly gasped. Finn kept talking as though oblivious to her shocked reaction. "He was right. My brother was the golden boy. He was everything my parents could want. Derek and I were quite different."

Tears slipped down her cheeks. It was horrific that his father would spew such mean and hurtful things, but the fact that Finn believed them and still did to this day tore her up inside. How in the world did she make him see what a difference he continued to make in others' lives?

And then a thought occurred to her. She pulled his hand over to her slightly rounded abdomen. "This is the reason you're still here. You have a future. You have two little ones coming into this world that you can lavish with love and let them know how important each of them are to you. You can make sure they know that you don't have a favorite because they are equally important in your heart."

"What...what if I end up like my father and hurt our children?"

"You won't. The fact you're so worried about it proves my point."

His gaze searched hers. "Do you really believe that? You think I can be a good father?"

"I do." Her voice held a note of conviction. "Just follow your heart. It's a good, strong heart. It won't lead you astray."

"No one ever said anything like this to me. I... I just hope I don't let you down."

"You won't. I have faith in you."

His gaze dipped to her lips. She could read his thoughts and she wanted him too. Not waiting for him, she leaned forward, pressing her lips to his.

At first, he didn't move. Was he that surprised by her action? Didn't he know how much she wanted him? Needed him?

As his lips slowly moved beneath hers, she'd never felt so close to anyone in her life. It was though his words had touched her heart. He'd opened up and let her in. That was a beginning.

Her hands wound around his neck. He tasted sweet like the fresh batch of Christmas cookies that she'd left on a plate in the kitchen. She was definitely going to have to make more of those.

As their kiss deepened, her fingers combed through his hair. A moan rose in the back of her throat. She'd never been kissed so thoroughly. Her whole body tingled clear down to her toes.

Right now though, she didn't want anything but his arms around her as they sank down into the nest of blankets and pillows. While the storm raged outside, desire raged inside her.

Chapter 15

It could be better.

But it could have been so much worse.

The next morning, Finn returned to the safe room after a preliminary survey of the storm damage. He glanced down at the cocoon of blankets and pillows to find Holly awake and getting to her feet. With her hair slightly mussed up and her lips still rosy from a night of kissing, she'd never looked more beautiful.

She blushed. "What are you looking at?" She ran a hand over her hair. "I must be a mess."

"No. Actually you look amazing."

"You're just saying that because you want something from me."

He hadn't said it for any reason other than he meant it. However, now that she'd planted the idea into his head, perhaps now was as good a time as any to tell her what he had on his mind. He'd stared into the dark long after she'd fallen asleep the night before. He'd thought long and hard about where they went from here.

But now as she smiled up at him, his attention strayed to her soft, plump lips. "You're right, there is something I want." He reached out and pulled her close. "This."

Without giving her a chance to react, he leaned in and pressed his lips to hers. Her kisses were sweet as nectar and he knew he'd never ever tire of them. He pulled her closer, deepening the kiss. He needed to make sure that last night hadn't just been a figment of his imagination.

And now he had his proof. The chemistry between them was most definitely real. It was all the more reason to follow through with his plan—his duty.

When at last he let her go, she smiled up at him. "What was that about?"

"Just making sure you aren't a dream."

"I'm most definitely real and so was that storm last night. So, um, how bad is the damage?" She turned and started to collect the blankets.

"There's a lot of debris on the beach. It'll take a while until this place looks like it once did, but other than a few minor things, the house held its own."

"That's wonderful. How long until we have power?"

"I'm hoping not long. I plan to work on that first." They were getting off topic.

"Before I let you go, I do believe we got distracted last night before I could ask my next question."

"Hmm… I don't recall this." She sent him a teasing smile.

"Convenient memory is more like it."

"Okay. What's your question?"

Now that it was time to put his marriage plan in action, he had doubts—lots of them. What if she wanted more than he could offer? What if she wanted a traditional marriage with promises of love?

"Finn? What is it?"

"Will you marry me?"

Surprise reflected in her eyes. "We already had this conversation. It won't work."

"Just hear me out. It won't be a traditional marriage, but that doesn't mean we can't make it work. After all, we're friends—or I'd like to think we are." She nodded in agreement and he continued. "And we know we're good together in other areas."

Pink tinged her cheeks. "So this would be like a business arrangement?"

"Not exactly. It'll be what we make of it. So what do you say?"

She returned to folding a blanket. "We don't have to be married to be a family. I still believe we'll all be happier if you have your life and I have my own."

A frown pulled at his lips. This wasn't the way it had played out in his imagination. In his mind, she'd jumped at the offer. If she was waiting for something more—something heartfelt—she'd be waiting a very long time.

There had to be a way to turn this around. The stakes were much too high for him to fold his hand and walk away. He needed to be close to his children—

"Stop." Her voice interrupted the flow of his thoughts.

"Stop what?"

"Wondering how you can get me to say yes. You can't. I told you before that I didn't want to get married. That hasn't changed."

But the part she'd forgotten was that he was a man used to getting his way. When he set his sights on something, nothing stood in his way. He would overcome her hesitation about them becoming a full-fledged family, no matter what it took.

He wanted to be a full-time father to his kids and do all the things his father had been too busy to do with him. He would make time for both of his children. He wouldn't demean one while building up the other. Or at least he would try his darnedest to be a fair and loving parent.

And that was where Holly came into the plan. She would be there to watch over things—to keep the peace and harmony in the family. He knew already that she wouldn't hesitate to call him out on the carpet if he started to mess up where the kids were concerned.

He needed that reassurance—Holly's guidance. There was no way that he was going to let her go. But could he give her his heart?

Everyone he'd ever loved or thought that he'd loved, he'd lost. He couldn't go through that again. He couldn't have Holly walk out on him. It was best that they go into this marriage as friends with benefits as well as parents to their twins. Emotions were overrated.

The storm had made a real mess of things.

And Holly found herself thankful for the distraction. She moved around the living room where one of the floor-to-ceiling window panes had been broken when a shutter had been torn off its hinge. There was a mess of shattered glass everywhere.

So while Finn worked on restoring the power to the house, she worked on making the living room inhabitable again. But as the winds whipped through the room, she knew that as soon as Finn was free, she needed his help to put plywood over the window. But for now she was happy for the solitude.

If she didn't know better, she'd swear she dreamed up that marriage proposal. Finn Lockwood proposed to little old her. She smiled. He had no idea how tempted she was to accept his proposal. She'd always envied her friends getting married…until a few years down the road when some of them were going through a nasty divorce.

No, she couldn't—she wouldn't set herself up to get hurt. And now it wasn't just her but her kids that would be hurt when the marriage fell apart. She was right in turning him down. She just had to stick to her resolve. Everyone would be better off because of it.

So then why didn't she feel good about her decision? Why did she feel as though she'd turned down the best offer in her entire life?

It wasn't like she was madly in love with him. Was she?

Oh, no. It was true.

She loved Finn Lockwood.

When exactly had that happened?

She wasn't quite sure.

Though the knowledge frightened her, she couldn't deny it. What did she do now?

"Holly?"

She jumped. Her other hand, holding some of the broken glass, automatically clenched. Pain sliced through her fingers and she gasped. She released her grip, letting the glass fall back to the hardwood floor.

Finn rushed to her side. "I'm sorry. I didn't mean to startle you." He gently took her hand in his to examine it. "You've cut yourself. Let's get you out of here."

"I… I'll be fine."

"We'll see about that." He led her to the bathroom and stuck her hand under the faucet. "What were you doing in there?"

"Cleaning up. What did you think?"

"You should have waited. I would have done it. Or I would have flown in a cleaning crew. But I never expected you to do it, not in your condition."

"My condition? You make it sound like I've got some sort of disease instead of being pregnant with two beautiful babies."

"That wasn't my intent."

She knew that. She was just being touchy because… because he'd gotten past all of her defenses. He'd gotten her to fall in love with him and she'd never felt more vulnerable.

"What had you so distracted when I walked in?" Finn's gaze met hers as he dabbed a soapy washcloth to her fingers and palm.

"It was nothing." Nothing that she was ready to share. Once she did, he'd reason away her hesitation to get further involved with him.

"It had to be something if it had you so distracted that you didn't even hear me enter the room. Were you reconsidering my proposal?"

He couldn't keep proposing to her. It was dangerous. One of these days he might catch her in a weak moment and she might say yes. It might have a happy beginning but it was the ending that worried her.

She knew how to put an end to it. She caught and held his gaze. Her heart *thump-thumped* as she swallowed hard, working up the courage to get the words out. "Do you love me?"

His mouth opened, but just as quickly he pressed his

lips together. He didn't love her. Her heart pinched. In that moment she realized that she'd wanted him to say yes. She wanted him to say that he was absolutely crazy in love with her. Inwardly, she groaned. What was happening to her? She was the skeptic—the person who didn't believe in happily-ever-afters.

"We don't have to love each other to make a good marriage." He reached out to her, gripping her elbows and pulling her to him. "This will work. Trust me."

She wanted to say that she couldn't marry someone who didn't love her, but she didn't trust herself mentioning the L-word. "I do trust you. But we're better off as friends."

He sighed. "What I need is a wife and a mother for my children."

"You know what they say, two out of three isn't bad."

His brows scrunched together as though not following her comment.

She gazed into his eyes, trying to ignore the pain she saw reflected there. "We're friends or at least I'd like to think we are." He nodded in agreement and she continued. "And I'm the mother of your children. That's two things. But I just can't be your wife. I won't agree to something that in the end will hurt everyone. You've already experienced more than enough pain in your life. I won't add to it. Someday you'll find the right woman."

"What if I'm looking at her?"

She glanced away. "Now that the storm's over, I think I should get back to New York."

Finn dabbed antibiotic cream on her nicks and cuts before adding a couple of bandages. Without another word, he started cleaning up the mess in the bathroom. Fine. If he wanted to act this way, so could she.

She walked away, but inside her heart felt as though it'd been broken in two. Why did life have to be so difficult? Her vision blurred with unshed tears, but she blinked them away.

If only she could be like other people and believe in the impossible, then she could jump into his arms—she could be content with the present and not worry about the future.

Chapter 16

Two busy days had now passed since the tropical storm. Finn had done everything in his power to put the house back to normal. The physical labor had been exactly what he needed to work out his frustrations.

Toward the end of the day, Emilio phoned to say that the storm was between them and he couldn't get a flight out of Florida yet. Finn told him not to worry, he had everything under control and that Emilio should enjoy his new grandchild.

"Do you want some more to eat?" Holly's voice drew him from his thoughts.

Finn glanced down at his empty dinner plate. She'd made spaghetti and meatballs. He'd had some jar sauce and frozen meatballs on hand. He didn't always want someone to cook for him—sometimes he liked the solitude. So he made sure to keep simple things on hand that he could make for himself.

"Thanks. It was good but I'm full."

"There's a lot of leftovers. I guess I'm not so good with portions. I'll put them in the fridge in case you get hungry later. I know how hard you worked today. I'm sorry I wasn't any help."

"You have those babies to care for now. Besides, you cooked. That was a huge help."

She sent him a look that said she didn't believe him, but she wasn't going to argue. "I'll just clean this up."

He got to his feet. "Let me help."

She shook her head. "You rest. I've got this."

"But I want to help. And I'd like to make a pot of coffee. Do you want some?"

"I can't have any now that I'm pregnant."

"That's right. I forgot. But don't worry. I plan to do lots of reading. I'll catch on to all of this pregnancy stuff. Well, come on. The kitchen isn't going to clean itself."

When he entered the kitchen, he smiled. For a woman who was utterly organized in the office, he never expected her skills in the kitchen to be so, um, chaotic.

Normally such a mess would have put him on edge, but this one had the opposite effect on him. He found himself relaxing a bit knowing she was human with flaws and all. Maybe she wouldn't expect him to be the perfect dad. Maybe she would be understanding about his shortcomings.

Holly insisted on cleaning off the dishes while he placed them in the dishwasher. In the background, the coffeemaker hissed and sputtered. They worked in silence. Together they had everything cleaned up in no time.

"There. That's it." Holly closed the fridge with the leftovers safely inside.

After filling a coffee mug, he turned to Holly. "Come with me. I think we need to talk some more."

She crossed her arms. "If this is about your marriage proposal, there's nothing left to say except when can I catch a flight back to New York?"

He'd already anticipated this and had a solution. "Talk with me while I drink my coffee and then I'll go check on the helipad."

"Do you think it's damaged?"

Luckily the helicopter had been on the big island for routine maintenance when the storm struck. It was unharmed. However, with so many other things that had snagged his immediate concern, he hadn't checked on the helipad. Anything could have happened during that storm, but his gut was telling him that if the house was in pretty good condition then the helipad wouldn't be so bad off.

"Don't worry. The storm wasn't nearly as bad as it could have been."

The worry lines marring Holly's face eased a bit. With a cup of coffee in one hand and a glass of water in the other for her, he followed Holly to his office. Luckily the windows had held in here.

"Why don't we sit on the couch?"

While she took a seat, he dimmed the lights and turned on some sexy jazz music. Cozy and relaxing. He liked it this way. And then he sat down next to Holly.

Her gaze narrowed in on him. "What are you up to?"

He held up his palms. "Nothing. I swear. This is how I like to unwind in the evenings."

The look in her eyes said that she didn't believe him.

"Listen, I'll sit on this end of the couch and you can stay at the other end. Will that work?"

She nodded. "I don't know why you'd have to unwind on a beautiful island like this—well, it's normally beautiful. Will you be able to get it back to normal?"

She was avoiding talking about them and their future. It was as though she was hoping he'd forget what he wanted to talk to her about. That was never going to happen.

Still needing time to figure out exactly how to handle this very sensitive situation, he'd come up with a way to give them both some time. "I have a proposition for you—"

"If this is about getting married—"

"Just hear me out." When she remained silent, he turned on the couch so that he could look at her. "Can I be honest with you?"

"Of course. I'd hope you wouldn't even have to ask the question. I'd like to think that you're always honest—but I know that isn't true for most people." Her voice trailed off as she glanced down at her clenched hands.

She'd been betrayed? Anger pumped through his veins. Was it some guy that she'd loved? How could anyone lie to her and hurt her so deeply? The thought was inconceivable until he realized how he'd unintentionally hurt those that were closest to him. And he realized that if he wasn't careful and kept her at a safe distance that he would most likely hurt her, too. The fire and rage went out of him.

Still, he had to know what had cost Holly her ability to trust in others. "What happened?"

Her gaze lifted to meet his. "What makes you think something happened?"

"I think it's obvious. I shared my past with you. It's your turn. What's your story?"

She sighed. "It's boring and will probably sound silly to you because it's nothing as horrific as what you went through with your brother."

"I'll be the judge of that. But if it hurt you, I highly doubt that it's silly. Far from it."

Her eyes widened. "You're really interested, aren't you?"

"Of course I am. Everything about you interests me."

Her cheeks grew rosy as she glanced away. "My early childhood was happy and for all I knew, normal. My father worked—a lot. But my mother was there. We did all sorts of things together from baking to shopping to going to the park. I didn't have any complaints. Well, I did want a little brother or sister, but my mother always had an excuse of why it was best with just the three of us. I never did figure out if she truly wanted another baby and couldn't get pregnant or if she knew in her gut that her marriage was in trouble and didn't want to put another child in the middle of it."

"Or maybe she was just very happy with the child she already had." He hoped that was the right thing to say. He wasn't experienced with comforting words.

"Anyway when I was ten, my father stopped coming home. At first, my mother brushed off my questions, telling me that he was on an extended business trip. But at night, when she thought I was sleeping, I could hear her crying in her room. I knew something was seriously wrong. I started to wonder if my father had died. So I asked her and that's when she broke down and told me that he left us to start a new family. Then he appeared one day and, with barely a word, he packed his things and left."

"I'm so sorry." Finn moved closer to Holly. Not knowing what words to say at this point, he reached out, taking her hand into his own.

"My mother, she didn't cope well with my father being gone. She slipped into depression to the point where I got myself up and dressed in the morning for school. I cooked and cleaned up what I could. I even read to my mother, like she used to do with me when I was little. I needed her to get better, because I needed her since I didn't have anyone else."

"That must have been so hard for you. Your father... was he around at all?"

Holly shook her head. "I didn't know it then, but later I learned my stepmother was already pregnant with Suzie. My father had moved on without even waiting for the divorce. He had a new family and he'd forgotten about us...about me."

Finn's body tensed. He knew what it was like to be forgotten by a parent. But at least his parents had a really good excuse, at first it was because his brother was sick and then they'd been lost in their own grief. But Holly's father, he didn't have that excuse. Finn disliked the man intensely and he hadn't even met him.

"When the divorce was finalized, my father got visitation. Every other weekend, I went to stay with him and his new family. Every time my parents came face-to-face it was like a world war had erupted. My mother would grouch to me about my father and in turn, my father would bad-mouth my mother. It was awful." She visibly shuddered. "No child should ever be a pawn between their parents."

"I agree." Finn hoped that was the right thing to say.

Just for good measure, he squeezed Holly's hand, hoping she'd know that he really did care even if he didn't have all of the right words.

"I don't want any of that for our children. I don't want them to be pawns between us."

"They won't. I swear it. No matter what happens between us, we'll put the kids first. We both learned that lesson firsthand. But will you do something for me?"

"What's that?"

His heart pounded in his chest. He didn't know what he'd do if she turned him down. "Would you give us a chance?"

Her fine brows gathered. "What sort of chance?"

That was the catch. He wasn't quite sure what he was asking of her—or of himself. Returning to New York with the holiday season in full swing twisted his insides into a knot. The reminders of what he'd lost would be everywhere. But it was where Holly and the babies would be.

He stared deep into her eyes. His heart pounded. And yet within her gaze, he found the strength he needed to make this offer—a chance to build the family his children deserved.

He swallowed hard. "I'd like to see where this thing between us leads. Give me until the New Year—you know, with us working closely together. That will give Clara time for an extended honeymoon and to settle into married life. And we'll have time to let down our guards and really get to know each other."

"I thought that's what we've been doing."

"But as fast as you let down one wall, I feel like you're building another one."

She worried her bottom lip. "Perhaps you're right. It's been a very long time since I've been able to count on someone. It might take me a bit of time to get it right." She eyed him up. "But I have something I need you to do in return."

"Name it."

"Be honest with me. Even if you don't think that I'll like it, just tell me. I couldn't stand to be blindsided like my mother. And there was a guy I got serious with while I was getting my degree. Long story short, he lied to me about his gambling addiction and then he stole from me to cover his debts."

"Wow. You haven't had it easy."

She shrugged. "Let's just say I have my reasons to be cautious."

"I promise I won't lie to you." She meant too much to him to hurt her. "Now, I need to go check on the helipad."

"What about the recommendation?" When he sent her a puzzled look, she added, "You know, for that other job?"

"You still want to leave? Even though we agreed to see where this leads us?"

"What if it leads nowhere? It'll be best if you don't have to see me every day."

His back teeth ground together. Just the thought of her no longer being in his life tied his insides up in a knot. For so long, he'd sentenced himself to a solitary life. And now he couldn't imagine his life without Holly in it.

"Let's not worry about the future. We can take this one day at a time." It was about all he could manage at this point.

"It's a deal." And then she did something he hadn't expected. She held her hand out to him to shake on it.

It was as though she was making this arrangement something much more distant and methodical than what he had in mind. He slipped his hand into hers. As her fingertips grazed over his palm, the most delicious sensations pulsed up his arm, reminding him that they'd passed the business associates part of their relationship a long time ago.

He needed to give Holly something else to think about. Without giving himself the time to think of all the reasons that his next actions were a bad idea, he tightened his fingers around her hand and pulled her to him.

Her eyes widened as he lowered his head and caught her lips with his own—her sweet, sweet lips. He didn't care how many times he kissed her, it wouldn't be enough.

And then not wanting to give her a reason to hide behind another defensive wall, he pulled away. Her eyes had darkened. Was that confusion? No. What he was seeing reflected in her eyes was desire. A smile tugged at his lips. His work was done here.

He got to his feet. "I'll go check on the helipad."

With a flashlight in hand, he made his way along the path to the helipad. He had no idea what to expect when he got there. If it was clear, there was no reason Holly couldn't leave in the morning. The thought gutted him.

He'd just reached the head of the path when the rays of his flashlight skimmed over the helipad. As though fate was on his side, there were a couple of downed trees, making the landing zone inaccessible. But luckily it didn't appear they'd done any permanent damage—at least nothing to make the helipad inoperable.

It was much too dark now, but in the morning he'd have to get the chain saw out here. He imagined it'd be at least a couple of days to get this stuff cleared. It was time that he could use to sort things out with Holly.

Chapter 17

A pain tore through Holly's side.

The plates holding cold-cut sandwiches clattered onto the table. Holly pressed a hand to her waistline, willing the throbbing to subside. She rubbed the area, surprised by how much she was actually showing. But with twins on board, she figured that was to be expected. Thankfully when they'd visited the big island, she'd picked up some new, roomy clothes. They were all she wore now.

The discomfort ebbed away. Everything would be okay. It had to be. She was in the house alone. Finn had gone to the helipad first thing that morning to clear the debris. He didn't say exactly how bad it was, but she had a feeling he had a lot of work ahead of him if it was anything like the beach area.

She'd offered to help, but he'd stubbornly refused. So she set about cleaning the patio and washing it down so that it was usable again. All in all, they'd fared really well.

In a minute or so the discomfort passed. Realizing she might have overreacted, she shrugged it off and moved to the deck. She loved that Finn had installed a large bell. It could be rung in the case of an emergency or to call people for lunch, as she was about to do.

She wrapped her fingers around the weathered rope and pulled. The bell rang out.

Clang-clang. Clang-clang.

"Lunch!" She didn't know if he'd hear her, but hopefully he'd heard the bell.

She turned back to go inside the house to finish setting the table for lunch. She smiled, wondering if this was what it felt like to be a part of a couple. She knew they weren't a real couple, but they were working together. And she was happy—truly happy for the first time in a long while. She glanced around the island. Wouldn't it be nice to stay here until the babies were born?

A dreamy sigh escaped her lips. If only that could happen, but the realistic part of her knew it wasn't a possibility. Soon enough this fantasy would be over and she'd be back in New York, settling into a new job and trying to figure out how to juggle a job and newborns.

One day at a time. I have months until these little ones make their grand entrance.

At last, having the table set, she heard footsteps outside. Finn had heard her. Her heart beat a little faster, knowing she'd get to spend some time with him. Sure it was lunch, but he'd been gone all morning. She'd started to miss him.

Quit being ridiculous. You're acting like a teenager with a huge crush.

No. It's even worse. I'm a grown woman who is falling more in love with my babies' daddy with each passing day.

"I heard the bell. Is it time to eat?" He hustled through the doorway in his stocking feet. "I'm starved."

She glanced up to find Finn standing there in nothing but his jeans and socks. She had no idea what had happened to his shirt, but she heartily approved of his attire. Her gaze zeroed in on the tanned muscles of his shoulders and then slid down to his well-defined pecs and six-pack abs. Wow! She swallowed hard. Who knew hard work could look so good on a man?

His eyes twinkled when he smiled. "Is something wrong?"

Wrong? Absolutely nothing. Nothing at all.

"Um…no. I… I made up some sandwiches." Her face felt as though it was on fire. "The food, it's on the table. If you want to clean up a bit, we can eat." Realizing that she hadn't put out any refreshments, she asked, "What would you like to drink?"

"Water is good. Ice cold."

It did sound particularly good at the moment. "You got it."

She rushed around, getting a couple of big glasses and filling them with ice. Right about now she just wanted to climb in the freezer to cool off. It wasn't like he was the first guy she'd seen with his shirt off. Why in the world was she overreacting?

Get a grip, Holly.

She placed the glasses on the table and then decided something was missing. But what? She glanced around the kitchen, looking for something to dress up the table and then she spotted the colorful blooms she'd picked that morning. They were in a small vase on the counter. Their orange, yellow and pink petals would add a nice splash to the white tablecloth.

A pain shot through her left side again. Immediately her hand pressed to her side as she gripped the back of a chair with her other hand.

"What's the matter?" Finn's concerned voice filled the room, followed by his rapid footsteps.

She didn't want to worry him. "It's nothing."

"It's something. Tell me."

"It's the second time I've had a pain in my side."

"Pain?" His arm wrapped around her as he helped her sit down. "Is it the babies?"

"I… I don't know." She looked up at him, hoping to see reassurance in his eyes. Instead his worry reflected back at her. "It's gone now."

"You're sure?"

She nodded. "Let's eat."

"I think you need to see a doctor. The sooner, the better." He pulled out his cell phone. "In fact, I'm going to call the doctor now."

"What? But you can't. Honest, it's gone."

"I'll feel better once I hear it from someone who has experience in these matters."

A short time later, after Finn had gotten through to the doctor who'd examined her on the big island, Finn had relinquished the phone to Holly. She'd answered the doctor's questions and then breathed a sigh of relief.

When she returned the phone to Finn, his brow was knit into a worried line. She was touched that he cared so much. It just made her care about him all the more.

"Well, what did he say?"

"That without any other symptoms it sounds like growing pains. But it was hard for him to diagnose me over the phone. The only reason he did was because I told him we were stranded on the island due to the storm."

The stiff line of Finn's shoulders eased. "He doesn't think it's anything urgent?"

She shrugged. "He said I needed to make an appointment and see my OB/GYN as soon as possible just to be sure."

"Then that's what we'll do. We'll be out of here by this evening."

"What? But we can't. What about the trees and stuff at the helipad?"

"I just got the motivation I need to clear it. So you call your doctor and see if they can squeeze you in for tomorrow, and I'll call my pilot and have him fuel up the jet. We'll leave tonight."

"But you don't have to go. I know you don't want to be in New York for the holidays."

"That was before."

"Before what?"

"You know."

Her gaze narrowed in on him. "No, I don't know. Tell me."

"Before you and me...before the babies. We agreed we were going to give this thing a go and this is me doing my part. You haven't changed your mind, have you?"

He cared enough to spend the holidays with her in the city. Her heart leaped for joy. Okay, so she shouldn't get too excited. She knew in the long run the odds were against them, but Christmas was the season of hope.

* * *

Things were looking up.

Finn stared out the back of the limo as they inched their way through the snarled Manhattan traffic. He could at last breathe a lot easier now. The babies and their mother were healthy. It was indeed growing pains. The doctor told them to expect more along the way.

Signs of Christmas were everywhere from the decorated storefronts to the large ornaments hung from the lampposts. As he stared out the window, he saw Santa ringing a bell next to his red kettle. It made Finn wish that he was back on the island. And then, without a word, Holly slipped her hand in his. Then again, this wasn't so bad.

She leaned over and softly said, "Relax. You might even find you like the holiday."

"Maybe you're right." He had his doubts, but he didn't want to give her any reason to back out of their arrangement. He only had until the first of the year to convince her that they were better off together than apart.

"We turned the wrong way. This is the opposite direction of my apartment." Obvious concern laced Holly's words. "Hey!" She waved, trying to gain the driver's attention. "We need to turn around."

"No, we don't," Finn said calmly. "It's okay, Ron. I've got this."

"You've got what?" She frowned at him.

"I've instructed Ron to drive us back to my penthouse—"

"What? No. I need to go home."

"Not yet. You heard the doctor. You have a high-risk pregnancy and your blood pressure is elevated—"

"Only slightly."

"She said not to overdo it. And from what you've told me, your apartment is a fifth-floor walk-up with no elevator."

"It… It's not that much. I'm used to it."

He wasn't going to change his mind about this arrangement. It was what was best for her and the babies. "And then there's the fact that your mother is out of town. There's no one around if you have any complications."

"I won't have any." Her hand moved to rest protectively over her slightly rounded midsection. "Nothing is going to happen."

"I sincerely hope you're right, but is it worth the risk? If you're wrong—"

"I won't be. But…your idea might not be so bad. As long as you understand that it's only temporary. Until my next appointment."

Which was at the beginning of the new year —not far off. "We'll see what the doctor says then. Now will you relax?"

"As long as you understand that this arrangement doesn't change anything between us—I'm still not accepting your proposal."

He wanted to tell her that she was wrong, but he couldn't. Maybe he was asking too much of her—of himself. He couldn't promise her forever.

An ache started deep in his chest.

What if he made her unhappy?

Maybe he was being selfish instead of doing what was best for Holly.

Chapter 18

It didn't feel like Christmas.

Holly strolled into the living room of Finn's penthouse. There was absolutely nothing that resembled Christmas anywhere. She knew he avoided the holiday because of the bad memories it held for him, but she wondered if it would be possible to create some new holiday memories.

She'd been here for two days and, so far, Finn had bent over backward to make her at home. He'd set her up in his study to monitor the final stages of Project Santa. And so far they'd only encountered minor glitches. It was nothing that couldn't be overcome with a bit of ingenuity.

That morning when she'd offered to go into the office, Finn had waved her off, telling her to stay here. Meanwhile, he'd gone to the office to pick up some papers.

He'd said he'd be back in a couple of hours, but that was before lunch. And now it was after quitting time and he still wasn't back.

Perhaps this was the best opportunity for her to take care of something that had been weighing on her mind. She retraced her steps to the study where she'd left her phone. She had Finn's number on it because he refused to leave until he had entered it in her phone with orders for her to call if she needed anything at all.

Certain in her plan, she selected his number and listened to the phone ring. Once. That's all it rang before Finn answered. "Holly, what's the matter?"

"Does something have to be the matter?"

"No. I just… Oh, never mind, what did you need?"

"I wanted you to know that I'm going out. There's something I need to take care of."

"I'm almost home. Can I pick something up for you?"

"It's more like I have to drop off something."

"Tonight?" His voice sounded off.

"Yes, tonight."

"I just heard the weather report and they're calling for snow. A lot of it."

Holly glanced toward the window. "It's not snowing yet. I won't be gone long. I'll most likely be home before it starts."

"Holly, put it off—"

"No. I need to do this." She'd been thinking about it all day. Once the visit with her family was over, she could relax. It'd definitely help lower her blood pressure.

Finn expelled a heavy sigh. "If you aren't going to change your mind, at least let me drive you."

He had no idea what this trip entailed. To say her family dynamics were complicated was an understatement.

It was best Finn stay home. "Thanks. But I'm sure you have other things to do—"

"Nothing as important as you."

The breath caught in her throat. Had he really just said that? Was she truly important to him? And then she realized he probably meant because she was carrying his babies. Because she'd asked him straight up if he loved her and he hadn't been able to say the words.

"Holly? Are you still there?"

"Um, yes."

"Good. I'm just pulling into the garage now. I'll be up in a minute. Just be ready to go."

She disconnected the call and moved to her spacious bedroom to retrieve the Christmas packages and her coat. Her stomach churned. Once this was done, she could relax. In and out quickly.

She'd just carried the packages to the foyer when Finn let himself in the door. She glanced up at him. "You know I can take a cab."

"I told you if you're going out tonight, I'm going with you."

"You don't even know where I'm going."

"Good point. What's our destination?"

"My father's house. I want to give my sisters the Christmas presents I bought while we were in the Caribbean."

He scooped up the packages before opening the door for her. "So we've progressed to the point where I get to meet the family." Finn sent her a teasing smile. "I don't know. Do you think I'll pass the father inspection?"

She stopped at the elevator and pressed the button before turning back to him. "I don't think you have a thing to worry about."

His smile broadened. "That's nice to know."

"Don't get any ideas. In fact, you can wait in the car. I won't be long."

"Are you sure you want to take the presents now? I mean Christmas isn't until the weekend after next."

"I don't spend Christmas with them. I usually spend it with my mother. But after talking with my mother and aunt, I decided to give them something extra special for Christmas—a cruise." It would definitely put a dent in her savings, but it was worth it. This was her mother's dream vacation.

"That was very generous of you."

Holly's voice lowered. "They deserve it."

"And what about you?" When she sent him a puzzled look, he added, "You deserve a special Christmas, too. What would you like Santa to bring you?"

"I... I don't know. I hadn't thought about it."

The elevator door slid open. Finn waited until Holly stepped inside before he followed. "You know without your mother around, perhaps you could spend the time with your father."

She shook her head. "I don't think that would be a good idea."

Finn had no idea about her family. Thankfully she'd thought to tell him to stay in the car. She didn't want to make an awkward situation even more so.

Something was amiss, but what?

Was she really that uncomfortable with him meeting her family? Or was it something else? Finn glanced over at Holly just before he pulled out from a stop sign. The wipers swished back and forth, knocking off the gently falling snow.

The sky was dark now and all Finn wanted to do was turn around. He wasn't worried about himself. He never let the weather stop him from being wherever he was needed. But it was different now that he had Holly next to him and those precious babies. He worried about the roads becoming slick.

"We're almost there." Holly's voice drew him from his thoughts.

It was the first thing she'd said in blocks. In fact, she hadn't volunteered any details about her family. Why was that?

As he proceeded through the next intersection, Holly pointed to a modest two-story white house with a well-kept yard that was now coated with snow. "There it is."

He pulled over to the curb and turned off his wipers. "You've been awfully quiet. Is everything all right?"

"Sure. Why wouldn't it be?"

"You haven't said a word the whole way here unless it was to give me directions."

"Oh. Sorry. I must be tired."

"Sounds like a good reason to head back to the penthouse and deal with this another day."

"No." She released the seat belt. "We're here now. And I want to get this over with."

"Okay. It's up to you."

When he released his seat belt and opened the door, she asked, "What are you doing?"

"Getting the packages from the trunk."

She really didn't want him to meet her family. Why was she so worried? He didn't think he made that bad of a first impression. In fact, when he tried he could be pretty charming. And if they were going to be a family, which they were because of the babies, he needed to meet her father. He was certain he could make a good impression and alleviate Holly's worries.

With the packages in hand, he closed the trunk and started up the walk. Every step was muffled by the thin layer of snow.

"Where do you think you're going?" Holly remained next to the car.

He turned back and noticed the way the big flakes coated the top of her head like a halo. "I presume we're taking the presents to the door and not leaving them in the front yard."

"There's no *we* about it."

"Listen, Holly, you've got to trust me. This will all work out."

"You're right. It will. You're going to wait in the car." Her tone brooked no room for a rebuttal.

Just then there was a noise behind him. "Who's there?" called out a male voice. "Holly, is that you?"

She glared at Finn before her face morphed into a smile. "Yes, Dad. It's me."

"Well, are you coming in?"

Obediently she started up the walk. When she got to Finn's side, she leaned closer and whispered, "Just let me do the talking."

Boy, she was really worried about having him around her family. "Trust me."

He wasn't sure if she'd heard his softly spoken words as she continued up the walk. He followed behind her, wondering what to expect.

They stopped on the stoop. Her father was still blocking the doorway. The man's hair was dark with silver in the temples. He wore dark jeans and a sweatshirt with the Jets logo across the front. Finn made a mental note of it. If all else failed, maybe he could engage the man in football talk—even though he was more of a hockey fan.

"Who's at the door?" a female voice called out.

"It's Holly and some guy."

"Well, invite them in." And then a slender woman with long, bleached-blond hair appeared next to Holly's father. The woman elbowed her husband aside. "Don't mind him. Come in out of the cold."

Once they were all standing just inside the door, Finn could feel the stress coming off Holly in waves. What was up with that? Was she embarrassed of him? That would be a first. Most women liked to show him off to their friends. As for meeting a date's family, he avoided that at all costs. But Holly was different.

"Here, let me take your coats." Holly's stepmother didn't smile as she held out her hand. She kept giving Finn a look as though she should know him but couldn't quite place his face.

"That's okay." Holly didn't make any move to get comfortable. "We can't stay. I... I brought some gifts for the girls."

"Suzie! Kristi! Holly's here with gifts."

"I hope they like them. I saw them while I was out of town and thought of them."

"I'm sure they will." But there was no conviction in the woman's voice. "You can afford to go on vacation?"

Holly's face paled. "It was a business trip."

"Oh."

Her father retreated into the living room, which was off to the right of the doorway. A staircase stood in front of them with a hallway trailing along the left side of it. And to the far left was a formal dining room. The house wasn't big, but it held a look of perfection—as though everything was in its place. There was nothing warm and welcoming about the house.

Finn wanted to say something to break up the awkward silence, but he wasn't sure what to say. Was it always this strained? If so, he understood why Holly wouldn't want to spend much time here.

"Who's your friend?" Her stepmother's gaze settled fully on him.

"Oh. This is Finn. He's my—"

"Boyfriend. It's nice to meet you." He held out his hand to the woman.

"I'm Helen." She flashed him a big, toothy smile as she accepted his handshake. "I feel like I should know you. Have we met before?"

"No."

"Are you sure?" She still held on to his hand.

He gently extracted his hand while returning her smile. "I'm certain of it. I wouldn't have forgotten meeting someone as lovely as you."

Her painted cheeks puffed up. "Well, I'm glad we've had a chance to meet. Isn't that right, Fred?" And then at last noticing that her husband had settled in the living room with a newspaper, she raised her voice. "Fred, you're ignoring our guests."

The man glanced over the top of his reading glasses. "You seem to be doing fine on your own."

"Don't I always?" the woman muttered under her breath. "Lately that man is hardly home. All he does is work." She moved to the bottom of the steps and craned her chin upward. "Suzie! Kristi! Get down here now!"

Doors slammed almost simultaneously. There was a rush of footsteps as they crossed the landing and then stomped down the stairs.

"What do you want? I'm busy doing my nails." A teenage girl with hair similar to her mother's frowned.

"And I'm on the phone." The other teenager had dark hair with pink highlights.

"I know you're both busy, but I thought you'd want to know that your sister is here."

Both girls glanced toward the door. But they were staring—at him.

Both girls' eyes grew round. "Hey, you're Finn Lockwood." They continued down the steps and approached him. "What are you doing here?"

His stomach churned as they both batted their eyes at him and flashed him smiles.

"He's your sister's boyfriend."

Surprise lit up both sets of eyes. "You're dating her?"

He nodded. "I am. Your sister is amazing."

"I brought you some gifts." Holly stepped next to Finn. "I found them when I was in the Caribbean and I thought you would like them."

Each girl accepted a brightly wrapped package.

"What do you say?" prompted their mother.

"Thank you," they muttered to Holly.

"I'm Suzie," said the blonde.

"And I'm Kristi."

Helen stepped between her daughters. "Why don't you come in the living room and we can talk?"

"We really can't stay." Holly glanced at him with uncertainty in her eyes.

He smiled at her. "Holly's right. We have other obligations tonight, but she was anxious for me to meet you all."

"How did she bag you?" Suzie's brows drew together. "You're a billionaire and she's nothing."

Ouch! Finn's gaze went to the stepmother, but Helen glanced away as though she hadn't heard a word. That was impossible because Suzie's voice was loud and quite clear.

His gaze settled back on Suzie. "Holly is amazing. She is quite talented. And she spearheaded the Project Santa initiative."

"The what?"

"It's nothing," Holly intervened. "We really should go."

Finn took Holly's hand in his. "We have a couple of minutes and they haven't opened their gifts yet."

Both girls glanced down as though they'd forgotten about the Christmas presents. They each pulled off the ribbons first and then tore through the wrapping paper. They lifted the lids and rooted through the bikinis and cover up as well as sunglasses and a small purse.

Kristi glanced up. "Does this mean you got us tickets to the Caribbean? My friends are going to be so jealous. I'll have to go to the tanning salon first. Otherwise I'll look like a snowman in a bikini."

Suzie's face lit up. "This will be great. I can't wait to get out of school."

"Oh, girls, we'll have to make sure you have everything you need. I'll need to go to the tanning salon, too."

"You?" The girls both turned to their mother.

"This is our gift, not yours," Suzie said bluntly. "You aren't invited."

"But—"

"Um, there is no trip," Holly said.

"No trip?" All heads turned to Holly. "You mean all you got us was some bikinis that we can't even use because if you hadn't noticed, it's snowing outside—"

"Suzie, that's enough. I'm sure your sister has something else in mind." Her stepmother sent her an expectant look.

Wow! This family was unbelievable. If Finn had his choice between having no family and this family, he'd be much happier on his own. He glanced around to find out why Holly's father hadn't interceded on his daughter's behalf, but the man couldn't be bothered to stop reading his paper long enough.

Finn inwardly seethed. As much as he'd like to let loose on these people and tell them exactly what he thought of them and their lack of manners, he had to think of Holly. For whatever reason, they meant enough to her to buy them gifts and come here to put up with their rudeness. Therefore, he had to respect her feelings because it certainly appeared that no one else would.

"There is one other thing." Finn looked at Holly, willing her to trust him with his eyes as he gave her hand a couple of quick squeezes. "Do you want me to tell them?"

"Um…uh, sure."

"You know how Holly is, never wanting to brag. But she used her connections and secured tickets to the Mistletoe Ball for the whole family."

For once, all three females were left speechless. Good. That was what he wanted.

"You did that? But how?" Her stepmother's eyes reflected her utter surprise. "Those tickets cost a fortune and I heard they sold out back in October."

Holly's face drained of color. "Well, the truth is—"

"She has an inside source that she promised not to reveal to anyone," Finn said. "They'll be waiting for the four of you at the door of the museum."

The girls squealed with delight as Helen yelled in to her husband to tell him about the tickets to the ball. If a man could look utterly unimpressed, it was Holly's father. And through it all, Finn noticed that not one person thanked Holly. It was though they felt entitled to the tickets. A groan of frustration grew down deep in his throat. A glance at Holly's pale face had him swallowing down his outrage and disgust.

He made a point of checking his Rolex. "And now, we really must be going."

As they let themselves out the front door, the girls were talking over top of each other about dresses, shoes, haircuts and manicures. And he had never been so happy to leave anywhere in his entire life. Once outside, Finn felt as though he could breathe. He was no longer being smothered with fake pleasantries and outright nastiness.

Chapter 19

Big fluffy snowflakes fell around them, adding a gentle softness to the world and smoothing out the rough edges. Finn continued to hold Holly's hand, enjoying the connection. When they reached the car, he used his free hand to open the door.

She paused.

"Holly?"

When she looked up at him, tears shimmered in her eyes. The words lodged in his throat. There was nothing in this world that he could say to lessen the pain for her.

Instead of speaking, he leaned forward and pressed his lips to hers. With the car door ajar between them, he couldn't pull her close like he wanted. Instead he had to be content with this simple but heartfelt gesture.

With great regret he pulled back. "You better get in. The snow is picking up."

She nodded and then did as he said.

Once they were on the now snow-covered road, Finn guided the car slowly along the streets. He should have been more insistent about putting off this visit, not that Holly would have listened to him. When she set her mind on something, there was no stopping her. Although after meeting her family, he could understand why she'd want to get that visit out of the way.

As the snow fell, covering up the markings on the street, his body tensed. This must have been how it'd been the night his parents died. The thought sent a chill through his body.

"Are you cold?" Holly asked.

"What?"

"I just saw you shiver. I'll turn up the fan. Hopefully the heat will kick in soon." After she adjusted the temperature controls, she leaned back in her seat. "What were you thinking by offering up those tickets to the ball? I don't have any connections."

"But I do. So don't worry." He didn't want to carry on a conversation now.

"You…you shouldn't have done it. It's too much."

"Sure, I should have." Not taking his eyes off the road, he reached out to her. His hand landed on her thigh and he squeezed. "I wanted to do it for you. I know how much your family means to you."

"They shouldn't, though. I know they don't treat me… like family. I just wish—oh, I don't know what I wish."

"It's done now so stop worrying." He returned his hand to the steering wheel.

"That's easy for you to say. You're not related to them."

"But they are related to you and the babies. Therefore,

they are now part of my life." He could feel her eyeing him up. Had that been too strong? He didn't think so. Even if he never won over her heart, they would all still be one mixed-up sort of family.

"You do know what this means, don't you?"

His fingers tightened on the steering wheel, not liking the sound of her voice. "What?"

"That you and I must go to the ball now. And it's a well-known fact that you make a point of never attending the ball."

"For you, I'll make an exception." The snow came down heavier, making his every muscle tense. "Don't worry. It'll all work out."

"I'll pay you back."

Just then the tires started to slide. His heart lurched. *No! No! No!*

Holly reached out, placing a hand on his thigh. Her fingers tightened, but she didn't say a word.

When the tires caught on the asphalt, Finn expelled a pent-up breath. This was his fault. He promised to take care of his family and protect them like he hadn't been able to do with his parents and brother. And already he was failing.

Finn swallowed hard. "If you want to pay me back, the next time I tell you that we should stay in because of the weather, just listen to me."

She didn't say anything for a moment. And then ever so softly, she said, "I'm sorry. I didn't think it'd get this bad."

His fingers tightened on the steering wheel as he lowered his speed even more, wishing that they were closer to his building.

Just a little farther. Everything will be all right. It has to be.

His gut twisted into a knot. It was going to take him a long time to unwind after this. The snow kept falling, making visibility minimal at best. The wipers cleared the windshield in time for more snow to cover it.

His thoughts turned back to Holly. The truth was that no matter how much he'd fought it in the beginning, he'd fallen for Holly, hook, line and sinker. He couldn't bear to lose her or the babies. From now on, when they went out, he'd plan ahead. He'd be cautious. He'd do anything it took to keep them safe.

From here on out, they were a team. He had Holly's back. And he already knew that she had his—the success of Project Santa was evidence of it. Now he just had to concentrate on the roadway and make sure they didn't end up skidding into a ditch or worse.

What an utter disaster.

Back at the penthouse, Holly didn't know what to say to Finn. He'd been so quiet in the car. He must be upset that she let him walk into such a strained situation and then for him to feel obligated to come up with those tickets to the ball. They cost a small fortune. She didn't know how she'd ever repay him.

Now she was having second thoughts about telling Finn that they had to go to the ball. She didn't know how she'd explain it to her family, but she'd come up with a reason for their absence. Besides, it wasn't like she even had a dress, and the ball was just days away.

When she stepped into the living room, she found Finn had on the Rangers and Penguins hockey game. That was good. After the cleanup on the island, the work at the office and then meeting her family, he deserved some downtime.

She sat down on the couch near him. "I hope you don't mind that I ordered pizza for dinner."

"That's fine." His voice was soft as though he was lost in thought.

"Tomorrow I'll work on getting some food in the fridge."

He didn't say anything.

She glanced up at the large-screen television. She had to be honest, she didn't know anything about hockey or for that matter any other sport, but she might need to if these babies were anything like their father.

"Who's winning?"

He didn't say anything.

What was wrong with him? Was he mad at her? She hoped not. Maybe he was just absorbed by the game. "Who's winning?"

"What?"

"The score. What is it?"

"I don't know."

He didn't know? Wasn't he watching the game? But as she glanced at him, she noticed he was staring out the window at the snowy night. Okay, something was wrong and she couldn't just let it fester. If he had changed his mind about her staying here, she wanted to know up front. She realized she came with a lot of baggage and if he wanted out, she couldn't blame him.

She placed a hand on his arm. "Finn, talk to me."

He glanced at her. "What do you want to talk about?"

"Whatever's bothering you?"

"Nothing's bothering me." He glanced away.

"You might have been able to tell me that a while

back, but now that I know you, I don't believe you. Something has been bothering you since we left my father's. It's my family, isn't it?"

"What? No. Of course not."

"Listen, I know those tickets are going to cost a fortune. I will pay you back."

"No, you won't. They are my gift. And so is your dress and whatever else you need for the ball."

"But I couldn't accept all of that. It... It's too much."

"The ball was my idea, not yours, so no arguments. Tomorrow we'll go to this boutique I know of that should have something for you to wear. If not, we'll keep looking."

"I don't know what to say."

"Good. Don't say anything. I just want you to enjoy yourself."

"But how am I supposed to after tonight? I'm really sorry about my family. It's complicated with them. I was less than cordial to my stepmother when she married my father I blamed her for breaking up my parents' marriage since he had an ongoing affair with her for a couple of years before he left my mother."

Finn's gaze met hers. "And your mother didn't know?"

Holly shrugged. "She says she didn't, but I don't know how she couldn't know. He was gone all the time. But maybe it was a case of *she didn't want to know so she didn't look*."

"Sometimes we protect ourselves by only seeing as much as we can handle."

"Maybe you're right. But I think my mother's happy now. I just want to keep her that way, because she did her best to be there for me and now it's my turn to be there for her."

"And you will be. I see how you stick by those you love."

"You mean how I still go to my father's house even though I'll never be one of them?"

"I didn't mean that."

"It's okay. I realize this, but as much as they can grate on my nerves, I also know that for better or worse, they are my family. I just insist on taking them in small doses. And I'm so sorry I let you walk into that—I should have made it clearer to you—"

"It's okay, Holly. You didn't do anything wrong."

"But you didn't talk on the way home."

"That had nothing to do with your family and everything to do with me and my poor judgment. I'm forever putting those I care about at risk."

Wait. Where did that come from? "I don't understand. You didn't put me at risk."

"Yes, I did. And it can't happen again. We shouldn't have been out on the roads tonight. We could have…"

"Could have what? Talk to me."

He sighed. "Maybe if I tell you, you'll understand why I don't deserve to be happy."

"Of course you do." She took his hand and pressed it to her slightly rounded abdomen. "And these babies are proof of it."

"You might change your mind after I tell you this."

"I highly doubt it, but I'm listening."

"It had been a snowy February night a year after my brother died. I'd been invited to my best friend's birthday party, but I wasn't going. I was jealous of my friend because my Christmas had come and gone without lights and a tree. I'd been given a couple of gift cards, more as an afterthought."

Holly settled closer to him. She rested her head on his shoulder as she slipped her hand in his. She didn't know where he was going with this story, but wherever it led, she'd be there with him.

"My birthday had been in January—my thirteenth birthday—I was so excited to be a teenager. You know how kids are, always in a rush to grow up. But my parents hadn't done anything for it. There was no surprise party—no friends invited over—just a store-bought cake that didn't even have my name on it. I was given one birthday gift. There were apologies and promises to make it up to me."

Her heart ached for him. She moved her other hand over and rested it on his arm.

"When the phone rang to find out why I wasn't at my friend's party, my mother insisted I go and take a gift. Our parents were close friends, so when I again refused to go, my mother took back the one birthday gift that I'd received but refused to open. She insisted on delivering it to the party, but the snow was mounting outside and she was afraid to drive. My father reluctantly agreed to drive, but not before calling me a selfish brat and ordering me to my room."

Finn inhaled a ragged breath as he squeezed her hand. She couldn't imagine how much he'd lived through as a child. The death of his brother had spun the whole family out of control. No wonder he was such a hands-on leader. He knew the devastating consequences of losing control.

Finn's voice grew softer. "They only had a few blocks to drive, but the roads were icy. They had to cross a major roadway. My father had been going too fast. When he slowed down for the red light, he hit a patch of ice and slid into the intersection…into the path of two on-coming vehicles."

"Oh, Finn. Is that what happened tonight? You were reliving your parents' accident?"

He nodded. "Don't you see? If I had gone to that party, I would have been there before the snow. My parents would have never been out on the road. And tonight if I had paid attention to the forecast, I would have known about the storm rolling in."

"No matter how much you want to, you can't control the future. You had no idea then or now about what was going to happen. You can't hold yourself responsible."

"But you and those babies are my responsibility. If anything had happened to you, I wouldn't have known what to do with myself."

"You'd lean on your friends."

He shook his head. "I don't have friends. I have associates at best."

"Maybe if you let down your guard, you'd find out those people really do like you for you and not for what you can do for them." Her mind started to weave a plan to show Finn that he didn't need to be all alone in this world.

"I don't know. I've kept to myself so long. I wouldn't know how to change—how to let people in."

"I bet it's easier than you're thinking. Look how quickly we became friends."

"Is that what we are?" His gaze delved deep into her as though he could see straight through to the secrets lurking within her heart. "Are we just friends?"

Her heart *thump-thumped*. They were so much more than friends, but her voice failed her. Maybe words weren't necessary. In this moment actions would speak so much louder.

Need thrummed in her veins. She needed to let go of her insecurities. She needed to feel connected to him—to feel the love and happiness he brought to her life. She needed all of Finn with a force that almost scared her.

He filled in those cracks and crevices in her heart, making it whole. And not even her father's indifference tonight, her stepmother's coldness or her stepsisters' rudeness could touch her now. In this moment the only person that mattered was the man holding her close.

So while the snow fell outside, Holly melted into Finn's arms. She couldn't think of any other place she'd rather be and no one else she'd rather be with on this cold, blustery night.

Chapter 20

This was it.

Holly stared at her reflection in the mirror. The blue sparkly gown clung to her figure—showing the beginning of her baby bump. She frowned. What had she been thinking? Perhaps she should have selected something loose that hid her figure. But Finn had insisted this dress was his favorite. She turned this way and that way in front of the mirror. And truth be told, she did like it—a lot.

She took a calming breath. She was nervous about her first public outing on the arm of New York's most eligible bachelor. A smile pulled at her lips as she thought of Finn. He'd been so kind and generous supplying her family with tickets to the ball, and now she had a surprise for him.

It'd taken a bit of secrecy and a lot of help, but she'd

pulled together an evening that Finn would not soon forget. To put the plan into action, she'd needed to get rid of him for just a bit. Unable to come up with a better excuse, she'd pleaded that her prenatal vitamin prescription needed refilling. To her surprise he'd jumped at the opportunity to go to the store. She might have worried about his eagerness to leave if her mind wasn't already on the details of her surprise. She liked to think of it as Project Finn.

She smoothed a hand over her up-do hairstyle. It was secured by an army of hairpins. Nothing could move it now. She then swiped a wand of pink gloss over her lips. She felt like she was forgetting something, but she couldn't figure out what it might be.

The doorbell rang. It was time for the evening's festivities to begin. She rushed to the door and flung it open to find Clara standing there on the arm of her new husband. They were each holding a large shopping bag.

"Hi." Holly's gaze moved to Clara's husband. "I'm Holly. It's so nice to meet you."

"I'm Steve." He shook her hand. "Clara had a lot to say about you and Finn—all good, I swear."

Holly couldn't blame Clara. From the outside, she and Finn appeared to be an overnight romance. No one knew that it started a few months ago.

Then remembering her manners, she moved aside. "Please come inside. I sent Finn out on an errand. Hopefully he won't be back for a little bit. Is everything going according to plan?"

Clara nodded. "It is. Are you sure about this?"

"Yes." Her response sounded more certain than she felt at the moment. "This is my Christmas present to Finn."

"I didn't know he did Christmas presents."

"He doesn't, but that's all going to change now."

"Isn't this place amazing?" Clara glanced all around. "I'm always in awe of it every time I stop by with some papers for him. And as expected, there's not a single Christmas decoration in sight." Clara sent Holly a hesitant look. "Do you really think this is going to work?"

"As long as you have the ornaments in those bags, we're only missing the tree."

"Don't worry. I called on my way over and the tree is on its way."

"Oh, good. Thank you so much. I couldn't have done this without you. But no worries. If it doesn't go the way I planned, you're safe. I'll take full responsibility."

Holly thought of mentioning the baby news. She was getting anxious to tell people, but she didn't know how Finn would feel about her telling his PA without him. So she remained quiet—for now.

After pointing out where she thought a Christmas tree would look best, Holly asked, "Where's everyone else? I was hoping they'd be here before he gets back."

As if on cue, the doorbell rang again.

"That must be them. I'll get it." Clara rushed over and swung open the door. "I was starting to wonder what happened to you guys."

A string of people came through the door carrying a Christmas tree and packages. Some people Holly recognized from the office and others were new to her. They were all invited to Finn's penthouse before attending the Mistletoe Ball. In all, there was close to a dozen people in the penthouse. Clara made sure to introduce Holly to all of them. Everyone was smiling and talking as they set to work decking Finn's halls with strands of twinkle light, garland and mistletoe.

Holly couldn't help but wonder what Finn would make of this impromptu Christmas party.

As though Clara could read her mind, she leaned in close. "Don't worry. He'll like this. Thanks to you, he's a changed man."

Holly wasn't so sure, but she hoped Clara was right. Instead of worrying, she joined the others as they trimmed the tree.

How long does it take to fill a prescription?

Finn rocked back on his heels, tired of standing in one spot. He checked his watch for the tenth time in ten minutes. There was plenty of time before they had to leave for the ball. Not that he wanted to go, but once he'd invited Holly's family there was no backing out.

He made a point of never going to the ball. Publicly, he distanced himself as much as he could from the event. He liked to think of himself as the man behind the magic curtain. He never felt worthy to take any of the credit for the prestigious event. He carried so much guilt around with him—always feeling like a poor replacement for his family. But Holly was changing his outlook on life. Maybe she had a point—maybe punishing himself wasn't helping anyone.

He strolled through the aisles of the pharmacy. When he got to the baby aisle, he stopped. He gazed at the shelves crowded with formula, toys and diapers. All of this was needed for a baby? Oh, boy! He had no idea what most of the gizmos even did.

Then the image of the twins filled his mind. His fingers traced over a pacifier. He finally acknowledged to himself that he had to let go of the ghosts that haunted him if he had any hopes of embracing the future. Because deep down he wanted Holly and those babies more than anything in the world.

In no time, he was headed back to the penthouse with two pacifiers tucked in his inner jacket pocket and roses in his hand. He knew what he needed to do now. He needed to tell Holly how much he loved her and their babies—how he couldn't live without them.

But when he swung open the penthouse door, he came to a complete standstill. There were people everywhere. In front of the window now stood a Christmas tree. It was like he'd stepped into Santa's hideaway at the North Pole.

Where had all of these people come from? He studied their faces. Most were his coworkers. The unfamiliar faces he assumed were significant others. But where was Holly?

He closed the door and stepped farther into the room. People turned and smiled. Men shook his hand and women told him what a lovely home he had. He welcomed them and gave the appropriate responses all the while wondering what in the world they were doing there.

And then a hand touched his shoulder. He turned, finding Clara standing there, smiling at him. If this was her idea, they were going to have a long talk—a very long talk.

"Oh, I know who those are for. Nice touch." Clara sent him a smile of approval.

"What?"

She pointed to his hand.

Glancing down at the bouquet of red roses he'd picked

up on his way home, he decided to give them to Holly later—when it was just the two of them. He moved off to the side and laid them on a shelf.

Finding Clara still close at hand, he turned back to her. "Looks like I arrived in time for the party."

"What do you think? Holly went all out planning this get-together."

Holly? She did this? "But why? I don't understand."

Clara shrugged. "Holly didn't tell me what prompted this little party. Maybe she just thought it would be a nice gesture before the ball. All I know is that she asked me to pull together all of your close friends."

Close friends? He turned to his PA and arched a brow. "And now you take directions from Holly?"

"Seemed like the right thing to do. After all, I'm all for helping the course of true love."

He turned away, afraid Clara would read too much in his eyes. True love? Were his feelings that obvious?

"Just be good to her. She's a special person." And with that, Clara went to mingle with the others.

His close friends? He glanced around the room. Yes, he knew many of these people. They'd been the ones to help him when he'd been old enough to step into his father's role as CEO. He'd had lunch or dinner with all of them at one point or another. He'd even discussed sports and family with them. He'd never thought it was any more than them being polite and doing what was expected, but maybe he hadn't been willing to admit that those connections had meant so much more.

Finn recalled the other night when he'd been snuggled with Holly on the couch. They'd been discussing friends and he'd said he didn't have any. Was this Holly's way of showing him that he wasn't alone in this world? That if he let down his guard, this could be his?

"Finn, there you are." Holly rushed up to him. "I have some explaining to do."

"I think I understand."

Her beautiful eyes widened. "You do?"

He nodded before he leaned down. With his mouth near hers, he whispered, "Thank you."

And then with all of his—their—friends around, he kissed her. And it wasn't just a peck. No, this was a passionate kiss and he didn't care who witnessed it. He was in love.

Chapter 21

Holly couldn't stop smiling.

A 1950s big-band tune echoed through the enormous lobby of the Metropolitan Museum. It was Holly's first visit and she was awed by the amazing architecture, not to mention the famous faces in attendance, from professional athletes to movie stars. It was a Who's Who of New York.

It also didn't hurt that she was in the arms of the most handsome man. Holly lifted her chin in order to look up at Finn. This evening was the beginning of big things to come—she was certain of it.

Finn's gaze caught hers. "Are you having fun?"

"The time of my life. But you shouldn't be spending all of your time with me. There are a lot of people who want to speak with you, including the paparazzi out in front of the museum."

"The reporters always have questions."

"Did you even listen to any of them?"

"No. I don't want anyone or anything to ruin this evening."

"You don't understand. It's good news. In fact, it's great news. Project Santa was such a success that it garnered national attention. The website is getting hit after hit and tons of heartfelt thank-yous from project coordinators, outreach workers and parents. There have even been phone calls from other companies wanting to participate next year. Just think of all the children and families that could be helped."

Finn smiled. "And it's all thanks to you."

"Me?" She shook her head. "It was your idea."

"But it was your ingenuity that saved the project. You took a project that started as a corporate endeavor and put it in the hands of the employees and the community. To me, that's the true meaning of Christmas—people helping people."

His words touched her deeply. "Thank you. I really connected with the project and the people behind the scenes."

"And that's why I think you should take it over permanently. Just let me know what you need."

Holly stopped dancing. "Seriously?"

"I've never been more serious."

This was the most fulfilling job she'd ever had. She didn't have to think it over. She knew this was her calling. Not caring that they were in the middle of the dance floor, she lifted on her toes and kissed him.

When they made it to the edge of the dance floor, Finn was drawn away from her by a group of men needing his opinion on something. Holly smiled, enjoying watching Finn animated and outgoing.

Out of excuses, Holly made her way to her family. It was time she said hello. She made small talk with her stepmother and sisters, but her father was nowhere to be seen. As usual, they quickly ran out of things to say to each other and Holly made her departure.

On the other side of the dance floor, Holly spotted her father dancing too close with a young lady. He was chatting her up while the young woman smiled broadly. Then her father leaned closer, whispering in the woman's ear. The woman blushed.

The whole scene sickened Holly—reminding her of all the reasons she'd sworn off men. They just couldn't be trusted and it apparently didn't get better with age.

Her stepmother was in for a painful reality check when she found out that she'd been traded in for a younger model just like her father had done to Holly's mother. The thought didn't make Holly happy. It made her very sad because she knew all too well the pain her half sisters were about to experience.

Deciding she wasn't in any frame of mind to make friendly chitchat, she veered toward a quiet corner. She needed to gather herself. And then a beautiful woman stepped in her path. Holly didn't recognize her, but apparently the woman knew her.

"Hi, Holly. I've been meaning to get a moment to speak with you." The polished woman in a red sparkly dress held out a manicured hand.

"Hi." Holly shook her hand, all the while experiencing a strange sensation that she should know this woman. Her confusion must have registered on her face because the woman said, "I'm sorry. I should have introduced myself. I'm Meryl."

Surely she couldn't be Finn's ex, could she? But there was no way Holly was going to ask that question. If she was wrong, it would be humiliating. And if she was right, well, awkwardness would ensue.

"If you're wondering, yes, I am that Meryl. But don't worry, Finn and I were over ages ago. I saw you earlier, dancing with him. I've never seen him look so happy. I'm guessing you're the one to do that for him. He's a very lucky man."

At last, the shock subsided and Holly found her voice. "It's really nice to meet you. Finn has nothing but good things to say about you."

Meryl's eyes lit up. "That's good to know. I think he's pretty great, too."

Really? Finn had given her the impression that hard feelings lingered. Her gaze scanned the crowd for the man they had in common, but she didn't see him anywhere.

"Ah, I see I caught you by surprise." The woman's voice was gentle and friendly. "You thought there would be lots of hard feelings, but there aren't. I assure you. Finn is a very generous and kind man. He just doesn't give himself enough credit."

"I agree with you."

Holly wanted desperately to dislike this woman, but she couldn't. Meryl seemed so genuine—so down to earth. There was a kindness that reflected in her eyes. Why exactly had Finn let her get away?

"And the fact that you were able to get him to attend his very own ball is a big credit to you."

"His ball?"

The woman's eyes widened in surprise. "I'm sorry. I said too much."

"No, you didn't." Holly needed to know what was going on. "Why did you call this Finn's ball? As far as I know, he's never even attended before this year."

"I thought he would have told you, especially since he just told me that he intends to marry you."

"He told you that?"

The woman nodded as her brows scrunched together. "Anyway, I do the leg work for the ball, but he's the drive behind it. It's not made public but the ball is done in memory of Finn's mother and brother. He says that he remains in the background underwriting all of the associated expenses because he's made a number of unpopular business deals as far as the press is concerned, but I think it's something else."

The thought that this woman had insights into Finn that Holly lacked bothered her. "What do you think his reasons are?"

"I think the ball reminds him of his family and for whatever reason, he carries a truckload of guilt that he survived and they didn't."

And that was where Holly was able to fill in the missing pieces, but she kept what Finn had told her about his past to herself. She knew all about his survivor's guilt. And now she realized how much it'd cost him to come here tonight.

But what other secrets was he keeping from me? Tears stung the backs of her eyes. *Stupid hormones.* "There appears to be a lot I have to learn about Finn."

"I'm not surprised he didn't mention it. Finn doesn't open up easily."

Just to those that are closest to him. Holly finished

Meryl's statement. After all of their talk about being open and honest with each other, he let her come here not knowing the facts. He'd lied to her by omission. Now she wondered what else he was keeping from her.

"I… I should be going." Holly was anxious to be alone with her thoughts.

"Well, there I go putting my foot in my mouth. Sorry about that. Sometimes when I'm nervous I talk too much."

"It's okay. I've really enjoyed talking with you."

Meryl's eyes lit up as a smile returned to her face. "I'm really glad we met. I think we might just end up friends, of course if you're willing."

"I'd like that."

But as they parted company, Holly didn't think their friendship would ever have a chance to flourish. She doubted they'd ever run into each other again.

She turned to come face-to-face with her father. He was the very last person she wanted to speak to that evening. "Excuse me."

Her father stepped in front of her. "Not so fast. I did a little research into that boyfriend of yours. And I think I should get to know him better."

Not a chance. Her father caused enough destruction wherever he went. She wasn't going to give him a chance to hurt Finn.

Holly pointed a finger at her father. "You stay away from him."

Her father's eyes widened with surprise. "But it's a father's place to make sure the guy is worthy of his daughter."

She clenched her hands. "And you would be an expert on character and integrity?"

"What's that supposed to mean?"

"I saw you—everybody saw you flirting with that young woman who's what? My age? How could you?"

"I didn't mean for it to happen."

"You never do."

Her father at least had the decency to grow red-faced. "You don't understand—"

"You're right. I don't. I have to go."

She rushed past her father. Suddenly the walls felt as though they were closing in on her and it was hard to breathe. She knew not to trust men. Her father had taught her that at an early age. And he'd reinforced that lesson tonight.

What made her think that Finn would be different? No, he wasn't a womanizer, but he was a man. And he only trusted her so far. Without complete trust, they had nothing.

Except the babies, which she'd never keep from him. But they didn't have to be together to coparent. Because she refused to end up like her mother and blindsided by a man.

The fairy tale was over.

It was time she got on with her life—without Finn.

She headed for the door, needing fresh air.

What in the world?

Finn had caught glimpses of Holly and Meryl with their heads together. His gut had churned. *Nothing good will come of that.*

He tried to get away from a couple of gentlemen, but they were his partners in an upcoming deal and he didn't want to offend them. But for every excuse he came up with to make his exit, they came up with a new aspect of their pending deal that needed further attention.

He should have forewarned Holly that Meryl would be here. But honestly, it slipped his mind. Between the news of the babies and then Holly's surprise holiday gathering at the penthouse, his thoughts were not his own these days.

He breathed easier when the women parted. But the next time he spotted Holly, she was having a conversation with her father and if the hand gestures and the distinct frown were anything to go by, it wasn't going well.

"Gentlemen, these are all great points. And I look forward to discussing them in great detail, but I promised my date I wouldn't work tonight."

The men admitted that they'd made similar promises to their wives. They agreed to meet again after the first of the year. With a shake of hands, they parted.

Finn turned around in time to witness Holly heading for the door. He took off after her, brushing off people with a smile and promising to catch up with them soon. It wasn't in him to be outright rude, but his sixth sense was telling him Holly's fast exit was not good— not good at all.

He rushed past the security guards posted at the entrance of the museum, past the impressive columns, and started down the flight of steps. Snow was starting to fall and Holly didn't have a coat. What was she thinking?

When he stepped on the sidewalk, his foot slipped on a patch of ice. He quickly caught his balance. He glanced to the left and then right. Which way had she gone?

And then he saw the shadow of a person. Was that her? He drew closer and realized the person was sitting on the sidewalk. His heart clenched. He took off at a sprint.

When he reached Holly's side, he knelt down. "Holly, are you all right?"

She looked up at him with a tear trailing down her cheek. "No. I'm not."

"Should I call an ambulance?"

"No." She sniffled. "I just need a hand up. I... I slipped on some ice."

"Are you sure it's okay if you stand? I mean, what about the babies?"

"Just give me your hand." He did as she asked.

Once she was on her feet, she ran her hands over her bare arms. He noticed the goose bumps, which prompted him to slip off his jacket and place it over her shoulders. "Thank you. But you need it."

"Keep it. I'm fine." He had so much adrenaline flooding through his system at that particular moment that he really didn't notice the cold.

"Do you want to go back inside?"

She lifted the skirt of her gown. "I don't think so. My heel broke."

He glanced down, finding her standing on one foot as the other heel had broken and slipped off her foot. Without a word, he retrieved the heel and handed to her. Then he scooped her up in his arms.

"Put me down! What are you doing?"

"Taking you home."

"Finn, stop. We need to talk."

"You're right. We do. But not out here in the cold."

Chapter 22

So much for making a seamless exit.

Holly sat on the couch in Finn's penthouse feeling ridiculous for falling on the ice and breaking her shoe. The lights on the Christmas tree twinkled as though mocking her with their festiveness. She glanced away.

She'd trusted Finn and yet things about him and his past kept blindsiding her. How was she ever supposed to trust him? How was she supposed to believe he'd never hurt her?

Falling in love and trusting another human was like a free fall and trusting that your parachute would open. Holly wasn't sure she had the guts to free-fall. Her thoughts strayed back to her father. She inwardly shuddered, remembering him flirting with that young woman, and then he didn't even deny he was having an affair with her. Her mother had trusted him and then her stepmother. It was to their utter detriment.

Finn rushed back in the room with a damp cloth. "Here. Let me have your hand."

She held her injured hand out to him. He didn't say anything as he gently cleaned her scrapes and then applied some medicated cream before wrapping a bit of gauze around it.

"Did you hurt anything else?"

"Besides my pride? No."

"I wish you'd have talked to me before you took off. Anything could have happened to you—"

"If you hadn't noticed, I'm a grown woman. I can take care of myself."

He arched a brow at her outburst.

"Hey, anyone can slip on ice," he said calmly. "I just wish you'd have talked to me. Why did you leave? Was it Meryl? Did she say something to upset you?"

"No. Actually she didn't. Not directly."

"What is that supposed to mean?"

"Why didn't you tell me she would be there? That you still interact with her?"

He shrugged and glanced away. "I don't know. I didn't think of it."

"Really? Is that the same reason you didn't tell me you're the mastermind behind the Mistletoe Ball? That without you, there wouldn't be a ball?"

"I guess I should have said something. I didn't think it was a big deal. I wasn't keeping it a secret from you, but I've been distracted. If you haven't noticed, we're having twins."

"What else haven't you told me?" Her fears and insecurities came rushing to the surface. "What else don't I know about you that's going to blindside me?"

His facial features hardened. "I'm sure there's lots you

don't know about me, just like there's a lot I don't know about you." When she refused to back down, he added, "Do you want me to start with kindergarten or will a detailed report about my last five years do?"

She glared at him for being sarcastic. Then she realized she deserved it. She was overreacting. She'd let her family dig into her insecurities and her imagination had done the rest.

"You know what? Never mind." Finn got up from the couch. "If you don't trust me, this is never going to work. Just forget this—forget us. I was wrong to think it could work."

Her heart ached as she watched him walk out of the room. She didn't even know the person she'd become. It was like she was once again that insecure little girl who realized her father had lied to her—learning that her father had secretly exchanged his current family for a new one. And now her father was about to do it again.

But Finn hadn't done that. He hadn't done anything but be sweet and kind. Granted, he might not be totally forthcoming at times, but it wasn't because he was out to deceive her or hurt her. She couldn't punish him for the wrongs her father had done to her over the years.

If she was ever going to trust a man with her heart—it would be Finn. Because in truth she did love him. She'd fallen for him that first night when he'd invited her here to his penthouse. He'd been charming and entertaining.

Now, when it looked like she was going to have it all—the perfect guy, the amazing babies and a happily-ever-after—she was pulling away. In the light of day, the depth of her love for Finn scared her silly. Her instinct was to back away fast—just like she was doing now. And if she wasn't careful, she'd lose it all. If she hadn't already.

Still wearing Finn's jacket, she wrapped her arms around herself. She inhaled the lingering scent of his spicy cologne mingled with his unique male scent. Her eyes drifted closed.

There had to be a way to salvage things. Maybe she could plead a case of pregnancy hormones. Nah. She had to be honest with him about her fears and hope he'd be willing to work through them with her.

It was then she noticed something poking her. There was something in his inner jacket pocket. She reached inside and pulled out not one but two packages of pacifiers. One was pink and one was blue. Happy tears blurred her eyes as she realized just how invested Finn was in their expanding family. She had to talk to him—to apologize.

She swiped at her eyes and got to her feet, heading for the kitchen.

Chapter 23

What was he doing?

Finn chastised himself for losing his cool with Holly. Every time she questioned him, she poked at his insecurities about being a proper husband and father. He had so many doubts about doing a good job. He didn't even know what being a husband and father entailed. All he knew was that he wanted to do his best by his family.

And he wasn't a quitter. He fought for the things he believed in. Sometimes he fought too long for his own good. But this was his family—there was no retreating. He would somehow prove to Holly—and most of all to himself—that he could be there for her and the babies through the good and the bad.

Certain in what he needed to do, he turned on his heels and headed back to the living room, hoping Holly hadn't made a quick exit. If she had, it wouldn't deter him. He would find her. He would tell her that he loved her. Because that was what it all boiled down to. He was a man who was head over heels in love with the mother of his children.

When he entered the living room, he nearly collided with Holly. He put his hands on her shoulders to steady her. "Where are you going in such a rush?"

"To find you. There's something I need to say."

"There's something I need to say to you, too."

At the same time, they said, "I'm sorry."

Finn had to be sure he heard her correctly. "Really?"

She nodded before she lifted up on her tiptoes and with her hands on either side of his face, she pulled him down to her. The kiss wasn't light or hesitant. Instead her kiss was heated and demanding. Need thrummed in his veins. He never wanted to let her go.

It'd be oh, so easy to dispense with words. His hands wrapped around her waist, pulling her soft curves to his hard planes. A moan grew in the back of his throat and he didn't fight it. Holly had to know all of the crazy things she did to his body, to his mind, to his heart.

But he wanted—no, he needed to clear the air between them. Christmas was in the air and it was the time for setting aside the past and making a new start. That was exactly what he wanted to do with Holly.

It took every fiber of his being to pull away from her embrace. Her beautiful eyes blinked and stared at him in confusion. It'd be so easy to pull her close again and pick up where they'd left off.

No, Finn. Do the responsible thing. Make this right for both of you.

"Come sit down so we can talk." He led her to the couch.

"Talk? Now?"

"Trust me. It's important."

"As long as I go first," she said. "After all, I started this whole thing."

"Deal."

She inhaled a deep breath and then blew it out. She told him about running into her family and how her father's actions and her stepsisters' words had ripped the scabs off her insecurities. "I know that's not a good excuse, but it's the truth. I've spent most of my life swearing that I would never end up like my mother—that I'd never blindly trust a man."

"And then you ran into my ex and found out I'd left out some important details about my life."

Holly shrugged and glanced away. "I just let it all get to me." She lifted her chin until her gaze met his. "I know you're not my father. You are absolutely nothing like him. I trust you."

"You do?"

She nodded. "I can't promise that every once in a while my insecurities won't get the best of me, but I promise to work on them."

"I love you, Holly."

Her eyes grew shiny with unshed tears. "I love you, too."

He cleared his throat, hoping his voice wouldn't fail him before he got it all out. "I would never intentionally hurt you or our children. You and those babies mean everything to me. I'm really excited to be a father."

"I noticed." She reached in his jacket pocket and pulled out the pacifiers. "I found these. And they're so sweet. Our babies' first gifts."

"You like them?"

She nodded. "How could I have ever doubted you?"

"I promise you here and now that I'll work on being more forthcoming. I've spent so many years keeping things bottled up inside me that I might slip up now and then. Will you stick by me while I work on this partnership thing?"

She nodded. "As long as you'll stick by me while I learn to let go of the past."

"It's a deal." Then recalling the flowers, he jumped to his feet. "I have something for you." He moved to the bookcase and retrieved the flowers. "I got these for you when I went to the pharmacy earlier." He held them out to her.

She accepted the bouquet and sniffed them. "They're beautiful."

This was his chance to make this Christmas unforgettable. He took her hand in his and gazed up into her wide-open eyes. "Holly, the most important thing you need to know about me is that I love you. And I love those babies you're carrying. I want to be the best husband and father, if you'll let me. Will you marry me?"

A tear splashed onto her cheek. She moved his hand to her slightly rounded abdomen. "We love you, too. And yes. Yes! Yes! I'll marry you."

His heart filled with love—the likes he'd never known. And it was all Holly's doing. She'd opened his eyes and his heart not only to the spirit of the season, but also to the possibilities of the future.

He leaned forward, pressing his lips to hers.

This was the best Christmas ever.

Epilogue

There—that should do it.

Finn stepped back from the twelve-foot Christmas tree that stood prominently in front of the bay windows of his new house—correction, *their* house…as in his and Holly's home. This was the very first Christmas tree that he'd decorated since he was a child. Surprisingly it didn't hurt nearly as much as he'd thought. The memories of his brother and parents were always there, lingering around the edges, but now he was busy making new memories with Holly and their twins, Derek, in honor of his brother, and Maggie, in honor of his mother.

"How's it going?" Holly ventured into the room carrying a twin in each arm.

"I just finished putting on the lights. And how about you? Is Project Santa a go?"

Holly's face lit up. "Yes. And this year will be even

bigger than last year, which means we're able to help even more children."

"I knew you were the right person to put in charge."

Maggie let out a cry. Holly bounced her on her hip. "Sounds like someone is hungry."

"Did I hear someone cry out for food?" Holly's mother strolled into the room, making a beeline for Maggie.

Finn glanced over at his mother-in-law, Sandy, who now lived in a mother-in-law apartment on the other side of their pool. When Holly had suggested her mother move in, he had to admit that he'd been quite resistant to the idea. But when Holly really wanted something, he found himself unable to say no.

In the end, he and Sandy hit it off. The woman was a lot more laid-back than he'd ever imagined. And she doted over her grandchildren, which won her a gold star. And with the help of a nanny and a housekeeper, they were one big, happy family—unless of course the twins were hungry or teething.

"I can do it, Mom," Holly insisted, hanging on to the baby.

"Nonsense. I wasn't doing anything important." Sandy glanced over at the tree. "And from the looks of things in here, your husband could use some help."

Holly smiled. "I think you're right." She handed over the fussing baby. "Thanks. I'll be in shortly."

"Don't hurry. I've got this." Sandy started toward the kitchen. "Isn't that right, Maggie? We're buddies."

Holly stepped up beside Finn. "Are you sure you bought enough lights to cover all of the tree?"

"Yes. I'll show you." He bent over and plugged them in.

His wife arched a brow at him as though she knew something that he didn't. This was never a good sign.

"You should have tested them before putting them on the tree."

"What?" He turned around to find the top and middle of the tree all lit up, but the bottom section was dark. But how could that be? "I swear I tested them before I strung them."

Holly moved up next to him and handed over Derek. "Maybe it's just payback."

He glanced at his wife, trying to figure out what payback she was referring to. And then he recalled that last Christmas he'd shared the story of how he and his brother had swiped a strand of lights from the Christmas tree in order to light up their blanket fort.

A smile pulled at Finn's lips at the memory. It was the first time he'd been able to look back on his past and smile. That was all thanks to Holly. Her gift to him last year was giving his life back to him. Instead of walking around a shell of a man, he was taking advantage of every breath he had on this earth.

"Perhaps you're right. Maybe Derek's playing tricks on me."

"Did you hear that?" Holly leaned forward and tickled their son's tummy, making him giggle and coo. "Are you playing tricks on your daddy?"

Finn knew she was adding a bit of levity to the moment to keep things from getting too serious. Finn liked the thought that his brother might be looking down over them and smiling. Right here and now the past and the present came together, making Finn feel complete.

"Would you do that?" Finn placed his finger in his son's hand. "Would you steal the lights from the Christmas tree to make a fort?"

"Don't give him ideas," Holly lightly scolded. "I have

a feeling your son will get into enough trouble of his own without any help from you."

"I think you might be right."

"And if he has a little brother, we'll really have our hands full."

This was the first time Holly had ever mentioned having another baby. It was usually him going on about expanding their family because to his surprise and delight, he loved being a dad. He'd even considered quitting the day job to be a full-time parent until Holly put her foot down and told him that someone had to keep the family business going to hand down to their children. But he no longer worked from morning till late at night. He took vacations and weekends. He had other priorities now.

"I think it'd be great to have another baby. Just let me know when you want my assistance. I'm all yours."

"Oh, you've done plenty already."

"Hey, what's that supposed to mean?" Derek wiggled in his arms. "Oh, you mean the twins? What can I say? When I do something I go all out."

"Well, let's just hope this time around I'm not carrying twins or you might just be staying home to take care of all of them while I run the office."

Surely he'd misunderstood her. She couldn't be—could she? "Are…are you pregnant?"

She turned to him and with tears of joy in her eyes, she nodded. "Merry Christmas."

Finn whooped with joy before leaning forward and planting a kiss on his wife's lips. He'd never been so happy in his life. In fact, he never knew it was possible to be this happy.

"You give the best Christmas presents ever, Mrs. Lockwood."

"Well, Mr. Lockwood, you inspire me." She smiled up at him. "I love you."

"I love you the mostest."

* * * * *

"I didn't fall," she announced with a wide smile as he returned the crutches.

"You did great." He looked at her with a huge smile.

"That was silly," she said as they started down the walk toward his car. "Maneuvering down a few steps isn't a big deal, but this is the farthest I've gone on my own since the accident. If my parents had their way, they'd encase me in Bubble Wrap for the rest of my life to make sure I stayed safe."

"It's an understandable sentiment from people who care about you."

"But not what I want."

He opened the car door for her, and she gave him the crutches to stow in the back seat. The whole process was slow and awkward. By the time Grace was buckled in next to Wiley, sweat dripped between her shoulder blades, and she felt like she'd run a marathon. How could less than a week of inactivity make her feel like such an invalid?

As if sensing her frustration, Wiley placed a gentle hand on her arm. "You've been through a lot, Grace. Your ankle and the cast are the biggest outward signs of the accident, but you fell from the second story."

She offered a wan smile. "I have the bruises to prove it."

"Give yourself a bit of…well, grace."

"I never thought of attorneys as naturally comforting people," she admitted. "But you're good at giving support."

"It's a hidden skill." He released her hand and pulled away from the curb. "We lawyers don't like to let anyone know about our human side. It ruins the reputation of being coldhearted, and then people aren't afraid of us."

"You're the opposite of scary."

"Where are we headed?" he asked when he got to the stop sign at the end of the block.

"The highway," she said without hesitation. "As much as I love Rambling Rose, I need a break. Let's get out of this town, Wiley."

HARLEQUIN

Heartfelt or suspenseful, inspiring or passionate, Harlequin has your happily-ever-after.

With new books published
every month, you are sure to find the
satisfying escape you know you deserve.

SIGN UP FOR THE HARLEQUIN NEWSLETTER

Be the first to hear about great new
reads and exciting offers!

Harlequin.com/newsletters

Love Harlequin romance?

DISCOVER.

Be the first to find out about promotions,
news and exclusive content!

 Facebook.com/HarlequinBooks

Twitter.com/HarlequinBooks

Instagram.com/HarlequinBooks

Pinterest.com/HarlequinBooks

ReaderService.com

EXPLORE.

Sign up for the Harlequin e-newsletter and
download a free book from any series at
TryHarlequin.com

CONNECT.

Join our Harlequin community to
share your thoughts and connect
with other romance readers!
Facebook.com/groups/HarlequinConnection

THE 2020 CHRISTMAS ROMANCE COLLECTION!

5 FREE TRADE-SIZE BOOKS IN ALL!

RaeAnne THAYNE

Christmas at Holiday House

MAISEY YATES

brenda novak
A California Christmas

'Tis the season for romance!
You're sure to fall in love with these tenderhearted love stories from some of your favorite bestselling authors!

YES! Please send me the first shipment of **The 2020 Christmas Romance Collection**. This collection begins with 1 FREE TRADE SIZE BOOK and 2 FREE gifts in the first shipment (approx. retail value of the gifts is $7.99 each). Along with my free book, I'll also get 2 additional mass-market paperback books. If I do not cancel, I will continue to receive three books a month for four additional months. My first four shipments will be billed at the discount price of $19.98 U.S./$25.98 CAN., plus $1.99 U.S./$3.99 CAN. for shipping and handling*. My fifth and final shipment will be billed at the discount price of $18.98 U.S./$23.98 CAN., plus $1.99 U.S./$3.99 CAN. for shipping and handling*. I understand that accepting the free books and gifts places me under no obligation to buy anything. I can always return a shipment and cancel at any time. My free books and gifts are mine to keep no matter what I decide.

☐ 260 HCN 5449   ☐ 460 HCN 5449

Name (please print)

Address   Apt. #

City   State/Province   Zip/Postal Code

Mail to the Harlequin Reader Service:
IN U.S.A.: P.O. Box 1341, Buffalo, NY. 14240-8531
IN CANADA: P.O. Box 603, Fort Erie, Ontario L2A 5X3

XMASR20